SACRAMENTO PUBLIC LIBRARY
828 "I" STREET
SACRAMENTO CA 95814
10/2019

D0896448

My Name is Trouble

JAMES TAYLOR

story by JAMES TAYLOR & MARCO SPARKS

My Name is Trouble

Copyright 2019 © by James Taylor & Marco Sparks. All rights reserved. No parts
of this book may be used or reproduced in any manner whatsoever without written
permission except in the case of brief quotations embodied in critical articles or
reviews. For more information, visit:
mynameistrouble.com

Print ISBN: 978-1-7330662-0-4
eBook ISBN: 978-1-7330662-1-1

Cover artwork by Michael Manuel

First Edition, 2019

For friends and lovers

Table of Contents

TROUBLE AWAITS...

Chapter One

Stranger Than Fiction

THERE WAS A QUOTE IN THE DEDICATION OF RJ VALENTINE'S latest book, *Trouble Eight Days a Week*:

> "For Trouble. Authors must tell lies to reveal a greater truth."

For 16 years, whenever anyone asked about her father, Jennifer Valentine told the truth.

The facts were these: she was born on March 10th at Santa Rosa Memorial Hospital in California. Her mother died a short time later, and Jenny was raised by her Aunt Shelly. Dad was never in the picture. These were all true statements, and yet to tell it like that, leaving out all the good parts, made her a goddamn liar.

Jenny wasn't above lying when it served her needs, and she liked keeping secrets. She had a big one, too. When her mom filled out the birth certificate, Laura Onishi blessed her daughter Jennifer with the middle name Trouble. It was an old joke between mom and dad, giving a kid a hard-boiled name like Trouble or Danger or the like—how could the kid *not* grow up to be cool? They weren't married.

RJ Valentine was a literature professor, she was his grad student. According to Aunt Shelly, the affair was a real scandal. Especially to dad's wife, Valerie.

Valerie Valentine had just given birth to a son of her own, and she refused to let dad even *see* his new daughter. Laura was determined, though. She packed infant Jenny—then only five days old—into a car seat and took off down Highway 12 on a grim, stormy afternoon. They never made it to RJ. A slippery road and a thick redwood tree got in the way. Or maybe another car forced them off the road? Jenny was too young to remember; it was a miracle she even survived. Mom wasn't so lucky. After the accident, Jenny would spend her first months in a UCLA dorm room with mom's sister Shelly. They'd been driving each other crazy ever since.

"Jenny!" her aunt shouted from the living room. "Did you move that box! The fridge guys will be here soon, and they need that path clear!"

Jenny ignored her. She was rummaging in the kitchen for a can of WD-40. There was a bay window in her new bedroom that opened wide enough to fit through. Wide enough for Jenny, at least, who at 16 was still smaller than everyone but her aunt. The window squeaked like crazy, though, which was a highly undesirable feature when you were trying to sneak out at night. Or back in, as the case may be.

They had just moved to Blackbird Springs from Glendale the day before. Shelly had a new job at the local charter school, and Jenny's grandparents were letting them stay in the family house while they took an extended vacation in Okinawa. Shelly had no idea that Jenny had been mailing her aunt's résumé to schools up here for two years. It was a close thing, too, since Jenny had just been kicked out of another school in Los Angeles, and Shelly was threatening boarding school.

It was hard enough not being a scamp when your middle name was

Trouble, and the book RJ published when Jenny was three certainly didn't help. *My Name is Trouble* was a junior readers book about a girl detective named Trouble who solved mysteries in the spooky hamlet of Blackbird Springs, California. And that, of course, was key. Because RJ Valentine lived in the real Blackbird Springs, and now Jenny finally did too.

She was staring at a box cutter she'd found in the junk drawer and wondering if she should take it when the doorbell rang.

"Get that! That's probably them! And move that box!" shouted her aunt.

Jenny yawned and moped to the entryway. It was only 10:00 AM on a Sunday, and she hadn't slept well last night. Too excited.

"Ow fuck!" she yelped, tripping over a box of books and stumbling into the door. She yanked it open like she'd planned the maneuver, expecting some delivery men with a new fridge. "Yeah?"

It was some blank-faced old guy in an actual chauffeur outfit.

"Jennifer Valentine?" he asked.

"...Yes?" Jenny said.

"Your presence is requested at Valentine Manor."

An electric charge coursed down Jenny's spine. She was in the back seat of the black town car before she knew it. The interior was all rich, supple leather. Was this what dad smelled like? She had totally forgotten to even tell Shelly where she was going. Probably for the best. Shelly's opinion of RJ Valentine had always been dismal.

After mom died, dad couldn't see Jenny, so he created a fictional world where they could be together. The pint-sized Trouble in his books never came across a mystery she couldn't solve, but only before making things ten times worse in the process. Eternally 11 years old, always wearing a purple trench coat that was a little too big, and her father's red fedora. She was a best-selling sensation. Dad wrote

11 more. *Here Comes Trouble, Trouble Always Finds Me, Trouble in Paris…* Trouble became a literary rite of passage, a natural stepping stone between Harriet the Spy, Nancy Drew, and Miss Marple. Every little girl read the *Trouble* books, and RJ made a fortune off the sales and merchandising.

Nobody knew there was a real Trouble too. No one except RJ and Shelly. It had to be that way. Laura Onishi's car accident was very convenient if you were Valerie Valentine. Maybe too convenient. Dad kept quiet and kept Jenny safe. Aunt Shelly, meanwhile, was determined to discipline the Trouble right out of her. Jenny grew up in anonymous obscurity: RJ Valentine's greatest plot twist, just waiting for her big reveal. As the driver rolled up the privacy screen, Jenny was sure that moment had finally come.

She could barely sit still, so she tried to distract herself from her anxiety by studying her new stomping grounds as they drove through town. She'd read about this place on the internet, but it was never the same as actually being there.

In the *Trouble* books, Blackbird Springs was a sleepy one-cop town full of eccentric locals, suspicious characters, and mysteries around every corner. Daily activities ranged from lemonade stands and bake sales to dognapping, smuggling, and jewel-thievery. The murder per capita must have been off the charts.

The real Blackbird Springs was nestled in the heart of Napa Valley. Jenny had spotted four wine bars, and she wasn't even counting for them. She'd seen three police cruisers and a meter maid. Jenny would keep her fingers crossed for a good dognapping or two, at least.

Tomorrow was Labor Day, and the brunch crowd was out in full force for the last good weekend dining of the summer. Bougie hipsters milled around on the corner checking their phones while waiting for a table at Rosie's. There was a big burly guy pacing on the sidewalk, checking the train schedule. City workers nearby were installing new traffic lights hand-crafted in wrought iron to look old-fashioned and rustic. Women sporting designer workout gear were walking their well-bred pocket dogs. An elderly man with a snow-white beard was climbing out of his Mercedes and handing off the keys to a valet. This town had lots of money. Lots of it. Jenny did not.

As if to remind her of this fact, they left the downtown shops behind and Jenny caught her first glance of Dad's mansion in the distance. Valentine Manor sat on the low shoulder of a hill covered in golden-green grapevines, just past the edge of town. The villa was only two stories high but sprawled out wide on the property.

Jenny glanced at her reflection in the side window, hoping she looked presentable. Her outfit felt stupid now; she'd worn her purple trench coat over a black shirt and jeans. Trouble's standard outfit; she couldn't help herself. She kept her hair in a short pixie cut to make it easier to wear wigs, and went heavy on the eyeliner, as was her manner. The black hair and deep brown eyes she got from her mother's Japanese ancestry. Her sharp cheekbones and thick eyebrows came from RJ, who was something of a Caucasian mutt. Adults would call her "striking" or "unique" and think they were paying her a compliment. What they really meant was that she was different. She didn't fit in. That was fine, she didn't want to. She was Trouble.

The driver turned east off the highway onto Cellar Drive, a smooth two-lane road running between rows of grapevines, following the signs to Valentine Vineyards. After another quarter mile, a pair of massive gates loomed across their path, each sporting a giant ostentatious V in wrought iron. Dad was a dramatic bitch, just like her.

An old-fashioned well marked the center of the roundabout where the driveway ended. Several cars were already parked out front, including a Blackbird Springs Police SUV.

"Why are the police here?" Jenny asked.

"Not sure," said the driver as he opened the door for her. "But head on in."

The air smelled sweet and earthy up here, like a glass of grape juice on a freshly-cut lawn. Jenny gawked at the grand entrance to the mansion. The steps were glazed coral flagstone, roughly hewn for that authentic Tuscany look. There had to be at least 20 bedrooms in this place. Was she about to get rich? According to Wikipedia, RJ's fortune from book sales and licensing was north of $250 million.

She tapped out a quick coded message on her Apple Watch and popped an Adderall before marching up the stairs. Jenny reached out to knock on the heavy mahogany door when it abruptly swung inward, and she found herself face to face with a tall, pretty blonde girl.

"Oh!" the girl shouted in surprise.

Her hair was up in a bun, two thick golden tendrils hanging down to frame her heart-shaped face. Jenny was smitten.

"S-sorry," Jenny stuttered out, trying not to stare.

"No, I was just leaving," said the girl.

"Dinah, would you just wait!?" said a male voice, calling from within.

Dinah's eyes flashed, and she offered Jenny a conspiratorial smile.

"Ignore him. I'm Dinah, by the way. Dinah Black."

"Jenny."

Dinah cocked her head, as though giving her a second appraisal.

"See you around, Jenny." Dinah smiled and trotted past her as a tall teenage boy in a suit rushed up to the front door.

"Oh, umm hey," he said, before brushing past her. "Come on, hang on a sec!"

"Forget it!" Dinah said. "I'll call you later. Maybe."

"Fine!" Jack shouted.

Dinah got into an Acura and drove off. The boy stood on the porch stewing for a few moments before remembering that Jenny was there too. He was tall and handsome, with dark hair and high cheekbones. He seemed a very serious boy with his furrowed brow, set jaw, and tired, bloodshot eyes. Just now, he was studying Jenny and frowning.

"Have we met?" he asked.

"No," said Jenny, managing to keep her voice from wavering. Because there was only one person this could be: Val's son, her half-brother. "It's—It's Jack, right?"

"Yeah," he said, looking past her as though he'd already lost interest. "Um, can I help you?"

"Oh, I'm…" she paused, not sure what to say. "I'm Jennifer—Jenny. The driver brought me here?"

His face gave away no sign of recognition. As she'd suspected, he had no idea who she was.

"Right," he said, glaring at Dinah's departing car one last time before taking Jenny by the arm and pulling her inside.

"Something wrong with you and her?" she asked.

Jack began to answer, and then stopped himself. It didn't matter. Jenny was too busy absorbing every inch of her father's house, in awe of the subtle wealth on display. The tile was marble, and gold lamé wallpaper lined the walls. All the furniture looked authentically handmade by master craftsmen. It was like stepping into an older, richer, better world.

"Come on, we're all in the study," he told her.

"Wow," was all she could manage.

"Yeah yeah." Jack rolled his eyes and pulled her under the double-staircase balustrade. Jenny gawked at the oil paintings and fancy wall sconces as Jack marched them briskly down the hallway. In a moment they had turned a corner and stopped at a tall door. Jack pushed it open and gestured inside.

With one last nervous breath, Jenny stepped in, ready to meet her father for the first time in her life.

INSIDE, SHE FOUND HERSELF IN A LARGE STUDY OR LIBRARY. THERE must have been no second story here because bookshelves at least 13 feet high lined the walls, complete with a rolling ladder to access the upper stacks. On the far side of the room, three massive arched windows looked out onto a courtyard, a wide lawn, and countless rows of grapevines beyond, running up the ridge.

Jenny had the sensation that the whole hill might come rushing in through the windows at any moment. She gasped involuntarily at the arresting view.

To the left was a fainting couch for thinking, a few Louis XIV chairs, and a mini bar. A fireplace was crackling from a blazing wood fire within. The high-backed chair behind the massive oak desk was empty, though.

"Where is he?" she asked.

Several others were in the study, including a tall woman dressed all in black who could only be Valerie Valentine. She was beautiful, but in a sharp, unfriendly sort of way, like God was pressing down too hard on his pencil when he'd sketched her into being. Val had already helped herself to a martini from the mini bar, the early hour be damned. She was standing rather close to a wiry ginger guy wearing a navy blazer over a *Nasty Woman* t-shirt.

"Who's this, Junior?" asked Val in a bored, husky voice, sipping her cocktail and tapping on her phone.

"I guess Dad wanted a Trouble cosplayer here," said Jack. "It was

Jenny, right?"

"Yeah," said Jenny, watching Val closely and feeling a growing rage rising within her. Here she was at last, the author of all Jenny's misfortune. At the mention of Jenny's name, Val looked up and narrowed her eyes.

"So glad you could make it," said a smooth, deep voice behind her. He was a thin man with a hawkish nose and horn-rimmed glasses. "I'm Mr. Webb, RJ's lawyer," he said and snapped his fingers. A business card appeared in his hand. It read:

Hamilton Webb, Esq

and had a phone number on the back. That was all.

"I wish we were meeting under better circumstances," he said.

"What do you mean?" asked Jenny. She glanced around the room. The cop by the window, two randos looking solemn on the couch. Jack and Val all in black. The man in the blazer with downcast eyes. Everyone was pointedly studying the carpet. This was all wrong. Jenny didn't want to solve this riddle, but the deductions came unbidden. "Where's RJ?"

"No one's told you, have they?" The lawyer winced. "I'm so sorry."

"Sorry for what?" Jenny asked, but she already knew by the look on his face.

"RJ Valentine passed away last night."

Chapter Two

Dramatis Personae

JENNY WAS FROZEN IN SHOCK. HOW COULD THIS BE? DAD WAS barely in his 40s. Jack was staring at her again, frowning.

"I was going to meet him today..." Jenny mumbled. It was cruel. Too cruel! She'd waited 16 years for this! And now they were telling her she was a day too late! "Are you sure?"

"Hamilton, what's this about?" asked Val. "Who is she?"

"This will all make more sense in a moment," said Mr. Webb. He hefted a large leather-bound suitcase he'd been carrying and brought it around to RJ's desk.

Val scowled into her cocktail. The barrister set his suitcase down and consulted the mini bar, mixing something brown and neat in a crystal tumbler.

Jenny glanced around the room numbly, finally taking in the rest of the occupants. It was a trick her last therapist taught her: focus on the details until you're ready to handle the big picture.

Dad...

She tried to focus. A tall black woman—like basketball tall—wearing a pantsuit and a braided ponytail was sitting on the couch, towering over a crimson-haired teenage girl who sat next to her. The redhead's dumpy skirt reached all the way to her feet, but when she crossed her legs, Jenny realized with a start that her right leg was a prosthetic. She looked all goth-ed out, dressed in black with lots of eye shadow and dark nail polish to go with her black lipstick. This, certainly, could not be Tori Valentine, Val's older daughter from a previous marriage. Jenny knew from the internet that Tori had dark hair and looked just like her mom.

The fashionable man in the blazer was sipping from a wine goblet. He had a short beard that gave him a rakish, charming look. His tight jeans were the kind of pricy designer duds she saw guys wearing when she went to The Grove or the Third Street Promenade in Santa Monica. Jenny's immediate impression was: town bicycle.

The final member of the group was a cop. He was standing in the back, staring out one of the arched windows. In the reflection he looked uneasy, his shoulders tight under his police uniform. Jenny was about to look away when she noticed his name tag: **Lockhart**.

In the books, Sheriff Lockhart was a minor but recurring presence in Blackbird Springs. Paunchy and dim-witted, with thinning hair and a nose full of rosacea. That's how dad always described Lockhart, anyway. But this real-life Lockhart—even hiding behind aviator sunglasses—was handsome and ripped. Graying at the temples but clean shaven and near bursting out of his crisp, freshly-starched uniform. Jenny never knew Sheriff Lockhart was a real person and not just a supporting Trouble character, and she instantly hated him for it. It was another thing she'd have to ask dad about. Except now she couldn't. Ever. A black glacier of despair descended on her thoughts…

"Well then," Mr. Webb clapped his hands, startling her. "Thank you all for coming on this dark day. I think this completes our roster. Get the door if you would, Jack. This little soirée is for your eyes only."

Jack closed the door behind her. Jenny noted that it was designed on the inside to look like part of the wall.

"Is this a bad time to remind you that I'm a reporter?" the tall woman asked.

"We are aware, Ms. Griffin." Mr. Webb curled his lip, a twinkle in his eye. "Why don't we get to the will and then you can decide whether or not you're here as a journalist."

"I hardly see what all the pomp and circumstance is for, Hamilton," said Val. "I've read Johnny's will. It's nothing unexpected. What is this all about?"

The will. That's why she was here. Had dad left her something?

"On the contrary, Val," said Mr. Webb. "You've only read the *alternate* will. The decoy, you might say."

"No," said Val.

"Yes!" said Mr. Webb with glee. "He was your husband, Val. I don't need to remind you of his flights of fancy. Mr. Valentine was very excited when I helped him draw up this will. Notarized, of course. You're welcome to verify it."

"I certainly will," Val replied acidly. "With *my* lawyers."

"As it happens, this will would only supersede the alternate under certain conditions. Once RJ Valentine regrettably expired, a proper autopsy could be performed, and lo, those conditions were met. But I get ahead of myself."

Jenny's mind was racing. What conditions could he mean? Everyone was looking at each other, trying not to appear nervous. The redhead raised her hand timidly.

"Are you sure I'm supposed to be here?" she asked in a high, child-like voice. "I didn't even know him."

"Mr. Valentine's instructions were quite specific in this regard, Alicia," Mr. Webb told her. "I assure you, you're exactly where you're supposed to be."

"If you say so," the fashionable man said.

Alicia the redhead lowered her hand slowly, not really convinced. Mr. Webb leaned over the suitcase and looked up with an impish smirk.

"Who can guess what's in here?" he asked theatrically. The room had gone silent as a blank page. "No guesses?"

Mr. Webb shrugged and did something with his hands to the case that none could follow and it popped open. He lifted the lid and began retrieving items, which he lined up on the desk in front of him.

A bottle of wine.

A framed photo.

A noose.

A worn hardcover book.

A small onyx statue of a bird.

A tarot card.

And lastly, an old-fashioned brass key.

Jenny shivered. Her arms were covered in goosebumps, despite the room becoming stuffy with fire and all these bodies present.

Mr. Webb had also retrieved some papers and an optical disk from the suitcase. He unfolded a legal document and adjusted his horn-rimmed glasses.

"Let's get the boilerplate out of the way first," he said, sipping his scotch, and began to read. "I, Johnathan Valentine, now residing in the County of Calistoga, state of California, and being of sound mind and memory, and not acting under fraud, menace, duress or the undue influence of any person whomsoever, do hereby make, publish, and declare this to be my Last Will and Testament. Dated August 5th."

The words died in the stale air, vanishing into the books that surrounded them. That was less than a month ago. Was this the last thing RJ Valentine had ever written?

"Pursuant to these wishes, please play the video on the enclosed media," Mr. Webb continued from memory, spinning a disk on his finger. "Do you mind, Val?"

Valerie Valentine let out an exaggerated huff and walked to the shelves opposite the desk. She slid her hands along the bottom of a waist-high shelf, and with a click, a wide section pulled out from the wall and rose up to reveal a high-definition TV behind it.

"He loved hiding in here on Sundays to watch football and avoid church," Valerie said to no one in particular. She held out a hand for the disk—and just about snarled when Hamilton Webb pulled it away and moved to operate the TV himself.

Moments later, they were all watching as RJ Valentine appeared on screen, healthy and hale, sitting at the desk in this very study. He looked just like his author photo: sharp cheekbones, dirty blond hair, and a mischievous smile tugging at the corner of his mouth. Those seven odd objects, the book, photo, statue, noose, key, tarot card, and bottle of wine were arranged in front of him just as they were now.

"Hello everyone," RJ Valentine said. "If you're seeing this, then I'm sorry to say I had to leave you."

Jenny sucked in a breath. With every word he spoke, the loss became more real, and more painful.

"I promise this will all make sense in a minute," he said with a warm smile. "But first, let me get to my bequeathments—which *is* a word, ask Webb. To my loving wife Valerie Isabel Valentine, I leave a bottle of *Ressort Rouge 1998*, in memory of our better times."

"What?!" Valerie demanded.

On screen, RJ Valentine lifted and admired the bottle of *Ressort Rouge*—a dark vessel topped with red foil—before setting it back down.

"It was a good year, for wine," he added.

Mr. Webb dutifully delivered the bottle of wine to the visibly-quivering Valentine widow.

"Please, Viv," said RJ, anticipating his wife's objections. "Save all your questions until the end. To my dear son Johnathan Renard Valentine, I leave the Onyx Blackbird he has almost broken so many times running up and down the hall."

Again, RJ lifted the heirloom on video as Mr. Webb passed out the real one. Jack's eyes got misty, which just about shattered Jenny. He pulled it together and considered the blackbird statue. On the video, her father continued:

"To Blake Henry Lockhart, I leave a reminder of our disagreement and a plea to reconsider."

This time it was the white rope noose that Mr. Webb passed out to the cop, who looked to be barely containing his fury as he accepted it. The reporter raised an eyebrow at this but said nothing. Then it was her turn.

"To my old friend Yvonne Ambrose Griffin," her father said. "I leave an original copy of *The Stranger of Sausalito*. I'm going to miss our nightcaps."

Ms. Griffin smiled—no, she was almost smirking—when she took the old, worn book from Mr. Webb. There was an illustration of some big-chinned, hard-boiled gumshoe on the jacket cover.

"To Declan Ezra Dillion, I pass on this vintage tarot card," said RJ. "Be careful, it may be cursed."

The slick blazer guy accepted an ornate Death card from Mr. Webb with a wolfish grin.

Now there were only two heirs left: Jenny and that weird redhead Alicia. On the video, RJ Valentine twirled the large brass key between his fingers.

"No mystery is complete without the following," he paused for a beat and Jenny shot a glance over at Alicia, who was doing the same back at her. Jenny wanted the key. Maybe it went to a treasure chest he'd hid for her or something. "So to Alicia Anne Aaron, I leave this antique skeleton key."

Damn it! If Alicia was anything other than baffled, she hid it well. Mr. Webb handed her the brass key, and then only the framed photo was left. It must be for her. Was that all? She looked back at the screen to find her father addressing her directly for the first and last time.

"And lastly... To my pride and joy, and my greatest regret. To my daughter Jennifer Trouble Valentine, I leave an old family photo for you to remember us by."

Everyone's eyebrows raised in curiosity, except for Mr. Webb who was grinning like the cat who ate the canary as he handed her the picture frame. Webb had known, obviously, but no one else did. Lots of girls saw themselves in Trouble, the tiny girl detective with a penchant for biting off more than she could chew. But Jenny *was* Trouble, and now her secret was out.

The others were just putting this together. Jack's jaw hung open, mouthing the word "daughter" in confusion. She grinned through her grief like a madwoman and did a little curtsey for Val.

"I thought you died in the accident," her wicked step-mother said.

"Don't be mad, Valerie," said Jenny. "At least you made the author bio."

Val looked like one of those cartoon characters whose head was about to start venting steam. Her glare was so fierce that Jenny relented and looked down at the photo she'd been left in the will. It was an old picture of RJ Valentine and a pretty young Japanese woman smiling in front of a bookstore. The woman was wearing a halter top and making a peace sign. The bookstore was the Poison

Pen, recognizable by its logo of a quill dipping into an inkwell with a skull on it. It was a popular tourist destination, and referenced often in the *Trouble* books. Neither Mom nor Dad was exactly looking at the camera, and there was something odd about the photo that Jenny couldn't put her finger on.

The woman was Jenny's mother Laura, obviously, but Jenny had never seen this photo before. As nice as it was to see her mom and dad together, she couldn't help but feel slightly disappointed. Was this it?

"Now then," said the video of RJ Valentine. "The rest of my estate shall be apportioned according to the terms worked out with Mr. Webb and explained forthwith."

He stopped to look around, as though he could somehow see them through the screen. For a chilling half-second, Jenny entertained the idea again that he actually could, and this was all some elaborate stunt. That he was still here. She knew it was a childish hope.

"I'm sure you're wondering what these heirlooms are for, and Val is no doubt furious with me right now. I'm sorry, Viv, but allow a dead man his fun." RJ leaned forward, the grin curling wider at the corners of his mouth. "I'd like you all to play a game. A dangerous game. You each in your hands hold a clue to a mystery. Solve it, and you just might solve the mystery of who killed me, too."

Valerie choked on her cocktail.

"I don't know how it went down, but I'll bet Sheriff Lockhart ruled it an accident," in the video, RJ turned to his right, which happened to be just where Lockhart was standing. "Less paperwork, right Blake?"

The Sheriff shivered.

"I assure you: I was murdered," her father continued. "Whoever solves the mystery of my death—and avoids a murder most foul themselves—will be awarded the remainder of my estate, mansion and vineyard included, which my accountant tells me is worth quite a lot of money. Oh! And all the rights and royalties to Trouble, including the final manuscript."

"This can't be legal," Val shook her head, dismissive.

"At this point," RJ Valentine said on the video, "Val is probably protesting the legality of all this. Well, honey, remember how you made me sign a prenup before we got married? It turns out they work both ways. Happy sleuthing!"

RJ let out a cackle and the video faded to a title card of his signature: the big ostentatious V, white on black. Then it was over. A sudden silence fell over the room as everyone tried to chew over what they'd just heard. Murder. A king's fortune up for grabs. $250 million, according to the internet. The mansion and the vineyard. And Trouble.

"Any questions?" asked Mr. Webb.

Chapter Three

A Dangerous Game

ACTING FAST, JENNY TUCKED HER FRAMED PHOTO UNDER HER ARM and got her phone out, taking pictures of the other heirlooms before their stunned new owners could pick their jaws up off the floor.

"What are you doing?" asked Jack.

Alicia was the first to figure it out and hid her skeleton key before Jenny could snap a photo of it.

"Is this against the rules?" asked Alicia.

"Ignore her," said Val. "No court would ever uphold this idiocy."

"If I report this, it'll be chaos in Blackbird Springs," said Ms. Griffin.

"How the hell is this a clue?" said Declan Dillion, waving his tarot card.

"Don't expect the department to help out with this nonsense," said the sheriff.

"I do know how to do my job, Blake," said the lawyer.

"What are the victory conditions?" asked Jenny.

"What do you mean?" asked Jack, who was lost.

"You solve the mystery," said Alicia, who was not.

The strange goth girl appeared eager to play. Noted. Jenny's mind and heart were racing each other to new conclusions, and she could hardly keep a thread straight as she considered all the different angles of this new game.

"Yeah, Hamilton," said Ms. Griffin. "What does 'solving the mystery' mean in a legal sense? Arrest? Conviction? Confession?"

"I think it's time you all got out of my house," said Val.

"Mom, let him talk," said Jack.

"If you don't care, could I have a look at that bottle of wine?" asked Jenny. "Is there any special significance?"

The widow glanced at the bottle and tucked it under her arm, hiding a private smile. Declan cackled.

"Don't you dare," Val said. "This bottle is worth more than your whole mongrel family's entire life savings."

A red wave of fury broke over Jenny. Sheriff Lockhart had to step in and catch her as she flew at Val, shrieking curses at the awful woman.

A loud piercing horn interrupted the scuffle, and everyone turned and glared at the source of the noise. It was Mr. Webb, holding up a disposable airhorn canister. Webb adjusted his tie and read from the will, raising his voice to command the room.

"Clause number two!" he shouted over the protests. "The executor shall give the heirs—hereafter referred to as 'contestants'—three minutes to argue and dispute the will before deploying the enclosed noise maker as he sees fit."

Shaking, Jenny pushed herself off the sheriff and came around to the lawyer's side. She wanted a better look at that will.

"You'll all receive digital document packs of this, don't worry," Mr. Webb told her, still not giving her a peek. "Now let's talk about the rules. First: a contestant wins when they've convinced the executor—in this case, *me*—of the murderer's identity, or the circumstances of

RJ Valentine's death, beyond a reasonable doubt. I'm talking motive, means, and opportunity. A murder weapon wouldn't hurt, either. I'm your jury."

"Come on, you're hardly an impartial party," said Val.

"I'm a sworn officer of the court," Mr. Webb said. "However, it is the right of the contestants to request arbitration from a panel of pre-selected judges if there is a dispute over my ruling.

"I should also add…" the lawyer made eye contact with all of them. "If I die or become incapacitated, steps have been taken to transfer my duties to another suitable neutral candidate. So don't get any ideas."

"Get bent," said Lockhart.

"Come on, Mr. Webb," said Jack. "You're practically family."

"Sure, for a hundred thousand dollar retainer, he is," said Val.

"Question," Ms. Griffin raised her hand.

"I'm getting there," the lawyer said. "Second: only contestants can win. If anyone who is not in this room solves the mystery, the money goes to charity. Also, if there is no winner after 100 days, the money goes to charity. You're welcome to report what you want, Yvonne, but if I were you, I'd sit on it."

"So would I," the sheriff said. "The last thing this town needs is a bunch of crazed nut jobs showing up thinking this is all a fun game."

"I don't know," said Declan. "It could be good for business."

"Lastly, the money," said Mr. Webb. "Effective immediately, all of RJ's assets have been frozen and placed in a trust, to be awarded, as I said, at my discretion. That includes the vineyard and manor, Valerie. You have 60 days to vacate the premises."

Val uttered a curse that made even Jenny blush.

"Dad wouldn't do that," Jack insisted.

"All assets that Valerie Valentine, née Stratford brought to the marriage remain with her. Also, you can keep your cars and personal possessions, jewelry, etc. A stipend will be provided to furnish you both with accommodations until Jack graduates. Housekeeping and staff will be retained to maintain the facilities until a winner is declared and the estate awarded. Which, by the way, is currently estimated at $272 million."

The money shut them all up. It was hard to ignore a massive payout like that. Jenny would never need to hear Aunt Shelly worry about money again. No more clothes from thrift-stores, using hand-me-down phones and having to pass up on class trips because they couldn't afford them. Jenny wanted that money, and really, she ought to have it. Was anyone else more worthy of the *Trouble* fortune than Trouble herself?

"If there really is a killer, this contest puts us in danger," Alicia said aloud, as much to herself as to the others.

"I think it's time I switched to the hard stuff," said Declan, returning to the mini bar. "Anyone else?"

"Don't worry," said Lockhart. "It's just a stupid joke from a world-class asshole. No offense, Valerie, may he rest in peace."

"None taken, Blake."

Jenny's mind shifted to the recurring villain of the *Trouble* series. *The Stranger* popped up every few books to stalk Trouble. The guy behind the guy behind the guy, the one she never caught. *A tall, dark, and Strangesome menace. Beware.* Her heart was beating rapidly in her chest. If she was Trouble, was there a real-life Stranger out there too?

"She's right," Jenny said. "If the killer knows we're after him…"

"All the more reason to keep it a secret, eh?" Mr. Webb retrieved a second document from the suitcase. "Now, RJ wished for you all to start the game on the same page, so I'm to give you a brief accounting of the facts."

"That's it?" Val frowned. "There's nothing in there for Victoria."

"…No," the lawyer looked down and offered no further explanation. Many questions formed on Val's lips, but she was too proud to ask them.

Victoria was Val's daughter from a previous marriage, Jenny knew from her internet sleuthing; she was older than Jack and Jenny by several years. Tori, as she commonly went by, appeared to split her time between grad school and rehab.

Mr. Webb was consulting a photo now and looking around the room. Not for the first time, Sheriff Lockhart involuntarily turned toward the mini bar before stopping himself. Clearly, he wanted a drink. Declan Dillion was wandering around the study holding up his Death card, as though it might reveal a secret at any moment.

"I have a funeral to plan, Hamilton," Valerie said to end the silence. "Are we quite finished with this ghoulish spectacle?"

"We're getting there," Mr. Webb replied, more serious now.

The lawyer walked over to the rolling ladder attached to the bookshelves by a rail. He wheeled it over so that it was next to RJ's desk. Next, he lifted his crystal tumbler and downed the last gulp of scotch. Consulting the photo again, he bent over and set the glass down on its side on the carpet.

"Jack, do you mind?" asked Mr. Webb.

Her half-brother's eyes widened in understanding, and he smiled sadly and joined the lawyer in front of their father's desk. Mr. Webb showed him the photo, and Jack gulped.

"Legs kinda out that way," Mr. Webb said, pointing at the carpet.

"I know," Jack said. "I was there."

Jack crouched and laid down on the carpet next to the desk and tipped-over crystal tumbler. Jenny and Val both cried out in horror. The two locked eyes, both surprised at the other and looked away fiercely.

"Junior!" Val admonished her son.

"It's okay Mom," Jack said from the floor. "I used to do this for dad when he needed help blocking out a crime scene."

"It's in extremely poor taste," said his mother.

"I know, he'd love it," replied her son. He craned his neck to look at Jenny. "I can't beat your middle name, but I did get to play the dead conductor from *Trouble on the Orient Express* for a whole afternoon while dad figured out how the murder happened."

Now he was playing his own father, it seemed. So it had happened here?

"As I was saying before," Mr. Webb continued, "here are the facts. On the evening of August 10th, RJ Valentine was working here in his study. There was a benefit gala being held by the Valentine Foundation at the Fairmont downtown. Valerie, you and Tori were both in attendance, correct?"

"Yes," confirmed Val.

"Blake, you were there too?" asked Mr. Webb

The sheriff nodded slowly, and Jenny thought he might have flicked his gaze to Alicia Aaron.

"As was I," said Declan.

"The only people at Valentine Manor that night were Jack, the housekeeper, and the gardener. And RJ, here in the study," Webb flipped a page and read on. "At approximately 6:15 PM the gardener, Jose Cooper, was working on the hedge out back and reported seeing Mr. Valentine through the window. According to Mr. Cooper's statement, RJ was working at his desk. Mr. Cooper finished trimming the hedge and left at 6:30 PM. Multiple witnesses can put Mr. Cooper at Champs Sports Bar for the next few hours, starting at 6:45 PM. Watching the A's game.

"The housekeeper, Mrs. Rivas, stated that when she was vacuuming in the hall at 7:45 PM, she could hear Mr. and Mrs. Valentine arguing in the study behind closed doors."

Jenny raised an eyebrow at this. Valerie cut in, annoyed.

"I was on the intercom, calling from the gala," Val explained. "I was upset with him for not making an appearance."

"Yes, I was getting to that," said Mr. Webb. "This is confirmed by several eyewitnesses at the gala who saw you making the call from your table in the ballroom. Mrs. Rivas is a new hire and unfamiliar with the intercom. Jack, meanwhile, was upstairs in his room doing homework."

Jenny thought she detected a slight blush from her brother when he nodded in confirmation from the floor.

"Jack came downstairs and knocked on the door to the study at about 9:10 PM, and there was no answer," Mr. Webb went on. "The door was locked. Jack tried the intercom, then called Valerie to check on RJ's whereabouts. While on the phone, Jack walked around the side of the house and looked in through the window and saw RJ lying prone inside. He then ran back inside and busted the door down to find Mr. Valentine like so."

He waved to Jack on the carpet. Jenny shivered.

"An empty glass lay next to RJ on the ground, with the bookshelf ladder right here. He was bleeding from an injury to the back of his skull. Paramedics arrived and rushed Mr. Valentine to the hospital where he would fall into a persistent vegetative state and never recover. Later that night, the police found bits of hair and skin from RJ on the corner of the desk here. It was written up as an accident. The theory was: he'd been drinking, and slipped and fell while climbing up the ladder here and hit his head on the desk."

Mr. Webb grimaced and tossed the report he was reading back into the suitcase.

"And that's it," the lawyer retrieved his glass and helped Jack stand. "A real locked-room mystery."

The room had gone quiet. Everyone was staring at the spot where they'd found RJ Valentine.

"But that was three weeks ago," said Jenny.

"It… took that long," said Jack in a small voice.

"Out of respect, I've held off on reporting about the accident until now," said Ms. Griffin.

Jenny swallowed and tasted that tangy, metallic sensation: fear. She understood with a jolt that she was having a panic attack. She couldn't breathe.

Jenny hadn't had an attack in weeks, but the feeling was all too familiar. She needed to get out of here. Her feet had mutinied, though, and remained firmly planted on the carpet. She could move her arms a little, and her searching hand reached out to Jack for support, but he yanked it away, suspicious. No one else seemed to notice her, but then Declan Dillion guided her into her father's desk chair.

Everything else had gone hazy, so she forced herself to focus on the desk. There was dad's pen holder on the left, then a large crystalline paperweight in the shape of a bishop chess piece. In the middle, a green banker's lamp with brass fixtures. A blotter calendar stretched out in front of her. Jenny found herself staring at a drawing of a little man's nose and hands peeking out from the bottom of the desk pad. A caption next to him read:

It was a well-known doodle from the *Trouble* books, sort of a calling card that the Stranger left behind. Had dad drawn this on his calendar— *or had the Stranger?* Fiction and reality blurred in her mind. Someone squeezed Jenny's shoulder.

"Are we *sure* RJ didn't have an accident?" asked Declan Dillion behind her.

"It wasn't ruled a homicide," said Lockhart. "And I see no reason to reopen the case."

"Well, how you run your shop is your business," said Mr. Webb. "But there are a couple reasons why we believe this to be a murder. Yes, this is important, Val, and then we can go."

Mr. Webb mixed himself another drink and walked back to his suitcase.

"First, there's the matter of the death threats," he said, holding up photocopies of handwritten notes in big, blocky letters.

"Johnny got those for years," said Val, rolling her eyes. "They're just stupid fans having a laugh."

"Perhaps," said Mr. Webb. "But these were different. More... personal, you might say. Blake knows this. RJ showed them to you."

"Sure," said the sheriff. "But that's not the first time he got some pretty aggressive ones. You remember that stalker? She was a kook, but not dangerous."

"Yes, and she had an alibi, by the way," said Mr. Webb.

"What was it?" asked Jenny.

"She slit her wrists. Three months ago."

"Oh," said Jenny.

"Second," said the lawyer, "the autopsy revealed not one but two indentations to the skull. Previously, the doctors believed there was only a single injury. It took a high-resolution X-ray and examination of the body to reveal the other. The first indentation was consistent with

27

striking the corner of this desk, and would not have been a serious wound. A mild concussion at best. The second, however, fractured the skull and pushed it inward, causing massive, irreversible brain trauma. This indentation was created with considerably more force from a narrow, pointed object."

"Like an icepick?" Alicia Aaron asked.

"Maybe," said Lockhart, leaning over Webb's shoulder to stare at the report. "But blunter, like a rock hammer or maybe a railroad spike."

"Yes, or perhaps the pommel of a knife," said Mr. Webb.

"Why not just stab him?" Jack said softly, a queasy frown on his face now. He probably didn't like thinking about dad as a collection of flesh, bone fragments, and gray matter instead of a living being. Neither did Jenny. She stood up shakily and walked over to the fireplace, clutching her framed photo. She hoped the heat would stop her shivering.

"There is one final clause in the will," Mr. Webb said. "RJ asked me to read this last after you'd had some time to consider things."

They all turned to listen.

"Call it the 'take your doll and go home' clause," said Mr. Webb. "Should all seven contestants agree to decline the game, they may return their heirlooms and receive a monetary sum instead, to be half of the Valentine fortune, divided seven ways. The other half would go to the Foundation."

Nobody spoke. They were all doing the math.

"About $19 million each," said Jack first.

The sheriff whistled.

"I could retire tomorrow," said Ms. Griffin.

"What about the house?" asked Alicia Aaron.

"Donated to the foundation," said Mr. Webb.

Her brother nodded, considering.

"What do season tickets at the Giants go for these days?" asked Lockhart.

"Maybe $50 grand, for good seats," said Declan.

"Sorry, but I'm not giving away my family's home and savings so you all can retire early and waste our hard-earned money on booze and cheap thrills," said Val, glaring at them.

"This clause, by the way, expires in 24 hours," said Mr. Webb. "Unless you all agree to it and return your heirlooms, at this time tomorrow the only way to win the money is to find RJ's killer."

"I'm in," said Alicia, and limped over awkwardly on her fake leg to return the brass skeleton key.

"Same," said Yvonne Griffin, putting the book dad gave her back into the suitcase.

The sheriff wordlessly followed suit with the noose. Declan shrugged and tossed his tarot card in. Jack turned to his mother.

"Let's think about this," he said. "Do we really need more than $38 million?"

"We don't need to take any deals like some desperate grifters," said Val, shooting a look at Jenny. "It'll never hold up in court."

"Look, Val, it's your choice, but come on," said Declan. "You really think you've got a better shot by solving the mystery? It's unprovable. In 100 days, the money will just go to charity anyway."

Jack put his onyx blackbird statue into the suitcase.

"We can always challenge the will later," he said to his mother. "And you run the foundation anyway. We could just rent ourselves the house back. Easy peasy."

Val ground her teeth and let out a great sigh.

"You're a real son of a bitch, Johnny," she said to her wine bottle and returned it to Mr. Webb. "Fine, divvy it up, but expect a call from my lawyer."

Mr. Webb took the bottle and placed it back in the suitcase, perhaps a bit disappointed.

"It has to be unanimous," he said.

They all turned to Jenny, who was still warming herself by the fire.

"Of course she's in," said Val, scornfully. "She can't even afford a decent haircut."

Jenny giggled.

"Did he really call it the 'take your doll and go home' clause?" she asked Mr. Webb.

"Mmhmm."

"That was for me, I think," Jenny said. "Book five. The snooty little heiress at the tea party."

Blank stares all around.

"You're all gonna have to brush up," she said, shaking her head.

"Come on, Jenny," said Jack, his pallor shading a bit green. "Let's settle this, and I'll give you a tour of the place."

"Haven't you guys been paying attention?" she asked incredulously.

Spinning around, Jenny hurled her heirloom into the fireplace. With a crash, the glass in the frame shattered on the bricks. Gasps of surprise rang out behind her as it went up in flames.

"My name is Trouble!" Jenny said with delicious satisfaction. "Happy sleuthing, bitches."

Chapter Four

At the Sign of the Poison Pen

Val wasted no time expelling Jenny from the mansion, shrieking about getting a judge to have the will thrown out and a restraining order filed. Everyone else was too pissed at her to notice the switcharoo: she'd tucked her own photo frame inside her coat and smashed a picture of RJ and Val instead. Amateurs. When she checked her phone, it was blowing up with aggravated texts from Shelly, but Jenny ignored them and ordered the chauffeur to take her to the Poison Pen, downtown. The game was afoot, and there was no time to waste.

Her emotions were all over the place. This game, this mystery, it was like her whole life had been building to this moment. She'd read all the books a hundred times. She had a collection of wigs and disguises, just like Trouble. She could pick locks and dust for fingerprints. She'd tried her hardest to be a good girl detective, but in real life, people didn't like it when you followed them around and exposed all their shit. Now she finally had an honest-to-god mystery to solve. All it cost her was her father.

Dad... There was a small black and white photo of RJ Valentine in the corner of the Poison Pen storefront. Above, an over-sized poster of the original *My Name is Trouble* cover dominated the window, with the other *Trouble* titles spread out like a deck of cards underneath. *Trouble Comes Knocking, Trouble Always Finds Me, Trouble and Treble,* and all the rest. Each book cover was illustrated with different scenes of Trouble in action: hunting for clues with a magnifying glass, hiding from a burglar behind a door, opening a secret passage…

Jenny blinked her eyes, hoping her mascara didn't run. She stared at her own reflection in the window, overlaid on top of Trouble's. "We can do this," she told herself.

There was something off about the Pen. She studied the photo RJ left her until she got it: this was a different building. The one in the picture of Mom and Dad had a brick facade between storefronts. There was a cafe next to their Poison Pen, but hers shared a block with a mortuary. The bookstore must have moved at some point in the past 17 years.

Jenny turned and stepped off the curb into the street, pulling her phone out to google it. She never saw the car coming.

Lucky for her, someone else did.

Strong arms wrapped around her waist and yanked her back to the curb. She yelped in surprise as a blue Dodge Challenger with white racing stripes blew by. It never slowed, leaving a huge gust of air in its wake that sent early fall leaves whirling all over the sidewalk. She kicked her legs reflexively and felt her stomach somersault as gravity spun and she landed with a crash on her back.

A male voice grunted in her ear. Jenny scrambled up and unleashed a torrent of foul language at the Challenger as it sped away.

"He didn't even brake!" she cried.

Her mysterious savior was dusting himself off as he got to his feet: it was the guy she'd seen checking the train schedule this morning on the ride to the mansion. He was tall but much younger up close—probably her age—with golden skin from what she guessed was Latino heritage. His close-cropped hair looked newly cut, and he was hiding those strong arms under a loose Blackbird Springs Academy pullover.

"Yeah, that was Mason's car," said the boy, panting. "He's kind of a bad driver."

"Holy shit, you saved my life!"

Jenny threw her arms around the big guy. Dude was solid. He smelled like a pine tree and didn't hug back. This was awkward now.

"Oh fuck!" she yelped.

That crash when she landed: it was her heirloom. The glass in the frame had shattered on the ground. Jenny scrambled to pick up the biggest shards.

"Fuck fuck fuck!" she said, before cutting her finger and swearing some more.

"Um careful," said the boy, no doubt baffled by this crazy bitch getting weepy over some glass. But for all she knew there was a secret message embedded in the frame.

She needed something to put this mess in. The guy was holding a thin paper bag from the Pen.

"Gimme that!" Jenny snatched the bag from his hands before he could stop her and dumped out the book he'd purchased. Carefully, she deposited her photo frame and the shards of glass inside.

"Sorry," he said.

"It's not your fault," Jenny stood, sucking the cut on her ring finger. "Mason, you said his name was?"

"Yeah. Mason Lockhart," he said. "He's a senior."

"Is he related to the sheriff?" she asked, suspicious.

"Yeah, that's his dad," he said.

Interesting. Coincidence? Or was dad already trying to thin the competition? "He's dead," she spat.

He nodded, grinning. Jenny was about to give him the business for patronizing her when she noticed the book in his hand. The one she'd dumped out of his bag. It was a Turtleback cover edition of *I Knew You Were Trouble.*

"That for your little sister?" she said, pointing.

"Only child," he replied, not embarrassed in the slightest. "Been looking for this edition for a while. I'm a collector."

Jenny's watch vibrated. She checked the message and sighed. The news about Dad had hit the wires. "Aren't those sort of girl books?" she asked, suspicious.

"Hey, danger has no gender," he said.

"Yeah, I don't know about that," said Jenny. "Who the fuck are you, anyway?"

"I'm Drew," he said and nodded at her outfit. "Drew Porter. You must be Trouble."

Jenny beamed. "Why thank you."

"Of course, the real Trouble doesn't have a tattoo and wear 'fuck you' eyeliner," said Drew, smirking. "But we get all types here."

Jenny smiled and rubbed the Ace of Clubs tattoo on her wrist. It was a recent addition and still itched. She loved it. "That's only because RJ didn't make her grow up," she said. An idea occurred to her. Maybe he'd be useful. "So you live here, huh?"

"Born and raised. I assume you're just visiting?"

"No, this is me now," said Jenny. "Just moved in yesterday."

"Sophomore?" he asked.

"Junior."

"Cool, me too," said Drew. "BS Academy, right?"

She nodded, and he made an exaggerated *phew!* expression.

"Good," he said, favoring her with a bemused head tilt. "You seem too interesting to be one of those Harbor High losers."

Oh, Jenny knew *that* look.

"Hey, just so you're not barking up the wrong tree, you should know I'm only for girls," she said. Jenny had found it was best to get this out of the way early with dudes.

"Me too!" he said, then grimaced. "Sorry, that was a douche thing to say. But it's all good. Actually, I should go…"

"You're fine, the train doesn't get here for 20 minutes," said Jenny. "I'll clear out before your hot date shows up, but you know, it might help you out a little if I didn't."

He was flabbergasted. They always were. Jenny loved it when she guessed right.

"Okay, how'd you know that?" he asked.

Jenny ran an eye over him.

"New haircut, new shoes," she nodded to his clean white kicks. "You normally wear glasses, but today you're wearing contacts. You keep touching the bridge of your nose like you're pushing up your glasses, but they're not there. It's a tick, you're nervous. Let me guess: she's been gone all summer and gets back today from uh, let's say Cheer Camp?"

"Journalism camp," said Drew. "Do I really seem nervous?"

"Little bit."

He sighed. "She's just a friend. Ya know, I think I'll stay on your good side, cause you're low-key terrifying."

Jenny missed the compliment because she was watching a distraught lady in her 20s put a tulip down in front of the *Trouble* display in the Poison Pen window. Suddenly, she wanted to be far away. She grabbed Drew's hand and pulled him into the street, looking both ways this time.

"Cool," said Jenny. "Now do me a favor and show me where the

Poison Pen *used* to be."

"Uh sure," he said, his long strides catching up with her. "But tell me your real name first."

"I already did."

Jenny spun out her backstory as they walked through town. He refused to believe her until she shoved her ID card in his face. Then he was ready to worship her. That would do.

"As you know, Trouble doesn't normally have a sidekick, but I'd be willing to make an exception if you prove your worth," she said with a wink. She was only half-kidding. "Anyway, I go by Jenny," she told him. She'd left out the part about the game. And RJ's death, though he'd learn about that soon enough.

Up ahead, half the road was blocked off with cones. Two city workers were using a cherry picker to work on the street lights. Drew was telling her about being teammates with her brother Jack on the school baseball team.

"Are you guys friends?" she asked.

"Jack has no friends, only people who want something from him," said Drew. "Be sure to call him Junior. He hates it."

Jenny snickered, even though she really just wanted to talk to Jack. Get to know him. The lift beeped as a worker with a salt-and-pepper beard came back down, carrying an old stoplight. The other worker, a big tall guy, was screwing in a fancy cylindrical lightbulb into a new wrought iron fixture. Drew led her past them, ducking under the cherry picker.

"Hung this one myself in 1992," said the older one, whose name tag read **ANDY**.

The other whistled. "Great season for Eck," he said.

"It was a good year, for wine," said Andy.

"Hey what's that mean?" asked Jenny, after they passed. RJ had said it on the video.

"Oh uh, it's like a saying here," said Drew, shrugging. "It's a wine thing. I don't know, ask my mom, she's a sommelier."

"What's that?"

"A wine expert. Okay, I'm pretty sure this is it." He pointed to a bakery on the corner up ahead.

Jenny opened the Poison Pen bag and disentangled her photo from the broken frame. The building looked right. It still had those brick facades and molding at ground level.

"Wow, he looks so young," said Drew looking on. "Is that your mom?"

"Uh-huh," Jenny said, biting her lip as she compared the picture to the real thing. "Something's still off."

"It's the focal length," Drew said. She raised a questioning eyebrow. "I shoot sports for the school newspaper," he explained. "This was shot with a long lens. May I?"

Curiosity won out over reluctance, and she handed him the photo. He held it up and walked backward, looking for a matching angle.

"Maybe right about here," he said, squinting out of one eye.

Jenny looked back and noticed with a start that there was a map drawn on the back of the photo. She'd prefer Drew didn't see it and was about to snatch the picture away when a passing shadow caught her eye.

It was the cherry picker. The platform was empty now, and swinging out into the road overhead… Jenny looked up in fascination as it smashed right into the stoplight directly above them in a squeal of crunching metal.

"Look out!"

Jenny lunged, pushing Drew to the side. His foot caught on hers, and they both tripped and went down. The stoplight crashed into the asphalt, missing them by inches. Jenny felt her calves sting under her jeans as shards of broken glass sprayed her legs.

"What the hell?" said Drew.

His eyes were wide in shock. She rolled off him as the workmen ran up in a panic. The tall one, whose name tag read **DAVE**, kept asking if Jenny was okay. A small crowd had stopped to watch the excitement.

"I don't know what happened!" Dave insisted, helping her and Drew up and brushing them off. "The lift was locked down, it should never have moved like that."

Jenny looked over to the curb, at the unmanned lift controls. She tried to shrug at Andy, but her knees were shaking. Maybe someone bumped it? Or a malfunction? Adrenaline was making her woozy for the second time in a handful of minutes. The car and now this… It was as though Blackbird Springs was trying to bump her off.

Maybe it was, Jenny thought with a frown. She scanned the crowd and rotated casually, alert for ill intent. Only blank and unfamiliar faces stared back. Many were already turning away, the spectacle no longer interesting.

She was turning back to Drew when she saw the Stranger.

He was standing beside the old town hall on the other side of the park, his face shrouded in shadow—if he was even a he. A foreboding figure in a dark coat with the collar up, wearing a black fedora.

Or thought she saw him. When Jenny looked back to get a better look, he was gone.

She was probably just imagining things. Years of reading and re-reading the Trouble series had caused that black rogue to appear in Jenny's dreams with great frequency when she was younger. Maybe being here now with all this excitement was letting him run wild in her thoughts again.

"*A tall, dark, and Strangesome menace. Beware.*" Jenny quoted to herself absently. Some fan theories had it that the Stranger was really just Trouble's father keeping an eye on his daughter, but Jenny didn't care for that interpretation. Especially not now.

No, she probably just imagined him. Looking down, she snatched up the heirloom photo where Drew had dropped it and tucked it into her pocket. She'd check out the map later in private.

"Heya, maybe we should get our stories straight," said Andy, running a nervous hand over his buzzcut.

"Let's pretend I was never here, and we'll call it square," she told him.

"Deal," said Andy with a thumbs up.

Jenny gave the hapless workmen a sarcastic salute and looked around for Drew. She found him hunched over on the sidewalk, hands on his knees, taking big gulps of oxygen.

"You okay?" she asked.

"I almost just died!"

"So we're even now," Jenny said.

He gave her a courtesy chuckle and straightened up, looking at Jenny with new wonder and gratitude.

"Thank you. This is like kismet or some shit. Friends for life?"

He held out his hand. Jenny gave him a fist bump and looked away shyly. Gratitude wasn't an emotion she was used to anyone showing her. Truth be told, she'd never really had any close friends. Trouble was a lone wolf.

Drew brushed some dirt off his sweater, biting his lip. "You know I gotta say Jenny, speak of the devil, this whole thing where we both almost get killed in the span of minutes is giving me some crazy Trouble vibes right now. Like in *Double Trouble* when those accidents keep happening to people on their birthday. Is it your birthday?"

Jenny snorted.

"No, I was born in March."

Drew continued to impress. *Double Trouble* was terrible. A one-off comic book written for an ill-fated promotion with Pizza Hut, and not counted among the canon novels. Only a true fan could pull that reference from their back pocket, but she kept that to herself.

Her watch vibrated again with another text. She couldn't avoid this any longer.

"Hey, I gotta split."

"Yeah, me too," said Drew, smoothing his hair. Then followed some awkward attempts at hugs or handshakes until they mutually settled on a fist bump and parted.

"Go smash that puss!" Jenny called after him. His ears burned red, which pleased her. "See you in school?"

"For sure," he said, looking back. "I wanna know more about that surveillance photo."

"The what?" she frowned.

"Your mom and dad?" he said, walking backward. "Look again. They're not posing."

Chapter Five
A Little Night Music

SOMETIME LATER, JENNY WALKED ON TIRED FEET UP TO THE PORCH of her new home.

"Okay, talk later," she said into her ancient iPhone 7 and hung up. After a moment's hesitation, she eased the door open.

The house smelled like kimchi and stale nicotine. Jenny wrinkled her nose, pausing on the doorstep. A day outside in lush Blackbird Springs had done wonders for her sinuses after years in smoggy Los Angeles. Now her revitalized senses were reminding her that her grandparents had been smokers. She leaned back for one last breath of pleasant air before walking into her new home.

"Hello?" a voice called from inside.

"Just me," said Jenny.

She found her aunt in the living room, enmeshed in a rats nest of cables from behind the entertainment console, covered in dust.

A year ago, Jenny went through a growth spurt and gained an inch on her aunt. Shelly could pass for Jenny's sister, were it not for her unflatteringly-broad shoulders and big round head. Everything about her, from her cell phone holster to her dorky bob haircut seemed calculated to embarrass her niece.

"I thought you said not to touch any of that," said Jenny.

"I told *you* not to," said Shelly. "I'm fixing the WiFi, so don't tattle."

"What are they gonna do, ground you?" said Jenny.

She could see the tendons in Shelly's neck tense as she bit back a reply.

"Don't get smart with me," said her aunt. "Where were you?"

Shelly and her grandparents didn't get along. It was weird not being the most disappointing scion of the Onishi clan for once. With Jenny, they were polite but withdrawn; they'd never totally forgiven Shelly for putting college on hold to adopt her, though. Shelly was the smart one, the good girl. She was supposed to be rubbing elbows with Paul Krugman by now, not teaching high school Econ.

"Well?" her aunt asked again. "Where've you been? I've been texting you for hours."

"I um…" Jenny knelt and pulled out the photo of her parents, wordlessly sliding it into Shelly's view.

Shelly took the photo and stared at it for a while. All at once, she thrust it back into Jenny's hands and turned around, busying herself with an ethernet cable. When her aunt spoke again, her voice was husky.

"I told you not to go see him," she said.

"I didn't," said Jenny. "Not really."

"How's that?"

Jenny couldn't bring herself to say the words. Speaking the truth would make it real. She could feel the dam behind her eyes ready to burst, and she wasn't about to give Shelly the satisfaction.

"Just… google it," she bit out. "Congrats, you always hated him."

Jenny stormed off before her aunt could respond and retreated to her new bedroom upstairs. Sinking deep into the mattress, she was suddenly exhausted. That black glacier was pressing hard on her brain again. This time, she stopped fighting and slipped under. The inky darkness enveloped her, and she knew no more.

It was well past midnight when she set off to follow the next clue. A quick internet search revealed that the map dad left Jenny on the back of the photo led to an undeveloped parcel of land next to Valentine Vineyards. She stole into the night on her bike and rode north.

The sky was clear, with barely a sliver of the new moon to light her way. She shivered and pedaled harder to keep warm. Instead of turning left toward the mansion, or right toward the vineyards, she rode on until she reached the berm at the end of Cellar Drive. The land beyond was vacant, but a dirt path continued into the wooded hills, just like the map showed.

She hefted her bike over the berm and followed the trail. What could this have to do with RJ's killer? The path soon joined a narrow stream that snaked between a small copse of oak trees, and right in the middle was a big treehouse. She double-checked the map. The treehouse was right where the big X marked, just like in *Trouble Eight Days a Week*.

A makeshift ladder of bolted on two-by-fours ran up the tree trunk to a small cabin, built onto a wide platform, about 20 feet above. She parked the bike and climbed up, dimly aware of the danger if she fell—and savoring it. The breeze up here after that ride should have chilled her to the core, but anticipation burned within, keeping her warm. There was a hatch in the floor at the top of the ladder. It was weather stripped and lifted open with a squeak as she broke the seal and let the air rush in.

"Lumos," she muttered and switched on flashlight mode on her phone.

She climbed inside and found herself in a tiny but functional studio apartment. There was a small camp bed in the corner and a narrow table next to a sink. A few dishes were stacked in a cupboard. Below, a small radio sat silent on the counter next to a compact heating pad. Was this RJ's little hideaway?

On the table was a manilla folder with Jenny's name on it. She looked inside and raised her eyebrow. There was a copy of her birth certificate, her old address, even a photo of her, taken with a telephoto lens, in front of—

A shiver ran down her spine. So he knew Jenny's secret. And he'd been watching her. Recently. Did he think *she* was a suspect?

Anger flared in her chest, but she had to admit it made sense. Family members always had a motive. Regardless, this didn't help: she had an airtight alibi for the night of the attack, so the killer was certainly not her. Which meant this clue was a dead end.

Well, maybe not. This treehouse could be useful. There was a thin layer of dust on everything, so it was unlikely that anyone else came here regularly. She waved her flashlight around the room and spotted a black rotary switch like the timed dial in their old apartment complex's laundry room. Crossing her fingers, she turned it clockwise.

A bulb in the ceiling lit up the room. The radio crackled and "Clair de lune" emanated softly from a classical music station. This treehouse had electricity: nice! She tried the faucet: running water too. There was even a cramped powder room with a toilet. From the window on the west, she could just see the lights from Valentine Manor through the trees. Yes, this would suit Trouble very nicely.

Another thought occurred: Dad wanted Jenny to find this place. To find that file. Maybe RJ never *really* suspected her. Maybe this was his way of telling her that every contestant was also a suspect. He wanted her to have this knowledge, to have this hideaway, and use it. Yeah, that sounded like RJ all right.

She smiled and tested out the camp bed. It was nearly as soft as a real mattress. The piano tinkled on the radio as she lay there, staring at the ceiling, considering the next move.

There was still the question of the photo Dad left Jenny. Who would have taken that picture of Mom and Dad if they weren't posing for it? If they didn't know someone else had been watching? A private eye? She could think of only one person who had reason to hire one: the jealous wife.

Valerie Valentine.

Chapter Six

Black Mirrors

JENNY HAD NEVER BEEN TO A FUNERAL BEFORE. SHE WAS PRETTY sure they didn't normally have giant wine tents serving 2016 Valentine Merlot in commemorative goblets etched with the initials **RJV**, but Dad had been a long time dying. Val had weeks to plan his service.

Or maybe longer, if the theory about her clue was correct. Val had an airtight alibi, putting on the Valentine Foundation Gala the night of Dad's attack, but she was also the richest lady in Blackbird Springs. If she could hire a PI to spy on Mom and Dad's affair all those years ago, could she hire some goon to off him now? It certainly seemed possible.

Jenny scanned the crowd for her evil stepmother. It seemed like the entire town had shown up to Black Rock Cemetery—and probably more than a few Trouble super fans as well. Jenny hadn't decided yet whether she loved or hated their presence. Maybe both.

"Let's get our seats now," said Shelly, pointing to a security checkpoint blocking access to the good chairs up front. Her aunt had apologized profusely once she learned about RJ's death. Jenny

46

appreciated it but wasn't looking to get all weepy with her any time soon. She hadn't mentioned the will, either. If Shelly knew about the game, she'd never let Jenny out of the house.

Jenny clutched her shoulders tightly, wishing she'd worn a sweater. She didn't own any black dresses, so she'd borrowed Shelly's sleeveless cocktail number. Her eye makeup was in full raccoon mode today; Jenny was half-hoping the eventual tears would make it run so she'd look fashionably broken. She even wore black lipstick, such was her mood.

"Friends and family only," said a lady cop, holding her palm outward to stop them from entering the VIP area.

"Bitch, I'm his daughter!" Jenny shrieked at her.

"Jennifer—" Shelly growled through gritted teeth.

"Peña! Let her in!" called a commanding voice. It was the sheriff, Lockhart.

Jenny smirked at Peña and slipped past.

"Thanks!" she told the sheriff.

Such was the expressiveness of his face, and the natural charisma he exuded, that a frosty glare was somehow communicated behind his aviators. Dad must have hated this guy.

"You're not still mad, are you?" she sassed him.

"$19.5 million…" he grumbled through tight lips.

"What's this?" asked Shelly.

"Shelly, this is the real-life Sheriff Lockhart, Blackbird Springs' designated punchline. As Trouble's legal guardian, you might as well get to know him now."

She scampered away, looking for the tent where the viewing was being held. Jenny had a nasty business she needed to attend to, and Dad would understand, but it still made her stomach churn. She ducked between two elderly mourners and nearly walked right into

Dinah Black, the pretty blonde from the mansion yesterday.

"Oh!" Jenny yelped, stumbling to the side in her flats.

Dinah dodged the other way, somehow keeping the wine glasses in her hands from spilling. A quick glance down confirmed to Jenny that, one: Dinah had stayed upright in three-inch heels, and two: she looked amazing, even in funeral attire. Her black dress was unadorned and had a modest neckline, but the hem only brushed her knees. She wore long black gloves and a black beret with a half-veil, which to Jenny made Dinah seem impossibly sophisticated.

"We have to stop meeting like this." Dinah smiled for a moment, then caught herself, mortified. "Oh my God, I'm so insensitive."

"It's okay." Jenny shrugged, trying to be cool. "Gimme one of those, and we'll call it even."

"This was supposed to be for Jack." Dinah pursed her lip in a coy smile and handed Jenny the glass in her left hand. "He'll be cross, but all right."

The wine was sour on her lips, but with a lingering sweetness that filled her throat with spicy, silky sophistication. It was a taste she would always remember, and would quite never recapture.

"Okay, I must ask," said Dinah. "Are you *really* a distant relative of the Valentine family?"

"Distant?" said Jenny. "I'm Jack's half-sister."

"Another one? Seriously?"

Jenny smirked. Dinah had no idea.

"Well, you can't possibly be as dreadful as Tori. So was RJ...?" Dinah winced. Jenny nodded again, with less mirth. Dinah embraced her. "I'm so sorry," said Dinah. "How awful. Jack is a mess, I can only imagine."

"Thanks." All this sincerity was going to make Jenny cry, so she changed the subject. "Jack didn't tell you about me?"

"That boy's been keeping secrets," said Dinah, appraising her further. "I can see it in the cheekbones, I think. So that's why they let *you* into that big to-do will reading, but what was Alicia Aaron doing there?"

"Sorry, I don't know myself."

Which was half-true.

"Such a mysterious family." Dinah twinkled an eye as if knowing that Jenny could say more but wasn't. Behind her, Jack approached in a custom-tailored black suit. Not the same one he wore yesterday, Jenny noted. What a fancy boy. He looked wary as he sidled up next to Dinah and put a possessive arm around her waist, keeping his eyes on Jenny.

"I see you've met Jenny," he said.

"You mean your *sister*?" asked Dinah. "I have."

Jack grimaced.

"*Distant relative?*" Jenny said.

"Did you tell her your other name?" Jack asked her.

Dinah raised an eyebrow, but Jenny demurred. "Hush," she purred at Jack.

"Dinah, can I borrow my… *sister* for a moment?" he said, chewing over the word like a bitter cough drop.

"Of course." Dinah smiled, ignoring his tone, and handed him her wine glass. "Here, take mine, I'll go find another."

She turned to Jenny and rummaged in her purse.

"We absolutely must hang out on a happier day than this." Dinah reached out and took Jenny's left hand and began to write on it with her cherry red lipstick. "Text me before you wash your hand."

She'd written numbers on her palm. Something looked odd about them, but Jenny was too delighted to investigate at the moment.

"I'll never wash it again," she said, joking—but also not joking.

Dinah drifted away, and Jenny glumly turned back to Jack.

"Let's go see Dad," Jack said and yanked her toward the viewing tent.

THE LINE TO THE CASKET WAS NEARLY EMPTY NOW. SERVICE WAS about to begin. The dread slowly built in Jenny's stomach as they neared the body.

"Did you tell Dinah about the will?" Jack asked suddenly. "You know, the contest and all that."

"No," Jenny told him. "But I think she's curious—"

"Hush, it's our turn."

They walked to the casket together. She glanced behind them, noting that they were last in line. No one else was in the tent now except a balding, pale man with a small, sharp nose, standing in the corner near the exit. He wore a black suit dulled with the sheen of too many trips to the dry cleaner. He had the sort of bland officiousness of Help about him, but his eyes were unsmiling, and it gave her a shiver.

This wasn't helping the dread inside Jenny—which was full to bursting by now—but then she saw RJ Valentine at rest in his coffin, and all her anxiety fled. Dad looked so vibrant and peaceful. She'd thought this would be wretched, but now her heart was soaring to see him like this.

"My compliments to the Undertaker," she said, and the pale man turned to her and bowed a little. She stretched up to whisper in Jack's ear. "Oh shit, that's him! Are you supposed to tip them?"

"No," Jack said. "Relax."

They stood over their father together. The mortician had even gotten the slight smirk RJ Valentine always wore in the left corner of his mouth just right. It made Jenny feel slightly better about what she

50

had to do.

"Okay. Don't freak out."

Jenny fished her phone out of her purse, careful with the lipstick on her left palm, and turned her body to shield them from the Undertaker as much as possible. Then she reached out with the phone and held the black screen under her father's nostrils. Jack reacted about as expected.

"What are you doing!?" he whispered, glaring at her.

"Come on," said Jenny. "Tell me you didn't wonder. We need to be sure."

"I *am* sure. I did it at the morgue—without the Undertaker watching. This is how rumors spread!" He was whisper-shouting, but the pale man took no notice, politely looking away.

"He can't see, relax," she said. "Understand, I can't really trust you right now."

"How so?"

"We have only your word that Dad was injured when you found him," said Jenny.

"He was!" Jack whispered, eyes flashing.

"Says you. Why weren't you at the Gala downtown with your mom and sister?"

"I hate those things. I never go if I can help it."

"What were you doing in your room?"

"Reading."

"What book?"

He hesitated. "Walden."

"I know you're lying," said Jenny. "But I don't think you did it, either."

Jack scowled. "Gee, thanks for the endorsement, Trouble."

"Just doing my job," said Jenny. "Gotta check every angle."

"Right. So you can steal my family's house."

"Not steal. Win. Don't you dare take it out on me. If you've got a problem, take it up with him."

She nodded to their dad, resting quietly under their noses. It had been long enough, so she pulled the phone back. Jenny found not even the faintest hint of fog on the glass. She let out a long sigh. It was always a fool's hope. What a grand twist it would have been, but not even RJ Valentine could pull off his own surprise resurrection.

Jack took another sip of wine and grimaced. "I hope *you're* enjoying this," he told his father.

"Of course he is," Jenny leaned over and kissed Dad on the cheek. "This may well be his masterwork."

Jack patted Dad's hand. They stood in silence.

"Is Val really gonna try to sue to get the will invalidated?" Jenny asked after a while.

"She's gonna try but…" Jack shrugged. "Mr. Webb said all he needs to get her case tossed out is her prenup and the Magna Carta."

"What's that mean?"

"I don't know. I guess she has a bad case. Way back when, she was the one worried about Dad getting *her* money."

"It doesn't have to be a competition, you know." She tried to be as casual as possible for the proposition she was about to make. "You and I could always team up. Pool our clues and resources together…"

Jenny studied his face, but Jack's shields were up.

"Seems like Dad wouldn't want us to," Jack replied. "Trouble doesn't have a sidekick."

"Is that why you didn't tell your girlfriend?" she asked.

"No," said Jack. "And you shouldn't either."

"Why, don't you trust her?"

Jack bit the inside of his cheek, turning it over in his mind. He took a sip of wine and a bouquet of melancholy spread across his face.

"She doesn't really love me."

"Oh. Sorry."

As they left, Jenny stopped to talk to the Undertaker.

"It's all right if I kissed him, right?" she asked.

"Him?" his eyes drifted to Jack, then back to Jenny, and he shrugged. "I don't judge."

"No, the body, you freak. I don't have like poison on my lips now or something?"

"Not literally, no," the Undertaker told them in a high, cold voice. "You should go join the other pallbearers, Mr. Valentine. We're about to begin."

Jack handed the empty wine glass to the Undertaker and took off without a word.

THE FUNERAL SERVICE ITSELF WAS A BORING BLUR. AN UNENDING parade of RJ's old colleagues from Calistoga University took the mic, and Jenny felt like she was at a political rally for *Books!* Jack never spoke. Jenny didn't see his older sister Tori anywhere. Perhaps she was back in rehab again. Valerie Valentine's remarks veered into a fundraising pitch for The Friends of the Library at times, but she managed to bring it home with a story about RJ bringing her flowers she was allergic to on their first date. Jenny suspected it was made up, but just in case, it might do to stock up on daisies.

As the service wound down, Shelly bid Jenny farewell after having a chat with the caterers about not serving her niece any more wine. Jenny insisted on waiting around to see the coffin interred. She wasn't sure what she was expecting to happen, but a good girl detective was patient and thorough.

After the tents came down and staff cleared out, a couple city workers showed up with a small crane to lift RJ's casket into the crypt. Jenny recognized the workers as the two from the stoplight debacle in Town Square. This time, thankfully, they performed their job without any mishaps. The Undertaker supervised as a massive slab of marble sealed RJ inside forever.

Jenny sauntered closer as the men packed up their gear. How many souls had these men locked away in their final resting places over the years? Was there ever a mistake?

"You guys ever have to open one of these up?" she asked the tall one named Dave.

"Hah, yeah, once!" he said, turning back to his colleague. "You remember that, Andy? Opening up the Klein tomb?"

"What a clusterf—fudge that was," said Andy, belatedly taking note of Jenny's age.

"What happened?" she asked.

"Some amateur investigator had a cockamamie theory about the Klein case," said Dave. "Sweet talked the sheriff into disinterring the body. Said he could prove they got the wrong guy with a new autopsy."

"Did he?"

"Nope."

The workmen grimly chuckled. The Undertaker cast a disapproving glare at them but held his tongue.

"When was this?" Jenny asked.

"What do you think, Andy?" Dave said. "2005?"

"2006," Andy corrected. "Last time the A's made it to the ALCS. Not that I'm superstitious."

"I still say Zito was injured," groused Dave.

"We should get going," said the Undertaker. "It'll be dark soon."

Jenny had one more question. "Do you remember who the amateur investigator was? That one who was wrong?"

"Course," said Andy, nodding back to the brand new crypt behind him. "Him."

After the workmen and the Undertaker left, the Valentines could finally have a moment alone. A long time she stood there, making oaths and forming plans. Her sorrow returned, but it was changed now. Charged with purpose. Which one of the five stages of grief did revenge fall under?

BEFORE SHE WENT TO BED, SHE REMEMBERED THE LIPSTICK ON HER palm. Seized by a bold notion, Jenny grabbed her phone and stood in front of her bathroom mirror. The face that stared back looked haggard and grim. Jenny found that if she mussed her black hair and smiled just right, her red eyes made her look like an unhinged badass.

Holding up her palm to the mirror, the numbers from Dinah finally looked correct when read backward in reflection. Using her other hand, she added the number to her contacts and switched to the camera app. Jenny might have spent the next 20 minutes posing, taking, and rejecting pictures, but no one was around to tease her, so who cared?

Feeling particularly extra, she undid a few buttons on her black cocktail dress. Just enough to catch the eye without being too slutty. She wiped off the black lipstick and did her best to approximate RJ Valentine's customary smirk, then she held up her palm again and took another photo of her reflection. She sent it to Dinah immediately, before she lost her nerve.

That night Jenny received two messages. The first was from Dinah. It was only a winking emoji sticking its tongue out, but it would have been enough to keep Jenny giddy all night—if not for the second message that came in a few minutes later.

D: Spot the difference

Followed by three images of people in formal attire attending a masquerade.

From the metadata, it looked like they were from someone's Facebook page. Each photo showed a tall woman in a stylish black gown posing with various other men and women. All wore half-masks covering their eyes, but the woman was easily recognizable with her dark hair and razor-sharp features. She could only be Valerie Valentine.

A large banner in the background of one shot read *Valentine Foundation*. This was the charity gala held the night of RJ Valentine's attack.

So what was the difference?

Jenny's eyes crawled over the photos, looking for the clue she was missing. The people were different in each, but that was too obvious to be it. Which one of these was not like the others? Val wore the same dress in each. Same black masque, same earrings, same elaborate updo hairstyle. Same black clutch with pearl accents that Jenny was now determined to steal...

Was there a bloodstain on one or something? No, that would be too easy. In one photo, Val had a reddish-brown scuff mark on the toe of her pumps, but so what?

Frustration was setting in, but Jenny refused to ask for a hint. She was Trouble, dammit! She should be able to figure this out! When Jenny finally got it, she smacked her head ruefully. Of course!

In the first two pictures, Val was holding a glass of pink wine. But in the third, she was drinking a diet Pepsi. That wasn't a drink you switched to after rosé. It was what you drank when you were out of rehab and avoiding alcohol.

Now that she knew what to look for, the differences became more apparent. This Val's features were a tiny bit softer. More comely. This Val's posture wasn't so rigid. And this Val wore that black gown to perfection, keeping it tighter in all the places a girl knew it was toughest to hide. Because this wasn't Val at all.

"Hello, Tori," she whispered.

Chapter Seven

Sink to the Bottom

MORNING CAME WAY TOO SOON. JENNY HAD BARELY SLEPT, staying up to research. She wasn't finding anything on Tori she didn't already know, so she tried a google search on Casey Klein and ended up down a Wikipedia true crime rabbit hole.

Casey Klein was only 11 years old when she went missing on the way home from school. She was a cute white girl with dirty blonde hair, so it made all the NorCal papers. They didn't find her body for five months. When they did, the neighbor's gardener had a really hard time explaining why his receipt from an old oil change was in Casey's coat pocket. She must have grabbed it from under his car seat at some point. Smart girl, but not smart enough. Cause of death: strangulation by rope. Deputy Blake Lockhart made the big break in the case. This must be what dad's noose clue to the sheriff was about. Did RJ think the real killer was still out there?

That question would have to wait because today was the first day of school. In the books, it must have always been perpetually summer or winter break, because Trouble was never in class. Lucky girl. Jenny groaned and rubbed her tired eyes under her sunglasses as Shelly parked the car in the teacher's lot.

"I need late arrival," said Jenny. "Human beings were not meant to be up this early."

"When I was in high school, I had zero period for FBLA," said Shelly.

"That's your fault."

"You won't have enough credits to graduate if you get late arrival."

Jenny sighed as dramatically as possible and levered herself out of the car and stretched on the sidewalk.

"You can always come hang out in the teacher's lounge till the bell rings," said Shelly.

"No thanks," said Jenny. "See you in class, Ms. Onishi."

Her aunt looked back. "Jennifer… I know this is a hard time. I get that. We will get through this together, but you've got to stay out of trouble."

Jenny cocked her head to one side and leveled her shades at her aunt. "Well, it is my middle—"

"—Finish that sentence, and you're grounded for a month," snapped Shelly.

Jenny cackled with delight. Shelly could only roll her eyes and shout "I mean it!" as she stomped off to her classroom.

As tempting as it was to go home and crawl back into bed, she needed to familiarize herself with Blackbird Springs Academy. Jenny crossed the student lot to the main gates into the campus, which were flanked by two massive sycamore trees in planters. She leaned up against the sycamore on the left, faced the parking lot, sipped her latte, and waited.

The lot filled up. Students streamed by. Rich kids sporting all the big brands, the new shoes, new bags. The air fairly reeked of mousse and AXE body spray. Jenny glanced down at her own outfit: a simple purple and black jersey t-shirt she'd shoplifted from Target, and fitted gray capri workout sweats. Jenny hoped this look conveyed "over it," instead of just "poor." She tried to remind herself that Trouble didn't care about fashion.

"Hey! Jenny!"

Drew was waiving as he walked over in the company of a tall black girl. She was sharply dressed and wore her hair in a braided ponytail.

"Hey um," Drew grimaced. "Sorry about the other day, I didn't know about your dad yet."

Jenny smiled sadly. "It's okay, I wasn't really ready to talk about it."

An awkward silence descended. The other girl cleared her throat.

"I'm Penelope Griffin, by the way," she said. "Penny."

"The girl I've heard so much about," Jenny said, making Drew blush and Penny beam. "You wouldn't be related to Yvonne Griffin, would you?"

"She's my mom," Penny said, raising a curious eyebrow.

"How do you know—" Drew started to ask, but was cut off by the screech of tires on asphalt.

That goddamn blue Dodge Challenger with the white racing stripes was racing through the parking lot, headed right for them. For a panicked second, Jenny thought it might mow them down. They all sprang back in alarm as the car skidded into a disabled spot inches from them.

Behind the wheel, some big beefy boy was braying like an ass at them. This must be Mason Lockhart. Jack was sitting next to him, watching Jenny coolly. Dinah glared at Mason from the backseat. She'd died her two blonde tendrils purple and black today: the school colors.

"Oh good," said Jenny. "I forgot I had this score to settle."

She stepped onto the low hood of Mason's car and marched right up to his windshield, leaning over to peer down through the moonroof. Mason flipped out.

"Hey! HEY! What the—"

"You almost hit me with your car on Sunday."

"Bitch, this ain't a complaint window!"

Jack rolled his eyes and helped Dinah out. That cheerleader outfit Dinah had on was *working* for Jenny, but she needed to focus on Mason right now. Even behind the wheel, she could tell he was tall and ripped, bigger and brawnier than Drew. His biceps looked thicker than her thighs. Face was sorta oafish, though. She stared down at him, knowing this angle would be a rarity for her.

"You could have killed me, asshole! Apologize, and watch the goddamn road next time!"

"Get off my car, you psycho!" Mason yelled.

Jenny shrugged and held out her cardboard coffee cup, tilting it slightly to threaten pouring it right through his moonroof. Mason's eyes widened in terror. "No! NO NO!"

"Apologize!"

"This is assault! No—wait! I-I'm sorry!" He scrambled out of the Challenger and tried to grab the cup. Jenny snatched it back and laughed at him, then threw the cup right in his face. It bounced off his forehead and fell to the asphalt with a clatter because of course, it was empty.

"Apology accepted," Jenny said and stepped off the car.

"Oh, I like her," said Penny.

Mason shoved past her to examine his hood. "If this is dented, you're gonna pay, you witch!"

Jenny was vaguely aware of some other kids nearby gawking at the commotion, so she put on her most confident smirk and winked at Dinah, who nodded back in approval.

"I don't think you understand who my father is," Mason was saying to her.

"I don't think you understand who *I* am," she shot back.

Jack intervened, stepping between her and the big brute and backing him away as he glared at Jenny. "Leave it, Mace! You too, Jenny!"

Jenny rolled her eyes and let cooler heads prevail. Dinah gave her a reluctant pout as Jack pulled her along with Mason. The trio squeezed through a gap in the crown of onlookers and walked off.

"Okay, show's over," said Jenny, tired of them all staring. She picked up her latte cup and tossed it in the garbage before falling in with Penny and Drew as the bell rang.

"I've got Physics," Penny said and headed off to the right. Drew waved, watching her go.

"You choked, didn't you?" said Jenny.

Drew let out a long exasperated sigh. "It's just… I don't want to ruin our friendship if she says no."

"Then maybe you should just be friends," she said. "Talking of which, I thought you said Jack didn't have any friends."

Drew shrugged. "I mean, we all kinda hang out on the team, but Jack keeps everyone at arm's length. Even Dinah."

"What team?" Jenny asked, trying to keep her face neutral at the mention of Dinah. She knew the absolute last thing she should be doing is trying to steal her brother's girlfriend away, but the way Dinah smiled at Jenny…

"What's so funny about being on the baseball team?" Drew asked, glaring. "That's my ticket to a full ride if I keep my stats up."

"Nothing, sorry," said Jenny, banishing visions of Dinah and those blonde hair tendrils from her thoughts. For all she knew, Dinah didn't even like girls. "Was thinking of something else. What's your first class?"

"Economics."

"Sweet, me too," she said. "You can meet my aunt. She's the new Econ teacher."

"Oh, is she cool?"

"No," said Jenny.

THE DAY PASSED BY IN A BLUR OF ROLL CALLS, SYLLABI, AND ICE breakers. Where did you go for summer vacation? What are your favorite movies and TV shows? Tell us two truths and a lie? Jenny was good at that one, even though she had to keep her best truths a secret. Word had already spread that she was RJ Valentine's daughter, but it still felt weird revealing to people that her name was Trouble too, so she kept that to herself. As far as she was aware, only the heirs and Drew knew.

After Econ came Precalculus. Jenny was terrible at math but had tested into this class with the help of a tutor. Mr. Stephenson called her name.

"Present," she said.

More heads turned. Some gawked. Some snickered.

At lunch in the cafeteria, Jenny sat with Drew and Penny, ignoring her food to watch her classmates as they watched her. RJ's big plot twist was landing with a thud. It felt like everyone was sort of embarrassed for her. She was supposed to be a lovable scamp, not a depressing charity case.

Drew slid over his slice of pizza in sympathy.

"I don't think she wants pizza right now Drew," said Penny.

Chemistry was the same. A beaker bubbled on a bunsen burner in front of Jenny. Alicia Aaron was assigned as her lab partner.

Jenny could feel the girl's nervous eyes moving from the beaker to her and back as they did a basic condensation experiment. Whispers surrounded her, and everywhere she looked, the backs of heads were turning away. Her Chemistry teacher Mr. Finch watched her with suspicion.

Once, Jenny tried to whisper a question to Alicia about the game, but the girl quickly shot her down with a curt, "I'd rather not talk about it."

In P.E., they made everyone stretch and do pushups and run a mile to see what shape they were in. Jenny hadn't done any exercising like this since freshman year, but she needed two years of physical education to graduate at this school, so she struggled along on her short legs. As first days went, it pretty much sucked.

THE REST OF THE WEEK WAS NO DIFFERENT. ICE BREAKERS GAVE WAY to lesson plans and ungodly amounts of homework. This was one of those hoity-toity charter schools with higher academic standards than she was used to. Jenny was kept busy enough just trying to keep up in Precalculus. Mr. Stephenson assigned 40 problems a day, and they had to work them all out by hand, no calculator, and show their work. If she didn't have a math tutor, she'd be totally lost.

Whenever she could, she reviewed the document packet Mr. Webb had given everyone. The evidence, the photos, the eyewitness accounts. Jenny was dying to learn more about Tori Valentine, but Jack was avoiding her, and all of Tori's social media was private.

On Wednesday, she finally found something.

Jenny was walking with Drew and Penny to the Journalism room when a plaque caught her eye in the school trophy case. Victoria Valentine had her name on half a dozen plaques and trophies within.

Track and Field, the State Science Fair, even two Golden Quill national student journalism awards.

"Did you guys ever meet Tori?" Jenny asked, her breath fogging the trophy case glass as she stared greedily at the awards.

"No, but Mr. White always talks about her," said Penny, mentioning the Newspaper Adviser. "Says she was the smartest student he ever taught."

"Hmmph!" said Jenny. "I guess she peaked early."

"You don't know anything about her," said a voice behind her.

Jenny spun to see Jack glaring at her behind dark Ray-Bans. He was wearing tight Levis and a fitted charcoal t-shirt. Some small part of her brain howled at the undeniable truth that he was prettier than she was.

"Oh, are you talking to me again?" she said sourly.

He swooped forward, boxing out Penny and Drew and cornered Jenny against the trophy case. "Leave Tori out of this!" he hissed. "You have no idea what she's been through."

"She might be more *in* this than you know, big brother," said Jenny.

"You need to stop," he whispered. "Mom's talking about hiring armed guards who will shoot to kill."

"What the hell are you talking about?" Jenny was baffled.

"I know it was you," said Jack, taking off his sunglasses to burn the words into her.

"Me what?" she was baffled. "What am I getting blamed for this time?"

He moved closer, eyes blazing in a cold fury. "You tried to break into our wine cellar!"

"I did not!"

She really didn't!

"You must have thought Mom would put the *Ressort Rouge* down there," his voice was full of scorn and pity. "You clearly don't know shit about wine."

Jenny's stomach churned. It took all her effort to keep him from seeing how hurt she felt. "I. Did n—not. Break. Into. Your. House. Or—or cellar."

He studied her keenly, his eyes full of doubt. "Then explain this."

He dug into his jacket pocket and pulled out a small ziplock bag. There was a clove cigarette stub in it. The filter was darkened by lipstick. Black lipstick. Jenny's eyes widened.

"I don't smoke," Jenny said, dimly aware that Drew and Penny were watching all this in fascination.

"You sure about that," said Jack. "You smelled like it yesterday."

"I—I probably walked past the theater kids outside," she told him, knowing as she said it how lame it must have sounded. "I only wore that shade once, for the funeral."

He wasn't buying it.

"Here's a freebie," Jenny said. "We know someone else who wears that shade. And I'll bet she smokes."

"Who?"

"Alicia Aaron!"

"It wasn't *her*," said Jack, rolling his eyes. "They ran away when the alarm went off. How's she gonna do that on one leg?"

"Maybe…" a light bulb exploded in Jenny's head. "Maybe that's not really a prosthetic!"

Jack stared at her, nonplussed. "*How?*"

"Okay, maybe that's a stretch—"

"Yo, Valentine!" someone shouted.

"What?!" said Jenny and her brother at the same time, turning towards the voice. It was Mason Lockhart, looking as muscle-bound and as stupid as ever.

"Not you! Why are you talking to this trash?" he asked Jack.

"You know we're related, right?" Jenny was planted between them and refused to move.

"I guess your side got all the trash, bastard," said Mason, laughing at his own dumb insult.

Jenny's eyes flashed. "Is that a racial thing? Cause I will rip your balls off!"

"You wish!" Mason said for some reason.

"Can you guys just lay off for one day?" Jack said in exasperation. "Jesus!"

Jack turned Mason around and put in his AirPods to let Jenny know the conversation was over.

"Anyone ever tell you that you look like a hot dog that got left in the microwave for too long?" Jenny called after Mason.

Mason made a lurid gesture and followed Jack.

"This is my new favorite TV show," said Penny.

Drew said nothing, watching Jenny closely.

On Friday the weather turned, with scattered showers and grey skies. It was all the excuse Jenny needed to wear Trouble's purple trench coat to class. A few kids might have snickered at her, but she felt better in her familiar ensemble.

After P.E., Jenny took her time changing, tying and re-tying her shoes, overcome with melancholy. By the time she stood up, the locker room was empty. She shoved her gym clothes into her backpack and was just zipping it up when she remembered the item she'd put in her bag this morning for good luck. She reached in and pulled out her personal copy of *My Name is Trouble*. It had arrived in the mail with no return address when she was three years old, signed by RJ himself.

No one could see, so she held the book close and let out a small whimper. She'd never even gotten a chance to see him. "*Crying doesn't solve mysteries,*" she quoted to herself. Jenny shoved the book back into her bag and zipped it shut.

The locker rooms emptied into the gym, but there was a back exit too that led into the Natatorium where the indoor lap pool and diving pool were. The smell of chlorine assaulted her nostrils, but at least there were no other people here. Jenny was walking around the diving pool when a door opened at the far end. Light flooded in over a silhouette. Someone tall, with an angry gait.

"I know what you did!" shouted Mason as he stomped toward her. Jenny pulled her house keys from her purse and clutched them tight between her knuckles, taking no chances that Mason was the kind of guy who wouldn't hit a girl.

"Not really in the mood, dude," she said.

She tried to walk past, but he juked to cut her off. She juked too, but he was spry for a big guy. Center fielder, she guessed.

"You're gonna pay for what you did to Bonnie," he said.

"Who? What?"

"You keyed my Challenger! That car was a gift for my sweet sixteen!" Mason said, fuming.

Jenny couldn't help but giggle. "Your *super* sweet sixteen?"

"I ain't playing!"

"Well I am, and I didn't do anything to your stupid car."

"Then who did?" He loomed over her, and she could feel his enraged breath snorting into her face. "People saw you in the parking lot during first period yesterday. I know it was you."

Jenny was pretty sure she hadn't keyed Mason's car, though she had been in a pretty foul mood and honestly who could blame her if she had? She waved her arms in a big shrug. Mason jerked a big paw out and grabbed her right wrist.

"Hey! Let go!"

He wrenched the keys out of Jenny's hand and examined them.

"What is your deal?" she said, stepping back. "Maybe it's time to cycle off the HGH."

"You're gonna pay for this," he said, scowling at her keys.

"Sounds great, now gimme back my keys."

"Sure, go fish."

He tossed her keys into the diving pool next to them and leered at her. The keys quickly sank to the bottom and Jenny could only watch in frustration as Mason left the way he'd come.

"Okay," she said to the closing door he'd just blown through. "You're on my list."

Jenny was alone again. She leaned over the pool. Those keys were way down there. There was a skimmer net hanging from hooks on the wall. Jenny tried using it to fish her keys out, but the pole was too short to reach the bottom. She stared down at the keys, biting her lip.

"Shit."

She glanced this way and that. No one was around, and there was only one way those keys were coming back to her. Before she lost her nerve, she doffed her coat, blouse, and leggings, stripping down to her underwear. She stashed her clothes and backpack behind a nearby trash can. This should only take a minute.

Jenny dove into the water. Aunt Shelly would have been pleased to see all those years of summer swimming lessons paying off with a textbook forward dive. Her whole body tingled as the cold water woke up a million nerve endings in her skin, and she blinked away the chlorine. It was the first time she'd felt alive all week.

Deeper and deeper she dove. Her ears popped; it got darker; the bottom, with its blue-tiled Xs, edged closer. Then she was there, snatching her keys in triumph.

But it kept getting darker. She looked up in horror to discover that the pool cover was closing above her. In the books, Trouble's heart was always "*freezing to the core*" when a big twist or surprise happened. Jenny was getting all too familiar with the sensation.

She worked her arms to spin back upright and launched herself off the bottom of the diving pool. Above her, precious oxygen was waiting, but the cover was going to beat her.

She surfaced in the middle of the pool. There was enough of a gap to push up the vinyl cover and grab a breath of air before it drove her back down. She kicked harder and surfaced again, gasping and coughing, and managed a cry for "Help!"

She slipped under and tried punching at the vinyl. It hardly budged.

"Anybody!?" she sputtered, surfacing again.

No one was coming for her. She dove and swam to the edge of the pool. Could she pull the cover back? No dice. Nothing to grip. It was probably electric and ran on a track. There was barely a gap for air over here. She coughed and sucked in half a lungful of water this time.

Jenny Valentine was about to drown, and she knew it.

Chapter Eight

Killroy Was Here

THE WATER SLOSHED AROUND LEAVING NO ROOM TO BREATHE. Bitter resentment washed over Jenny. To die like this, just beginning to unravel the mystery: that was a bad ending, surely Dad would agree. Maybe she'd be seeing him soon to find out.

No. Fight!

She wrapped her fist around her keys and punched up. There wasn't much of an edge on the key, but it was enough to punch through the vinyl cover. This might work!

Pushing hard, she tried to cut a wider opening.

Spots were forming in her vision.

Finally, her key found the right angle and cut a big gash. She knifed both hands into the gap and tore through the vinyl, lifting her head through the tear and gasping for air. Her lungs were burning. Jenny didn't think she had the strength to struggle through the breach, but then strong arms reached in and fished her out.

Her body squeezed through the vinyl tear; she had a sudden mental image of being birthed anew from the depths. She lurched over the tiled edge, choking and coughing for air as the chlorinated water wretched out of her throat.

"What the hell is going on?"

Her rescuer towered over her. She rolled on her back and looked up to see familiar eyes staring down from a big, burly guy in a Blackbird Springs hoodie. Drew.

"Are you okay!?" said Drew.

"Just goin' for a swim." Jenny smiled and spun the keys on her finger, surprised that she'd held onto them through all that. He must have noticed what she was wearing—just a sports bra and boyshorts—because his face reddened and he looked away. Jenny remembered too now, and covered up as best she could, mortified.

"Is there a towel?" she asked.

"I'll go look!"

He bolted away to the boys' lockers. Jenny stood up and slicked back her hair to squeegee some of the water off, making sure to keep facing away. Drew came huffing back and handed her a fresh white towel over her shoulder.

"I came out of the locker room and heard you screaming," he told her. "Who closed the pool cover?"

Jenny wrapped the towel around her and turned to look him right in the eye, just to be sure. "How do I know it wasn't you?"

He raised his hands in surrender. "I swear! This place was empty when I came out."

Jenny sighed and windmilled her arms to air dry.

"Okay, I believe you," she said. "You didn't maybe see Mason Lockhart lurking around anywhere?"

"No, you think it was him?"

"I'm not sure," said Jenny, walking over to the trash bin to get her clothes. They weren't there. Neither was her copy of *My Name is Trouble*. She unleashed a vicious stream of curses that echoed through the natatorium.

Drew winced, unsure how to respond. Jenny rifled through her bag to no avail.

"My stuff! You're sure you didn't see anyone?"

"You lost your clothes?"

"Screw my clothes, they took my book!"

Her priceless namesake. One of her only connections to her father. Murder entered her heart, someone would pay. But who? This didn't seem like the work of a dumb oaf. This felt like someone sending her a message. The Stranger?

"What is going on?" Drew asked, arms crossed.

Jenny considered her options. Trouble didn't normally have a sidekick, but she could use some muscle, and Drew knew the town in ways she couldn't learn from researching online. A thin smile spread across her cold lips.

"Do one more thing for me, and I'll tell you," she said.

Drew smirked. "I mean, I've only saved your life twice now."

"Anyone can be a hero. I need a *troublemaker*."

His eyes twinkled. "Bitch, I'm the fan club president."

"Good, cause I need more info on Tori Valentine and you're gonna get it for me."

OTHER STUDENTS GAWKED AS JENNY MARCHED ACROSS CAMPUS IN A towel with Drew in tow. School was out, and the office would close soon, so they needed to hurry.

"Are you sure about this?" he asked. "If I get caught, they could kick me off the team."

"You won't," she said. "Consider this your initiation."

"No team, no scholarship, no college, and then I spend the rest of my life as a busboy."

"You said your dad worked his way up from busboy to head chef."

"I can't cook!" he whined. They were getting off-topic.

"Look, what if I told you I could pay your way through college?" she said.

He raised an eyebrow, full of questions.

"After," she said, pushing open the door to the school office and dropping her towel. Drew stayed outside and counted to 30 as instructed.

The main office had a big wood veneer countertop that wrapped around the secretary's desk. Behind, deep filing cabinets lined the back walls. Cabinets which, Jenny hoped, still contained files on former students. The secretary, a middle-aged woman with a picture of a pug on her sweater, gasped at Jenny's appearance.

"What—?" she started before Jenny cut her off.

"Some mean girls stole my clothes!" Jenny wailed, letting the fake waterworks flow. "Is there a lost and found?"

"Oh my dear," said the secretary, scrambling up to help Jenny. "I think we have some loaners for dress code."

On cue, Drew entered. Jenny shrieked and covered up.

"Drew?! What are you—?" said the secretary.

"Uh, sorry," Drew said, turning a convincing shade of magenta.

"Is there so-somewhere p-private!?" Jenny stuttered, backing away from Drew.

"I just need to check the course catalog," said Drew. "Coach wants me to—"

"Hold on!" said the secretary, frazzled.

She hustled Jenny into a back room. "Okay okay," the secretary said, pulling out a bin from the bottom shelf of a cabinet. Inside were lots of truly hideous school spirit shirts and long skirts. "What happened, you piss off Meghan May and her Bitchy Brigade?"

"Who—who's that?" asked Jenny as she rummaged through the loaner clothes.

The secretary snorted. "You must be new here. I'll just let you pick something out." She turned to leave. It was too soon. Drew needed more time.

"No, don't, please? Just help me pin this." The skirt Jenny selected had a waist about six inches too large.

"I have some pins in my desk," the secretary said, turning to the door again.

"Wait! Don't you think this one is cuter?" Jenny blurted out, pulling the woman away from the door again. How did Trouble ever keep from laughing during these cons?

Jenny stalled with the lady for as long as she could before returning to the front office in a long plaid skirt and an oversized purple t-shirt with Billy the Blackbird—the school mascot—on it. Drew was nowhere to be seen. She thanked the secretary again and stepped outside.

"We've got a problem," said a voice behind her.

Drew was leaning up against the wall, tapping on his phone.

"You didn't get it?" Jenny's heart sank. She'd just made a fool of herself to the school secretary for nothing.

"No, I got it," he said, putting his phone away. "Come on."

He headed for the campus gates. Jenny followed, waiting for him to elaborate. Once they were off school grounds, he checked around him and unzipped his jacket. Inside was a green folder. The label on the tab read: **VICTORIA JEAN VALENTINE.**

"What's up?" she asked. He handed her the folder. Inside was a single piece of paper. **You're getting colder** was written in the center of the page, and underneath was RJ Valentine's signature with the big V flourish. At the bottom was another one of those little cartoon drawings of a man peeking over a wall.

KiLLROY WAS HERE

"What does it mean?" Drew asked.

Jenny frowned. "I'm not sure."

IT WAS A 15-MINUTE BIKE RIDE TO DREW'S HOUSE FROM THE SCHOOL. His family lived on the edge of town, in an older and presumably cheaper neighborhood. The house was small, single-story home nestled into a comfortable lot big enough for a large oak tree with a tire swing out front. Instead of inviting her in, he led her around the side of the house to a detached garage in the back.

"Are your parents here?" she asked.

He shook his head. "The Winchester is open late on the weekends." Both his parents worked at one of the pricy restaurants in town.

It was dark now. Jenny had given Drew an abridged version of Dad's will, the clues, and the contest in the school parking lot. He was predictably enthralled by the locked-room mystery, but he'd had baseball practice to get to, so they agreed to meet at his place later to continue the conversation.

Drew unlocked the side door to the garage and ushered her into a neglected workshop. One wall was lined with tools and a workbench and the detritus from abandoned metalworking projects. The rest of the floor was cleared for a baseball tee and a large, heavy blue tarp that was suspended from the ceiling.

"Mom and Dad barely come in here anymore," Drew said. "So I use it to work on my swing."

"I want to try!" Jenny demanded at once.

Drew smirked and retrieved a special baseball that he attached to

76

the tee with a short cord. He set the ball on top and handed her a bat.

"Face that way," he pointed at the tarp.

Jenny lined herself up to swing left-handed and aimed for the ball. Her first swing missed entirely. He snickered, which only encouraged her to grit her teeth and try again. This time she connected, driving the ball into the ground. It bounced once and hit the tarp, which stopped it easily.

"Double-play," said Drew. "So: RJ's will. What are you gonna do?"

"What do you think?" she said. "I'm going to win."

"You better," Drew rubbed his chin, thinking. "If I help, do I get a cut?"

"Trouble doesn't normally have a sidekick," said Jenny, appraising him. "But I'd be willing to expand the canon for oh, say... ten percent?"

"I don't know," he said, "I feel like if I had an agent, he'd be telling me to ask for more."

Jenny retrieved the ball. "Okay, ten percent, plus you'll be guaranteed a room in the Valentine Mansion. Like a sick-ass room, with your own bathroom, and a huge closet with one of those fancy shoe cubby hole rigs..."

Really, Jenny was thinking of her own fantasy now. A massive closet with tons of clothes and wigs and shoes for any persona she wanted to adopt. Glamorous Trouble, Sporty Trouble, Road Crew Trouble, Jungle Adventure Trouble... Open up a pro bono detective agency for hard cases...

"It better be hella sick," said Drew. "With one of those whirlpool spa tubs with the little jets that shoot water up your ass—"

"I didn't need to hear that!" Jenny could feel her cheeks warming.

"Wow, I didn't know you *could* blush," he said smugly.

"Then it's a deal?" Jenny asked.

"Deal, but I can't miss practice, and I'll have games in the spring," said Drew.

"That's fine, I've got my math tutor after school anyway," said Jenny. "Oh, and we only have 94 days left to solve this anyway."

They shook on it.

"Dope, now let's make a Big Board," said Jenny. Trouble always made a big board of suspects to solve her mysteries. "I printed out of the stuff Mr. Webb gave me, but we need to make sure no one else sees this. If Shelly finds out, she'll lose her shit and probably try to move us back to LA. Oh! And that includes Penny too. Her mom is one of the contestants."

"Way ahead of you," said Drew, pulling back the tarp. Behind it, a big wide screen like for watching movies or slideshows from a projector was hanging from the garage door. "We can just roll it up when we're not here," he explained, very pleased with himself.

"Brilliant!" Jenny said clapping her hands.

They got to work sorting out the documents for the wall.

"So what do you think your clue means?" he asked, setting aside the pictures of the other heirlooms.

"Oh, it turned out to be a dead end," Jenny lied as casually as possible. "Val hired a PI guy way back when, but I checked with Webb, and he's been dead for years."

This wasn't true at all, but there were some secrets, like the treehouse and the files within, that she didn't want even Drew knowing about. A girl needed an ace or two up her sleeve. She'd have to check on potential PIs on her own time.

"Are you sure?" Drew asked. "We should cover all our bases, just to be safe."

"I'm sure," Jenny said firmly. "If anything, it just points back at Val as a suspect."

"It's too bad they think you burned it, then," Drew said. "We could have had them chasing a red herring."

"Look, I didn't want them digging shit up about my mom," she said. "The less they know, the better. Anyway, no freebies. This will keep them guessing. Trust me."

Drew shrugged like he wasn't totally buying it, but he let it drop. "We need a lamp back here, or everything's gonna look blue," he said, noting how the light filtered through the tarp onto their big board.

"You work on that, I'll start taping up stuff," said Jenny. "How about suspect photos across the top with the heirlooms underneath? That gives us six paths to victory, and we start on the most likely culprit first."

"Uh, I think your math is off, Jennifer," said Drew.

"What?"

"It's seven suspects, not six."

He held up a piece of paper, glancing between it and her. After a moment he flipped it around for her to see. Jenny's own face was staring back at her from a color photo.

"Oh well done, Andrew," she said, newly appreciative of his nerve. "You're right. We have *seven* paths to victory."

She set about taping up the photos while Drew went to work hanging a light behind the tarp. He insisted on using a stud-finder, tape measure, and centerpunch before drilling a single hole.

"It's just a work light!" Jenny said in exasperation as she took the centerpunch and passed him a drill.

"You should see me in the batter's box," he said with a laugh.

"Oh God, you're one of those guys." Jenny groaned. Drew laughed, undeterred.

"Stomp the back of the box twice," he said, pantomiming his routine. "Tighten left batting glove, then right. And then—this is very important—whack the bat barrel hard to shake off any dust, then tap it twice on the part of the plate you think the pitch is coming over. Three times, if you think it'll be a curve."

"This is why you lost your nerve with Penny," Jenny teased. "You over-think everything."

"I'm just gonna write her a letter," he said.

"*Don't* write her a letter!" Jenny shook her head.

"You speak from experience?" Drew asked, grinning.

Jenny flushed, recalling a disastrous note she'd written sophomore year. "Yes. Trust me."

With the work light finally hung securely enough to survive the Big One, Jenny surveyed the board with her new sidekick.

"So this is what I'm thinking," she said. "Each heir is also one of dad's suspects."

"Maybe," said Drew skeptically.

"Think about his mysteries," Jenny said. "Never a loose thread. He always ties everything up."

"But he didn't know who was after him," said Drew, "or he would have said so."

"He had clues, and he had suspects," said Jenny. "Obviously he didn't know for sure, or he would have solved it himself. He knew he was in danger and he knew he was running out of time. I saw his blotter, he met with Webb to make that will only a few days before the attack. These were the best leads he had."

"Even if he's right," said Drew, "six of those clues won't lead anywhere. Or at least not to his killer. *And!* If one of you *is* the killer, then wouldn't you just *not* investigate your own clue?"

He raised another suspicious eyebrow at her.

"I have an alibi," she said, bristling. "Shelly can vouch. But you're right, which is why the smart players won't just be working their own heirlooms. We need to branch out."

"I'm guessing you have a theory?"

Jenny smiled and explained the social media photos she'd found of Val and Tori as she taped them up.

"It's always the spouse," said Jenny. "It's always always always the spouse. Her family's money was running out. Dad loathed her, I'm sure. Tori and Val pulled a switcharoo at the Gala so Val could sneak back into the study and whack him with a perfect alibi. I don't know how, maybe a secret passageway or something."

Drew twisted his lip. "You're forgetting the note RJ left in Tori's file."

"Yeah, I don't know what to make of that," she admitted. "Unless it wasn't Dad that left it. You saw the Killroy drawing."

Drew was skeptical. "I mean, I always got the impression from Jack that Tori was RJ's favorite."

"*I* was Dad's favorite," Jenny insisted.

"Still…" said Drew, treading carefully. "Maybe he doesn't want us poking around in her shit. Kinda like you with your mom—"

A muffled crash sounded nearby.

Drew sprang to the door and rushed outside. Jenny followed, the adrenaline coursing through her veins becoming a familiar sensation. The yard was pitch black under the tree canopy. She could just make out the tire swing nearby. Maybe it was only the wind that had set it swaying.

"Check it out," said Drew. He was crouched over a shattered terra-cotta flowerpot. Soil and a cactus the size of a baseball lay amongst the broken pottery.

"Do you have a cat?" she asked, crouching down. The butt of a cigarette was still smoldering in the grass.

"The neighbors do." He sniffed and wrinkled his nose. "Do you smell that?"

Jenny placed her shoe over the cigarette butt. "I have a cold," she lied. It was time she had a private chat with a certain clove smoker.

They stared down the street, listening to the whistling wind, but heard nothing more.

"We're probably just freaking ourselves out," said Jenny.

Drew shrugged, still wary. They headed back inside.

"I should go, actually," said Jenny. "Will you agree at least that we should focus on Val first?"

"Yeah, I guess," he said.

"Good," she told him. "Then you need to introduce me to your mother."

"Why?" he asked, frowning.

She tapped the photo of *Ressort Rouge 1998* under the sneering portrait of Valerie Valentine.

"Because as my snob of a brother so kindly reminded me, I don't know shit about wine."

Chapter Nine

Pinefall's End

BY THE TIME AUNT SHELLY MADE HER WAY DOWNSTAIRS THE NEXT morning, Jenny had already scarfed down a bowl of Grape Nuts and was lacing up her sneakers.

"What's this?" Shelly said, narrowing her eyes at Jenny's attire. Jenny had worn her favorite pair of stretch leggings and an old tank top over her sports bra.

"I thought I'd go for a run."

"I didn't know Trouble went on runs?" Shelly said crisply, watching Jenny as though she had just announced she was on her way to rob a bank.

"Yeah, well Trouble could eat two-scoop butterscotch sundaes whenever she wanted and never gain a pound," said Jenny, referencing her fictional counterpart's favorite dessert. "The rest of us have to sweat a little to keep it tight."

"When can I expect you back?" Shelly asked.

"I wouldn't wait up."

"Jennifer."

"Michelle."

They stared each other down for a while. Jenny broke first.

"God, I don't know. Later. I'm meeting Drew for lunch." Jenny leaned over and strained to grab her toes, feeling her under-worked calf muscles complain as she stretched.

"I might be gone when you get back," her aunt said airily like it was hardly worth mentioning. "There's leftover chicken and rice in the fridge."

"Where will *you* be?" Jenny asked, now suddenly the suspicious one.

"I'm having dinner," Shelly said, pretending to look for something in the fridge.

Jenny narrowed her eyes. "You slut!"

"Really, Jenny."

"Even I haven't moved that fast," Jenny put her hands on her hips to give her aunt the business until she realized that Shelly was doing the same back at her. "Who is it?"

"Mr. Lockhart," Shelly said. "He works at the Sheriff's Department."

"*Blake??*" Jenny could feel her stomach somersaulting.

Shelly regarded her with renewed wariness. "I suppose I shouldn't be surprised that you're already on a first name basis with the local law enforcement?"

"You know he's—" Jenny shut her trap as reason caught up with her big mouth.

"He's *what?*" asked Shelly.

He's only pretending to be interested in you to spy on me, was what Jenny had been thinking, but that would have only prompted more questions. She hoped Sheriff Lockhart had the good sense to keep *his* trap shut about the game too. Besides, telling her aunt that Lockhart's intentions weren't honest would be cruel. Even if it was true.

"He's—got a kid," Jenny said instead. "Lotta baggage there."

"I'm not trying to marry him," Shelly said, laughing.

"I'm gonna go run before I vomit," said Jenny, putting in her earbuds and jogging right out the front door.

She wasn't lying, she really was going for a run. If someone was trying to kill her, Jenny needed to be in peak condition and a week of P.E. had made it plain that she wasn't.

It was another gorgeous day in Blackbird Springs. Jenny headed for town, passing tarot card readers and wine lounges and hydroponics stores and the kinds of gift shops that sold $80 cheese knives. She crossed over to the park in Town Square and did a lap on the walking path. That old man with his cane and bushy white beard was out for a stroll. A young mother and daughter tossed bread to the ducks in the small pond. The city workers were replacing another traffic light fixture. She gave them a wave and a wide berth. They even waved back.

Jenny ran on, a big happy grin on her face. Her whole life in LA, she'd felt crowded out and unwelcome. Here, she belonged. She headed north from Town Square, her eyes on the big ranch mansion in the distance that dipped in and out of view between the trees. By the time she reached her treehouse hideaway, her side was burning from a stitch in her abdomen.

Yeah, she really needed to get in better shape.

After climbing up and collapsing on the small camp mattress to rest her cramping sides for a bit, Jenny gave herself a hobo shower in the sink and changed into street clothes. She'd already stashed some clothes and her school books here. The peaceful quiet of the oak forest was perfect for studying, and by the time the sun reached its zenith, she'd completed all of next week's homework.

Precalculus was still a bear for her, but she found Chemistry surprisingly engaging once she was away from Mr. Finch's somnolent drone. On her tutor's suggestion, Jenny pretended it was Potions class, and the work flew by.

It was, perhaps, a bit more studious than Trouble would approve of. Then again, eleven-year-olds didn't have to worry about college applications. Jenny lay back on the camp bed, snuggling in for a nap...

In a blink, her alarm beeped. It was time to go find out about a bottle of wine.

THE WINCHESTER WAS ONE OF THOSE JOINTS THAT WAS SO FANCY that they closed between lunch and dinner. They even had valet service out front, but the drivers were taking five now that lunch was over.

Jenny knocked at the take-out door as instructed and Drew let her in. She blinked in the dim light, her eyes struggling to adjust to the murky lighting after the bright sunshine outside.

"They just closed, so they'll be cleaning, but we should be fine," said Drew. He led her through a sea of tables, all covered in glowing, bleached-white tablecloths. Jenny wondered what happened if someone spilled red wine on one. Would they throw you out? It almost seemed like a dare.

They passed a few waiters who smiled at Drew as they bussed dishes. Jenny snagged a buttercream mint from the hostess desk, and they huddled into a small booth in the corner.

"My mom should be here in a few," Drew told her, looking absently at a menu. "She had to meet with a wine seller."

"Cool."

They killed time gawking at the outrageous prices on the menu until the front entrance door swung open and an elegant woman with raven-black hair and an olive complexion walked in pushing a hand truck loaded with cases of wine. She was wearing a chartreuse evening dress and wayfarers.

"Oi, let's have some light," she said and swatted at some switches behind the front desk. Dozens of lights hidden in recessed sconces lit up all over the restaurant, making the place look rather plain without all the moody ambiance.

"Be with you in a moment, Drewboo," she said, calling over to their table. "I just need to store these."

Drew blushed scarlet as his mother went into the kitchen. "She always does this when she meets my friends," he said.

"Aww, Drewboo!" said Jenny.

He sighed deeply but didn't fight it. Drew's mom had an interesting accent, vaguely Mediterranean.

"French?" she asked.

"Spanish," Drew said. "Basque, actually, but don't get her started on that."

She returned a moment later with a basket of steaming artisanal bread, some small saucers, and a bottle of wine under her arm.

"Oh, you're not Penny," she said with a coy smile.

"Mom, I told you, this is Jenny," said Drew.

"A pleasure, Jenny," said his mother, holding out a slender arm weighed down by many silver bangles.

"Hi Mrs. Porter," Jenny said.

"Please, call me Mirai," she said with a vampish smile. "My son says you want to know about a bottle of wine?"

"Uhh, yeah," said Jenny, wondering how much Drew had told her. "For a uh research project."

"He also says 'don't embarrass me,'" Mirai Porter leaned over to fix Drew's collar. "I do my best."

"You sure do," Drew muttered.

"You won't understand about the *Ressort Rouge* unless you know about wine," Mirai Porter said. She produced a wine key from somewhere and went to work on the bottle she'd brought over. Her long fingers deftly handled the small blade at the end of the tool and sliced off the top of the foil cover.

"Un repas sans vin est comme un jour sans soleil," said Mrs. Porter. "'*A meal without wine is like a day without sun.*' But it must be enjoyed properly." She gave them each a stern look in turn. "And responsibly."

She held Jenny's gaze a moment longer—to let her know she meant it—before screwing the wine key into the cork. "First we must eat a little— Oh! And we need glasses."

Mrs. Porter retrieved some small wine goblets from the bar as Drew pulled a piece of bread from the basket.

"Is there any butter?" he asked.

"Tut!" She frowned at her son. "Who embarrasses who now? You're in the Winchester, not an Olive Garden."

Mrs. Porter passed out small saucers and grabbed the bottles of olive oil and balsamic vinegar from the center of the table. She poured a little of each into their saucers and ground some pepper over the mixture.

"Eat. It's good," she said and showed Jenny by dabbing a chunk of bread into the oil and vinegar. Jenny followed her example and was pleasantly delighted by the taste. The warmth of the bread and the oil melted together in her mouth, and the vinegar added a crisp sweetness that didn't linger. She instantly ate another bite, with Mirai nodding in approval.

"Everyone knows about the red and the white," Mrs. Porter said, uncorking the bottle she held. "But it's the type of grape that makes all the difference. This is our Table Red from Campion Vineyards: a blend of merlot, pinot, gamay... All grapes low in tannins so the wine can be paired with a wide variety of foods. Not like your cabs or shiraz, which will dry your mouth out."

Mrs. Porter poured them each a finger of red wine.

"Now, drink," she instructed them. Jenny tried not to let on how blown away she was at being served booze by an adult. Mirai Porter was awesome. "Not too much, but give yourself a mouthful. Enough to soak into the palate. A good table wine is light and soft, not too intense to overwhelm the food. What do you taste?"

Jenny and Drew dutifully drank the wine, and Jenny tried hard to think about how it felt on her tongue.

"Sweet, and... sort of fruity. Like berries," she said. "It almost reminds me of Dr. Pepper a little."

Mrs. Porter laughed. "Yes, there is a touch of cola and cherries and some earthy mineral notes. That would be the pinot noir."

"Honestly, it all tastes the same to me," said Drew. "Kind of sour and vinegary."

"That's because you haven't developed your palate," said his mom. "All that whey powder you drink, it kills your tastebuds. Anyway, these things matter to wine connoisseurs, which brings us to *Ressort Rouge*."

"I don't know, Mirai, are you sure this is a story for children?"

A wiry ginger with designer jeans stepped out from the kitchen: Declan Dillion.

"Declan, darling, we're closed," said Mrs. Porter, rolling her eyes. Drew shifted uncomfortably.

"I know, I had to bribe your husband to cook me a steak," said Mr. Dillion, scanning the bar.

"Do you work here too?" Jenny asked.

"Oh, no," he said. "Just grabbing a bite."

"He's uh self-employed," said Drew, nonplussed.

"What a coincidence," said Mirai. "I was just talking to Declan about the *Ressort Rouge* the other day."

"Oh really?" Jenny favored him with a piercing glare. He gave her a toothy smile, unabashed. So she wasn't the only contestant investigating Val's clue. "And what is it you do?"

"I provide my clients with… whatever they need," he said.

"What, like a weed dealer?" Jenny asked.

"Haha. I got your dad the last bottle of *Ressort Rouge* on the west coast, for one," Mr. Dillion said.

"Oh come sit down and stop ruining my story," said Mrs. Porter.

Declan squeezed in next to Drew, who looked none too happy and reached for the bottle of Table Red. Mrs. Porter snatched it away. "You're having steak, go get a cabernet," she said.

"Table red is okay," frowned Declan.

"For a tourist, maybe," said Mrs. Porter archly.

"Okay okay," Declan said, retreating to the bar. "First rule of fine dining," he said, calling over his shoulder, "is always trust your sommelier."

Mrs. Porter chuckled to herself. This seemed to be an ongoing joke between them.

"Blackthorn cab?"

"Much better," said Mrs. Porter, nodding in approval. "Now, about your question. Do you guys know about the disaster at Pinefall?"

Drew and Jenny both shrugged. Mrs. Porter sighed. "I suppose it was before your time."

"1998," said Declan Dillion, rejoining them with a dark bottle of cabernet. "That was a good year, for wine."

"Sure, and 2001 was a good year for skyscrapers," said Mrs. Porter, her eyes flashing.

"What happened?" asked Drew.

"First," said Mr. Dillion, "you have to understand that this wasn't any old winery. Pinefall was the jewel of the valley. All their wines were world-class superstars, but the secret recipe for their red blend: the *Ressort Rouge*, well... it was legendary."

"It wasn't just the recipe," said Mrs. Porter, getting excited despite herself. "*Ressort Rouge* means Red Geyser, and Pinefall sits in the runoff of the Minutemen Hot Springs. There was something about that water, the exact amount of sulfur and nitrates, mixing perfectly with the roots and soil of the pine trees as it flowed into the valley... We call it the *terroir*. No one else, even following that secret recipe, would ever be able to duplicate the taste.

"I had a sip once, just a sip. Long ago, in Bilbao when I was young. It was the finest petite sirah I ever sampled. Just that sip and a bite of rib-eye was a meal fit for a queen. At the height of their production, a bottle would go for $10,000, easy."

"How??" Drew couldn't believe it. "It's just wine!"

"Supply and demand," said Mr. Dillion with a gleam in his eyes. "My Dad said they used to joke: three paychecks for the diamond if you loved a girl, and six for the bottle of *Ressort Rouge*, if you weren't sure she loved you back."

"A girl would say yes to anything after a sip of *Ressort*," said Mrs. Porter. Declan cackled. She glanced at Drew and reddened. "Don't tell your father that."

Drew looked like he wanted to crawl under the table and die. But Jenny was nodding, understanding a little more now.

"And 1998 was the last year they made it?" Jenny guessed.

Mrs. Porter nodded gravely. "Every year, the Martins hand-bottled their vintage and packed up half the batch to sell to the wine merchants in Paris. So on a foggy Sunday morning in May they all piled into a big rental van, one hundred cases of wine in a trailer behind them. The whole family, except for Wilford Martin, the grandfather who ran the family business—"

"—And his aunt Rachael, but she was in a nursing home," added Mr. Dillion.

"Wilford had stayed behind to finish up some last minute work," said Drew's mother, shaking her head. "He was supposed to meet them in Paris the next day. But they never made it to the airport.

Mrs. Porter let out a long, sad breath and squeezed Drew's hand. Jenny could barely breathe, guessing what came next.

"Drunk driver," said Mr. Dillion. "Ironic, right? The fog, and that low angle of the sun when you come over the ridge on Highway 12… The guy lost control and swerved into the Martin family's van. Pushed them across the median. Right into an oncoming semi truck."

Jenny's heart froze to the core. The story had suddenly gotten far too familiar. Memories flashed unbidden in her mind. *A young woman driving fast, tears in her eyes. Raindrops pounding on the windshield. A screech of tires. And a small newborn child in the car seat…*

"They were all gone," said Mrs. Porter. "The Martins, the wine, all of it."

"They say the whole highway ran red that day," Mr. Dillion added. "One last red geyser of blood and wine."

"Wilford was crushed," said Mrs. Porter. "It broke him. Completely. He loaded up the crop duster with Bromacil pesticide and rock salt and dumped it all over Pinefall. Then he filled the pesticide tanks with gasoline and fertilizer and dive-bombed into the family estate. No more Martins. No more Pinefall. No more *Ressort Rouge*."

"That's hardcore," said Drew.

"So you see why it's so rare now," Mrs. Porter said. "Declan sourced a bottle for RJ Valentine a few years ago, for his 15th anniversary. It might have been the last bottle in Napa Valley. Cost him fifty thousand."

Jenny dug her fingernails into her palm, feeling her pulse race. Was that the bottle he left Val?

"Arturo was so jealous," said Mrs. Porter. "He refused to cook steaks for a month afterward. I caught him twice watching RJ and Val dine from behind the kitchen door."

The idea of a romantic dinner between her father and that awful witch made Jenny's stomach turn. Fifty grand for a bottle of wine, but nothing for her? She bitterly willed the thought away.

"Wait," Jenny said. "They drank the wine?"

"Well of course," said Mrs. Porter. "A well-marbled steak like that... you see, when you eat meat, the fat makes a thin layer in your mouth that the wine breaks down..."

"So where'd he get the other bottle?" Drew wondered aloud.

"A good question," said Mr. Dillion behind a wolfish grin. His phone vibrated on the table and Jenny could see from the caller ID that it was Valerie Valentine on the line. "I better go check on my steak," he said, covering his phone and retreating with a smile that didn't reach his eyes.

"I should get to work too," said Drew's mother, standing as well.

"Thank you so much for the lesson," said Jenny. "I think I learned a lot."

"Bring Penny next time, too," she said, grabbing the wine bottles and bussing the plates. "We can't have only the rich kids knowing about fine dining."

Jenny didn't speak until they'd ducked out the front entrance, blinking in the bright sunshine.

"New theory," she said. "Declan Dillion and Valerie Valentine are having an affair."

Drew mulled it over, biting his lip.

"It's thin."

"That was her on the phone," Jenny said. "Dad had a bottle of wine that should have been impossible, and Declan Dillion knows something about it. I'm sure of it!"

"We're gonna need more than 'I'm sure of it,'" said Drew.

"You'd really never heard about Pinefall?" she asked. "I would think that would be legendary around here."

"You know, I have," he said, rolling his eyes. "Just not by that name. Everyone calls it the Haunted Vineyard. People take their dates up there to scare them and make out. Or so I've heard."

Jenny missed his smirk because she'd just received a new text on her watch that made her heart skip a beat.

"Yeah," she said, trying not to smile. "Something else to check out. I gotta go, talk later?"

"Sure."

Jenny waved and walked off. She waited until she rounded the corner into Town Square before she allowed herself to smile and pulled out her phone to check her messages.

Dinah: What are we doing tonight?

She bit her lip, beyond thrilled. After a moment, she typed:

Jenny: We're going ghost hunting.

Chapter Ten

The Haunted Vineyard

B ACK AT HOME, JENNY TOOK A NAP TO FADE HER WINE BUZZ. WHEN she arose in the twilight, Aunt Shelly was gone on her date. After a quick shower to freshen up, Jenny dressed in her favorite slinky black shirt with the three-quarter-length sleeves, and dark, durable jeans. She went heavy on the mascara, hoping Dinah was into that look and donned her red wig because Trouble always went sleuthing in a good disguise.

It hadn't taken much effort to learn that Declan Dillion drove a silver BMW. Jenny watched Mr. Dillion pull up in his beamer outside of Champs Sports Bar and leave the keys with a valet. Inside, the high-def TVs were so big that Jenny could follow the game from her seat at a table by the window in the coffee shop across the street. Trouble's first rule of following someone: get there first.

Champs seemed to be the local watering hole for baseball fans. It was where Jose Cooper went to watch the game after gardening at the Valentine mansion on the night Dad was attacked. Was it just a coincidence that Declan was here now?

She sipped her tea, researched on her laptop, and watched Declan

Dillion watching the game. Near as she could tell, no one was selling *Ressort Rouge* anymore. The last bottle sold at auction went for $60,000 a few years back. Declan mixed amongst the fans like he was salt of the earth: bashing forearms with those city workers after a home run, yelling at the ump, and buying a round of shots.

There was an obituary in the Blackbird Times for Rachael Martin, dated three years ago this October. Survived by no one; the last of the Martins of Pinefall was gone. The remainder of the Martin estate had been auctioned off and proceeds donated to Mothers Against Drunk Drivers.

Jenny studied the way Declan interacted with the women near him. He seemed friendly and gregarious, but uninterested. Maybe because he was already seeing Valerie Valentine in secret? Now that Jenny thought about it, Val and Declan had been standing a bit close to each other at the will reading.

Cool, slender fingers reached out from behind and covered Jenny's eyes.

"Guess who?"

Jenny's heart fluttered. She'd been keeping an eye out, but somehow Dinah had snuck up behind her. She covered Dinah's hands with her own and pretended to think.

"Um… Penny?"

"No, but close!" Dinah laughed and pulled her hands away. Her breath was warm on Jenny's neck. "Love the hair. Who's that, your boyfriend?"

Jenny blushed. She had a photo of Jose Cooper open on her laptop: a middle-aged Latino man with crinkly eyes and a thick mustache.

"No!" she said, slamming the lid of her MacBook Pro shut.

Dinah giggled to herself and came around to sit across from her. She was dressed all in black, as Jenny requested. However, in lieu of jeans, she'd worn a short black skirt and knee-high Steve Madden boots.

"No? Was it the mustache?" Dinah smiled at her, eyes sparkling between the twin tendrils of hair that spilled out from under her black pageboy cap.

"The mustache, the age…" Jenny glanced over at the bar again. She could no longer see Declan. "…The fact that he's a man…"

She shot a quick look back at Dinah to gauge her reaction and caught a saucy eyebrow wiggle in return. Jenny's heart pounded in her chest.

Was Dinah flirting?

Jenny wasn't sure if she could point to an exact moment when she knew she preferred girls. Maybe something with Sally Draper when her aunt let her stay up to watch *Mad Men*. But for sure, she'd never felt the faintest inkling of interest for guys. Trouble didn't care about boys either, so it just felt natural.

After coming out to Shelly, she wasn't usually this shy about it, but she'd been writing lots of fanfic about her and Dinah in her head, and she didn't want the story to end too soon.

"So whose ghost are we hunting?" Dinah asked, twirling one of her hair tendrils around her finger. Jenny couldn't help staring. She had the distinct impression that Dinah knew exactly what she was doing, and she wanted it to continue.

"Wilford Martin's," said Jenny.

Dinah's eye twitched in surprise.

"Is this another Valentine secret?"

"Something like that."

THEY DROVE UP THE HILL IN SILENCE, LISTENING TO SOME CANADIAN art-rock band. The lead singer had a breathy voice which made Jenny think of Dinah's neck and her throat and her lips. The car had heated leather seats and smelled like a vanilla cookie. Like Dinah.

The road into the late Martin estate was blocked off and gated. They could have hopped the fence, but it was quicker to go around and come in through the Minutemen Hot Springs at the top of the ridge.

Dinah eased her Acura into a parking spot in the empty visitor's lot next to the geyser field. The hot springs lay before them, beyond a short wooden railing. Steam was venting from fissures in the earth, covering the hilltop in an eerie fog.

The two got out and stretched their legs. Jenny felt her skin prickle in the cool, humid air. The wood railing triggered a memory. On her phone, she brought up an old picture Aunt Shelly had given her of Shelly and Jenny's mom Laura at the hot springs as teenagers. She held up her phone and compared the scene. Mom had once stood right here.

"She was pretty," said Dinah beside her.

Jenny quickly tucked her phone back into her pocket.

"Sorry," said Dinah.

"It's fine," Jenny said. "I just— I guess I never really talk about her much."

Dinah nodded and swung her legs over the wooden railing. Jenny followed her into the steaming geyser range. The ground was soft and spongy.

"Is this safe?" Jenny asked.

"Sure," Dinah nodded, running her fingers over a jet of vapor rising up from a fissure. "As long as you don't hear a whistle."

"Why, what's that mean?"

"It means the hot springs are a minute from erupting. Always a minute, like clockwork. Hence—"

"The *Minutemen* Hot Springs," Jenny said, getting it. She found a nearby vapor jet and ran a hand through it. Cold, then hot, then cold again in the autumn air. Jenny imagined that she was walking on the surface of some alien planet.

"Did she come here a lot?" asked Dinah. "Your mom?"

"I… I don't know," said Jenny.

They walked on.

"She died when I was only five days old," Jenny said. "My aunt doesn't like bringing her up. She adopted me when no one else would. I— I think I sort of ruined her life."

"I'm sure you didn't," said Dinah.

They walked on. Jenny was taking a meandering route across the field. It felt good to walk over the thermal vents.

"Jack said he'd never heard of you," said Dinah after a while.

"I believe it," said Jenny. "Valerie wouldn't want any reminders that Dad loved someone else. I was *her* dirty little secret as much as I was his."

"Almost sounds like one of his books," said Dinah.

"You have no idea," Jenny said.

"What do you mean?" asked Dinah.

Jenny hesitated, absentmindedly rubbing the Ace of Clubs tattoo on her wrist. There were secrets, and then there were *secrets*, and then there was her *big big secret*. Her middle name was only a minor secret, and she wanted Dinah to know it. She wanted Dinah to know her.

But she also wanted to flirt a little.

"Do you trust me?" Jenny asked her.

"Jack told me not to," Dinah said.

"Funny, he told me the same about you."

Dinah's lips curled into a sly smile, betraying nothing. "He was quite curious when I told him we were gonna hang out," she said. "I kinda got the impression that he wanted me to spy on you."

"Are you?" Jenny asked.

"Of course," she said, tucking a tendril of hair behind her ear. "But what should I report back?"

"Only enough to make him jealous."

"You Valentines," Dinah said in a low purr. "Nothing but trouble."

Jenny snorted and grinned. "Not him. Just me."

As they left the geyser range and descended through the redwoods, Jenny told Dinah all she could. Her middle name, her amateur detective mishaps. She left out the part about the will, the game, and the Stranger who might be trying to kill her. Dinah was delighted and indignant all at once.

"He cursed you!" she said as they picked their way down the hill. "That's some *Boy Named Sue* shit!"

Jenny laughed and waved her concerns away. "Everyone goes through life thinking they're the star of their own story," she told Dinah. "The only difference is: *I actually am.*"

"If RJ were still alive I'd put him back in that grave," Dinah said, shaking her head. "He never contacted you? Not even once?"

"He couldn't," Jenny said, feeling defensive. Dinah didn't understand. "He was protecting me from Val."

"Val's a house cat," Dinah replied. "You just have to know how to handle her."

"Yeah," said Jenny. "Well, at least Dad had the last laugh."

"How so?"

"Umm— Oh, look, we're here."

She was saved from her big mouth by their arrival at the edge of a vineyard. Pinefall.

In the dark, the vines looked almost normal. Only when taking a few steps closer could Jenny see that they were dried and cracked and brown and bereft of fruit. Dead. A whole vineyard of dead grapevines stretched before them. In the distance, she could just make out the outline of a misshapen building. A former grand Tudor house, burnt to cinders, with a savage wedge cut into the side by Wilford Martin's last flight. In the moonlight, the mist took on an ethereal glow.

"Welcome to the Haunted Vineyard," said Dinah beside her.

Jenny picked at one of the dead leaves. It crumbled away into dust. They walked slowly in the direction of the fire-blasted mansion, their footsteps barely making a sound in the close, heavy mist that hugged the ground.

"Well Jennifer," said Dinah softly, "why have we come to this grim desolation of a once great house? First and finest of the Big Six."

"The big what?"

"The Big Six," Dinah repeated like it was self-evident. "They're like the original wineries that put Blackbird Springs on the map."

"Who are the others?"

Dinah glanced away, unexpectedly shy. "Well, there's Woodhall, Carnegie, Campion, Rosewood, and of course Pinefall."

"That was only five," said Jenny.

Dinah bit her lip, embarrassed. "Jack really didn't tell you?"

"Jack doesn't talk to me. Come on."

"Blackthorn," Dinah said. "Owned by the Black family."

"As in the *Dinah Black* family?" Jenny asked, delighted. Dinah gave a slight nod. "Oh, so you're a rich bitch!"

Dinah feigned offense and for a heartbeat, Jenny feared she'd crossed a line. But then she let out an infectious laugh which Jenny felt deep down in her stomach.

"Not *that* rich," she said. "We sold off half the business years ago. But we do okay."

"I'm sure," said Jenny. She had figured Dinah was well off, like most kids in town were, but this made her seem almost like nobility. "So who's dating below their station, you or Jack?"

"Definitely Jack," said Dinah. "My God, I mean you saw that house. We have a housekeeper, they have a staff."

"Not for long," Jenny muttered.

"Okay, come on," Dinah said, halting abruptly. "You keep dealing me these cards from the back of the deck and acting all coy. Out with it."

Jenny hesitated. She wanted to tell but knew she shouldn't. "I'm not supposed to say."

"But you clearly want to," Dinah's mood had shifted, and now Jenny felt like an asshole for bringing it up. "Does this have anything to do with Valerie Valentine tying one on with a bottle of *Ressort Rouge* the other night? Or why Jack barely speaks to me anymore?"

"She *drank* it? Wait, how do you know?"

"I'm over there a lot," Dinah took a step closer, and Jenny got a whiff of her vanilla perfume. "You're changing the subject."

Something caught Jenny's eye behind Dinah, near the mansion.

"I— don't hate me, but I gotta change it again," she breathed, trying to keep her voice calm. "Why do you guys call this place the Haunted Vineyard?"

"Because of the ghosts," Dinah said sarcastically. "Supposedly. The souls of the Martin clan, forever trying to make these dead vines blossom again. Woooo. Why?"

"Cause I think I see one over there," Jenny said, pointing behind Dinah at the bobbing light she had spotted a moment ago. In the fog, it was dim and diffuse, but it appeared to be floating along over the vines near the main Pinefall house a few hundred feet away.

Dinah shrieked.

There was a high-pitched clink of breaking glass, and the light stopped moving.

Had the Stranger come to Pinefall with Jenny? She was sick of waiting around for another trap to spring to find out. Jenny leapt forward, charging toward the floating light.

It was moving again; retreating. Jenny ran harder.

All at once the light vanished. Jenny burst out from the dead vines into an open area on the side of the Pinefall mansion.

There was nobody there.

She gazed up at the empty husk of the mansion as Dinah ran up, panting.

"What was it?" Dinah asked.

"I don't know," said Jenny, drifting closer to the building. Had the ghost—or whatever it was—gone inside? She stepped into the gap where a side door used to be. The decayed wood groaned underneath her foot. It was pitch black within.

"Jenny, it's not safe," said Dinah.

Grimacing, Jenny stepped back and looked around. The eerie mist obscured her view in every direction, and the only sound came from the dead vines, rattling in the wind.

"Would you hate me if I said I wanted to go?" Dinah asked, huddling close and clutching her arm tightly.

Jenny winced, noticing that Dinah's face had gone pale. "Sorry. Yeah, let's get out of here." She took Dinah's hand, and they made their way back to the hot springs.

They were halfway across the geyser field before either spoke again.

"I didn't imagine that, did I?" Jenny asked, trying to sound casual.

Dinah chuckled nervously. "No, I saw it too."

"Good," said Jenny. "Well, not good, but Shelly says... Sometimes I guess I have trouble with, you know, my imagination."

Dinah glanced at her, kindness in her eyes. Jenny was about to say more when a shrieking whistle sounded.

"Oh crap!" said Dinah, yanking her forward.

"Wait!" cried Jenny, stumbling after her.

"We can make it! Hurry!!"

They were both running now, racing for the edge of a geyser range they could no longer see through the thick fog.

"What happens if we don't?!" Jenny shouted.

"Don't think, just run!!"

They ran on, blazing a trail through the thick, warm mist. Despite Jenny's very recent commitment to jogging, Dinah and her longer legs were outpacing her.

At any moment, a superheated blast of steam could boil them alive. Fog obscured visibility in all directions. Were they even going the right way? All at once the wooden railing loomed out of the haze. Dinah performed a textbook hurdle, kicking out her right leg and leaping over the fence.

Jenny heard a blast behind her; felt heat on her back; she leapt over the rail.

She was no track star. Her back foot caught on the top beam, and she pitched forward, falling into Dinah and knocking them both over. They hit the ground and rolled, tumbling across the gravel in the parking lot.

When the world stopped spinning, there were steaming geysers whistling in the distance. A hot wave washed over Jenny. She found herself on top of something soft and warm.

Dinah.

Her breath in Jenny's hair and their heaving chests pressed close together. Jenny could feel Dinah's heartbeat pounding through her black gabardine sweater, and her own heart pulsing back in response. Like saying hello.

Raising her head, Jenny noticed for the first time that Dinah's eyes were hazel. They locked gazes, and Dinah smiled up at her. Jenny felt herself reddening, and rolled off to the side, looking away.

Dinah giggled.

"Mom always warned me I'd end up on my back if I went to the hot springs at night."

Jenny found herself caught between wanting to make a joke of her own to play it off and rolling back over to give Dinah a big kiss. Maybe she was just being nice… In her indecision, she let out a kind of weird exhale that sounded embarrassingly like a moan and stared up at the night sky.

"So about that change of subject," said Dinah.

"Oh." Jenny glanced over. Dinah's expression was kind, but it was clear she wasn't going to drop this. "The answer is yes," Jenny said, choosing her words carefully. "Valerie and the bottle, Jack, this vineyard. It's all connected. I just don't know how yet."

"And let me guess, you can't tell me more."

"…Not yet."

Dinah sighed. "Okay, fine. For now." Her hand found Jenny's and squeezed for an intoxicating second before pulling her up. Jenny's red wig had gone all crooked, so she pulled it off.

"Oh! Your knee!" Jenny exclaimed, noticing a nasty red abrasion on Dinah's left leg.

"It's not too bad," said Dinah.

Jenny knelt, probing the wound gently. "This could get infected."

"You were right," Dinah said. "Next time, I'll wear pants."

"Next time let's just go shopping," Jenny said, looking up apologetically.

Dinah ran a hand through Jenny's short hair, and Jenny felt her insides tumble in delirious vertigo.

Somewhere close by, a throat cleared and a male voice said, "Evening, ladies."

They turned, startled, to see Declan Dillion leaning against the hood of his silver beamer.

"What are you doing here?!" Jenny demanded.

"More like who," Dinah muttered.

"A little stargazing," Declan said, pulling a small telescope and tripod from his trunk. "Good night for seeing, don't you think?"

Jenny glanced up at the fog that swirled around them. They might as well have been inside a cloud. "Sure," she said. "Great view."

"That's what the IR package is for," he said, patting a bulky plastic box attached to the base of the telescope.

"Ugh, my mom's calling," said Dinah, checking her phone. "We should go." She gave Declan a dirty look and walked to her car.

"Hey Trouble," said Declan, once Dinah had closed the door. Jenny looked back. The oily ginger had sidled forward, speaking in a low voice.

"Careful with that one," he said, nodding to Dinah's car. He reached out and put a small roll of paper in Jenny's hand.

Jenny frowned and unrolled the note, inside it was a wine cork with RR branded on one end. It was signed in sharpie with a big V. On the note was a phone number. "What's this?"

"An offering," said Declan. He shook the tripod at her. "There's safety in numbers, kid. Call me when you're ready to get serious."

Chapter Eleven
Player Two Has Entered the Game

THAT NIGHT, JENNY SLEPT FITFULLY, PLAGUED BY DREAMS OF A ghost chasing her through endless rows of dead grapevines. Just when she thought she was in the clear, a tall, dark and Strangesome menace appeared before her, throwing a noose around her neck and choking the life out of her. Sometimes the Stranger was Declan. Sometimes it was Valerie Valentine. Sometimes Alicia Aaron stood nearby, watching Jenny's murder, smoking a clove cigarette.

Why couldn't she have a good dream? One about Dinah?

Something was nagging her about the Haunted Vineyard. Those floating lights, the sound of broken glass, the Ghost of Pinefall disappearing into thin air near the mansion... Jenny grumbled and sat up in bed. The sun had risen, and she was sick of replaying the previous night. Stupid Declan Dillion showing up to ruin the moment.

She staggered downstairs—bleary-eyed, cranky, and looking for carbs—to find her aunt in workout leggings of her own, lacing some running shoes. They both stared at each other a while.

"Well well," Jenny said at last. "I guess the date went well."

Shelly flushed and tried to keep her face straight. "You know, I never did ask you about that girl who dropped you off last night."

Jenny allowed a coy smile, remembering the soft warmth of Dinah's body underneath her when they tumbled in the parking lot.

"She's Jack's girlfriend, Dinah," Jenny said, walking to the kitchen to grab a muffin.

"Oh yeah?"

"For now."

"*Oh yeah?*" Shelly raised an eyebrow.

Jenny rolled her eyes and took a big bite of her muffin. "Di Wockhar way annihin awout we?"

Shelly waited, nonplussed, until Jenny finished chewing and swallowed.

"Did Lockhart say anything about me?" Jenny repeated.

"No," Shelly said, her guard up now. "Should he have?"

"Of course not," Jenny said, smiling sweetly. "Anyway, watch yourself with this guy, he's still hung up on his ex."

Shelly's face darkened. "How would you know?"

"Well," Jenny paused, taking time to chew and swallow again. It was time to flex. "He's got a ring on a chain around his neck. You can see the imprint under his uniform. But there's a mark on his ring finger from where he used to wear it. And it's clear he hemmed his slacks himself: the stitching is clumsy, and the thread doesn't match. Somewhat recent bachelor. She probably left him within a year, I'd guess. Did he tell you what happened? Did he cheat? Or was it the drinking?"

A cold silence had descended over the Onishi household. Even the blackbirds outside had stopped singing. Shelly stared at her, mouth agape. She looked— she looked repulsed. Jenny began to entertain the idea that she might have made a mistake.

"Jennifer, his wife passed away," Shelly said, disgusted. "Breast cancer, three years ago."

"Oh," Jenny said lamely. "I guess I was close?"

"Jennifer!"

She wanted to stick the rest of her body into her mouth along with her foot and disappear completely. A Jenny black hole, a singularity of shame. Some monster she must have seemed to her aunt.

"Sorry," she said hoarsely. Aunt Shelly was studying her closely now, her dark eyes burning holes through Jenny.

"We're not having another problem, are we?" Shelly asked.

"No," said Jenny. Shelly glared harder. "No! I'm just an asshole, okay? Can I have $20? I need tampons."

"Bullshit," said Shelly.

"My Adderall scrip is up too," Jenny added.

"I'll pick it up when I'm out," said her aunt. "What do you need money for?"

Jenny scowled at the muffin, no longer hungry, and tossed it in the trash. "The finer things in life."

Shelly snorted.

"I need a new jacket," Jenny said, annoyed.

"What happened to yours?" asked Shelly.

"Someone stole it," said Jenny. "Probably your boy Blake's kid, Mason. Anyway, I'll bet the thrift stores here have lots of purple coats."

"Maybe we can go later," Shelly said, faking a yawn. Translation: don't hold your breath.

"Fine," Jenny sighed.

She should be thinking about the mystery. The ghost. Declan's mysterious cork. But her mind kept turning back to Dinah. Dinah, who didn't know she was a monster. She tried to recall the feeling of Dinah's fingers in her hair. The smell of her vanilla perfume...

"I'm gonna shower," she announced and retreated to her bedroom.

"HOW FAST CAN YOU RUN ON THAT FAKE LEG?" SHE ASKED ALICIA Aaron, leaning an arm against the side of the building and effectively cornering the little redhead into the wall.

It was Monday morning, and Econ had just let out. She'd been on her way to PreCalc when she spotted Alicia by the library. *Someone* had been there the other night at Pinefall. Someone watching Jenny and Dinah, and without any real leads, it was time to shake a few trees and see what fell out.

"What do you want?" Alicia said through gritted teeth in her high, squeaky voice.

"You're not the kind of girl who follows people around, are you?" she asked, leaning closer.

Alicia was undaunted. "I thought that was your department, *Trouble*."

"I'm serious," she said. "Say you were in danger. Like if a bear was chasing you, how fast could you go?"

"Oh, I would trip you, so speed wouldn't be an issue," Alicia said, flashing a nasty smile.

She grinned back, raising an eyebrow. "Well well. 10 points for Hufflepuff."

"I'm a Ravenclaw!" Alicia squeaked, her eyes flashing momentarily with childlike delight before her neck reddened and she glanced down at her legs. "You can get other kinds of them. You know, prosthetics, that are made for running. But they're expensive."

"When I solve the mystery, I'll buy you the fucking Cadillac of fake legs," she said, feeling a sudden kinship to the girl.

"*If* you win," said Alicia.

She smirked, reminding herself again that, unlike in dad's books, the other contestants actually *could* win this game. She wouldn't be able to count on convenient deus ex machina to save the day. No sudden influx of points to win the house cup. Alicia was in it to win it, possessing a clue Jenny hadn't even managed to get a photo of.

Alicia being the Ghost of Pinefall was a long shot, though. Declan Dillion, on the other hand… Could he really have made it all the way from the mansion to the geyser parking lot ahead of Jenny and Dinah? And what was the *Ressort Rouge* cork he gave Jenny supposed to mean? That he could be trusted since Dad signed it? Fat chance of that.

"Is there a problem here, Miss Valentine?" asked a teacher as he walked up.

"No problem," she said, turning away. "Just headed to math class." Jenny had a PreCalc quiz today, and she needed to pull a decent grade to keep Mr. Stephenson off her back.

"Actually, why don't you come with me," said the teacher.

Alicia Aaron snickered and limped away. The teacher was a willowy man with long, thinning hair. Late 50s, she guessed. He looked like a pushover.

"And who are you?" she asked, walking with him. He was leading her away from the Math building.

"I'm the Vice Principal, Mr. Carter," he said, holding the door to the school office open for her. She stepped inside warily. He motioned for her to follow him to his office. Inside, Mason Lockhart and his father Blake were waiting. Shit.

"Oh good," she said, feigning confidence. "Now you can tell this jerk to stop bullying—"

"The way we hear it, you threatened Mason in the parking lot and keyed his car," said Blake.

"I did not!"

"Not to mention the damage done to the diving pool cover," said the vice principal.

"This is bullshit! Did he tell you whose keys he threw into that pool? And then tried to drown?"

"Language, Miss Valentine," the vice principal said quietly, tenting his fingers and giving her a hard stare. "Now, Mason has something he'd like to say to you."

Mason turned to her, calm behind a mask of phony contrition. "It was wrong of me to confront you after you threatened me and damaged my car," he said robotically. "I'm sorry I threw your keys in the pool. Next time I will report any concerns to my father and Mr. Carter."

Blake patted his son's shoulder, watching her closely.

"Now it's your turn," said the vice principal. "And I'd like to see you both shake on it."

"I have nothing to apologize for," she said.

The vice principal sighed and pulled out a folder from his desk. It was Jenny's file. Oh boy.

"On the sheriff's suggestion, I had a chat with your old principal," the vice principal said, leafing through the file.

"Oh yeah? Is he still on house arrest?" she sneered.

"Not him, his replacement," said Mr. Carter. "It seems you've had quite the colorful high school career, Jennifer. That ends now. You'll find our tolerance for trouble at Blackbird Springs Academy to be very low."

She couldn't help but snicker. Even the corners of Blake's mouth curled a little.

"Yes, I'm sure this must all seem very amusing to you right now," said the vice principal. "After a five-day suspension, maybe you'll change your tune. Oh, and you'll have to reimburse the school for the pool cover damage. About $2,000."

"And another thousand for Bonnie's paint job," said Mason.

Aunt Shelly was going to be so pissed at Jenny.

"If I refuse?"

"Then you'll be expelled."

"So this is how you're gonna play?" she asked the sheriff.

"No one is playing here, Miss Valentine," Blake said, and winked when only she could see it.

Jenny didn't have $3,000. She doubted Shelly did either. But getting expelled would be a disaster. Mason held out his hand to shake, a shit-eating grin plastered all over his big dumb face.

"Bill me," she said, giving Mason a fist bump and walking out.

The sheriff escorted her to Shelly's room. Her aunt leaned out the door and listened to Blake explain the situation, refusing to even look at her niece while shaking her head in disappointment.

"Make sure she goes directly home," was all she had to say, and shut the door on them both.

Blake made her ride in the perp seat on the drive home.

"You might as well get used to it," he said.

"You think she's pissed at you, or me?" she asked.

"Definitely you," Blake said.

"Why the hell did Dad ever name a character after you?" she blurted out.

"It bothers you, doesn't it?"

"Yes, it does!"

His eyes found hers through the rear-view mirror. They were hard and piercing and full of fire.

"Well think about how much it bothers me," he said.

They drove on.

"If you think this suspension is going to stop me from winning, you're an even worse cop than Dad thought."

He smiled at that, a far-off look in his eye. "Look, you got spirit, kiddo. I'll give you that. You know who else had spirit?"

"Who?" she asked, not really caring.

"Casey Klein."

The strangled girl. Blake's big break. The one Dad talked him into disinterring. Their eyes met again, and he knew that she knew. "Dad thought you got that wrong."

"John thought lots of things that sounded better in children's books than police reports," said Blake with a scowl. "Trouble always finds the dognapped pooch alive and well, no worse for wear. She never had to come across her classmate's body in a ditch, throttled by a noose, face turned black and rotted half off."

She grimaced, thinking about poor Casey Klein. Blake wasn't done.

"An illegal search never sinks a case once Trouble retrieves the missing jewels. Oh, no. Trouble never had to watch her friend's brains get scraped off the asphalt after a drunk driver caused a 5-car pileup."

"Trouble's not that kind of book," she mumbled.

"No one gets cancer in RJ's Blackbird Springs…" he said and drove on in silence.

Another nasty retort died on her lips as she studied Blake's white knuckles gripping the wheel. They pulled up in front of Jenny's grandparents' house. Blake parked and twisted to look at her directly.

"Mason might be a dunce, but he's my dunce, and he's all I've got," he said. "Leave him out of it."

"Like you're leaving Shelly out of it? If you hurt my aunt—"

"Your aunt's a lovely lady, Jennifer," he cut her off. "You should really give her a break."

"If you hurt her, I'll…" she was racking her brain for the cruelest threat she could muster.

"Relax, kiddo," he smirked again and chuckled. "Such spirit. I'm a gentleman."

She leaned close to the grate that separated them, whispering softly even though they were alone.

"Casey Klein had spirit. I've got claws. If you hurt Shelly Onishi's feelings, I will hurt you."

He studied her for a beat and tipped his cap.

"Fair enough."

Chapter Twelve

Picaresque

SHELLY CAME HOME LATE IN THE AFTERNOON WITH A BUNDLE OF Jenny's classwork for the week.

"Mr. Stephenson wasn't happy about you missing the quiz," Shelly told Jenny as she prepared dinner, avoiding the larger suspension discussion for now. "He said he needs to see a big improvement in math this week or you'll have to transfer."

Wordlessly, Jenny moved to help chop vegetables. Her aunt regarded her for a moment and nodded, sliding the cutting board over to Jenny.

"I know," Jenny said. "I'm working on it. I found a tutor."

"Maybe it was a mistake letting you test out of Algebra II."

"I said I'm handling it. I had a bad week, you know."

"Is that why you keyed Mason Lockhart's car and destroyed the pool cover?"

"I didn't—"

"I don't have $2,000, you know," said Shelly.

"Mason is lying, I never keyed his car," Jenny said. "And the pool cover wasn't my fault."

"Blake said you agreed to pay for it."

"I had to, they were going to kick me out."

Shelly stared at her a moment, softening just a smidge.

"If you're telling me you got outsmarted by Mason Lockhart then I'm even more disappointed in you."

Jenny scowled and gave the carrot she was holding a big whack with the chef's knife.

"You're not gonna keep dating the sheriff, are you?" Jenny asked. "He's a bastard. And he hates Dad!" Jenny scraped the carrot slices into the pan. "Hated Dad," she corrected herself.

Shelly ran a hand over Jenny's shoulder. "I don't know. We'll see."

BEING SUSPENDED TURNED OUT TO BE QUITE PRODUCTIVE.

Growing up with a teacher for a parent meant Jenny had absorbed at least half an economics degree just by osmosis. She'd completed the whole week's Econ lessons and homework before bedtime, which buttered up Shelly enough that she agreed to let Jenny go out jogging every morning to fulfill her P.E. requirement.

Shelly didn't need to know that Jenny's run was a perfect cover to spy on Valerie Valentine.

Val had a typical rich trophy wife lifestyle: yoga in the morning at a studio in town, then brunch at Rosie's with some other ladies. Jenny felt fresh scorn welling within her as those blue blood bitches paid $50 a head to push some lettuce around on their plates for an hour.

The Valentine Foundation had an office a block from the Winchester. Near as Jenny could tell, Val spent most of her time there planning expensive parties for her friends and calling them fundraisers. After a couple hours in the office, Val went to spin class, which was notably also attended by Mr. Declan Dillion. As luck would have it, the gym they both attended sat across the street from the park in Town Square.

Jenny pretended to feed the ducks while watching from behind dark aviators and a brunette wig, styled in pigtail braids. The ducks quacked at Jenny, and Jenny quacked back. She liked ducks.

Declan Dillion stayed behind at the gym to lift weights while Val went to lunch. On Tuesday, Val had lunch with an older man in a pinstripe suit who Jenny thought might be her lawyer. On Wednesday, it was the brunch friends, who seemed to be some kind of bored housewives club. Val didn't take lunch on Thursday and instead went back to the mansion.

Drew thought she was wasting her time, but as Jenny explained in her emails, the first step to solving a mystery was knowing your suspect's routine. She had told him about the events at the haunted vineyard—with the sapphic bits edited out. Drew's theory was smugglers. It was always smugglers in the books, he said. Which, to be fair, was accurate: it was smugglers in like five of the 12. But this was different. The Ghost of Pinefall had been waiting there for Jenny, watching her. Was this, too, the Stranger?

Each day, Jenny would stop by the Poison Pen to look at the big display for RJ Valentine in the window. Fans were still leaving flowers and notes underneath. She had debated leaving one of her own, but a small, egotistical part of her didn't like to think of herself as just another fan. What would she even write? Better to honor him by catching his killer.

On Thursday, she was just turning away from the display window when she saw a sight to make her heart freeze. Headed right for her was that man from Dad's funeral: the Undertaker. Those same dead eyes, that threadbare suit that had buried too many souls… Her vision dimmed, and she felt another panic attack coming on. He was coming for her.

But then he merely nodded, gesturing with his Starbucks cup, and continued on. Jenny watched him pass, transfixed. He walked past the Pen and entered a shop. The sign read Carnegie Mortuary.

Jenny deflated, feeling foolish. This wasn't some karmic omen, the guy just worked next door. Blushing at her own lack of nerve, she jogged on and went back to snooping.

On Friday morning, Jenny tucked a bag with the last few slices of bread into her sleeveless blue workout hoodie for the ducks. She was feeling saucy today, so she wore the electric blue pixie wig. It was mildly scandalous when that tall city worker Dave whistled at her as she jogged by their latest streetlight replacement site. Later on, while she was feeding the ducks, Val and Declan finally interacted with each other at the gym.

Before this, an observer might have assumed they didn't know each other. They had never so much as looked in the other's direction the entire time Jenny had been spying on them. But today, Val came out of the locker room after spin class and found Mr. Dillion while he was doing curls. They chatted for a couple minutes, and Jenny would swear that Val was arching her back on purpose to stick her tits out at him. They parted with smiles, and Val patted him on the shoulder.

These two were totally fucking.

Soon afterward, Val walked to the courtroom at City Hall instead of going to lunch. Jenny shifted over to a park bench in front of the courthouse steps. One of the ducks had followed her over, so she split a slice of bread with him, chewing absentmindedly while she waited. Mr. Duck hopped up next to her and took a nap. Jenny was about to join him when Val finally reappeared.

She looked pissed.

Val was wearing a white pantsuit with black trim today, and wicked stiletto heels that brought her clomping down the steps in loud, angry *tap tap taps*. Jenny hid behind her copy of *Trouble Eight Days a Week* as Val marched right up beside Jenny's bench and lit a cigarette. Her evil stepmother took a few long drags, exhaling in frustration. She kept clenching and unclenching her empty hand like she wanted to hit something. Eventually, Val looked over and noticed Mr. Duck.

"Disgusting!" said Val.

"Quack!" said Mr. Duck.

The old man in the pinstriped suit made his way down to Val, in no hurry himself.

"We can always appeal," he said.

"We'll lose," said Val, throwing her cigarette down and crushing it with her heel.

Val marched off towards the Valentine Foundation office with her lawyer trailing behind, saying something about a motion to delay. Jenny craned her neck to watch them both walk all the way back down the street. She wished again that she could afford a camera with a telephoto lens.

"I did warn her," said a man's voice next to her.

Jenny jumped and whipped her head around with a start to find that Mr. Duck had vanished, and a thin man with a hawkish nose and horn-rimmed glasses had taken his place: Hamilton Webb, Esq.

"Are you a duck?" Jenny blurted out.

"No," said Mr. Webb. "Shouldn't you be in school?"

"I got suspended," Jenny said.

Webb wrinkled his nose, unimpressed.

"Sloppy."

"I don't need to hear it from you too," she told the lawyer. "Unless you have two grand I can borrow."

"Have you solved the murder?"

"Is it enough that I can blow apart Valerie's alibi?"

"No."

"Fine," Jenny said. "It's not for me. My aunt's getting billed for something that wasn't her fault. I could, like, do office work for you. Or serve someone papers."

"You're not old enough for that yet," said Webb. "But I'll see what I can do."

Jenny gave him a surprised smile. It was better than nothing.

"Thanks. What did you warn her about?" she asked him, nodding back in Val's direction.

"She tried to get the will thrown out," he said, buffing his nails on his suit jacket. "Let's just say Judge Santos booted her case so hard she left a footprint. The will is ironclad."

"Good," said Jenny.

Mr. Webb stood up. "Well, I'd tell you to stay out of trouble, but…"

"Mmhmm."

He was walking away when Jenny remembered something. "Hey, real quick?" Webb paused. "Can you get me the phone number of the Valentine housekeeper? The one who was there the night of the attack?"

"Well, I'm technically her boss now, so sure," said Mr. Webb. "But I need you to do me a favor."

"Sure, what?" asked Jenny, curious.

"Sooner or later, someone is going to ask you to betray me. When that happens… think fondly of me."

"Absolutely," said Jenny.

AFTER MR. WEBB LEFT, JENNY REPOSITIONED HERSELF TO SPY ON Val. Her usual bench by the Valentine Foundation was occupied by that old man with the snowy white beard. She peeked over his shoulder and saw that he was playing *Words With Friends* on his phone. Probably with a grandkid. That was nice, but now he was in her spot. She lingered nearby, pretending to check her watch when, quite unexpectedly, Declan Dillion walked out of the Foundation office across the street.

Jenny peered through the door as it closed and spotted Valerie inside. Declan walked swiftly away. He was still in his workout clothes: a tight Under Armour shirt and warmup pants, with his gym bag over his shoulder.

No, wait— Not *his* gym bag, *Valerie's!*

She'd been watching Val carry around that little black duffel with violet straps all week. The bag under Declan Dillion's arm was Val's, she was sure of it. With a sudden rush of intuition, she pictured the bottle of *Ressort Rouge* hiding within the bag. It was just the right size. Or the murder weapon. Was Declan hiding something for Val? Jenny froze. She had a decision to make: stay on Val, or follow Declan and the bag. Screw it. All her instincts were screaming at her to tail Declan.

She jogged off, weaving back and forth to keep her distance. Declan was heading away from the center of town. His silver BMW was nowhere in sight. Where was he going? He turned a corner and Jenny saw the Winchester up ahead. Declan looked to be headed to the service entrance. Jenny was regretting her electric blue wig choice now. She would be far too noticeable inside the restaurant.

An idea occurred to her, and she whipped out her phone, pulling up her contacts to text Declan.

Jenny: We need to talk. Go somewhere more private and I'll meet you there.

Watching from afar, she could see the slick ginger pause just outside the back door to the Winchester and check his phone. He frowned, looking around, and turned away from the door. Good. He was taking the bait. Jenny cut down an alleyway and beat him to the next cross street. She ducked into an ice cream shop and watched through the window.

Soon, Declan strode by, still carrying the duffel bag, continuing down Mission Street. Jenny mentally pictured the next block in that direction. The road would dead-end into some warehouses up ahead. She counted to ten and stepped back out. Up ahead, she caught sight of Declan again. He seemed to be disappearing into the earth.

The warehouse at the end of the block was an old building, fronted with a mossy, cobblestone facade. Instead of a flat roof, there were two arched canopies, sort of like an airport hanger. As she got closer, she saw that a groove was cut into the ground between the two arches, and stairs led down to a door several feet below street level.

A small sign made of tiles was set into the cobblestone wall: **The Cellars.**

The door was cracked open. Inside, the walls were lined with wooden barrels. Big ones, at least a yard across and almost as tall as she was, stacked three levels high. Rows and rows of them ran deeper into the dark warehouse. Wine barrels, she figured. It was cool and damp down here. Ideal conditions for aging. Dim light filtered in from gaps in the canopy high above.

The floor was smooth cement here, and the heavy air seemed to smother each step she took. Fifty feet down, there was a gap in her row. Jenny paused and looked around. To her right, more wine barrels, triple-stacked to the rafters. On her left though, the shelves gave way to an open space that ran all the way to the back wall.

Declan Dillion was standing in the center of the clearing, Val's bag hanging from his right hand. Too late, Jenny realized she'd been spotted.

"Nice wig," he said. "What's with the subterfuge?"

Jenny stepped out casually to greet him, hoping to convey a level of confidence she wasn't feeling.

"Hello, Mr. Dillion," she said. "Fancy meeting you here."

"Decided to take me up on the offer, have you?" he said, grinning.

"What? The cork?" she guessed.

"Looks like we were both on the right track with Pinefall," Declan said. "What do you say, 60/40?"

"Am I the 60?" Jenny asked. She had no interest in an alliance with Declan, but she wanted to keep him talking.

"Don't be greedy, babydoll," he said, narrowing his eyes. "And tell your friend to stop skulking and join us."

"What friend? And there's no way I'm getting less than 50 percent!"

"That friend," Declan said, pointing to the casks behind Jenny. "Who's that? Drew? Dinah? Come on, man, cards on the table." He withdrew his Death tarot card from his duffle and waved it at her. "I found a buyer online. He's willing to pay $2 million in hard cash now plus a cut later if we pony up."

The flesh on Jenny's bare arms prickled with goosebumps.

"I didn't come with a friend," she whispered.

Behind his red beard, the color drained from Declan's face.

"Shit," he said.

Her heart froze. Something was wrong. Deadly wrong.

A footfall sounded behind her and Declan's eyes widened in horror.

Jenny spun in time to see the blur of a large figure rushing toward her, all covered in black.

The Stranger.

Something silver, shiny, and sharp flashed in the Stranger's hand. Jenny stared dumbly as strong arms gripped her from behind and yanked her back. The knife whistled through the space where her neck had just been.

Declan shoved her behind him and shouted. Jenny rolled over and scrambled to her knees.

The knife sang again. This time, a wet tear followed, and a gasp that became a gurgle.

Declan Dillion spun around, and Jenny was hit with a jet of something hot and sticky. Blood. All over her face and chest. Streaming down Declan's workout shirt from a hideous gash in his neck.

His expression was confused. Scared. Pleading. When Jenny shrieked, he seemed to understand. He was dying.

"Go," Declan mouthed, baring his teeth in a familiar wolfish grin and pressing the tarot card into her hand. With the last of his strength, he threw himself back at the Stranger and tackled him.

It saved her life.

The dark figure fell, entangled with Declan's body. A long steel knife skidded across the concrete. For an instant, her assailant was overwhelmed, and the way out was open.

Jenny sprang past them, grabbed the knife, and ran for it. Down the aisle and through the door and up the stairs into daylight; a crazed fugitive from the underworld with the devil himself on her heels. She didn't stop until she reached Town Square and saw a police SUV pulling away from the curb.

Jenny threw herself in front of it and pounded on the hood, smearing blood all over the white paint. Through the windshield, she locked eyes with Blake Lockhart.

A heartbeat passed between them.

Some picture she must have looked to him. A dumb little girl with blue hair all covered in blood, a wicked knife in one hand and the Death card in the other, playing a game way out of her league. But she had spirit, all right.

"Get in!" he shouted.

Chapter Thirteen

Red Red Red

JENNY HURRIED AROUND TO THE PASSENGER DOOR, PANTING hard, and hopped in.

"Is that your blood?" Lockhart asked.

"No."

"Where?"

"The Cellars!" Jenny managed between heaving breaths. "Declan Dillion. Murdered."

Lockhart flipped his siren on and made a hard u-turn, peeling out as they whipped back around to face Mission Street.

"The Stranger," she said with a whimper. "Hurry."

Jenny had barely collected her thoughts when suddenly they were back at the Cellars. It couldn't have been more than 15 minutes since she'd come racing up those steps to get away from the killer. Lockhart muttered some jargon into his radio, frowning at the cobblestone-fronted building. He stashed the receiver and glanced at her.

"Stay put."

He hopped out and unholstered his pistol. Moving swiftly, his gun pointed down in a two-handed grip, Lockhart approached the warehouse and descended the stairs.

Jenny stared at the spot on the ground where his head had disappeared. She couldn't think straight. Every time she closed her eyes, she saw Declan Dillion's pleading look as the life drained out of him.

Declan. Dead. Because of her? She asked him to meet her. Made him take her somewhere private. Was the Stranger following her the whole time, just waiting for the chance to strike?

One thing she was sure of: he'd saved her life. She looked down at the blood-stained Death card, still held tight in her hand. That look on his face…

She was still staring at that spot on the sidewalk when Lockhart re-appeared, climbing back up the stairs with a hard, unreadable visage. His pistol was still gripped in his left hand, pointed at the ground. He walked over to her door and opened it. She flinched as his right hand reached out, but it went right past her to the glove compartment. He opened it and pulled out a latex glove.

"Let's have that," he said, pointing at the knife she was still clutching, white-knuckled.

Jenny blinked, and quickly handed the knife over, happy to be rid of it. Lockhart grasped it with a latex glove and holstered his pistol. Then he carefully deposited the blade into an evidence bag before reaching over to the radio receiver.

"Got a one-eight-seven, Mack," he said with a sigh. "10-79, over."

His eyes never left hers as he hung up the receiver. He pointed to the tarot card next. Jenny hesitated.

"It's evidence," he said sternly.

Numbly, she handed it over, knowing that if Lockhart wanted to, he now had possession of two heirloom clues. More sirens were wailing in the distance now, getting closer.

"Is he…?" Jenny asked.

"Yes," said the sheriff. "Come on down from there."

He coaxed her out of the cab. Jenny stepped gingerly onto the asphalt. The sun was still shining so brightly like nothing was wrong. She thought she might vomit soon.

"Are you hurt?" Lockhart asked.

Jenny shook her head.

"Okay, turn around," he said.

She turned in a daze. The shock was so complete that she didn't even realize she was under arrest until the second handcuff clicked tight over her wrist.

PROCESSING AT THE POLICE STATION TOOK HOURS. THERE WAS FIN-gerprinting. Photographs. Swabs for DNA in her mouth, and under her nails. Her bloody clothes were evidence now. The wig too. Her heart sank when they took her phone and her watch. That stung.

A female deputy gave her a loose BSPD t-shirt to wear, but they wouldn't let her wash up. Her face was still sticky with Declan's blood. She could feel it drying, tightening, cracking when she moved her eyebrows or heaved her chest.

Once the shock wore off, Jenny was furious with the sheriff.

He'd stuck her in an interrogation room, handcuffed to the table. The door was propped open, which somehow made it worse. She could sense the flurry of activity outside, but no one would tell her what was going on. Surely they'd called her aunt by now.

"You know I didn't do it you asshole!" she shouted when she spotted Lockhart walking by outside. He stopped long enough to close the door, shutting her out entirely.

Left alone with her thoughts, Jenny kept replaying the moment in her mind. Not the awful attack, but right before it.

"Looks like we were both on the right track with Pinefall," Declan had said. What did he mean? Who was this mysterious buyer he found online? Was there something she had missed at the Haunted Vineyard? She needed to go back, but first, she needed to not go to jail. Lockhart could get her school records. If he saw her medical records… But those were private, weren't they?

Jenny was close to another panic attack when the door finally reopened. The sheriff entered, rolling down a shade over the two-way mirror and taking a seat opposite her.

"I can prove it wasn't me," said Jenny. "You need to talk to the M.E. Get him to examine the angle of the cut."

Lockhart stared at her, inscrutable.

"I'm way shorter than Declan Dillion!" Jenny said, trying and failing with the handcuffs on to pantomime the attack. "If I did it, the cut would be at an angle. But the Stranger, he was tall. The cut would have been straight on."

Lockhart continued to stare.

"That's really how you think this works, huh?" he asked after a while.

Jenny's cheeks burned. "Fuck you."

"I know you didn't do it," Lockhart said, sliding something small and metal over to her. The key to her handcuffs.

"So you checked with the M.E.?" Jenny asked, grabbing the key and unlocking her cuffs.

"No," said Lockhart. "Declan had the voice recorder on his phone running. We heard the whole thing."

Jenny sagged in her chair, relieved.

"You're lucky," said the sheriff. "We had your prints on the knife, you were covered in his blood, and you'd sent him a text to meet you there. What were you thinking? This isn't a game."

It was, though. A dangerous game.

"You really thought I did it?" Jenny asked.

"No, of course not. But I can't exactly ignore the possibility when you show up holding a murder weapon."

"You prick," she said.

"Tell me more about the attacker," Lockhart said, ignoring the barb and pulling out a notepad. "I can't exactly put out an APB for a tall, dark and Strangesome menace."

Jenny tried to smirk, but the smile fled from her face, and she relived the attack. "He was big like I said. Tall. Black clothes. Black shirt. Black gloves. He had on like a ski mask or something, but with no eyeholes. I couldn't see any skin at all. He was like a phantom." She shivered.

"All right, come on," Lockhart said, rising.

She followed him to his desk in the police station bullpen.

"Your aunt's on her way," he said, pointing her to a chair. "What did Declan mean about Pinefall?"

"I don't know," Jenny said, which wasn't a total lie. He was about to protest when someone shouted, and Valerie Valentine came stomping into the office in her black and white power suit and stiletto heels.

"I want a restraining order!" she thundered, jabbing a finger at Jenny. "She doesn't come near my family, Blake!"

As luck would have it, Val's side of the family owned the Cellars. One of their few remaining assets. Val licked her lips and smiled.

"I want her on trespassing, vandalism, wrongful death!" Val went on and on as Lockhart sighed. "Throw the book at her."

"She's a minor, Val," Lockhart said. "Best you could possibly get is two grand restitution from her aunt."

Jenny's heart sank. Add that to the $3000 she owed the school and

Mason. Any more of this and they wouldn't be able to afford food. Shelly was going to be so mad at her.

"My aunt didn't do anything!" she said to Lockhart, but Val was having none of it.

"She didn't drive your mother to the clinic. That's enough for me."

Jenny whipped her hand around and hurled the handcuffs at Val's head. They bounced off her forehead with a satisfying *thunk!*

Val screeched and dove at Jenny, her acrylic talons out for blood. Lockhart ducked between them, and Deputy Mack pulled Val away. Jenny could swear Lockhart was close to cracking a smile as he re-cuffed Jenny. He enjoyed locking her up far too much, Jenny thought.

"Ask her about Mr. Dillion!" Jenny shouted, remembering their meeting earlier. "She was the last one to see him alive."

"What about it, Val?" the sheriff asked. "Did you see Declan today?"

Val took a step toward Jenny. The deputy put a hand on her shoulder, and she smacked it away in a huff.

"He stopped by the Foundation to drop off a check for the harvest festival," Val said, affecting a bored casualness that Jenny hoped Lockhart wasn't too thick to see through.

"It's a bit early for that," said Lockhart.

"He was headed out of town," Val said, faking a yawn.

"Liar."

Everyone turned back to Jenny.

"You gave him something," she said, staring with pleasure at the rising welt above Val's eyebrow. "He left with your gym bag. Black, with purple straps. I saw him."

"CoreFit gives those bags out to everyone," Val said, and Jenny felt her face reddening. "How long am I gonna have to put up with this trash, Blake?"

"As long as it takes for you to find some class, Valerie," said a voice behind them. Shelly had arrived. She and Val each tilted their head to regard the other, invisible lightning arcing between them.

"Shelly—" Jenny started, but her aunt cut her off with a withering glare.

"Not a word," Shelly turned to Lockhart. "What do I need to do to get her out of here?"

"Mack, could you escort Mrs. Valentine to number three?" Lockhart asked his deputy. He waited until Val was out of sight to unshackle Jenny again. "Look, I don't know how much Val's gonna push it, but you might have to talk to a JCO."

"Can I have my phone back?" Jenny asked.

"It's evidence," he said.

"Come on, Blake," said Shelly, giving the sheriff an expression Jenny had never witnessed from her aunt before: desire.

"Okay, hold on," he said, his cheeks shading a little.

"My watch, too!" Jenny called after him as he went to get her phone.

"You're grounded," Shelly said, back to her usual severe mood. "You were supposed to be staying at home studying. Who is this Declan person?"

Jenny was prepared for this lie. "My math tutor."

THAT NIGHT, JENNY SLEPT IN HER CLOSET. SHE'D SEEN THIS IN A movie once. Let the Stranger attack the wig and lump of pillows under her covers. She'd be fine here. She was small. It was comfy, even.

In the morning, she had a horrible neck ache. Aunt Shelly made it worse by announcing that Jenny was to spend the day doing community service. Trash pickup in the park. Apparently, Val was serious about making life hell for Jenny with a Juvenile Court Officer, so Jenny needed to burnish her image with some civic virtue.

Really, Jenny suspected that her aunt wanted someone to supervise Jenny for the day while she went on a lunch date with Lockhart. By the time she finished that afternoon, her back ached from all the leaning over, but no one had tried to murder her, at least.

"This came for you," Shelly said when she got home, sliding Jenny a small envelope from the stack of mail. It had Jenny's name on it, but no stamp. Jenny narrowed her eyes, examining the letter. It was barely bigger than a playing card; the sort of size people used for thank you notes. "Who's it from?" Shelly asked, still watching her.

"Dinah," Jenny lied and turned away. "You mind?"

She opened it in her room. Inside was a small card. A calling card, like the kind the Stranger left in the books. The little drawing of a peeking man in a hat, and:

KiLLROY WAS HERE

Below was a message for Jenny.

SORRY ABOUT THE MESS. GAME ON.

Chapter Fourteen

Return to the Haunted Vineyard

SATURDAY NIGHT PASSED IN SILENCE. NO ONE TRIED TO MURDER her, but she kept watch all the same.

In the morning, Aunt Shelly consented to letting Jenny go jogging with her. Jenny took them down a bike trail path Drew had shown her, coming around the long way into town. Shelly was dying by the time they stopped for lattes at a local beanery.

"I'm telling you, Jenny," Shelly said between breaths, her hands on her knees as they waited for their drinks. "Enjoy that youthful energy while it lasts."

"Whatever," Jenny rolled her eyes and turned away in time to notice a few patrons quickly looking elsewhere and avoiding eye contact.

The whole town knew about Declan Dillion's murder by now. Officially, Declan was mixed up in something shady, maybe drug-related. There was one witness, but no suspects. The papers had kept Jenny's name out of it because she was a minor, but word must be traveling around that the new Valentine girl was involved.

"I have a favor to ask," Jenny said.

"The answer is no," said Shelly.

"Drew and Penny need help with a yearbook project," Jenny said, putting on her best pout.

"Who are Drew and Penny?" Shelly asked. "And since when do you care about yearbook?"

"My friends," Jenny said, the words still felt strange on her lips. "And I don't really care, but if I have to sit around the house all day, I'm just gonna keep seeing Declan Dillion's face over and over. I barely slept last night."

Shelly bit her lip, not liking any of this.

"Come on, Drew's never even had detention," Jenny added. "And I think Penny sleeps with a copy of the AP Style Guide between her legs."

"Don't be gauche, Jennifer."

"I promise I'll check in every hour."

Her aunt sighed, and Jenny knew she had her.

"WHY IS HE CALLED *THE STRANGER*?" PENNY ASKED. THEY WERE traipsing through the geyser field outside Pinefall. Jenny and Drew had been having a coded conversation about the identity of the Stranger, which Penny took to be a purely book discussion.

"Because he's unknown," Drew said, confused. "And... strange?"

"But... that doesn't make any sense," said Penny.

Jenny exchanged glances with Drew. He shrugged. "How so?" he asked.

"He goes around leaving these calling cards, right? 'Killroy is here'?" Penny said, bugging her eyes out like her point was obvious.

"Yeah?" said Jenny

"So why don't they call him Killroy?" said Penny.

She tried to summon an explanation, but her Trouble knowledge failed her. Jenny had never actually considered this before. "Because he's the Stranger," she said, irritated.

"This is why I can't with those books," said Penny. "If a black girl did one-tenth of the shit Trouble pulled, the cops would've just shot her."

Jenny winced.

"Now you're sure Trouble's dad couldn't be The Stranger?" Drew said, raising his eyebrows.

"Absolutely positive," said Jenny. "I still say it was the evil heiress. She was tall, and goes—went to the gym regularly."

"The evil heiress has an alibi for the second murder, though," said Drew.

"Which book are you talking about?" asked Penny.

"Crap," said Drew, changing the subject. "My new kicks are getting all dirty."

"Stop whining," Jenny said. "If Dinah can walk through here in Steve Maddens, your dumb Nikes can take it."

"Are you and Dinah, like, friends?" Penny asked.

"Yeah, why?" Jenny replied.

Penny hesitated, so Drew chimed in.

"They're mortal enemies," he said.

"We are not," Penny said with a flicker of annoyance. She paused and shrugged at Jenny. "Dinah is my competition for Valedictorian."

"And she's winning," said Drew.

"Well some people can't afford tutors and study aides and trips to museums in Europe for extra credit," said Penny with more than a hint of bitterness.

They had arrived at the end of the geyser field. Jenny went first, picking her way down the steep slope through the redwood trees.

"She seems nice," said Jenny, feeling defensive.

"It's just... ugh!" Penny said in disgust. "Perfect little rich girl with her long legs and cheerleader skirts. She could at least do us the favor of being a ditz, but no. Can't confine herself to ruling the school with her sexy vampire boyfriend, she's gotta get in my lane too."

Jenny laughed at this description of Jack.

"I'll see what I can do about corrupting her," Jenny said with a devious smile.

In a few short steps, they came to the vineyard. Pinefall looked even more desolate without the silvery moonlight painting everything in deceptive monochromatic hues. A vast field of decay spread out before her, all rotting umbers, fetid browns, and scorched, crumbling red bricks under the clear blue sky.

"This place is creepy," said Penny.

"Don't worry," said Drew. "I don't think ghosts can come out in the daytime." He dug in his backpack for his camera and took a few shots of the mansion.

As far as Aunt Shelly knew, they were taking pictures of the Haunted Vineyard for a yearbook spread. As far as Penny knew, that was just a cover so they could search for clues about someone who played a prank on Jenny.

In the back of her mind, Jenny was keenly aware of how reckless this was. If the Stranger didn't like the idea of Jenny and Declan partnering up, what would he think of Penny and Drew helping her? She might be putting them in incredible danger. But on the other hand, Penny had a car, and Jenny didn't. And after the attack in the Cellars, Jenny was too scared to come here alone without someone big like Drew around.

Declan had said she was on the right track about Pinefall, so there must be something she missed. Still, lying to Penny was making her irritable, so the sooner she found the answer, and they got out of here, the better.

"Let's move around to the front," Jenny said and led onward.

A long driveway met the entrance to the mansion over on the right. Blackened marble pillars still stood, framing the grimy remains of the foyer. Drew took more photos and then insisted that Jenny take some of Penny and him by the entrance.

"Come on, put your arm around her," she commanded, smiling as Drew awkwardly draped an arm over Penny's shoulder. She motioned for them to move closer. "Stop hover-handing and give her a squeeze, Drew!"

"Did you get it?" Drew asked, his face frozen in a smile.

"What about this?" Jenny said. "We do a shot where like Penny's been injured in the fire, and you're carrying her to safety."

"Oh come on," said Penny, but Drew swept her into his arms like a blushing bride before she could protest further. Jenny cackled with laughter as Drew carried Penny over, which took seemingly no effort for him at all.

"My hero," said Penny with a smirk as he let her down. Drew was practically glowing.

"Let's check the side," said Jenny. "I think it was over here."

Jenny walked the length of the building, looking for the spot where she'd last seen the floating lights.

"It could have just been a drifter or a homeless guy," said Penny.

"Maybe," Jenny said, not believing it for a second.

She found the side door she'd stopped at that night and peered inside. This must have been the kitchen, judging by the rusted out ventilation hood over a half-melted oven.

"Maybe your ghost hid in here," Drew said.

But the floor here was just as grime-covered and filthy as the foyer had been and showed no recent signs of foot traffic.

"Hey Jenny, you said you heard glass breaking?" Penny asked behind them.

"Yeah," said Jenny.

"Check this out." Penny was crouched on the crumbling tile verandah next to some dead grapevines stacked up against the side of the house. As Jenny moved closer, she saw that Penny was examining a small scattering of broken red and blue glass shards.

"What do you think?" Penny asked, gingerly poking at the tiny shards with a pencil eraser. "One of those mini liquor bottles, maybe?" She laughed. "You probably scared some wino and ruined his binge."

"I don't think so," said Jenny, studying the pieces. "Wait! Don't move! Freeze!"

Penny and Drew frowned at her but stayed where they were. Perfectly preserved in the soil nearby was a footprint. The print was deep and well-defined, with a raised heel like a boot or dress shoe. The tread was marred by odd gashes across the arch. It could have been a man's or a woman's. Hard to tell.

"Come over here and put your foot right there," Jenny said, pointing at another patch of damp soil nearby.

Drew groaned but did as instructed. His print was much larger. Penny went next: too small, as was Jenny's.

"You think you found your ghost," Penny said.

"His footprint, at least," said Jenny. "We'll need to make a cast."

"A what?" asked Penny.

Jenny was digging in her backpack. "A plaster cast of the footprint. For evidence."

"I'm not driving all the way back to get some play-doh or whatever," said Penny.

"You won't have to," said Jenny, pulling out a pre-mixed plastic container of plaster of Paris and a bottle of water.

Penny laughed, turning to Drew. "Who carries around plaster of Paris in their backpack?"

"She does," said Drew.

IT TOOK HALF AN HOUR FOR THE PLASTER OF PARIS TO SET IN THE footprint. Jenny used a ziplock bag to collect the small shards of broken red and blue glass, in case they were important. They killed time playing a trivia game on Penny's phone. Drew was good at pop culture, but Penny crushed them in history and science. Jenny wasn't trying very hard; she was thinking of Declan and his telescope. It was too dark for stargazing that night. Perhaps his IR package let him see people down here. Did that mean he saw the Stranger? But why would the Stranger be hanging out after Jenny left?

The timer she'd set on her phone went off, and she carefully extracted the plaster footprint from the earth. "Perfect!" she declared, appraising the big hunk of white plaster half-covered in dirt. "So I'm betting whoever left this footprint is the one who closed the pool cover on me."

"I thought you said that was Mason," Penny said to Drew.

Jenny shrugged. "Mason says he didn't. We'll see if the print matches."

"Maybe there's an easier explanation," Drew said with a frown. "Who knew you would be here that night?"

"Just Dinah," said Jenny.

"And did Dinah tell anyone?" he asked.

"No. Well, Jack, I guess."

Drew grimaced, choosing his words with care. "Is it possible that they were the ones playing a joke on you?"

"That doesn't seem like Jack," said Penny.

"How would you know?" Drew asked a little too quickly.

"We worked on a project in World History last year," Penny said testily.

"Dinah would have told me if she found out Jack was here," Jenny said.

"Unless she was in on it," said Drew.

"I seriously doubt that," Jenny said with as much conviction as she could muster. Except now the seed of doubt was planted in her head. She glared at him. Damn you, Drew!

His shrug in response seemed to say: you'd be an idiot not to at least consider it.

If Penny caught any of this non-verbal exchange, she kept it to herself.

"Anyway, let's get out of here," Jenny said, standing to brush herself off.

For the first time in this case, she had some solid physical evidence. Now she only needed to match this footprint to one of Blackbird Springs's five thousand local residents. Piece of cake.

Chapter Fifteen

Sole Searching

Monday meant the end of Jenny's suspension. She was eager to go to class. She had a Precalc test to ace and some scores to settle.

"Really?" said Shelly as she came downstairs.

"What?"

Shelly ran an eye up and down her outfit. She'd picked out tight jeans and a black tank top that barely covered her bra, and she was wearing a brunette wig, braided in pigtails.

"No straps," said Shelly, pointing at her shoulders. "They'll send you home."

She rolled her eyes and returned to the closet to fetch a short-sleeve Boy Scouts uniform shirt Jenny had found at a thrift store. Jenny didn't wear it often because she'd sewn a "Trouble" name patch onto it, but everyone would be staring today anyway so she might as well own it. Let them snicker at her cheap wig, her fuck you Doc Marten's, and her Ace of Clubs tattoo. She was sick of hiding.

She got to school early and planted herself under the big sycamore on the right. More than a few classmates kept their distance as they walked by. It made her feel dangerous, which suited her quite nicely.

With ten minutes till the first bell, the Valentine town car pulled up. Jack and Dinah emerged from the plush leather interior like a celebrity couple on the red carpet. Dinah had dyed her hair tendrils crimson red today and looked like some kind of bizarro Rogue from the X-Men. Just as dangerous to touch, no doubt.

She let them pass, then followed swiftly and "accidentally" stepped on the back of Jack's right shoe. He stumbled and nearly fell, hopping on his left foot until his right foot came free of the shoe she'd pinned to the ground.

"What the hell?!" he cried as Dinah reached out to steady him.

"Oh sorry!" she reached down and snatched up his shoe, not sorry at all.

"Jenny!" said Dinah with surprise. "Ooh nice hair, I like the color."

She ignored her and studied the sole of Jack's shoe. It was a size 12 Reebok cross-trainer. Too big, and definitely not possessed of those odd creases in the footprint Jenny had found.

"Ugh," she threw down the shoe, annoyed. It figured. The footprint at Pinefall looked like it had come from some kind of boot. The kind you might wear in the woods, but not to school. She had to check, though. No more lazy assumptions.

"What are you doing?!" Jack demanded, snatching his shoe back. She stared at him appraisingly. They really did have identical cheekbones.

"Nothing, Junior," she said. Dinah hid a smirk. She was good, all right. "So who are you conning today, Dinah? Him or me?"

The smirk vanished into fear and confusion.

"I-I'm— What—?" Dinah stammered.

"Careful dawg, she's gonna steal your shoes," said Mason Lockhart, brushing past. He was wearing a garish orange San Francisco Giants t-shirt, one size too small to show off his pecs and biceps. She wondered if Blake taught him that move. "I hear you might be a little short on cash, bastard."

"I heard your mom might be short on cash," she snapped back and had the pleasure of seeing his big thick neck and face turn bright purple.

"Jenny! His mom— she passed away," said Dinah.

Now her own face was flushing with embarrassment. "I knew that," she muttered.

Jack darted in front of Mason before he could lunge at her. But Mason looked more hurt than angry, and now she felt like a jerk. She stared at the pavement, searching her brain for a change of subject.

"Speaking of shoes, Mace, where'd you get those?" she said.

He was wearing leather loafers, with thick soles—not like he needed the extra height. She smiled at him, eyes darting up and down from his face to his feet. Mason was still glowering, but confusion and fear were beginning to creep into his face now. He took a step back.

"Don't even," said Mason.

"Why?" she replied.

They locked eyes for a moment, then she dove for his leg.

"Jenny!" Dinah and Jack both screamed.

Mason bucked and kicked and tried to push her off. It took some effort, not to mention a layer of skin off the back of her left hand when it scraped the pavement, but she managed to wrench his loafer away. Before he could snatch it back, she turned it over to study the sole.

"Damn!" she shouted.

The loafer wasn't a match. Too big again, and no horizontal creases.

"What has gotten into you?" asked Dinah. "Do you want to see mine too?" She held a leg out.

"No thanks," she said, dismissing Dinah's proffered foot. It couldn't have been Dinah that left the print, and besides, she was wearing pink Keds.

"I'm beginning to think Mom was right about you," said Jack.

"Shut up, Junior," she said.

"Don't call me that," he said angrily.

Mason made a swipe for his shoe and missed as more kids gathered to watch. Drew and Penny were among them. Drew shot her a concerned frown, but she ignored it.

"Dad always raised me not to hit a girl," Mason said through gritted teeth. "But—"

"Good." She threw Mason's shoe over his head across the quad. The growing circle of onlookers all "oohed" at her chutzpah.

"You bitch," he said.

"Go on, you know you want to," she said.

But he couldn't. Not with all these people watching.

"Is there a problem here?" said a voice. It was the vice principal.

"No problem," she said casually, pretending to yawn. The vice principal stepped between her and Mason anyway.

"Your suspension just ended, Miss Valentine," he said. "Are you looking to add some detentions?"

She shook her head, avoiding eye contact. The last thing she needed was this guy up her ass again, keeping her after class for hours to polish the trophy case or whatever. Jack pulled Mason away, frowning sternly at her. Dinah's eyes had narrowed too. It was probably better this way—fewer distractions—but she couldn't deny the pang of regret she was feeling now.

"Okay, let's get to class everyone," the vice principal was saying.

Just then, she noticed a shock of red hair over Dinah's right shoulder. Alicia Aaron was watching from the edge of the crowd too. Her eyes traveled from the strange girl's red hair to her prosthetic leg.

145

The shoe on that leg was a black leather buckle flat, with a thick sole and a low heel.

Alicia's eyes widened, and she took a step back and booked it to class as fast as her limping gait would carry her.

"I was thinking of something a little more subtle for the footprint," Drew said with a nervous chuckle. Penny stood close by, saying nothing, her chin jutted out in disapproval.

"Does Alicia Aaron ever take her leg off?" she asked.

"Girl, you are off the hook," said Penny with an exasperated laugh.

"I mean, probably to shower, I would guess," Drew said with a shrug.

"Look, I've seen this episode of *Friends*, and it doesn't end well," said Penny. "Let's get to class."

Maybe Dinah hadn't been scamming Jenny after all. She wanted to hope so.

Chapter Sixteen

Trouble For Hire

Meanwhile, Jenny had her finances to look after. Mr. Webb texted her and told her to meet him at the Poison Pen that afternoon for a job opportunity.

This was the first time Jenny had actually ventured inside the bookstore. The shelves were high and the aisles narrow—and a little claustrophobic. The lady at the counter had a crabby attitude and the cat-eye glasses that came with it. She pointed Jenny to the back, where Mr. Webb was browsing the Literature section. As she approached, he closed the book he was reading: *Fight Club*, Jenny noticed with a smirk.

"All you dudes love that book," she said, reaching behind him to pull a copy of *Gravity's Rainbow* off the shelf. "What do you got for me?"

"A job, maybe," he said. "Are you Jenny today, or Trouble?"

"I contain multitudes. But I can behave myself if that's what you're asking."

"The owner of this place needs a new stock boy," he said, re-shelving *Fight Club*.

"Really?" The dark clouds that had been following Jenny around since the attack finally seemed to be parting. Working at a bookstore always seemed like a cool job.

"We cross paths now and then," the lawyer said. "Four hours on Tuesday evening, eight hours on Saturday. You might clear a hundred a week."

"At that rate, it'd take me a year to pay off the school," Jenny said, her mood rapidly deflating.

"You gotta start somewhere," said Mr. Webb.

"Do you do pro bono work?" Jenny asked. "I think Val's gonna try to rail me for 'trespassing' at the Cellars. I have this hearing coming up with a Juvenile Court Officer."

"Tell you what," he said. "See if you can hold this job down for a while without getting fired and I can probably get Val off your back."

"What's in it for you?"

Webb smiled and looked over his shoulder before moving closer and leaning down to speak softly. "Sometimes RJ's stuff comes through here. Signed copies, rare first editions, that sort of thing. I want you to keep an eye out for me."

"And do what? If I see stuff like that?" she asked.

"Give me a heads up, that's all," Webb said, inscrutable as ever.

"Sure. I can do that," Jenny wasn't sure who was doing who the favor now, but liked the idea of watching for Dad's rare collector's items. She probably would have been looking for them anyway.

"John always said that was his favorite book, you know," Webb said, nodding to the Pynchon book in her hand.

"I know," Jenny said. "I don't get it. I've tried reading it three times. It's totally impenetrable."

"Between you and me, I think he was joking," Webb said. "Come on, let's go meet your new boss."

Jenny put the book back and followed Mr. Webb up to the front of the shop, where that old man with the snowy white beard was chatting with the bookseller.

"Jenny, this is Mr. Carnegie," Webb said as the old man turned to greet them, a twinkle in his eye.

"Oh, it's you!" Jenny said.

"It's me!" Mr. Carnegie said with a titter.

"Sorry," said Jenny. "I've seen you around town is all."

"As have I," the old man grinned. "You're quite the jogger, but how are those muscles? Lifting boxes of books is hard work."

"I'm scrappy, I can manage," Jenny said confidently.

"Excellent! You're hired!" Mr. Carnegie held his hand out, and they shook on it. "Heidi here can get your paperwork sorted away."

Heidi, the bookseller, had a sour look on her face, but Jenny was too busy beaming to care.

"Carnegie?" Jenny said, holding a finger to her chin. "That name sounds familiar."

"Oh, I don't know," said the old man with another chuckle.

"Modesty doesn't become you, Horace," said Mr. Webb. "He's one of the Big Six."

"That's right!" Jenny exclaimed. She knew she'd heard the name somewhere before. He must own one of the original wineries in town.

"Big Five now, sadly," said Mr. Carnegie. "But you might see my name around town, here and there."

"Mr. Carnegie has his fingers in a lot of pies here in Blackbird Springs," said Mr. Webb with a wink. Jenny was worried Mr. Webb was going to anger the old man, but Mr. Carnegie boomed with laughter again.

"Diversification, m'boy," Carnegie said. "I keep telling you to branch out more."

This seemed to be an old joke between the two of them. Jenny did her best to nod and smile.

"I'm quite happy where I am," Mr. Webb said. "And talking of which, I have other work to attend to. Jenny."

Webb shook Jenny's hand and left with Mr. Carnegie.

"Thanks," Jenny called after him. "You won't regret it."

She looked down at her palm. Mr. Webb had passed her a slip of paper as they shook hands. It was one of his business cards, and scribbled on the back was:

Mrs. Rivas 707-482-4893.

The Valentine housekeeper. Excellent. Maybe things were finally starting to go her way.

WORK TURNED OUT TO BE A TOTAL PIECE OF CAKE. IT WAS MOSTLY moving boxes around and putting new books on the shelves. She was becoming a wizard with her box-cutter. It was too bad Jenny only had 12 hours on her schedule. She felt she could have easily managed twice as much.

The only downside was running into that damned Undertaker again. His office was next door, and she realized now that Carnegie must own the funeral parlor too. From what little she could get out of the store clerk Heidi, it sounded like the Undertaker was an in-law of the Carnegie family or something. He gave her the creeps. There was just something not right about people who were cool working around dead bodies all day. She thought of asking Dinah about Mr. Carnegie, but then she recalled that she'd made a huge ass of herself in front of Dinah at school, and they hadn't texted since.

She finished early on Tuesday evening, so Heidi had her going around straightening the shelves. She spent extra time making sure the Trouble display looked just right. No special items that Mr. Webb was interested in had come in yet, but she was dutifully keeping her eyes peeled for them.

Jenny's return to class was going well too if you didn't count that incident with the shoes. Everyone was doing this thing where they pretended not to know she was a witness to and person of interest in a homicide. Those stolen glances of curiosity had given way to a practiced disinterest. It was nice.

Mr. Stephenson slid her math test back with a smile. "Great improvement, Jennifer," he said proudly. "That tutor is really paying off."

She looked at her grade: an A-

Awesome!

Econ was a breeze as usual, and Jenny was developing a fun rapport with her Chemistry teacher Mr. Finch. He seemed to appreciate having a student he could mess with who wasn't going to get all butthurt and run to the principal.

"Safety goggles, everyone," he said. "And watch out for your shoes, I hear there's a little goblin running around campus trying to steal them."

The class snickered, and Jenny said, "Mr. Finch, when do we get to the chapter that covers the wax you use on your bald spot?"

More snickering, but her teacher just laughed it off. "That's more of a physics question. Talk to Mrs. Finch next door."

Some men just liked being dominated, Jenny concluded.

She perked up a little when they worked with iodine. It came in little blue bottles with eyedroppers, making Jenny think of the blue and red glass shards they had found at the Haunted Vineyard. But there were no red bottles to match, and they would have noticed the iodine smell at the vineyard, Jenny reasoned.

School was good, work was good. No one had even tried to kill her in the past few days. But she was getting nowhere on the mystery. Calls to Mrs. Rivas had gone straight to voicemail, and though she'd left several messages, she'd received no response. Jenny still hadn't figured out a way to get a look at Alicia Aaron's shoe, either.

On Thursday, Drew was in a foul mood in Econ but wouldn't say why. When Jenny brought her lunch to the Journalism room to eat with him and Penny, only Penny was there.

Penny seemed superficially cordial but guarded, as they sat together and ate lunch, chatting with Mr. White, the Journalism teacher, about college majors. When Jenny finished her PB&J sandwich, Penny stood up and smoothed her skirt. She'd been dressing more girly lately, Jenny had noticed. Penny certainly had the legs for it. "I'm going to the ladies room," she announced. "Come with, Jenny?"

"Uh sure," said Jenny.

As soon as they entered the bathroom, Penny ducked to check under the stalls to make sure they were alone. Then she wheeled on Jenny.

"What is your deal?" Penny said, hands on her hips.

"Umm," Jenny wasn't sure what she meant. "I think they call it solipsism."

"Drew asks me out, so you start flirting with him shamelessly right in front of me. What are you playing at?" Penny was shaking.

"Whoa whoa, you guys are going out?" Jenny asked, delighted.

"Not anymore!" Penny said, full of righteous anger.

Jenny's face fell. "Oh. But I have not been flirting with him!"

"You were sitting in his lap at lunch yesterday and joking about painting his nails!" Jenny wanted to laugh, but Penny was a good deal taller than her and didn't look like she was in the mood for jokes.

"Look, I don't know why I did that," she said as sincerely as she could manage, "but I wasn't trying to flirt. He knows he's not my type."

"Does he?"

"I'm not gonna take responsibility for his feelings," Jenny said, annoyed now. "He likes you, and he knows full well he'd be barking up the wrong tree. I'm a lesbian. I like girls."

"That doesn't seem to stop you from encouraging his little fanboy obsession with you. That's right, I heard about your middle name."

"Oh I get it," said Jenny. "You're jealous. You want my advice—"

"No, I don't," Penny snapped. "Advice from a nutcase like you is the last thing I want!"

Jenny closed her eyes and focused on breathing like she'd been taught. Punching Penny in the face wasn't going to solve anything, even if it might feel good.

"Well, I'm glad we understand each other now, Penelope," she said, allowing a bit of the fiery rage that lurked deep within to surface behind her eyes. "Sorry you couldn't hold his attention."

She spun on her heal and marched out, immediately feeling shitty. It wasn't Penny she was mad at. She'd been careless with Drew's adoration because it made her feel like a celebrity and now she'd screwed up his and Penny's friendship.

Jenny had taken several steps, lost in her own self-loathing before she noticed someone was watching her. Alicia Aaron was leaning against a tree near the edge of the pavement, past the Journalism room. She was brazenly smoking a clove cigarette, staring at Jenny behind Lolita sunglasses.

Alicia held out the pack to her. Jenny waved it off.

"Aren't you worried about getting caught?" Jenny asked.

Alicia rolled her eyes and answered in a voice full of bitter scorn, "What can they do to me?"

She looked down at her feet. Jenny noticed now that Alicia Aaron had changed shoes on her prosthetic leg. It was no longer a black buckle flat, she'd switched to pink Keds, just like Dinah wore. Jenny frowned and met Alicia's eyes again. The girl had a nasty smile on her face now.

The bell rang.

Alicia Aaron flicked her cigarette away and brushed past Jenny, limping back toward the center of the campus. "I'vvvve been working on the raillllroad…" she sang in a surprisingly lovely voice as she drifted away. "Alllll the live-long dayyyyy…"

DRAGGING HERSELF OUT OF BED AND DOWN TO THE PEN ON Saturday morning was a real struggle. Heidi was already in a foul mood because that creepy Undertaker had let himself into the break room to bogart some coffee filters. He treated Heidi like he owned the place—because his father-in-law in fact did—and in turn, she took her frustrations out on Jenny, who was having trouble remembering some of her training four days later.

"I'm sorry," Jenny said with a wince after having to ask again about how to punch out for lunch. "I don't always remember the first time, but I definitely will if you tell me twice. It's been a long week."

The shift passed quickly. Heidi kept her busy stocking shelves, but Jenny managed to chat up a few *Trouble* fans under the guise of helping them find a book. She was straightening shelves in the romance section when she sensed someone's presence behind her and spun around. It was Dinah.

"Oh!" said Dinah in surprise. Her hair tendrils were back to blonde today.

"How did you know I worked here?" said Jenny, suspicious.

"I didn't. I…" Dinah looked past her, blushing.

"Ah," said Jenny. "Well, if you're looking for romance, you're in the right section."

Her hand shot up to cover her mouth. Dinah raised her eyebrows.

"I didn't mean—" said Jenny.

"What *do* you mean?"

"What?" Jenny belatedly put her defenses up. Dinah's tone wasn't unfriendly, but it wasn't playful either.

"I mean it seems like you're mad at me, and I'm not sure why, because I've done nothing to deserve it," Dinah said.

"I—" Jenny hesitated, unsure of what to say. Dinah's hazel eyes had gone steely. "I thought maybe that ghost in the vineyard was Jack. That you two were playing some kind of joke."

"Well we weren't—at least I wasn't for my part," Dinah said. "I don't think Jack was either, but if he was, he hasn't mentioned it. You'd know that if you had just talked to me instead of jumping to conclusions with your little sidekicks Penny and Drew. I don't play games, Jenny."

"I do. Sometimes."

Dinah gave her a long, appraising look, and Jenny felt as though she was being judged like an outfit on the rack at Macy's. Judged and found lacking.

"I'm sorry," Jenny said when she couldn't take Dinah's glare any longer. "I have trust issues. Blame RJ."

She was hoping to ease the tension, but Dinah's stony face didn't even twitch.

"Come on, we've all got secrets," said Jenny, starting to feel annoyed by all this self-righteousness. "I'm sure you've got them too."

Dinah relented and looked away. "Sure," she said. "I thought we were friends, though."

"I don't want to be your friend," Jenny said before she could stop herself. Dinah looked up in surprise, and Jenny's breath froze in her lungs. Her eyes filled with longing and terror as the tall, pretty cheerleader stared down at her, equally stunned. An eternity of confused emotions hung in the air between them. Jenny didn't dare to speak.

"Jennifer, we have another box back here," Heidi called from a row over.

The voice startled Jenny out of her trance, and she turned to glare through the stacks at her cranky boss.

"B-be there in just a sec, Heidi."

When she turned back, Dinah's blonde ponytail was already retreating to the store exit.

"Dinah…" she said, but weakly and without hope. The bell on the front door chimed as it opened, and Dinah was gone.

AFTER WORK, JENNY WENT TO THE TREEHOUSE AND TOOK A MUCH-needed nap. She was fairly exhausted after her first eight-hour workday and was eager to put all things Dinah out of her mind. When she awoke, the sun was going down in the west, and her phone was buzzing with texts from her aunt.

Getting the job at the Pen had gone a long way toward removing the stick that was lodged up Shelly's ass. Nothing pleased her quite like a participating member of the economy. Or maybe it was the date Shelly had with Lockhart tonight, but Jenny preferred not to think about that. She checked her phone.

Shelly: "Where are you?"

> Shelly: "Blake is coming over for dinner. Should I set you a place?"
> Jenny: "haha fat chance"
> Jenny: "I'll be home at 9"
> Jenny: "by that I mean I expect to walk in the door at 9 and not see anything that will scar me 4 life"
> Shelly: "Grow up, Jennifer"
> Jenny: "Something something hold the pill between your knees for best results"
> Shelly: "You always said you wanted a sister"
> Jenny: "OMG STOP"

Jenny dropped her phone, repulsed, and moved to the window to stare at her future mansion some more. From her reconnoitering, it appeared that Mrs. Rivas, the Valentine housekeeper, lived in one of the servants' quarters on the premises. She rarely left the mansion, but she'd be in town tomorrow for church. Mrs. Rivas hadn't returned any of Jenny's messages, so Jenny would just have to intercept her after service.

She glanced at her phone again. Drew had gone radio silent after the Penny drama, and Dinah…

"Should I text Dinah?"

She already knew the answer. If the damage was done, it was done. And if not, maybe Dinah needed some space to think.

Her attention shifted, as it often did at the treehouse, to the cork from a bottle of *Ressort Rouge* that Declan had given her. She'd examined it from every angle she could think of: with a blacklight, under a magnifying glass, blindfolded and feeling for oddities by touch. Near as she could tell, it was just a cork. Seemingly the one from the bottle that Declan obtained for Dad for his 15th anniversary.

It felt like Jenny had been nibbling around the edges of the wine bottle clue for weeks and gotten nowhere. Some broken glass and a footprint that might mean nothing. Maybe Dad's clue was about more than just the bottle itself. Something with Pinefall, or with Valerie Valentine and their anniversary. Maybe how they met...

The wind whistled outside, and Jenny shivered. A fuse had blown recently, and the heater in the treehouse no longer worked. With a groan, she set the cork aside and pulled out her Precalculus book and tucked back under covers for an evening of polynomials.

Chapter Seventeen

A Break in the Case

THE NEXT MORNING, JENNY FOLLOWED MRS. RIVAS TO CHURCH on her bike. The housekeeper went right into the chapel, so Jenny parked across the street and waited.

And waited. And waited.

Feeling sure the housekeeper must have slipped her, Jenny peeked in, only to spot Mrs. Rivas doing childcare. The sun was drifting to the west from its zenith by the time she left the building.

"Thanks for wasting my whole morning, lady," Jenny grumbled to herself as she followed Mrs. Rivas from the church to the cafe across the street. When Mrs. Rivas reached into her purse to pay for her coffee, Jenny darted in with a crisp $10 bill she'd liberated from Shelly's wallet and offered to cover it.

"My treat," Jenny said, putting on her most innocent smile from under a long, straight, raven-haired wig. In her dowdy thrift store gingham dress she looked like a 12-year old Japanese school girl. "I just have a few questions."

The housekeeper eyed Jenny warily.

"I shouldn't be talking to you," Mrs. Rivas said, but she allowed

Jenny to pay.

"Don't worry, I'm in disguise!" Jenny said with a wink and led Mrs. Rivas to a table. The housekeeper was middle-aged, small and sturdy. A lifetime of service work had given her graying hair and a slight hunch in her shoulders.

"I guess you kinda look like him," the housekeeper said. "Jack, I mean. I didn't know Mr. Valentine well."

"But you were there the night of the atta— the night of the accident."

Mrs. Rivas nodded, letting out a tired sigh and giving an exact recitation of her testimony from the police report: vacuuming in the hall and hearing dad argue with Val on the intercom through the closed study door.

"What did you do after vacuuming?" Jenny asked, feeling the flesh on her forearms pimple up as her mind traveled through the events of that fateful night.

"I went to the service kitchen to make myself dinner, then I went to my room and watched TV," said Mrs. Rivas.

"What'd you have for dinner?"

"Tacos. We had some leftover chicken in the fridge."

"Initially, you told the police that you heard Val and my dad arguing in the study—"

"I know. I was wrong, it was the intercom," said Mrs. Rivas. "And no one told me to say that. I was mistaken because I was new there and didn't know about the intercom yet."

"You're sure?"

"I'm sure." Mrs. Rivas smiled sadly at Jenny. "I'm sorry, hon. I only knew him a short time before the accident, but he seemed like a good man. He was the one who hired me after my previous posting ended. He didn't have to, but he wanted to help me out."

"What happened at your old job?" Jenny asked.

There was a ripple in the housekeeper's expression before her years of service work smoothed it over.

"What?"

"Nothing," said the housekeeper.

"Come on, spill."

"It's not something you usually discuss in my line of work," Mrs. Rivas said.

"But I'll bet you're dying to." Jenny gave her a conspiratorial grin. The housekeeper exhaled in resignation.

"It wasn't my fault," she said, some long-buried irritation resurfacing. "Twelve years of service and they let me go over a stupid bottle of wine."

Jenny nearly dropped her coffee cup, an electric shock jolting through her body. She did her best to keep her voice casual as she dug deeper.

"What bottle of wine?"

"Mr. Valentine, it was his birthday coming up," said Mrs. Rivas. "Mr. C—my old boss—told me there was a bottle of wine in his office. 'Wrap it up and send it over from us,' he says. These rich folks, they're always trading bottles of wine back and forth on birthdays and Christmas, so they never have to go buy anything.

"Well, I go into Mr. C's study, and there's a bottle on his desk, so I wrap it up and send it over. It's only later he comes home and starts freaking out. 'Where's the bottle? You sent the wrong bottle!' Turns out there was another bottle of wine on a side table that I was supposed to send instead. How was I supposed to know? I guess the one I sent your dad was really expensive, and Mr. C was too embarrassed to ask for it back. And poof! Just like that, I'm out on my ass. Twelve years..."

Jenny could hardly breathe. This was how Dad got the bottle of *Ressort Rouge*. It must be.

"That sucks," said Jenny. "This bottle, did it have a red foil cap?"

"…I think so, yes," Mrs. Rivas said.

"What was his full name, Mr. C?" Jenny asked. "Come on, I pinky swear I won't rat you out."

"Horace Carnegie," Mrs. Rivas said. "Bah! Ungrateful cheapskate."

Mr. Carnegie? Was this why Mr. Webb had embedded Jenny at the Pen? And what did Carnegie have to do with Val? It was, after all, Val's clue.

Jenny thanked the housekeeper and retrieved her bike from the rack. She needed to talk to someone who knew the locals. Dinah was out of the question, so it was time for her anointed sidekick to stop sulking about Penny and get back in the game.

DREW'S MOTHER ANSWERED THE DOOR WHEN JENNY RANG THE BELL. She looked as effervescent and sophisticated as ever in a violet cocktail dress and a black pashmina.

"Jennifer!" Mrs. Porter exclaimed. She was holding a goblet of white zin in one hand and a bottle of L'oreal mascara in the other, one eye still unpainted. "Oh, but Drewboo isn't here right now. He went to the batting cages."

"Oh, shoot, sorry," Jenny said.

"It's fine, come in, before I forget to do the other one," Mrs. Porter said.

The Porter house was small and cozy. The decor was pure Mediterranean: terra-cotta tile, warm yellow and red walls, and beautiful exposed wood everywhere. Jenny instantly loved the place. So much more homey and welcoming than her grandparents' stale kimchi shrine to yuppie interior decorating from the '80s.

Mirai led them into a back room, and Jenny blushed as she realized this was Drew's parents' bedroom. The bed was unmade, and it smelled like— well, what she imagined sex smelled like. She blushed harder. It felt like she was encroaching on something private.

"I don't want to intrude," Jenny said.

"Don't worry," she said. "Mr. Porter is in Windsor today doing a wedding." When Jenny still hesitated, Mrs. Porter took a big gulp of wine. "Indulge me. I have only a big lug for a son, and that Penelope is too shy to come inside."

"Okay. Actually, do you mind if I change?" Jenny asked.

Mrs. Porter waved her to a changing screen and sat at the vanity to finish her makeup. Jenny had extra clothes in her backpack, and this was as good a place as any to change into snooping gear. She wasn't sure if she should bring up the whole Declan situation, but it felt like it would be poor form not to say *something*.

"Um, sorry to hear about Declan," she said as she pulled the cheesy church dress off and tossed it on the screen. "It seemed like you guys were friends?"

"Not exactly," said Mirai with a heavy sigh. "But he was a regular. Kind of an institution, you know. Lots of tourists come and go in this town, but we locals like to stick together. I always worried he'd get mixed up in something stupid. The Winchester is putting on a service for him this week. Sort of a wake for us in our racket to send him off."

"Oh, that's nice," Jenny said as she fished some dark jeans out of her pack and tugged them on. "You said Drew's at the batting cages?"

"Dusty's Batting Cages. Your google will show you, I'm sure," said Mrs. Porter. After a moment, her voice brightened. "How do you feel about some mascara?"

"Um, sure," Jenny said, feeling an outpouring of warmth for Mrs.

Porter. She pulled her favorite black shirt with the three-quarters length sleeves over her head. Jenny had paid full price for it at Forever 21, and now that her purple trench coat had been stolen, it was her most prized item of clothing. These were her sneaking clothes, and they made her feel like a super spy.

Mrs. Porter pointed her to a stool, ready with some eyeliner.

"I was thinking blonde, today," Jenny said, fishing her platinum wig out of her pack.

Mirai laughed. "A material girl," she said, leaning over to apply makeup. Jenny closed her eyes, trying not to let the pen tickle her. Mirai chuckled, "I'll give you my go-to '90s look. The boys could not resist." She waggled her eyebrows at Jenny saucily.

"Um, it's more the girls I'm interested in," Jenny said awkwardly.

"Wonderful!"

"It is?" Jenny hadn't come out to many people yet, but this usually wasn't the reaction she got.

"My son has a friend he won't be getting pregnant? Music to my ears."

Jenny laughed nervously, unsure as she replayed the conversation if it added up to a compliment. Mirai was still smiling warmly, at least.

"So… I'm working for Horace Carnegie now," Jenny said. "What's the word on him?"

"Bad tipper," said Mrs. Porter.

"Did you ever see him with my dad?"

Mrs. Porter shrugged. "Probably. They swam in the same rich guy circles. That was never RJ's crowd, though."

"What was his crowd?"

"Let's just say your father taught me as much about scotch at the Bad Egg as I taught him about wine at the Winchester." There was a wistful pleasure in Mrs. Porter's voice that made Jenny blush again. She tucked her head, pulling on the platinum wig to hide her reddening cheeks, and changed the subject.

"Hey um… I have to ask," Jenny said. "Not that's it's any of my business, but you kinda knew Declan and all…?"

"It is not your business, but what?" Mirai said tartly.

"Did Mr. Dillion…?" Jenny hesitated, it was mortifying to ask this, but what the hell? "Do you think he and Val ever… you know?"

Jenny tried to wiggle her eyebrows as Drew's mom had done earlier. Mrs. Porter blinked in surprise and let out a merry laugh.

"Those two??" said Mrs. Porter incredulously. "Now *that* would be a scandal. But who can say? That Declan… you wipe the toilet if he used it last, if you take my meaning. But I don't spread rumors."

She shrugged as if she had no opinion on the matter.

"Thanks, Mrs. Porter," Jenny said, fighting the giggles. "One more thing—"

"Why don't you stay for lunch," said Mirai. "I just opened a bottle of zin and the day is young."

"That sounds awesome, but I gotta go find your son first," said Jenny, thinking fondly of a chance for more wine and bread with Mirai. "But real quick, if I brought a cork from a bottle of *Ressort Rouge* to you, would you be able to tell if it was the real deal?"

"The cork?," asked Mirai. "Hmm. No, not by smell alone. My mentor could, maybe."

"Oh," said Jenny, her face falling. "Like in Spain?"

"No no, he is here," said Mrs. Porter. "Giuseppe. He no longer works. Bad eyes. Lives on the Rosewood grounds."

"Cool, thanks," said Jenny, moving to leave.

"If you want his help, bring him a wheel of high-moisture Monterey Jack from Vella Cheese Factory. He can't resist it," said Mrs. Porter. "Bring me one too, eh?" she added with a wink.

Dusty's Batting Cages was a half-mile from the Cellars, in a more industrial section of town. She almost rode past it because the parking lot was blocked off by those city workers Andy and Dave, changing another traffic light.

"Well if it isn't Blackbird Springs' Finest," said Jenny, leaning on her handlebars. "Drop a light on anyone today?"

"Not yet," said Andy, and they both cackled.

"Hey, you guys ever do any work on the Valentine Mansion when they were building it?" Jenny knew from her research that the mansion had been built about 10 years ago when her father was flush with cash from the success of *Trouble*.

"Nah, that was all private," said Dave, sniffing in indignation.

"The wicked witch farmed it all out to her brother's company," said Andy. "He's some kind of architect."

"What about the treehouse?" Jenny asked

"What treehouse?" said Dave.

"Never mind. Hey, how do you fix a blown fuse?" she asked.

"Probably just need to reset the breaker," said Dave.

Jenny blinked.

"Big gray box, probably in the garage," said Andy.

Fat chance of getting access to that, Jenny thought. It was going to be a cold winter in that treehouse if she couldn't get the electricity working again.

"Right. Cool. Cheers," she said, gesturing with her water bottle to the beer can in a 49ers koozie that Andy hid behind his back when she rode up.

They laughed nervously as she rode around to the small parking garage next door. A giant circular tent-like structure behind it housed

166

a ring of cages and pitching machines. The *clink* and *knock* of bats could be heard hitting balls around in staccato bursts. Jenny found a sturdy railing behind the elevator that she could lock her bike to. She flinched when she turned around and saw another drawing of that little cartoon man on the concrete wall behind her.

KILLROY WAS HERE

Adrenaline flooded her veins, and she whipped her head around the garage, searching for threats. But none came. Cautiously, she relaxed her posture and eased up on her fingernails, which were digging into her palms. Fans of the *Trouble* books were known to leave these calling card drawings all over town. This must be one of them. Not the Stranger's work. She hoped.

It didn't take her long to find Drew. He was mashing away in one of the cages, using far more force than he did on the tee in his garage.

"Hey," Jenny said softly.

He did a double-take at her new look and scowled. "Hey."

"I um. I think I made a big discovery in the case."

"Great," he said and took another big cut, which would have been more impressive if he hadn't missed entirely.

"Do you want to hear what it is?" she asked.

"Look, Jenny…" Drew said, lowering his bat. The next pitch sailed by between them.

"I'm sorry if I screwed things up with you and Penny," Jenny said, and really meant it. "I have this bad habit of not really knowing what I'm doing, or how it might seem to other people."

"Yeah, I'm getting that," Drew said, hunched over and looking wounded. "It's just… sometimes you send these mixed signals, I don't know how to react."

"Just be like… 'bitch, stop salting my game because you're horny for your brother's girlfriend,'" Jenny said ruefully.

Drew wouldn't even give her a smile at that. He let another pitch sail by.

"How's that going?" he asked.

"Horrible!" said Jenny.

"Good, we're even," Drew said.

"I could talk to Penny," Jenny offered, but he waved her off and turned to line up the next pitch.

"She says it was weird anyway, and we're better as friends," said Drew, smashing a pitch back at the machines. "Maybe she's right."

"I'm sorry," she said.

Silence hung between them as he annihilated another pitch.

"Back in LA... I never really had friends," Jenny said, her voice had gone small and sad. "I'm not... *good* with people. They never seem to like me. So it's easier if I make them hate me. But I don't want to do that here. I want Blackbird Springs to be different. This is my home. So... call me on my bullshit, but please don't give up on me. We're a team, right?"

"Are we?" He hit another pitch.

"Yes," she said, feeling annoyed by all this pouting. "Ten percent, remember? Ass jets?"

He couldn't hide the slight grin peeking out from the corners of his mouth.

"That's what I thought," she said.

Drew let out a long sigh and caught the next pitch with his left hand before dropping the ball at his feet.

"Look, I paid for an hour here, so I can't really talk right now," he said. "Maybe later?"

"Totally. Text me."

Jenny walked back to the parking garage in higher spirits. Drew was still a bit sore, but after he found out this new info she'd dug up on Carnegie, she was sure he'd be fully back in the game. She was just about to retrieve her bike when she spotted a familiar blue Dodge Challenger with white racing stripes parked in a disabled spot. Mason.

The garage was empty, and there were no cameras she could spot. No witnesses. Drifting over to Mason's car, she saw that his right door panel had been buffed and repainted. On a whim, she gripped her house key between her fingers and made a long scratch across the paint. She was grinning like a madwoman when she circled to the driver's side and found that Mason had left the window cracked.

Cracked too wide for her skinny arms. She reached in and was able to pop the lock after a bit of trying. Rookie mistake, Mason. Inside, the car smelled of leather and teenage boy. There was a plastic shopping bag in the passenger seat full of energy drinks, a big container of whey powder... and some blonde hair dye.

"Now what could you possibly need this for?" she said to herself.

Nothing in the glove except for a bunch of parking tickets and a pistol. Jenny felt a brief surge of hope when she spotted a book in the back seat, but it turned out to just be *Dune*, and not her missing copy of *My Name is Trouble* like she'd hoped.

The trunk was frustratingly empty too. Jenny was leaning in to check the spare wheel well when she heard voices approaching. With nowhere else to go, she pulled up her legs, rolled into the Challenger's trunk, and pulled it closed.

"Must have just missed her," said a man in a low voice. "You sure about this?"

Jenny's spine tingled. Was he talking about *her?*

"If Declan was asking around, other people might be too," said a high, cold male voice that sounded vaguely familiar.

Her skin had gone clammy. She couldn't breathe. Were Declan's killers mere feet away? Or were they his accomplices? Jenny badly wished to peek out and see who was talking, but she found her muscles were quite unwilling to move.

"Maybe someone did us a favor," said the other one.

"I like to know who's doing me favors," the familiar one said.

There was a pause, and something she couldn't make out from another voice.

"We don't know what he told her, or Val," said the cold voice. "But we can't count on getting that lucky again."

More arguing that Jenny couldn't make out.

"No, I'll do it," said the high voice. "It'll be real poetic. Valerie Valentine poisoned by her own shit wine. No one's gonna shed a tear over that."

"When?" asked the low voice.

Jenny couldn't make out the next part. The men seemed to be walking away. The only snatch she could recognize was "Declan's wake" and "The Winchester." The voices trailed off, leaving Jenny scrunched up in the trunk of Mason's car, heart pounding in her chest.

Before she could think of what to do with this info, more voices echoed across the parking garage. These she recognized.

"Hey, you wanna get dinner?" said her brother Jack.

"Nah, I er... I got a thing," said Mason Lockhart.

More footsteps, then a sudden laugh intermixed with a guttural howl.

"That bitch!" screamed Mason. "Again!?"

Jack was laughing hysterically.

"I just got Bonnie fixed!" whined Mason.

"You know, maybe it's not her," said her brother. "You sure you don't have a pissed off ex? Maybe that color guard girl?"

"Psh, please."

"Damn, that is messed up," said Jack. "Down to the bone."

"I'm gonna kill that bitch."

Jenny could hear the clunk of a car door opening.

"Well at least don't kill her without a good alibi first," Jack said.

Jenny's jaw dropped. How dare he!

Mason laughed, and she felt the car rock as he got in.

"Hey man," said Mason. "Sorry about… you know."

"It's fine," said Jack. Jenny couldn't see him, but from his voice, she could picture her brother closing off like he always did with her.

There was a clacking noise as the car door shut and then the Challenger's big, powerful engine turned over. Red lights illuminated the trunk as Mason backed his car out of the disabled spot.

Jenny was going for a ride.

Chapter Eighteen

The Cabin in the Woods

THE CHALLENGER'S ENGINE DRONED INTO A LOUDER, LOWER PITCH and Jenny could feel the car accelerating. They must have turned onto the highway. Mason turned his radio up, and Jenny was forced to endure his bad country music.

"Hi, this is Drew Porter's phone," said Drew's voice when Jenny called him. "I guess I couldn't take your call, so leave me a message and I'll try to get back to you."

"You're really falling down on your sidekick duties right now," she whispered in disgust and ended the call.

Small though she was, it was cramped in the trunk with her backpack on. She spent about a minute trying to guess by the turns which way they were headed before slapping herself on the forehead and pulling out her phone again. She fired off a text and watched with curiosity as her little blue dot in the maps app moved further into the outskirts of town.

Eventually, the car slowed and turned, and the ride got bumpy. Jenny guessed they were driving on a gravel road. Her phone was losing reception because they were out in the woods now, up off Castle

Road.

After a jarring couple of minutes, they slowed to a stop just as the car bounced and rolled smoothly again. Jenny pictured a paved driveway in her mind.

Mason shut the engine off and got out.

Jenny held her breath.

If he opened the trunk, she was ready. Her legs were coiled up to unleash a devastating kick to the first face she saw. She could hear Mason's heavy footfalls pass by as he circled the car. The passenger door opened. Getting his bag of hair dye and protein, Jenny guessed. The door closed and the footsteps faded away.

After counting to 100 and not hearing a sound, Jenny dug a screwdriver out of her pack and used it to pop the trunk open. Her raccoon eyes blinked in the sudden sunlight, and she found herself staring into a forest in the waning afternoon. She climbed out onto a dusty asphalt driveway large enough to fit a few cars and stretched her cramped muscles.

In front of the driveway sat a lone cabin.

The building looked several decades old, with stained wood siding and a steep red roof. Warm yellow light shone from inside the front windows. Feeling exposed, Jenny stopped stretching and ducked behind the Challenger. She waited again for a hue and cry to know she'd been spotted, but it never came. Only the occasional bird call and the wind in the trees.

The cabin was the only thing here; Mason could not have gone anywhere else. There was a single other car parked nearby: a used Subaru that Jenny didn't recognize. She snapped a photo of it with her phone.

"Okay, Trouble, what are your options?" she whispered to herself.

The simplest solution: get back in the trunk and wait for Mason to come out and drive back into town. It was a Sunday, and surely he'd go back home on a school night, right? But that kind of timid response wasn't worthy of her namesake. She'd already let fear get the best of her once today.

So the Trouble solution: sneak into the house, steal Mason's keys, and drive back herself. Jenny smiled. This was going to be beautiful.

"This is how you end up in the wood-chipper for sure," Jenny muttered to herself, popping an Adderall into her mouth and creeping closer.

Her first course of action was to reconnoiter the perimeter. The cabin was basically a big square box raised up a few feet, which let Jenny get close and sneak around under the windows. As she worked her way around the side, she would stretch up to peek through the windows, but so far all the rooms were empty. In the back, the ground fell away, and the cabin was built out on stilts, which meant that she couldn't see into the back rooms. The other side of the cabin was much the same. If Mason was inside, he must be in the back room.

Jenny reached for the handle on the front door and willed him to stay back there.

Luckily, a front window was cracked so there would be no noticeable change in air pressure as she eased the door open. She'd learned to pay attention for that in *Trouble Eight Days a Week*.

To her right was a small, homey kitchen with old Formica plates and cups in the dish drainer that had recently been washed. Someone was living here. On the left was the living room, carpeted in garish burnt orange shag. There was an odd scent here, something sour, Jenny decided. For some reason, she thought of Aunt Shelly.

From down the hall, old country western music emanated softly from a radio.

Jenny took a step, then paused. There on a table by the entrance were the clothes Mason had been wearing. They were folded up, with his shoes sitting on top, as though he'd stripped as soon as he entered. Next to Mason's clothes was another plastic shopping bag. She peeked inside, frowning.

They were lightbulbs. LEDs. Maybe a half dozen of them, big as softballs, made of beige plastic that flared out to a flat face, covered in tiny red and blue glass diodes. *Red and blue glass...*

Jenny let out a squeak before she could cover her mouth. She froze, begging the gods that Mason hadn't heard.

Seconds passed. There was no reaction from down the hall.

These lightbulbs, the broken glass they'd found at the Haunted Vineyard... Was Mason the Ghost of Pinefall after all?

An icy chill ran down her spine. She needed to get the hell out of here.

Mason's car keys were next to the shopping bag. Jenny tucked one of the lightbulbs into her backpack, snatched up the keys, and retreated. A minute later and she was sitting in Mason's Challenger, about to make a grand escape.

She hesitated.

What was Mason doing here? Cooking meth? Was this his serial killer dungeon?

She couldn't leave without knowing. It was simply in her blood to be nosy. Leaving her pack in the passenger seat and the keys in the ignition for a quick getaway, she slipped back into the cabin.

From down the hall, she heard a laugh. It was Mason.

Jenny crept closer, glad to have switched to her rubber-soled shoes earlier. The hall was long and narrow, and the last door on the left was cracked open. Purple light leaked out. There was a flicker inside as someone passed in front of the door.

Her heart was pounding again, but Jenny willed herself forward.

175

With one foot placed carefully in front of the other, she closed the distance, grimacing every time the hardwood floor made the tiniest of creaks, willing the soft country western radio to cover her approach.

When she was near enough, she held up her phone to the purple crack in the door with the video camera recording. Jenny watched the screen as she angled the phone around, taking in as much as she could.

Oh Mason, you big dumb idiot.

She almost felt bad about the leverage she had over him now. Almost.

By the time she got back to Mason's car, the sun had already sunk below the tree line. It would be dark before long, and the forest had gone silent.

Too silent. Jenny had the sudden sensation that she was being watched.

She spun around, eyes searching for a threat. They found only endless rows of trees in the darkening forest. She was getting paranoid. Nevertheless, she hurriedly slipped behind the wheel, eager to leave this place.

The bucket seats made her feel like she was in a race car. It was intimidating and exhilarating. Shelly had let Jenny drive the family Volvo around empty parking lots a few times, but she'd never actually driven in traffic before. With a turn of the key, the Challenger thrummed to life.

The engine was deafening, and Mason would surely hear it. Jenny shifted into reverse and eased out onto the gravel. The brakes felt funny, and for a panicked moment, Jenny frantically searched the instrument panel until she realized that the parking brake was still on. With a clunk, she yanked the release. It was time to go.

Jenny hit the gas. The car fishtailed on the gravel as she overcorrected. No matter, she was away, going as fast as she dared. It was nearly dusk, so she flipped on the headlights to see better.

After a minute, Jenny executed a lazy turn onto the highway, going too fast to stay in her lane. No one else was on the road, though, so who cared? Back on firm pavement, she sped up, thrilled as the Challenger leapt ahead and ate up the asphalt. Jenny giggled and turned on the radio. Mason's awful country blared out until she smacked enough buttons on the console to open the moonroof and change the station. Turning it up, Jenny gunned it and whooped as she raced down the highway.

Delight percolated through her body, from her heart to her limbs, down to the ends of her fingers and toes. She pumped a fist high through the open moonroof and let out another yelp of pleasure. This was living.

Her cheeks were freezing in the wind, and she realized she was crying. It was as though all her emotional valves opened up when she hit 80 miles per hour, and everything she'd buried away was bursting forth. Her terror when the Stranger attacked. Her fear that Drew and Penny didn't like her. Her complicated feelings for Shelly and Jack. For Dinah. For Dad…

The only problem was, the brakes had stopped working.

She first noticed it when she came to a curve in the road, and the car didn't slow down as she raced around the bend. She could feel the centrifugal force pulling her into the oncoming lane, and alarm punctured her reverie. She pulled as hard as she dared on the wheel. The tires squealed, but they held.

Her foot was smashing on the brake pedal now, but nothing was happening.

She realized with sudden, terrifying clarity that someone had cut the brake lines. Back at the cabin, she'd thought someone was watching her. She was right. They'd set this trap, and she'd driven right into it.

The road was getting windier, and signs cruelly reminded her that the speed limit was 55 mph. Jenny was doing 82. She winced and barely maintained control around another bend in the road, drifting fully into the oncoming lane. If she encountered another car out here on one of these turns, she was dead.

Her speed was dropping, but not fast enough. Another sign warned of an S-curve up ahead. Gripping the wheel tight, Jenny flew into the leftward turn and mashed on the parking brake pedal.

Metal shrieked as the Challenger grazed the right guardrail. Sparks danced across the windshield. Somehow, Jenny kept herself on the road. Her speed was down to 67 mph, but the other half of the S-curve was approaching way too fast. Her tires were screeching in protest, and she could smell burnt rubber through the open windows. Beyond the turn, a vineyard stretched into the distance over a low, rolling hill. Again, she pushed with all her strength on the parking brake, but this time it wasn't enough. Not even close.

At the last second, Jenny threw her hand up as the Challenger drove right through the guardrail on the far side of the road.

The crunch of metal was hideously loud.

Glass shattered; Jenny screamed; an airbag exploded in her face. She felt a sharp pain in her left arm. The car kept going, and her body was jostled like a rag doll as she plowed into row after row of grapevines.

She might have blacked out somewhere in there.

Vines snapped and tore apart as the car knifed deeper into the vineyard, spinning around and finally, mercifully coming to a stop.

THERE WAS NO ONE AROUND TO WITNESS THE CRASH. DUSK HAD fallen, and the last rays of sunlight were soaking into the cloudy horizon like a guilty glass of pinot noir staining a white blouse.

A stream of foul vapor whistled out from the wrecked hood and woke Jenny up. She blinked and opened her eyes. The sunset on the horizon was beautiful. Her mouth was full of acrid powder. From the airbag. Now she knew what it meant to see stars after a head injury. Her left arm was throbbing.

Slowly, and with great effort, Jenny marshaled her senses and took stock of her situation. She was strapped into the bucket seat of Mason's stupid car for his super sweet sixteen. Now it was smashed all to hell and spun around in the middle of a grapevine off Highway 12.

Through the shattered windshield, she could see the savage gash she'd just carved through the vineyard. Snapped vines and broken posts and shredded irrigation. The car's tires had cut deep trenches into the soil running all the way back to the smashed guardrail and burnt rubber skid marks veering off the road.

She needed to get the hell out of here. "Trouble" didn't begin to cover the mess she would be in if someone found her here.

Pushing the airbag away with her good hand, Jenny found the door latch and fell out of the car. The pain in her left wrist almost knocked her out. A primal groan escaped her clenched teeth, and she took several fast breaths to prevent the darkness from enveloping her completely.

Mason's car was making some ominous clicking and popping noises now, so she staggered away, trying to re-adjust her blonde wig and keep it out of her eyes. With some effort, she managed to get her shattered iPhone out of her back pocket. Mentally crossing her fingers, she hit the wake button. It still worked!

The screen was half a kaleidoscope of glitched out graphics, but she could manage. She'd have to. She opened up her FaceTime app and made a call. Or maybe it was the camera app. Her head was pounding, and she couldn't focus. She needed to get this on the record, just in case.

"My name is Trouble, and someone wants me dead."

Her head injury might be making her delirious.

"Oh my god," said the voice on the screen.

Behind her, the car caught fire with a decisive *whumpf*. Jenny glanced over her shoulder, angling her phone to get this on video too. Mason's Challenger was quickly engulfed in flames.

"I know, right?" Jenny said with a smirk.

In the distance, she could hear sirens approaching. It was time to bail. She hustled into the grapevines, still talking into her phone.

"I think someone cut the brakes," she told the camera, moving as fast as she could. With as much precision as she could remember, she recounted the details of Mason's cabin, Mason's secret, and the conversation she'd overheard earlier in the parking garage. By the time the sirens arrived at the accident, Jenny was a good distance away. She ducked behind a large oak tree and leaned against it to rest.

"Anyway, the pool, the traffic light, the Cellars, the Haunted Vineyard, this... It's all too much to be a coincidence. Plus, you know, Dad..."

She wiped her brow with her injured left arm and winced. With clumsy fingers, she found the source of the stinging pain in her scalp and yanked out a small shard of Mason's windshield. Jenny stared at it in fascination until a stream of blood ran down her forehead.

"Shit."

She got up and hurried on, holding up a tissue from her pocket to staunch the bleeding. She had a small first aid kit in her pack. If she could just—

"Oh no," Jenny said, feeling dizzy again.

"You forgot something, didn't you?"

"My pack. It's still in Mason's passenger seat."

Behind her, first responders were trying to put out the fire Mason's car had started.

"It's too late now."

"But if they find it…"

"Let's hope it burns."

"If not, I'm screwed."

"Not yet. There's still Mason."

True, she had leverage on the sheriff's son now.

After what she judged to be at least a mile from the crash, she turned left and headed back toward the highway. As she walked, she composed an email and sent off the video she'd taken in Mason's cabin. Just in case.

There wasn't a car in sight on the highway. Her phone beeped.

"My battery is dying."

"Hang in there, Trouble."

Jenny smiled and waved, saving her grimace for after she put the phone away. This was going to hurt like hell. She scrambled out onto the highway and rushed to the other side. There was a guardrail here, and the terrain dropped off steeply on the other side. Jenny took several fast breaths and counted down.

"3… 2… 1… Go!"

She threw herself over the railing, tumbling and rolling to the bottom of the hill. Her arm screamed in pain, and she thought her head might split in two. With her remaining strength, she tapped out a short message on her watch and rehearsed her story.

"Honestly, I was— No, not 'honestly,'" Jenny corrected herself. "I was out for a walk when this car ran me right off the road. Woulda hit me if I hadn't dived over the railing. It was like a sports car with, um, white stripes on it. On the side. …If I hadn't jumped over the railing, it would have hit me. It was blue and white, like a sports car. Nod convincingly."

She was fading now. A vehicle roared by on the highway up above. Her last memory was of a familiar shadow leaning over her.

Chapter Nineteen

Numb

WHEN JENNY CAME TO, IT WAS IN A DIMLY LIT HOSPITAL ROOM. She had the impression, maybe a memory, that her aunt had been here earlier, pacing nervously. Drew and Penny too. She was probably just imagining that Dinah had come by and kissed her on the forehead, though.

As consciousness slowly returned, she blinked her eyes open and a shadowy figure was waiting in the doorway. *A tall, dark, and Strangesome menace. Beware!* She blinked again, and he was gone. Instead, Sheriff Lockhart was sitting in a chair nearby, reading *The Smell of Trouble.* Jenny was suddenly aware that she was wearing only a hospital gown. She pulled the blanket up to her chin and saw that her left arm was in a splint, wrapped in ace bandages. Forcing her nausea down, she sat up.

"Um, hey," she said.

"Ah, you're awake," he said.

Jenny pawed at the IV tube taped to her wrist.

"You should take it easy," the sheriff said. "They've got you pumped full of opiates."

"Awesome!" Jenny said outwardly, but in her mind, she was cursing again as she remembered the backpack in Mason's car. Her Adderall pills were in there: a sure way to link her to the crime. She must have been pretty blitzed on painkillers though because even thinking about her impending arrest didn't ruin this good vibe she was feeling.

Maybe Dinah really did come by... Jenny smiled and rubbed her forehead where she imagined the cheerleader would have kissed it. This was covered in bandages too, of course. Jenny felt like a real badass.

"*The Smell of Trouble*," the sheriff gestured to the book. "In this one, the little brat tries to drive her dad's crown vic and backs right into a ditch."

"I always hated the title to that one," said Jenny, ripping out her IV.

"Sheriff Lockhart lets her off with a warning," he said, sneering. "What a putz."

"Not at all like the real Blake Lockhart," said Jenny.

"We know you were driving the car," he said.

"Who's we? And what car?" Jenny replied.

He glowered and flared his nostrils.

"Oh you mean the royal we," she said.

"The car you crashed," Lockhart said. "My son's car. The car he says you keyed."

Jenny shrugged and didn't even bother to hide her smirk. "I was out for a walk when this car ran me right off the road. If I hadn't jumped over the railing, it would have hit me. It was blue and white, like a sports car. That's the last thing I remember. Nod convincingly." Jenny frowned at that last part. There was something she was missing. Oh yeah. She nodded earnestly.

"I remain unconvinced," said Lockhart.

Jenny slid off the bed, taking care that her hospital gown covered her up, and rummaged through the cabinets in the room.

"Why don't you talk to Mason?" she said. "He almost ran me over once already a few weeks ago. He's kind of a bad driver— Wait, I'll bet *he* crashed that car!"

She smiled, very pleased with her deduction. In a drawer, she found some more ace wraps and bandages. She grabbed a handful and stuffed them into a handy plastic bag.

"He said he wasn't driving," said Lockhart. "Someone stole it from the parking garage. Hey, you can't just take those."

Jenny ignored him and scrounged for more supplies.

"Bandages need re-dressing. This ain't my first rodeo, chief." A thought occurred to her. "Wait. You don't know where he was, do you?"

This was perfect. She owned his son's dumb ass now. Before the sheriff could reply, the door opened, and a tall man with a hawkish nose and horn-rimmed glasses entered: Mr. Webb.

"Tsk Tsk," said the lawyer. "Interrogating a minor without her guardian present? Poor form, Blake. Especially if you want a third date."

"We were just having a chat," said the sheriff, rising to his feet. "Last chance to come clean, Trouble."

"Okay, I lied," said Jenny. "You are a putz."

"Suit yourself," said Lockhart, his lips spreading into a nasty smile. "I'll put you in that car, and then your ass is grass. Consider this strike two."

"Likewise!" she spat back at him.

The sheriff left, and Mr. Webb laughed to himself.

"You know, your hearing is tomorrow," he said. "Anything else I need to know about?"

Jenny tied her bag of medical supplies closed and hopped back on the bed, smiling in the buzz of hydrocodone the nurses had dosed her with.

"I was a mile away from the wreck when they found me," she said. "I don't think I need a lawyer to prove I couldn't have been driving the car."

"All the same, a lawyer would remind you that you couldn't know how far away from the crash you were and were merely guessing."

"Oh yeah, right."

"Your court date is at one, so get there at noon," he said. "Wear something nice and formal and boring—no wigs."

Mr. Webb allowed a slight smile and walked out of the room. Before the door could close, her aunt burst in, hands on her hips, furious.

"Three weeks! Three weeks and the sheriff's already got me on speed dial!"

"Aw, he likes you."

"I am not in the mood, young lady."

"This wasn't my fault!" Jenny said. "Someone tried to kill me! Again!"

Aunt Shelly let out a long, ragged breath and collapsed into a chair, suddenly looking very weary and concerned.

"Jennifer," she said, pausing to choose her words. "We cannot keep doing this."

"I know."

They sat in silence for a while.

"Okay, get dressed," Shelly said at last, tossing a bag with some clothes on her bed. "We can't afford an overnight stay."

Jenny dug through the bag, inspecting the loose sweats her aunt had brought her. "Wait, where are my other clothes?"

"They had to cut them off you," Shelly said.

"The shirt too?!"

Her aunt nodded. No amount of painkillers could lessen the sting of the dagger Jenny felt in her heart at losing that Forever 21 shirt.

"By any chance, were Drew and Penny here earlier?" she asked glumly as she pulled on the sweats.

"Yes, I sent them home," her aunt said. "It's not like you're dying."

Jenny snorted. "Thanks."

"There was another girl here too," Shelly said. "A blonde."

Jenny's heart swelled in her chest as Shelly raised an eyebrow.

"Oh?" She could feel her face warming, so she turned things back on Shelly. "How was your date with that creep?"

"You were right," said her aunt. "He's got a lot of baggage."

Something in Shelly's tone made Jenny wary.

"And?"

"I kinda like the baggage," Shelly said.

Jenny teased her aunt about the sheriff the whole way home. It wasn't until she was unwrapping her bandages to take a shower that she remembered the threat against Val. Someone was planning to poison her. Probably at Declan's wake. Jenny had said nothing to Sheriff Lockhart about it. As she leaned against the tile, letting the hot water wash over her bruised body, she thought long and hard about whether or not she should warn her stepmother, or let these mystery players take out her biggest competitor.

"DON'T YOU THINK IT'S GOING TO LOOK FAKE, DRESSING ME UP LIKE THIS?" Jenny asked her aunt while leaning into the fridge in search of breakfast. Shelly had mercifully let Jenny stay home from school, but was forcing her to wear a hideous dress that buttoned all the way to the neck, with a lace collar.

"It doesn't matter," said Shelly. "It's expected. Juvenile court officers have a lot of discretion, so you need to be on your best behavior and show respect."

Jenny settled on a yogurt and fumbled to open it with one hand in a sling. She felt like death. Her aunt saw her struggling and came over to help. Jenny smiled in gratitude and sat at the table, wincing in pain.

"I'll bet you're sore," said Shelly.

Jenny nodded.

"It feels like someone took all my organs out and shook them up like cans of soda," Jenny said.

"Yeah, that's usually how car accidents feel," Shelly said, glaring at her.

"Oh."

"Mmhmm."

"Maybe it's how it feels when you fall down a hill too?" Jenny said.

Shelly rolled her eyes in annoyance. "Did you take the pills they gave you?"

"No."

"Why not?"

"I was gonna sell them at school," Jenny admitted.

"Oh Jesus Christ, Jenny."

"Norco goes for $20 a pill," Jenny said. "We need the money, don't we?"

"Not that badly!" Shelly said, exasperated. "Take the pills, trust me. You're gonna feel like hell for a few days."

"How do you know?" Jenny asked. "You've never been in a car accident."

"No. But you have."

Jenny frowned, not getting it until lines of old grief rippled over her aunt's usually composed face.

"You cried for a week afterward," Shelly said, her voice catching in her throat.

Jenny popped two pain pills while Shelly pretended to busy herself with her school bag. A bold question formed in Jenny's mind, and she spat it out before caution prevailed.

"Why did you adopt me?"

Shelly didn't respond at first. Jenny knew she'd heard, though. A long silence passed between them. Shelly lifted her bag and stood there, frozen, shoulders scrunched up tight like she was bracing for something.

"Because my big sister was dead, and you were all I had left of her," her aunt said after a while. "Come on, we're going to be late."

Jenny thought about her aunt's answer for a long time afterward.

By the time they got to the courthouse, Jenny was feeling good and high with all the prescription opiates flowing through her veins. Mr. Webb was waiting for them on the court steps.

"It's gonna go like this," he said. "Declan said he wanted to show you the Cellars, you thought he owned the place. You're pleading no contest and are very sorry for trespassing on Valerie's property."

He must have sensed Jenny bristling at the last part.

"I'm serious," Webb said. "If the court officer doesn't sense contrition, he could decide to file a formal petition. You don't want that. This isn't like adult court where you have objections and admissible evidence and all that. Your reputation matters here."

Jenny let out a melodramatic sigh and swallowed another pain pill.

"I thought you were an estate attorney," said Aunt Shelly warily. "Have you represented kids in juvenile court before?"

"Not even once," Webb grinned.

"And why are you helping us?" Shelly was even more suspicious now.

"Shelly—" said Jenny.

"Your daughter is helping me out with another case," Webb said quickly. "In exchange, I told her I would represent her in this matter."

Shelly narrowed her eyes and appraised him darkly. "I see. Speaking of his estate—"

"Come on, we're gonna be late," Jenny said and dragged her aunt up the steps before she could ask more questions.

The third pain pill kicked in just before the hearing started, so Jenny didn't remember much of it afterward. Valerie Valentine was there, sneering through the whole thing in a navy pantsuit. The juvenile court officer seemed amused by the head bandage and arm sling Jenny was rocking, and stopped proceedings to ask if Trouble was really her middle name. Jenny proudly declared that it was. She was high as balls.

She did her best to act remorseful, and Val overplayed her hand by interrupting the officer too many times. In the end, Jenny got off without a formal petition. She agreed to pay Val a $500 fine and be on her best behavior from now on.

"I'll be keeping an eye on you, Miss," the officer told her.

Jenny didn't have $500, but she didn't have $2,000 even more, so she'd call it a win. She spent the rest of the day spacing out on the couch, feeling far too aware of all the organs and tissue inside of her that fit together to make up a whole Jenny.

In her hazy mind, the pieces of the mystery were beginning to fit together too.

She waited until Aunt Shelly went to get take out that evening and FaceTimed Drew from her laptop.

"Jesus, you look like hell," he said, gawking.

"Thank you!" Jenny said, feeling her head sway as her eyes tried to track Drew's jerky cell phone video.

"Sorry I missed your call yesterday, I forgot I had you on mute." He paused when her head drooped. "Um, are you okay?"

"Not dead yet," Jenny said.

Drew laughed nervously. She ordered him to his garage to show her the Big Board. Thankfully, he set his phone down to talk in front of it. She might have puked soon if she looked at any more handheld video.

"Okay, new theory," Jenny said. "Someone is growing something at the Haunted Vineyard."

She gave Drew a quick rundown of her discoveries about Mr. Carnegie and the red and blue LED light—without mentioning where she found it.

"That's what the glass was from: a grow light that the 'Ghost of Pinefall' was carrying," Jenny said.

Drew agreed. "They probably dropped it when you and Dinah startled them."

"And Declan knew about it, that's why he was there that night," said Jenny.

"But what would they be growing? Pot?" Drew asked. "I mean that's legal, isn't it?"

Jenny shrugged. "Maybe… poppies for opium?"

"That seems unlikely," he said, rubbing a hand over his new buzzcut. "Could they be making more wine there?"

"I thought about that, but according to your mom, even if they could get new grapes to grow, the taste would be awful," said Jenny.

"You have to admit, this is sounding less and less like Valerie Valentine is involved," Drew said.

"I don't know," said Jenny. "Val owns a winery. Maybe she and Declan were cooking up some bootleg *Ressort Rouge* on the side. They could make bank on it and still have a nice stack if she left my dad and he kept everything in the divorce."

"It would be easier to just repackage something off the shelf," said Drew, "since the taste wouldn't match."

Jenny bit her lip. She'd hit another dead end, unless... Her head lolled. It was hard to focus.

"Also, it doesn't explain how Mr. Carnegie had the bottle that RJ left Val," said Drew. "Honestly, I think the Haunted Vineyard is a red herring."

"Declan didn't."

"That guy once tried to sell my dad pirated Game of Thrones DVDs," Drew said, rolling his eyes. "He was probably trying to run a con on you."

"Okay fine," said Jenny. "I think I'm gonna pass out. Put up pictures of Mr. Carnegie and a grow light anyway," she said, pointing at the Big Board.

"Oh, real quick," Drew said. "I wanted to show you something."

Jenny shook her head. "Tomorrow. I'll need cheese."

She signed off and lay back. Her brain felt like it was marinating in a dish of warm hollandaise sauce. Her last thought before the darkness took her was that she needed to go see an old man about a cork.

Chapter Twenty

The Blind Sommelier

THE NEXT DAY, SHE GOT TO SCHOOL EARLY TO SEARCH FOR MASON. She had eschewed the head bandage and did her best with makeup on her forehead to look right. The splint on her wrist itched, and she was about to rewrap it when a big meaty hand grabbed her backpack from behind and yanked her into the boys' room.

"Out," growled Mason at some other boy who was standing at the urinal. She couldn't help watch as the dude zipped up. Urinals were so weird.

When the kid left, Mason reached under the sink and held out Jenny's backpack. Miraculously, it wasn't melted or burnt to a crisp. There was some soot on it, but other than that, it looked no worse for wear.

"Wow, I thought this would be toast," she said.

She took the bag and checked inside. The church dress, lightbulb, and Jenny's Adderall pills were still there. With a huge sigh of relief, she popped one in her mouth.

"For your troubles?" she said to Mason, holding one out for him.

He shrugged and took it.

"You're lucky the insurance is going to cover it," said Mason.

"You're lucky it wasn't you driving," she said. "The brake lines were cut, you know."

"Karma," Mason grumbled. "We're even, give me the video."

"Oh come on, Mason," she said with a cackle. "You know that's not how this works."

"I did what you asked!" he said, fear in his eyes. "No one saw me at the impound lot, but my dad will get suspicious if I ask to borrow his keys too many times."

"Don't worry," she said. "We're like a team now. It's in both of our best interests to keep this video off the internet, right?"

He gave her a dark and dangerous look but relented.

"Good. Now tell me about this," she said, pulling the LED bulb out of the pack. "This is what I think it is, right?"

"I mean, you saw at the cabin," said Mason. "Just a little side hustle. I got expenses."

"What were you doing at the Haunted Vineyard two weeks ago?" she asked.

"Huh?"

"Don't lie to me," she said, staring at him keenly for a tell. "I found the broken glass from one of these bulbs there."

Mason blinked, bewildered. "What the hell are you talking about?"

"Maybe I should go ahead and send this video to your dad," she said, pulling her phone out.

"Hey hey come on! I wasn't there!" Mason insisted, eyes bulging in panic. "Why the hell would I be out in the middle of nowhere?"

If Mason was lying, he was doing a fantastic job of it. She put her phone away. "Fine." She handed him the lightbulb. "Where did you get this?"

"The hydroponics store on Maple," he said.

"You ever see anyone else in there?" she asked.

Mason blew a raspberry. "I mean, yeah, sure. Lots. It's legal, you know."

"I'm sure Blake will be thrilled to hear that," she said, winking at his consternation. "Relax. Like I said, we're a team now. Let's get out of here before people start spreading rumors."

She hefted the second backpack, ducked out the bathroom door, and found herself face to face with Dinah Black.

"Jenny," said Dinah in surprise. "Uhh…" her eyes traveled past her to Mason exiting the boys' room behind her.

"It's not what you think," she said quickly.

"Come on, give me some credit," said Dinah, staring down Mason as he walked past and coughed "whore!" into his hand. She was about to go after him when Dinah grabbed her and yanked her back into the bathroom.

"Have you ever tried one of those Go Girl funnel things?" she asked, nodding to the urinals. Dinah snorted and shook her head.

"Look…" Dinah said, speaking softly. "We should— I wanted to talk."

Dinah looked up, her eyes full of nervous energy.

Oh hell.

"I thought a lot about what you said," Dinah continued, absently picking at her cuticles.

"I'm sorry," she said. "I shouldn't have been such a… such a…"

"Such a flirt?" Dinah asked with a small smile.

"Guilty as charged," she said, turning red. This was the last conversation she wanted to be having, especially in the boys' bathroom.

"It's okay," said Dinah, stepping closer. "I um… I've never—"

At that moment, some freshman kid walked in and probably shat his pants at the sight of Dinah Black and Jenny Valentine in the boys' room, inches away from each other. He just stood there, staring at them.

"Look," she said to Dinah, seizing on the interruption. "We should do this later. When we're not in the boys' bathroom, and I'm not all pumped up on Norco, and Colin Creevey here isn't staring at us like he just got his first boner."

She grabbed the frosh kid and shoved him into a stall.

"Oh, um. Okay," said Dinah, looking crestfallen.

She took Dinah's hand, hoping she hadn't already ruined things.

"It'll be better later, trust me," she said. "I'll text you. Is that okay?"

"S-sure," said Dinah, looking confused now, which only made her feel that much worse.

"Later, I promise," she said. "I gotta get to class."

She hurried out of the bathroom, feeling terrible. Dinah deserved Jenny's full attention, and she had other things on her mind right now. She hoped Dinah would understand.

"ARE YOU LUCID RIGHT NOW?" DREW ASKED WHEN SHE GOT TO ECON. There were still a few minutes before the first bell. Besides Aunt Shelly at her desk grading papers, the classroom was empty.

"I'm not saying I would recommend a concussion, but the drugs are pretty awesome," she said in a low voice. "But yes, I'm good. What's up?"

Drew dug into his backpack and pulled out an oversized chess piece. It was a bishop made out of clear plastic. She knew she had seen it somewhere before.

"What's that?" she asked.

"You probably recognize this," he said, handing the piece over. It was surprisingly light. "It's the paperweight from RJ Valentine's desk."

Her pulse quickened, and she turned the piece over in her hand.

"How did you get this?" she asked.

"eBay," Drew said.

She frowned.

"No, it's not the real one," Drew said. "It's a replica. They gave these out to everyone who attended the charity gala on the night of— well, you know."

"That's right, I've seen these in a few of the photos from the ballroom that night," she said. "The real one is still on Dad's desk."

Jenny had noticed the crystal paperweight when she sat at Dad's desk during the will reading.

"So what do you think?" he asked.

"What?"

"The murder weapon!" he exclaimed, before covering his mouth and sinking down in his chair. Shelly looked up and frowned, then went back to her paperwork.

"This?" she whispered.

"Well not this one exactly, but they gave out like 500 of these that night. Look at the top, the bishop's hat."

"I always thought that was a nose," she said.

"Well, whatever. It's narrow and blunt and rounded. Exactly the kind of thing RJ's killer could have used to deliver the fatal blow."

"Hmm," she thought it over. "That's kind of the perfect weapon. There are hundreds of identical ones, and you could just melt it down when you were done. eBay, you said?"

"Yeah, they go for about $300 a pop these days."

"Dude!" she looked at Drew in surprise. "You didn't have to buy this."

"It's fine," he said. "I didn't spend any money, I worked out a trade. I had an extra first edition of *My Name is Trouble*, signed and all that.

I've always wanted one of these."

"Dork," she said with a laugh. "Okay, so let's see then: Valerie Valentine takes her replica from the gala—"

"Or she takes Tori's," Drew suggested.

"Sure, or anyone's," she said, running through the night's events in her head. "Goes back to the mansion, sneaks into the study..."

She mimicked attacking with the transparent bishop in an overhand swing.

"Boom, and then she goes back to the gala, ditches the paperweight, and no one's the wiser. Someone else could have taken home RJ Valentine's murder weapon and never known it."

"Cool, right?" Drew smiled, pleased with himself.

The bell rang, and more students drifted in.

"Yeah, we just need to prove it now," she said.

They both went quiet, considering the still-daunting task. Just then, Jack walked between them and kicked Jenny's bag as he went by. She was sure it was intentional.

"Hey!" she yelled at him.

Jack ignored her and sat in the back, head down, glaring darkly at his desk.

"What's with him?" she asked Drew.

"You didn't hear?" Drew said.

"No. Hear what?"

"Jack and Dinah Black broke up," Drew said.

"Ohhhh," she said. It was all starting to make sense now.

"Rumor has it: she dumped him," said Drew.

"Aren't you a gossipy bitch," she said.

He shrugged and cocked an eyebrow at her.

"Let me guess, you're gonna tell me this is all another ploy to regain my trust?" she asked.

"It crossed my mind," said Drew.

"No. I think this is real," she said with a sigh of regret. "I just hope I didn't already screw things up with her."

It wasn't looking good. Jenny had texted Dinah as soon as she could, but school was out now, and there was still no response. Her fingertips were absolutely itching to send off another message explaining herself, but she sensed it would only make things worse. Dinah had tried to open herself to Jenny, and she'd completely missed it.

Maybe there was a big romantic gesture that Jenny could make to fix things. The trouble was, Trouble never had a romance, so Jenny had no guidance here. Thanks, Dad.

Jenny groaned and stuck a finger underneath her splint to itch her forearm. Her body was still aching all over, and she'd skipped her painkillers today to keep her wits about her.

"Um, hey!" said Penny.

"Oh hi," said Jenny.

Penny frowned, questions forming on her lips. This was probably because Jenny was sitting on the hood of her car in the school parking lot. It was after class, and Drew would have baseball practice right now, making this a perfect opportunity for Jenny and Penny to have some Girl Time.

"Look. I'm really sorry about the whole Drew thing," Jenny said. "You were right, I guess I liked the attention. But I let him know how it was in no uncertain terms, and he gets it."

Penny let out a long sigh. "I mean, thanks," she said. "But it actually made me see that it's better if he and I just stay friends."

"Can *we* still be friends?" Jenny asked, trying her hardest to seem contrite.

Penny snorted. "What do you want?"

"For starters," she said, hopping off the hood, "I need a ride to the cheese factory to get some moist Jack."

"Ew, isn't he your brother?" said Penny with a giggle.

"Oh gross!" said Jenny. "No, I need cheese to bribe this wine guy."

Penny shifted from one foot to the other, scratching the back of her calf with her shoe as she considered. She gave Jenny a funny look.

"Who are you right now, Trouble or Jenny?" she asked.

"Trouble."

Penny blinked, surprised. "Does Drew know you're doing this?"

"No."

"Good. Let's go."

As they drove to Vella Cheese Factory, Jenny explained about Giuseppe the sommelier and needing to ask him about the wine cork. She told Penny it was for a scavenger hunt.

"Sure it is," Penny said. "You know I told my mom about going to the vineyard with you and she lost her shit. Said it wasn't safe to hang out with you. I'm guessing this is related."

"This shouldn't be dangerous, I swear," said Jenny.

"Well, let's not ruin all the fun," said Penny, pulling into the Vella parking lot.

Five minutes later they were back in the car with two big wheels of high-moisture Monterey Jack cheese, half a paycheck lighter and headed for Rosewood Vineyards. Even though it was a Tuesday, there were still a handful of tourists gathered at the winery visitor center for tasting. When Jenny asked about Giuseppe, the hostess pointed them to a small hut up on the hill, on the other side of a large pond.

"Aww, I wish I had some bread," Jenny said as they rounded the pond. There were more ducks here. She quacked at them as they left the water's edge and hiked up to the small cottage. When they reached the door, it was closed. Penny shrugged and knocked.

"It's open," said the voice of an older man from within.

Jenny nodded at the door to Penny.

"No, after you, I insist," said Penny with a smile.

Jenny reached out and turned the doorknob. Inside, the room was dark, lit only by a few flickering candles.

"Who is it?" called the voice out of the gloom.

"Mirai Porter sent me," said Jenny, hesitating on the threshold. "My name is Trouble."

A low cackle rose from the darkness. Jenny and Penny exchanged nervous glances, though neither could help smiling at the weirdness of it all.

"We have cheese for you," said Penny.

"High-moisture Jack," said Jenny.

Penny snickered.

"Gross! Stop!" whispered Jenny.

"Sorry, but your brother can get it," Penny whispered back.

"Come in," said the old man.

Jenny grabbed Penny's wrist and pulled her inside. An old man was sitting in an armchair at the back of the main room, next to the dying embers of a fire. His pate was nearly bald save a few wisps of white hair behind his ears, and he was wearing dark sunglasses that wrapped around to completely block out the light.

Jenny and Penny sat in an old loveseat across from him. Giuseppe leaned forward, and the flickering flames lit his craggy face.

"Mirai sent you?" he asked. "Good girl."

Jenny held out a hand in front of the old man and waved it back and forth. He didn't react.

"He's blind," she whispered to Penny.

"But not deaf," he said.

"Mrs. Porter said there was no one in Blackbird Springs who knows wine better than you," Penny said in her most studious voice. "We need your help."

"And how can an old grape monger like me help you two young ladies?"

"We have a cork that we think was—"

"We wanted to know if you could tell what kind of wine it came from by the smell," Jenny cut in. For this smell test to be legit, he shouldn't know that Jenny thought the cork was from a bottle of *Ressort Rouge*.

"I see. Am I a parlor trick then?" he asked, his lips flattening into a thin line.

"Not at all," said Penny, shooting a glare at Jenny and pushing the cheese across the coffee table. "We think you'll understand why in a bit, but first, we brought you a wheel from Vella Cheese Factory. Mrs. Porter said it was your favorite."

"She's right," said Giuseppe. "You can't get a better Jack in all of Napa Valley."

Jenny whacked Penny with her bandaged arm to keep her from laughing. "That's what I hear," Jenny said with as straight a face as she could muster. The pain in her arm helped.

"Fine, fine. If I'm going to do my trick, I need to cleanse the palate. Would you like to try some of the cheese?"

"Sure!" they replied together.

The old man rose and made his way to the kitchen. Everything he did seemed to move in slow motion. Once he was busy, Jenny leaned over to Penny.

"What's with this sudden thirst for my brother?"

"Well, he's single now," Penny said.

"So you're really not gonna give Drew another chance?"

"It's not about that. It's just," she turned to face Jenny. "I know it's not all your fault, but the way he looks at you: Drew never looks at me that way. I don't want to just be old reliable, you know?"

"Does um... Jack look at you like that?" she asked.

Penny blushed. "I don't know. He's very intense."

"He does have great cheekbones," Jenny had to admit. Because she did too.

Giuseppe returned carrying a heavy wooden cutting board, a cheese knife, and a thin baguette.

"You haven't told me your names," he said.

"Penelope Griffin."

"Jennifer Valentine."

"Oh, of course," said the old man as he unwrapped the cheese wheel. "Did your father send you here?"

Penny cringed, but the idea made Jenny smile.

"You could say so, yeah," Jenny said.

Giuseppe sliced them each a thin piece of bread and a hunk of Monterey Jack. Jenny bit into the soft sourdough and softer cheese. He was right: she had never tasted a finer cheese.

"This is amazing," said Penny over a mouthful.

"Now let's have this cork."

Jenny dug into her pack and pulled out a napkin. Wrapped within was Declan's cork. She took his hand and guided the cork into it. He nodded, and she let go. The blind sommelier sniffed deeply, rotating it from end to end.

"Oh," he said.

He took another whiff.

"Now I understand.," he said. "You wanted to know if it was real."

"Is it?" Jenny asked.

"It's been years, but you don't forget a smell like that. The Red Geyser, *Ressort Rouge*. A 1998 vintage, if I'm not mistaken. That was a good year, for wine."

Penny prodded Jenny. She looked down to discover she was holding Penny's arm in a death-grip. Jenny eased up. That confirmed it. Declan's cork, the one from dad's 15th anniversary bottle, was from a real *Ressort Rouge*.

Giuseppe sniffed the cork again.

"Hmm, there is something strange," he said. "Where did you get this?"

Penny raised an eyebrow at her

"Long story," Jenny added. "The bottle was opened a few years back, and they saved the cork."

"Ahh, perhaps that is it," said the old man. "Maybe the age. I hope someone had a grand meal that day, I'd thought this vintage was all gone."

"Could someone have found a secret stash, maybe?" Penny asked.

"Unlikely," said the old man. "There were a few extra cases stashed in the basement at Pinefall that were untouched by the fire, but those were all found and sold off years ago."

Jenny's eye twitched. Pinefall had a basement?

"That's too bad," said Jenny, rising. "Thanks, you were really helpful."

"Bring your father next time," the old man said. "It's been too long since RJ came to visit."

Jenny's mouth hung open as she considered how to respond. Penny placed a hand on her shoulder.

"Um yeah. Sure thing," Jenny said.

Chapter Twenty-One

Into the Spider's Web

THAT AFTERNOON, SOMETHING INTERESTING FINALLY HAPPENED at work. Jenny's boss called her over to show off some new merchandise in the glass display case: a boxed set of the twelve existing *Trouble* books, signed by RJ Valentine. Also on display was another one of those replica glass chess piece paperweights, and a map of the fictional Blackbird Springs, also signed.

"Oh, I've seen one of those," she said, pointing at the chess piece.

Heidi was unimpressed. "Big deal. Check out the map. These are impossible to find now."

"Meh, not canon," she said. Then, after Heidi's incredulous reaction, "Seriously. Dad said so in an interview. The publisher made them without his input. This was before he reworked his contract."

"It's still a collector's item," Heidi insisted. "Good luck finding another signed copy."

"Yeah, sure..." her voice trailed off as she considered the likelihood of Dad signing one of those maps. "Where did you get this one?"

Heidi adopted a laughable poker face and mumbled something vague about private collectors.

"Are you gonna be able to work with that injury?" Heidi asked, nodding at her bandaged wrist.

"I'll be fine," she assured her boss.

As soon as Heidi took a smoke break, she was snapping pictures of the *Trouble* boxed set. She couldn't find any invoices for the collectibles, so she retreated to the stock room and went digging in the wastebasket.

"What are you doing?" a shrill voice asked.

She whirled around, box cutter in hand. It was just the Undertaker.

"Jesus! We need to put a bell on you," she said.

He rolled his eyes and walked past her to the refrigerator.

"Is there no fridge in your office?" she asked.

"You know how in the movies, the mortician is always, like, eating a ham sandwich right off an empty slab?" the Undertaker said.

"Yeah," she said.

"Yeah, nobody does that," said the Undertaker. "That's gross. I like to keep my food well away from my work." He took a Tupperware container out of the fridge and nodded to the wastebasket. "You lose something?"

"I need a thing for inventory," she said dismissively. A thought occurred to her. "Hey, lemme see your shoes. Are you the one tracking dirt in here?"

"No."

"Prove it, then," she demanded. "Revelio."

The Undertaker flapped his arms in a big show of exasperation and lifted up his right leg to show the bottom of his shoe. He was wearing loafers, and the sole was smooth and unblemished.

"Other one too."

He sighed again and showed her the left shoe. It was the same. Whatever Mr. Carnegie had to do with the mystery, it didn't include his weird son-in-law as the Ghost of Pinefall.

"What happened to your face?" he asked, staring rudely at her sketchy forehead makeup job.

"I took a little tumble. What happened to yours?"

"Oh, burn," he said, smirking. "But seriously, who taught you to use concealer? I think you're actually making it worse."

"Are you seriously mansplaining makeup to me?" she said.

"I mean, it's kind of my job," he said, affecting an air of professional superiority. "Feel free to stop by on your break if you want me to clean that up."

"Oh right," she said, crinkling her nose. "Cause you spruce up the bodies and all that. Wow, you are the worst. Thanks for the offer, though."

The Undertaker gave her a sarcastic salute and walked off with his food. She frowned and used her phone as a mirror to check on her head wound. Maybe it did look particularly sloppy after a long day at school. She'd fix it up soon, but first, Jenny had some photos to send to Mr. Webb.

If the info was what Mr. Webb was looking for, he didn't say, only sending a brief "thank you" in response. Despite the breakthrough Jenny had made with Mrs. Rivas, there was nothing at The Poison Pen to connect Mr. Carnegie to Declan or Val. It was highly likely that he'd accidentally given the bottle of *Ressort Rouge* to Dad, but that might have been the extent of it.

Jenny spent the evening working on her homework and trying to talk her aunt into doing something new with her hair.

"I am not getting an undercut," said Shelly.

"I'll bet Blake would like it," Jenny teased. "You just know that guy's got some weird fantasies."

Shelly threw the remote at her and went back to watching "Mr. Robot." Jenny smirked and returned to her latest project: creating an entire bespoke social media presence for a fake person she had created. If Tori Valentine wouldn't talk to Jenny, maybe she'd talk to "Dee Dee Sharp," a new student at Blackbird Springs Academy who wanted to be the bestest Yearbook student ever and was eager to pick Tori's brain for advice. Jenny affixed her blonde wig and tied it into a preppy ponytail.

Shelly gave her the stink eye as Jenny took a selfie. "What are you up to?"

"Nothing! Relax!" said Jenny.

She couldn't resist sending the photo to Dinah. After ten minutes with no response, she was regretting it, though, and didn't bother to protest when Shelly sent her to bed.

Morning found Jenny with an uneasy mind. She still hadn't done anything about the threat she'd overheard against Val, and Declan's wake at the Winchester was tonight. Jenny told herself she was strategizing for the best way to use the intel, but... Mom would have never been on that rainy highway if Val hadn't been trying to keep dad away from his daughter. Maybe this was karma. Val had probably hired the private eye to spy on her parents. Who knew what else she was capable of?

She was distracted and anxious all day at school, arguing with herself over what she owed her wicked stepmother. When class let out, she strode briskly to the parking lot, eager to stake out the hydroponics store for a few hours before Declan's wake.

"Hey, hold up," said a voice behind her, grabbing her by the elbow.

It was Jack. "My mother wants to talk to you."

His manner was brusque and unkind. He pointed to the family's black town car like it was an order.

"And what about you, Junior? Do you want to talk?" she said, yanking her arm away.

"Don't call me that," he said, and led her to the car.

Jenny was too curious not to follow. Once they were inside, Jack hit a switch on his armrest and a black privacy screen rose between them and the driver. They rode in silence for a while.

"I'm sorry about you and Dinah," Jenny said at last.

"Are you?" he asked.

"I want only good things for you, big brother," she said.

"Mom lost all her court appeals, you know?" Jack said. "We're going to have to move out soon."

"That's not my fault," said Jenny. "Maybe a little downsizing will do you good."

He looked away with a scowl and said nothing.

"You *did* say she didn't really love you," Jenny said.

"Well I was hoping I was wrong!" he said, seething.

"You're already scamming on Penny Griffin," Jenny said. "You'll be fine."

Jack gave a nasty laugh. "You hoping that I date Penny, so she won't get mad about you hooking up with Drew Porter?"

It was Jenny's turn for an evil cackle.

"No, I need you dating Penny so *you* won't get mad when I hook up with Dinah."

"Very funny," he said.

Well, Jenny had put it out there. If he didn't believe her, that was his problem.

"I still need to meet your sister Tori," she said.

"I don't think she took Dad's will too well," said Jack.

"Have you talked to her?"

Jack ignored her as the car slowed down and pulled into the circle in front of the Valentine mansion.

"What does your mom want?" Jenny asked.

"I don't know," said Jack. "But do me a favor and try not to piss her off. She's had a rough week."

The driver opened the door. Jenny had to twist awkwardly to offer the man her uninjured wrist as he helped her out.

"She should talk."

THE MANSION WAS AS SPLENDID AS EVER IN THE AFTERNOON SUN. Jenny was delighted when Jack led her down a different hallway from the foyer. Their path took them through the east wing, past a fancy dining room and a massive kitchen.

"What do you do if you just want, like, a sandwich?" Jenny asked.

"I just ring down for one," he said like it was normal to have a chef on call.

Jenny lingered at a large portrait of the Valentine family on the wall. Jack looked a few years younger in it, and there was Tori looking like a youthful clone of her mother, with Val and Dad behind the two kids. In the glass frame, Jenny's reflection fit right in next to her brother.

"Almost looks like a complete family photo," said Jack behind her.

"Almost," said Jenny.

He pushed her onward. She went as slowly as he would let her, trying to commit every detail of the east wing to memory.

"Where's your room?" she asked.

"Upstairs."

"Can I see it?"

"No."

They turned down another corridor.

"Did you tell Dinah I was spying on you at the hot springs?" Jack had his face screwed up in a most serious and wounded expression.

"Were you?" she asked.

"No!"

She was tempted to believe him.

"Well someone was," Jenny said. "I couldn't see who, but I got their footprint."

"Ohhh," said Jack, comprehension dawning in his eyes. "Jesus."

He led her to a door at the end of the hall and motioned her through it. Jenny was met by a blast of heavy, humid air. She was in a lush greenhouse. Large palm fronds and ferns hung from above. Shocks of pink and orange and yellow peeped out from the tropical green foliage. There were lady slipper orchids, white lilies, clusters of violet, red poinsettias. It smelled of earth and decay.

Valerie Valentine was waiting for them, a great spider in her web. She wore an apron and gardening gloves over a lacy black evening dress. Val ignored them for a few beats before looking up from the black and crimson roses she was trimming.

"I'll call for you when I'm done here, Junior," Val said, dismissing him.

Jack shrugged and walked back into the house. Jenny ignored Val and walked down another aisle to get a better look at some orange chrysanthemums. Everything was planted in reddish-orange soil.

"So what do you want?" she asked without bothering to face Val.

"I thought we might come to an arrangement."

"Oh?" Jenny turned, favoring Val with a look of smug condescension.

"This whole contest of RJ's. It's foolish and fruitless," said Val.

"There was no murder. He would have us spinning our wheels for five years chasing down inane 'clues' and for what? So we can lose it all to charity in five years?"

"I thought you ran a charity."

"Don't be obtuse, Jennifer," said Val.

"It's what Dad wanted," said Jenny. "He *was* murdered, and I'm going to prove it."

"You're never going to win," Val said. "Maybe I can make losing worth your while."

"How?"

"I can't challenge the medical examiner as long as Webb is the estate lawyer. But if he wasn't?" Val lopped off a rose. "Maybe a second look gets RJ's death ruled an accident again. Then the previous will supersedes this one."

"And it all goes to you?" Jenny scoffed and wiped her forehead, already sweating in the moist atmosphere. "No thanks."

"I would make it worth your while," said Val.

"How worth my while?" Jenny wasn't planning to say yes, but she couldn't help wonder how much she was worth to Val.

"Five million," said Val.

"Hah, it would have to be 40 at the absolute minimum," Jenny said. "In fact, you know what? It just became 50."

"Don't be greedy," said Val. "I can do 40. Maybe. If you moved back to LA. But you'd have to play your part."

"Which is what?" she asked. "You want me to kill Webb?"

Val's lips curled into a venomous sneer.

"Your aunt really did raise a little monster," she said. "No, if Webb dies, the M.E. report becomes permanent. I need him *replaced*."

"I don't follow," said Jenny.

"The estate lawyer can be replaced for cause," said Val. "A conflict of interest. Maybe he tried to cut a side deal with one of the heirs. Maybe he acted… inappropriately."

Jenny felt a twinge in her stomach. The air and Valerie Valentine were making her nauseous.

"You want me to lie," said Jenny. "Or set him up? Accuse him?"

"All men have weaknesses," said Val. "I'll leave the particulars up to you. Just make it happen."

Jenny pondered how far Val was willing to go. "Why didn't you ask Alicia Aaron?"

"For the love I bore your father, I went to you first," Val said, walking over to Jenny and holding out the black and crimson rose.

"Like you'd ever do me any favors," Jenny said, wary.

"I got your aunt a job at the high school, didn't I?" said Val.

Jenny frowned. "You didn't do that, I did."

"To be fair, when Johnny asked me to help get Shelly hired, I didn't know you were in the picture, but… You can't say I've done nothing for you. Take the deal. You know that white trash girl will if you don't."

Jenny didn't doubt it. "Sure, I just have to debase myself and dishonor my father." She reached out absentmindedly and took the rose.

"$40 million of Johnny's fortune is worth a whole lot more than your honor," Val said.

Jenny turned away and walked to the end of the aisle.

"I have questions," she said, staring at a patch of reddish-orange soil on the ground. "Did you really drink that bottle of *Ressort Rouge?*"

"Yes," said Val.

"Why?" asked Jenny, leaning down. There in the soil: faint arcs, like something had dragged across the dirt. A shelf leaned against the brick wall here, lightly burdened with gardening supplies.

"It was our anniversary," Val said. Jenny looked back and was surprised to see actual emotion in her stepmother's eyes. "I wanted to remember a time when our love was pure. Before you."

Jenny turned away and used her body to hide her phone as she snapped a photo of the shelf.

"Did you hire the P.I. to spy on their affair?" she asked.

"No," said Val.

"Who did?"

"I don't know," Val said. "They arrived by mail in an unmarked envelope. There was no note attached."

Jenny swallowed. "Did you have her killed?" she asked, her voice barely a whisper in the hot, heavy air.

Val's eyes filled with disgust and bitter resentment. She didn't answer.

"Have you ever considered that I'm not the one you should be upset with?" said Jenny.

"Have you?" said Val.

They regarded each other for a while, stepping lazily around the table between them.

"I'm going to need your decision now," said Val.

Jenny hesitated. The woman's expectation and entitlement kindled a fury within her.

"You really think I'd betray my father's legacy for a fraction of what he owes me?" Jenny said with a louder, shaking voice.

"I think you've only ever cared about yourself, you narcissistic bitch. Johnny all but guaranteed that when he named Trouble after you."

For the first time since she entered the greenhouse, Jenny could relax and breathe easy. Finally, the cards were on the table.

"I don't want $40 million. I want it all," she said, stepping into Val's personal space and forcing her to move backward. "And I'll start with this putrid greenhouse. No more rancid ferns and hideous peonies. Whatever your favorite plant is, I'll be sure to burn it—and film it for you to watch over and over. This will be my rock garden, with cherry trees and a koi pond. It'll be like you were never here. Oh, and daisies!"

Valerie pretended to yawn and withdrew her phone from her apron pocket.

"Suit yourself," she said, tapping on the screen. "I'm sure that one-legged trollop will see reason. Don't say I didn't give you a chance." She held the phone to her lips. "Junior, please come down here and take out the trash."

Jenny couldn't help but grin.

"What are you smiling at?" Val asked.

"I know something you don't," said Jenny.

"Sure you do," Val said with an eye roll. "I've invited Alicia Aaron to Declan's service tonight. In fact, I should be on my way now to oversee preparations. Have a good look around. It'll be the last time you ever see this place."

Val doffed her apron and gloves and headed for the outer door.

"Hey, Valerie?" Jenny called. "Have a nice glass of red."

Val gave her the finger and left just as Jack entered the greenhouse behind her.

"Making friends, I see," he said.

"She thinks she can buy me," said Jenny, steaming with outrage.

"Hey. I want to show you something," said Jack.

Chapter Twenty-Two

The Immolation Game

A WIDE STAIRWELL LED UP TO THE SECOND STORY OF THE MANSION. Jack opened a heavy wooden door on one side of the hall, and Jenny found herself in a massive bedroom. Jack's room. She almost drooled.

Jack lived in a corner room as big as the entire second story of Jenny's grandparents' house. The walls were covered in gold wallpaper, velvet-flocked in forest green, and the teakwood furniture was all hand-crafted, with brass fixtures. He even had a vanity.

Everywhere Jenny looked was some expensive piece of technology: a MacBook Pro, every video game system you could ever want and a whole shelf of games, DJ turntables, a big stereo system, a telescope by the window... Hanging over his bed was a huge oil painting of a British man-of-war in a naval battle against the Spanish Armada. On the opposite wall, he allowed three framed posters to express his pop culture interests: an Oakland Athletics baseball player, Daenerys Targaryen riding a dragon, and a brooding illustration of Kylo Ren.

What drew her attention, though, was the honest-to-god golden pillar and pedestal under the window, and the onyx blackbird statue sitting on top of it.

"Not that," Jack said.

He pointed her to his closet by the bed instead. It was just as obscenely large. Jenny was unsurprised but annoyed to discover that he owned more shoes than she did. Each pair had its own special lighted alcove on the right side of the closet. This could all be hers...

"If I were going up to the hot springs, I'd probably wear my Timberlands," he said, holding up the sole of a fancy hiking shoe for her to examine. "Or maybe my Vibergs."

He passed her another leather hightop that looked overpriced and unworn.

"My Moncler's are too nice for that area, but still," he flipped another set of leather hiking boots over. Jenny didn't fail to notice that none of them possessed the sole she'd captured a footprint of.

"What a goddamn fancy boy you are," she said, shaking her head. Some of the brands were so posh she'd never even heard of them.

"Of course there's my custom Nike cleats, my Reebok Crossfit Nanos, my Gucci Oxfords, my Prada derbies..." he went down the rows of shoes, flipping each of them in turn to show the tread.

"What is this?" Jenny said, getting annoyed. "You just like showing off?"

"Check them all," he said, his voice hot. "I wasn't spying on you."

"If you were, you could have just hidden that pair," she said, putting the shoes back in place.

"You don't believe me?"

"No, I do Jack."

"Then do me a favor and let Dinah know," he said, tossing the slipper over his shoulder.

"Jack..." Jenny pursed her lips. She needed to tread carefully. "Look, I don't want to speak for Dinah—and she hasn't told me *anything*, I swear—but I would guess it's more about her than about you."

"What do you mean?" he asked, baffled.

"I don't—I don't know," said Jenny, not wanting to continue this conversation any further. "But maybe it would do you good to not always get what you want."

He blew out an exasperated sigh.

"I mean it," said Jenny, walking back into the bedroom area and studying the giant naval painting. "Let me guess, you probably think of yourself some kind of gentleman. Good form and all that. Here's a chance to build some character. Show your quality."

"What would you know about that?" he sneered.

Jenny turned away, willing herself not to engage further before she well and truly hated her brother.

"Can I use the restroom?" she asked.

"Down the hall on the left," he said.

She left him to his toys.

"Don't wander," he called after her.

Jenny obediently found the bathroom and closed the door. Turning on the faucet, she counted to twenty and peeked out. The hallway was empty. With silent steps, she crept down to the door at the end of the hall.

It was the master bedroom. Valerie's domain.

Moving fast, she crossed to the armoire and rifled through the drawers. Other than a vibrator and a roll of money, there was nothing of interest to be found. Jenny badly wanted to take the cash, but who would she be to preach about good form if she were a common thief? She stole the batteries from Val's vibrator instead.

Crossing to another colossal closet, she poked around amongst more designer shoes and outfits. None of Val's boots matched the footprint either. Another swing and a miss.

Valerie had a special vanity in here for her makeup and hair. Jenny paused to regard herself in the mirror. Somewhere in all this family bonding, her mascara had run. She was about to move on when she spotted a card taped to the vanity on the right side.

It was a cheesy birthday card with Peanuts characters and some puns about a mother's birthday. Jenny peeked inside and saw that it was from her brother.

Happy Birthday Mom,

Love Junior

Jenny read it again, and a wave of guilt crashed over her.

"Show your quality," she repeated to herself, closing her eyes and letting out a ragged breath. "Goddamnit."

Already, she could feel the venom and hatred draining away. Jenny had found the line she wouldn't cross. She knew what she had to do now. This was going to suck.

"What are you doing?!"

Jack was standing in the doorway, furious.

"I need to go! Now!" Jenny cried, ignoring his anger and rushing past him.

"The driver is on his way back," he said, hurrying after her. "Why were you in here?"

Jenny raced down the hall to the stairwell with Jack on her heels.

"Forget about that, I need to leave now! Don't you have a car?"

"No."

"But you're rich!"

"I never needed one! What's going on?" Jack asked.

Jenny turned down the hall and found herself in the foyer. She skidded to a stop and faced her brother.

"Look," she said. "No matter what you hear, I'm not a monster. I have a plan."

She left Jack there in the Valentine Manor doorway with a bewildered scowl on his face. Before he found his voice, she was already down the stairs and sprinting back to town.

EVEN WITH HER RECENT CARDIO ROUTINE, IT TOOK HER 20 MINUTES to reach the Winchester. The valets were busy out front parking cars as guests arrived for the wake. Jenny rushed past them and into the restaurant.

She'd considered several different plans on the jog down here, but all of them depended on getting here in time to speak to Valerie beforehand. So it was to her great horror that she burst into the room with the event already in progress. Val stood at the back of the main dining area on a small stage, holding a microphone. She was in the middle of a toast, holding up a glass of red wine.

"Tonight, we celebrate Declan…" Valerie trailed off because Jenny was sprinting through the tables straight for her.

On the edges of her vision, she saw several familiar faces staring in surprise. The sheriff and Shelly were sitting together. Mr. Carnegie sat at a table with his Undertaker son-in-law and what must have been the rest of his family. There was Penny and her mom Yvonne, Heidi from the Pen, the city workers. Drew sat with his parents in dress attire.

And Dinah. Goddamnit, Dinah is here. Alicia Aaron had worn a dress to the event, flaunting her metal leg. She saw Mason and Mr. Webb. She half expected to see Mr. Duck in a chair with a glass of merlot in his wing, gawking at Jenny's reckless charge to the stage.

All of her ruined plans hinged on one crucial detail: it couldn't look like she knew the wine was poisoned. The only way this worked was if Jenny's intervention looked totally unrelated. She had to convince the killers that Valerie wasn't a threat, and neither was she. And to do that, she would have to set herself on fire.

"Murderer!" she screamed and hurtled onto the stage, slapping the glass of wine out of Val's hand. It crashed to the floor in a spray of red wine and broken crystal.

"What the fuck—" Val screeched as Jenny grabbed her by the throat.

"I'm onto you, you evil witch!" she screamed. Then, leaning in, she hissed in Val's ear so no one else could hear, "You're in danger. The wine is poisoned."

"What in the hell are you doing?!" Val yelled, shoving Jenny to the ground.

The room had gone deathly quiet. As Jenny rose to her knees, she saw a flicker of concern and hesitation in Valerie's face. She'd heard. Mission accomplished. Now to put on a show. Jenny gave a slight nod before turning to address the stunned crowd.

"Declan Dillion was murdered and Valerie Valentine did it!"

Murmurs of shock arose from the crowd. Jenny's gaze found Shelly among them; her aunt's face was frozen in horror. In heartbreak. Sorry, Shelly.

"You want to know why Valerie is at this service?" Jenny said as she grabbed the microphone from Val. "It's so you'd never suspect her, but I'm onto you. You and Declan were having an affair!"

More rumbles of consternation from the audience.

"They conspired to kill my father," Jenny told the crowd. "I checked the photos from that night. Declan Dillion isn't in a single one after 8:00 PM. He left the gala early to kill RJ Valentine. You thought you could get around the prenup by bumping him off, but the joke was on you when Dad changed the will."

Lockhart was inching towards her. Drew looked like he wanted to sink through his chair into the floor. Dinah held her face in her hands.

"You have no idea what you're saying!" Val shrieked.

"You were the last person to see Declan alive," Jenny continued. "You tricked him into meeting me in the Cellars, followed us there, and killed him! Thought you could frame it on me!? Nice and tidy for you, right!?"

"Jennifer, no," she heard her aunt plead.

"My name is Trouble!" she shouted back.

A middle-aged man with a horrified expression caught her eye: the juvenile court officer who had said he'd be unofficially monitoring her behavior. The sight of him made Jenny hesitate, and Val seized the moment to snatch the microphone away. When Jenny flailed to grab it back, strong arms grabbed her from behind to restrain her.

"Declan Dillion is my second cousin, you demented pervert!" Val shouted. There was thunder booming in her voice. "I am not sleeping with my cousin!"

"Oh," Jenny said. Someone snickered. "*Really?*"

Jenny found Drew in the crowd as she struggled in the Lockhart's iron grip.

"Why didn't you say so!?" she yelled.

"I didn't know," Drew said, biting his fist in embarrassment.

Next to him, Mirai and her husband were just as mortified. She could hear scattered titters of awkward amusement spreading through the room.

"Strike three, kiddo," the sheriff whispered in her ear.

"Declan met with me because he needed to borrow some money," Val said, delicious savagery on her face. "I loved the idiot, but he couldn't stay away from the pai gow table. I take care of my own. And several witnesses can confirm that I never left my office until I heard the awful news. News that YOU had been found, covered in blood, with the knife that killed Declan IN YOUR HAND!"

Jenny sagged to the floor, her face burning with shame.

"Blake, I want her arrested," Val said. "In fact, I'm beginning to wonder if maybe *she* attacked my husband. She's clearly deranged, you can't deny it."

"You're right, Mrs. Valentine, she's not well," said another voice. Jenny was surprised to see Penny Griffin walking forward. "I'm sorry, Jenny, but I looked at your chart when you were in the hospital."

Jenny's heart froze to the core. Would *that* have been on her chart?

"No," she said weakly. "Please."

Panic rose up inside her like a horrible sickness. She could suffer the indignity of her failure here, but this secret wasn't Penny's to tell.

"It's okay," said Penny. "I know you didn't hurt your father. You couldn't have."

Jenny couldn't breathe. She was having another panic attack, like before. Like she used to have, when...

"She was in the hospital the night of the charity gala," said Penny. "The psych ward. Getting treatment for Dissociative Identity Disorder. Sometimes she really *does* think she's Trouble, and she can't tell the difference between fiction and reality."

"Dude, Penny," said Drew, frowning.

Jenny could barely process it. She was focusing on the carpet pattern, trying not to throw up. It was hard enough to breathe, and now Lockhart had bumped her head, and she was feeling nauseous again. This was a nightmare.

"I'm better now," she said in a small voice.

"It's okay," said Penny. "You just need help."

"I think you've helped enough," said Shelly, coming to her side.

Jenny concurred by vomiting onto the carpet of the Winchester.

"Blake, let's get her outside," said Shelly.

Jenny felt herself being lifted up and carried away.

"Sorry folks," she heard Val saying. "We'll get this cleaned up in just a bit. Please, stay. For Declan." She let out a nervous chuckle. "You know, if he's looking down on us now, he's probably laughing his ass off."

Everyone thought that was hilarious.

Jenny felt the air change and a cool wind blowing in her hair as Lockhart set her down on the valet's chair outside. Shelly used a napkin to wipe her face.

"Later," she heard the sheriff say to someone.

She couldn't hold it in anymore. She fell into Aunt Shelly's arms and sobbed.

Chapter Twenty-Three
Days Go By

IN THE BOOKS, WHEN THE TITULAR GIRL DETECTIVE GOT INTO TOO much trouble, it usually meant having to give an awkward apology to old Mrs. Waverly for ruining her dinner party. Or repainting a house after throwing an egg at the jewel thief and missing. Or mowing lawns to pay back the chapel for the broken stained glass window.

That girl had it easy.

Jenny would kill to mow some lawns right now if only to get out of the house. She might even agree to apologize to Valerie Valentine. Well, maybe not. Why should she? She saved that ungrateful bitch's life.

Jenny was grounded, of course. All activities restricted. No iPhone, no TV, no computer. They even took her Apple Watch, which she sorely felt. Communication was now impossible unless it was face to face. Aunt Shelly escorted her to class every morning and took her right home after school. Even if she had wanted to sneak out, the ankle monitor her juvenile court officer insisted she wear prevented that.

No more trips to her treehouse to study and relax and spy. No more job at the Poison Pen. She had meetings with a court-assigned therapist every Wednesday and Friday, and random, mandatory drug tests. Shelly packed up all her *Trouble* books and hid them. Jenny hadn't spoken to her for three days after that indignity.

"How was school today?" the therapist asked. It was their second session.

"I can do this magic trick now where I sit down at a cafeteria table and then everyone else stands up," Jenny said, all sardonic wit.

Her therapist was toady and bureaucratic and made weird wheezing noises whenever she stood up or sat down. It was like being visited by the DMV. If she weren't so mad at her aunt, she'd feel bad that Shelly had to pay for these sessions.

"This was a problem for you at your old school, wasn't it?" said the therapist. "Do you think it's possible that you push people away because it makes it easier to pretend you're... you know who?"

"Trouble," said Jenny. "And no. You guys don't get it, none of you do. Check my birth certificate, I'm not pretending. I am literally Trouble. That's my name."

"And you don't think that's a problem?" the therapist asked.

"Take it up with my dead parents," Jenny said. "They named me. And also, I do have friends. I have Drew. He still sits with me."

She smiled. Drew's loyalty meant a lot. He hadn't even asked her any questions when she returned to class.

"What about the other one you mentioned?" asked the therapist. "Penny?"

Jenny took a steadying breath, quelling her rage. "Penny and Drew aren't getting along right now after she invaded my privacy like that. Plus, she and Jack are kind of— Anyway, the point is, my original diagnosis was bullshit. I'm not dissociative."

Her therapist raised an eyebrow and looked through the folder in her lap.

"That's not what the Glendale psych ward had to say," her therapist said, reading from her file. "Threatening your principal. Starting a fire in the school hallway. Coming home late at night, unable to account for your actions. Claiming you were solving a mystery…"

"Look, I was in a bad place then," Jenny admitted. She hated recalling that last dark year in L.A. "But not because of Trouble. This girl I liked… she did a cruel thing, and it messed me up. I was sneaking out to go clubbing every night, rolling on molly and trying to throw myself at any girl who even looked my way. Which I guess is a turnoff."

"And that made you threaten your principal?"

"He was sleeping with a student, and I exposed him," said Jenny. "That was the mystery. The fire was to catch him in the act. You guys all just took it out of context. I'm not crazy!"

She was getting angry again just thinking about it. The lack of freedom, the condescension, the meds that made her numb. Having to wear loose-fitting clothes with no belts; eating without any sharp utensils. She might have actually lost her mind, and then one day, a miracle happened. Shelly got the job in Blackbird Springs, Jenny found her strength again, and they had to let her go.

"You know, everyone else only wishes they could be a character in their favorite book," Jenny said, eyes flashing. "Attend Hogwarts, flirt with Mr. Darcy, go ice skating with Sally Hayes, behold the Cracks of Doom. But they can't. I can. And you all want to take away my fun. My identity!"

After that, they upped her meds, and Jenny was no longer allowed to eat lunch with Drew.

There was only one silver lining.

Well, two if you counted Valerie Valentine's continued ability to draw breath and walk the earth. Jenny's performance must have convinced the killers that Val wasn't a threat. So Jack still had a mom, and Jenny's conscience was clean. That had to count for something. And truthfully, whenever Jenny was feeling particularly depressed with her predicament, thinking of what she had done for her brother made her feel better.

But the real stroke of luck was that Alicia Aaron had rejected Val's deal too. Jenny was still in the game, even if she couldn't come out and play.

Days went by.

The leaves turned orange and umber and brown, the wind picked up, and the weather cooled. Jenny woke up. She went to school. She came home and locked herself in her room. Repeat.

Like a prisoner, she'd taken to doing crunches and one-armed pushups in front of her bed. There was nothing to do except homework. On a spiteful whim, she handed her aunt the completed tests for every chapter in her Econ book after two weeks in lockup.

"If you want to impress me, do better in math," was all Shelly said in response.

Jenny's grade in Precalc was slipping again. Her homework was solid, but she could only claim "lady emergencies" to Mr. Stephenson so many times before a quiz.

One morning, the school was abuzz with the news that the Valentines were moving out of their mansion to a posh hotel downtown. The official word was that Val wanted to turn the mansion into a museum for RJ's work, but Jack's ever-darkening moods hinted otherwise. Lately, he only seemed happy when Penny was around, "helping him study." Drew bristled whenever he saw the two together

228

but said nothing.

Dinah, though.

With their conflicting schedules and Jenny's unmasking as a volatile head-case, Jenny thought she might never see the tall cheerleader again. So she was both surprised and anxious when Dinah passed right by on Jenny's walk from Econ to Precalc. Their eyes met for a fraction of a second. Dinah walked on. Jenny was sure that Dinah would take a different route tomorrow.

But she didn't. This time, Dinah moved closer as she went by. Close enough to smell her wonderful vanilla perfume. And she smiled at Jenny. A secret smile.

On the third day, their hands brushed as they passed.

Soon, the walk between the Humanities building and Math class became the highlight of Jenny's day. By some sort of unspoken agreement, they never glanced each other's way for more than a moment. Dinah would walk past, always on Jenny's right, and Jenny would let her arm swing just so, with Dinah doing the same, and for a brief moment of electric excitement, their hands would touch.

After a week, Jenny risked passing Dinah a note.

Dinah,

I'm sorry you had to see me that way at the Winchester, and hear that stuff about me. I swear to God I'm not crazy. It's just hard being me sometimes. If I'm ever allowed to leave the house again, we should hang out. I miss you.

-Jenny

The next day, Dinah pressed a small, folded up note into Jenny's palm as they passed in the quad.

Jenny,

I don't think you're crazy. I do think you've got quite the story to tell, and I'd love to hear it sometime. I miss you too.

xoxo Dinah

PS. Your new mascara game is on point!

From then on, Jenny always had a note ready for Dinah, or vice-versa. Never a long letter, just a quick thought or two. Jenny would stare at the x's and o's in Dinah's signature and daydream about what her lips tasted like. The notes were probably the only thing keeping Jenny going. That, and the revenge fantasies she entertained when she imagined solving Dad's murder and having all that money at her disposal.

Days turned into weeks. Jenny got up, went to school, brushed past Dinah, went home, and studied in her room. Homecoming came and went. Jack and Dinah were elected Homecoming Prince and Princess, which was awkward because Jack had gone with Penny Griffin. Jenny wasn't allowed to attend. No one had tried to murder Jenny or Val. Alicia Aaron shuffled along, always an unkind little smile on her face whenever they locked eyes in Chemistry.

The bump on her head healed, along with her wrist. The splint gave way to a brace. The brace came off. Jenny's left forearm was a bit skinnier now than the right one, but no worse for wear. She switched to two-armed pushups and her strength returned.

Whether she knew it or not, her heart was healing too. The sight of Penny at school no longer enraged her, and she didn't even mind Mason's douchebag comments in Econ anymore. She might have even looked forward to them. Maybe this was just Stockholm Syndrome, and she was so desperate for human contact that she'd take it anywhere she could get it. Or maybe this little vacation from Trouble was giving her something she'd never known she'd been missing: an opportunity to write her own story.

But even as she grew stronger in body and soul, somewhere a clock was ticking. RJ had given them 100 days to solve the mystery. Soon, those days would be half gone. Her anxiety meds were an even bigger concern. They took four to six weeks to kick in, and she needed to be free of her pills, therapist, and juvenile court monitoring before that happened. She couldn't go back to being that Jenny, the one who was numbed and passionless, a guest of the Glendale Behavioral Health Center.

Finally, in late October, the chance to get back in the game presented itself: the annual Blackbird Springs Harvest Festival.

EVERY YEAR, THE HIGH SCHOOL HELD A FESTIVAL ON THE FOOTBALL field the week before Halloween. Proceeds went to pay for school supplies, though somehow Valerie Valentine had entangled the Valentine Foundation with the event to "promote literacy" or whatever. There were carnival booths, hayrides, pigeage (which Jenny learned was the fancy name for grape stomping), tarot card readings, face paint, bake sale treats for the students, and wine tasting for the adults. By long tradition, all the kids were allowed one modest glass of beer or red wine by their parents, and everyone looked the other way on the drinking age.

Jenny guessed that Aunt Shelly would not adhere to this tradition, but through a combination of begging, pleading, flattery, threats, and cajoling, she had talked her aunt into letting her work the beanbag toss booth. They cleared it with the juvenile court officer so that no one would flip out when Jenny's lojack ankle monitor showed her at school after hours. As long as Shelly was there to work the booth with her, Jenny could attend the festival with the rest of her peers.

The festival volunteers typically wore lederhosen or dirndl dresses to the event instead of costumes, to reflect the town's Germanic roots. Aunt Shelly, having no Germanic roots of her own, brashly showed up after school in a kimono that Jenny had helped her pin tight in all the right places. Shelly actually looked... hot. Too bad it was for Lockhart.

As for Jenny, she wore her long black wig, pulled up in a traditional bun and held together with tama kanzashi hair sticks and a fan. That was for Kenji and Reiko, her great-grandparents. For Dad's side, she wore the dirndl bodice and blouse. And for Trouble, a tartan skirt, knee-high socks, and Chuck Taylors. The big bulky ankle monitor really tied the look together.

Working the beanbag toss mostly entailed collecting tickets and trying not to laugh when little kids pathetically missed their throws. Still, it was glorious after being cooped up in her room for a month. They had a whole assortment of stuffed animals to give away, from tiny little teddy bears to giant stuffed penguins. Jenny had her eye on the big plush shark, which she planned on swiping if no one else won it first.

Jenny was retrieving a beanbag from some idiot freshman who'd thrown it too hard and hit the vinyl backstop when she heard a familiar voice at the counter.

"Miss Valentine, we've missed you," said Mr. Carnegie.

Chapter Twenty-Four

Grape Crush

JENNY LOOKED UP TO SEE THE OLD MAN WITH THE SNOWY WHITE beard leaning on his cane. Her ears were already burning. Ever since the incident at the Winchester it had been extremely embarrassing to encounter any adults who were in attendance that night.

"Uh, hi Mr. Carnegie," she said.

"I haven't seen you at The Poison Pen lately," said Mr. Carnegie.

Jenny couldn't tell if he was clueless or just rubbing it in.

"Um, yeah, I've kinda been grounded."

"Yes, that was quite the performance at the Winchester," he said. "I haven't seen Valerie that flustered since she lost control of her beamer during Driver's Ed and ran over my wife's azaleas."

Jenny laughed at the idea of Val ever being young and flustered.

"Not everyone found my niece's behavior amusing," said Shelly.

Mr. Carnegie tut-tutted and rapped his cane on the railing.

"Well you have to come back as soon as you're free," he said. "Heidi has been whining to me about the extra work, and you know, it just felt right having a Valentine there. RJ would always drop by unannounced to sign books, and the kids loved it."

Jenny nodded and shot a satisfied grin at her aunt.

"Yeah, totally. I'll come by as soon as I can," she said.

Mr. Carnegie held out a handful of tickets.

"I don't know if I'm good for a toss," he said. "How much for one of the little ones? My granddaughter loves frogs."

He pointed at one of the little plush frogs on the prize shelf.

"I'll play for you!" said Jenny.

She took the beanbags, and by her third toss had scored enough points to win Mr. Carnegie his frog.

"She names them all Ribbit!" he said with a smile and sauntered off.

Shelly allowed a "hmmpf!" and collected the beanbags.

"What? He's nice," said Jenny.

"It takes a special kind of privilege to see your mental breakdown as entertainment," she said archly. "Imagine being that rich."

"I'm working on it."

As the sun dipped low in the west, Jenny found herself looking down the midway to the southern goalpost where a brunette with big bushy hair and bigger sunglasses was picking her way through the crowd. She was wearing a school-girl outfit under black robes, and a big red and gold scarf. Jenny smiled at the costume. Game respect game.

A shadow passed in front of her. It was the sheriff strolling by in black police uniform instead of his usual tan.

"Hey mom, check it out," Jenny said. "This guy dressed up as bumbling Sheriff Lockhart for Halloween."

"I'm the T-1000," Lockhart said, miffed, and pointed at some foil taped to his shirt.

"What's that?" asked Jenny.

His look of disgust quickly melted away when he spotted Shelly in her kimono. He actually whistled.

"Can I trust you to hold down the fort for a little while?" Shelly asked.

"Not like I'm going anywhere," said Jenny, lifting her ankle to brandish her lojack bracelet.

Shelly glared harder.

"Yes, I'll be good," Jenny said. "Look, I'm not telling you to ho it up, but whatever you have to do with him to get this off me: I won't judge."

Shelly rolled her eyes but couldn't keep from blushing.

"As if," she said with a laugh. "Maybe I'm dating him to keep that thing *on* you."

"You would."

"Be right back, I gotta run and catch Mr. Stephenson real quick," said Shelly, dashing off in her red kimono.

Jenny raised an eyebrow and held out a beanbag to Lockhart as she took his ticket.

"Any luck on the case?" she asked.

"Which case?" he replied.

"You know the one," Jenny said.

The sheriff leaned closer.

"I thought your girl detective days were behind you."

"Between you and me," Jenny looked over both shoulders, a devilish smile spreading on her lips. "I'll always be Trouble."

"Oh, I know," he said and threw the beanbag over her head. It sailed perfectly through one of the high-score holes at the back of the booth.

"Not bad," Jenny said.

"I was All-American at QB," he said.

"Wow, how sad," Jenny sneered, retrieving that plush shark she coveted. "Give this to my aunt. And remember: if you hurt her, it's your balls."

He gave Jenny a crisp salute, full of rich menace and subtle hints of mockery. Shelly returned to the booth and just about melted into a puddle when Lockhart handed her the stuffed shark.

"He was All-American at QB," said Jenny.

"Aww, what's his name?" Shelly asked, hugging the shark.

"Uhh—"

"Casey Klein," Jenny said, marveling at the consternation she caused the sheriff.

"Someone's coming by to collect tickets," Shelly said, oblivious. "If I'm not back by then—"

"Yeah yeah, I got it," said Jenny. "Get lost, you two."

With one last look of concern, her aunt walked off with Lockhart. Jenny rolled her neck, glad to finally be free of a chaperone. It didn't take long for Drew to materialize out of the crowd.

"Sup? Out on parole?" he said, bounding up in his Blackbird Springs Academy baseball jersey. Drew had visited the face paint tent and had metal cyborg parts drawn on his cheeks and forehead.

Jenny lifted her leg again to show off her ankle accessory.

"It's a work release," she said. "Don't tell me that's your costume."

"Oh, it's a team thing. We're supposed to represent," Drew said. He grabbed a beanbag and tossed it, and missed badly.

"I guess that's why you're not a pitcher," Jenny said.

"Did you know they call this corn-holing in the south?" he said, grinning.

Jenny was too distracted by a vision over his shoulder to reply. Dinah was headed their way. She was wearing tight, high-waisted blue jeans and a tighter white t-shirt with a big red star on it. The Homecoming Princess tiara gleamed upon her brow. Drew caught Jenny's expression and followed her gaze.

"Oh," he said. "I guess I should…"

"Beat it," said Jenny.

"Imma go check out the grape stomp," Drew said. "I hear they give you an extra glass of wine if you do it."

Jenny barely heard him, basking in the warm glow of Dinah's smile.

"Hey stranger," Dinah said, her eyes traveling up and down Jenny's body. "That's a hell of a look."

"Thanks!" Jenny said. "You too! Nice crown."

"We're supposed to wear them," Dinah said.

"Is Jack wearing his?"

Dinah shrugged.

"Sorry about you and him," Jenny said.

"Are you?"

"No."

Jenny had been resting her hand on the booth railing between them. Dinah placed her hand on top of it, and Jenny's heart leapt into her throat.

"I um… I thought about what you said," Dinah said. "About not being friends."

"Sure," said Jenny, afraid to say anything else.

"I don't… I mean I never… I guess I've always been curious?" Dinah's face reddened. "God, I'm such a cliche."

"What are you saying?" Jenny asked. Her throat had gone dry.

Dinah squeezed her hand. It was shaking. So was Dinah's.

"I'm *saying*," said Dinah, a bashful smile widening on her face, "that maybe we could try not being friends? When you can come out and play, that is. If you still want to."

"Yeah," said Jenny. "Yes! I want to!"

"Good."

"I mean, I don't want to front," said Jenny feeling a rush of relief

237

and glee wash over her. "I've only ever *really* made out with one girl, and it was at a club in WeHo when I was spying on this bitch. And I was on molly—and God! Why am I telling you this?"

Dinah laughed and gave Jenny's hand a gentle caress.

"Well, there's a first time for everything," she said in a sultry voice that Jenny felt deep down in her belly.

She had to look away from Dinah's captivating hazel eyes, blushing furiously and loving it. Glancing around, she suddenly realized that Mrs. Rivas, the Valentine housekeeper, was standing at the booth across the aisle, waiting for her turn with the Fortune Teller.

"Hey, can I totally change the subject for a moment?" she asked.

"Yeah, sure," said Dinah.

"You're one of the Big Six, right?" said Jenny. "What do you know about Carnegie?"

Jenny quickly relayed the story Mrs. Rivas had told her about the accidental gift of *Ressort Rouge*. Dinah shook her head, incredulous.

"I'm not surprised," she said. "They send my dad a $30 bottle of white zin every year. Obviously, he'd shit a brick if he sent a *Ressort* by mistake. But what's it to you?"

"So my Dad's will…" Jenny said slowly. Was she really going to tell Dinah about this? Yeah, she was. "It said he was murdered. Whoever finds the killer wins his inheritance, and that bottle of wine is supposed to be a clue."

Dinah was speechless for a while, and Jenny could see the gears turning in her head.

"Oh, this explains so much," she said at last.

"What?"

"Just—your brother. Never mind him. *That's* why they're moving!?"

"Yep."

"So Carnegie and that bottle," said Dinah, pursing her lips to ponder. "I mean, I can say this for sure. I'd be surprised if that family could even afford a bottle of *Ressort Rouge* to begin with."

"He owns stuff all over town though," said Jenny.

"Believe it or not, there's not a ton of money in running a winery these days," said Dinah. "I mean we're doing fine, I can't complain. But we're not exactly Scrooge McDuck either. The Carnegie family owns a lot, but the taxes on these wineries are insane, it's why we divested. There's *no way* he'd have a bottle of *Ressort Rouge* just lying around like that. For God's sake, he eats at Arby's."

"Huh," said Jenny, trying to fit this new piece of information into the puzzle in her brain. Just then, the yearbook teacher Mr. White walked up holding a small lockbox.

"Oh, you probably want the tickets," said Jenny.

Dinah's phone buzzed. She frowned at the screen and moved aside for Mr. White as Jenny ducked under the counter to get the coffee can they'd been depositing carnival tickets into.

"Be back in a sec," Dinah said, slipping around the back of the booth to take the call.

"Haven't seen you in my room in a while," Mr. White said. "How've you been?"

"Oh, everyone thinks I'm crazy. Here you go." Jenny held out the coffee can of tickets.

"All teenager are a little crazy," said Mr. White with a grin. "Doesn't mean you can't come visit."

Jenny sighed. "Talk my aunt into letting me, and I—"

"HARBOR HIGH IN THE HOUSE!!!"

Four guys wearing flesh-colored body stockings charged past, whooping and hollering. Kids screamed and leapt out of their way. Mr. White shook his head.

"See? Duty calls." He rapped his class ring on the table and jogged off after the streakers.

Half a minute passed before Jenny realized that Dinah was gone.

"Dinah?"

There was no answer. Jenny ducked under the vinyl flaps at the back of the booth.

"Dinah?"

No one was back here. This part of the field was deserted except for a few pickup trucks that had backed in to unload supplies. It was almost quiet. The row of booths made the sounds of the festival seem far away.

"Dinah?!"

Nothing.

She slipped back into her booth, but Dinah wasn't there either. Would Dinah just leave like that? The hair on the back of Jenny's neck stood up. This wasn't crossed wires or a misunderstanding. Some primal, instinctual sense of dread blossomed in her stomach. She knew— she *knew* that something was wrong.

Some kid in an Iron Man mask walked up to play.

"We're closed!" she barked at him, and he ran off, terrified.

Lockhart and Shelly were nowhere in sight. She couldn't wait.

"Sorry, Shelly."

Jenny hopped over the railing and sprinted down the midway, hoping she wasn't too late.

HALFWAY TO THE GOALPOST, JENNY REALIZED SHE HAD NO IDEA where to look. She glanced around in a panic, hoping to spot that brunette in the Gryffindor scarf with the big sunglasses. Instead, she found only smiling families and young children. Despite her urgency, it pleased Jenny immensely to see a few little girls dressed as Trouble.

A big, wide, wooden cylinder rose up from the ground nearby, next to a pile of shoes. It was the pigeage, where you crushed grapes the old-fashioned way, with your bare feet. The current stompers were Mason Lockhart and her brother Jack. They were leaping up and down, laughing like idiots, staining their feet purple as they mashed grapes to a pulp.

Pinot Noir, Jenny guessed from the smell. Good with pasta and game birds.

There was a line next to the slatted wooden vat. Her peers were waiting with bare feet to stomp grapes and earn a free glass of red wine. Mr. Stephenson and Mr. Finch were next. They'd rolled their pleated slacks up past their knees. Behind them were those city workers, Andy and Dave, followed by Heidi from The Poison Pen. Drew and Penny were further back in line, doing their best to pretend they didn't notice the other.

Jenny felt a ringing in her ears. Something had been nibbling on the edge of her mind for weeks, and it felt like it was about to break through. Her jaw hung slack as she tried to understand.

She blinked and stared at the pile of shoes. Shoes from the grape stompers standing in line. In particular, a right-footed sturdy work shoe with a short heal and odd horizontal creases across the tread.

"Son of a bitch!" she exclaimed, her mind exploding with epiphanies, despite her panic.

Jenny saw Drew's Big Board in her mind. All those loose threads that she'd failed to connect to Val: Rachel Martin, the broken glass, Carnegie, the footprint, Declan's cork. Suddenly they formed a clear picture when she connected them to each other instead.

She ran on. If they'd taken Dinah, she wouldn't be out here. Not somewhere public. No, if they had her, they'd be trying to get away.

Jenny headed for the school parking lot. The festival had been running for hours, and the lot was nearly full. Jenny sprinted between rows, leaping up at intervals to see into the next lane. She made it to the end of the lot, but there was no sign of Dinah.

In the next row over, something shiny caught her eye. Jenny rounded a big black car and stooped over a glittering object on the ground.

It was Dinah's Homecoming Queen tiara.

"Oh perfect," said a familiar voice from behind her.

Powerful arms gripped her from behind, and a hand covered her mouth before she could scream.

"You just made my job much easier," said a high, cold voice.

There was a sharp sting in her neck. In an instant, Jenny's world faded away. The last thing she remembered before the darkness took her was a chilling laugh, and then the black.

Chapter Twenty-Five

The Red Geyser

WITH A ROUGH JOLT, JENNY SNAPPED AWAKE. SOMEWHERE nearby, she could hear rusty iron grinding with an eerie shriek on old hinges. Her head felt woozy and slow. The last thing she remembered was finding Dinah's tiara… and that familiar cold voice.

She knew who it was now. Only one person it could be.

"Jenny?"

Her eyelids shot open, and with her vision came searing stabs of pain in her skull. The pale face that swam in front of her was, quite literally, a sight for sore eyes.

"Dinah!" she whispered.

"Hey!" Dinah whispered back.

They were both lying on their side, facing each other in a dark compartment. A car, Jenny guessed. No, a hearse.

"What's going on?" asked Dinah.

Jenny wanted to reach out and comfort Dinah but found her hands were bound behind her back. Zip-ties, judging by the feel of the narrow bands cutting into her wrists.

"We're being kidnapped," said Jenny.

"Yeah, no shit!"

She became aware of the hearse's engine now as it shifted gears, and they began to move.

"Actually, no," Jenny said. "Not kidnapped. He's going to kill us. He has to."

"What did we ever do?" said Dinah. "Besides being young and hot?"

She couldn't help but giggle. She was either a total badass or so terrified she was losing her mind.

"What's so funny?" asked Dinah.

"He screwed up," said Jenny. "He should have killed us already. Don't worry, baby. Everything's gonna be okay."

"Oh, I'm totally chill."

"Good," said Jenny.

"Good," said Dinah.

They both giggled this time until their laughter turned to tears.

"We're so fucked," sniffed Dinah.

"The cavalry is probably already on its way," said Jenny. "I'm wearing an ankle monitor."

"Yeah, but how long until they notice you're gone?" said Dinah. "Most of the station is probably at the festival."

Jenny frowned. "What about your phone?"

"I think he took it," said Dinah.

"Shelly never gave me mine back," said Jenny. "Damnit! The one time I didn't bring my box cutter! It wouldn't stay put in my skirt."

"Mine was in my purse."

"Okay, I'm panicking now," Jenny admitted, her heart racing faster and faster as they felt the hearse slow to a stop.

"Hold on. Roll over," said Dinah.

Jenny twisted around. She felt Dinah doing the same, and their hands touched behind her back. The car door opened.

"Oh," said Jenny. "Are we holding hands?"

"That's sweet, but I was trying to untie us," Dinah said.

"I think they're zip-ties."

"Yeah. Damn."

"No matter what, just keep him talking," said Jenny, as they heard footsteps crunching on the ground outside. "Stall as long as you can and wait for my signal."

Jenny found Dinah's hand behind her back and squeezed. The back of the hearse swung open, and she felt goosebumps prickle on her arms as cool, damp air flowed into the cabin.

"Wakey wake," said that sinister voice.

A strong hand gripped her ankle and pulled. He dragged them out onto a crumbling asphalt driveway in the middle of a gloomy field. In the hazy moonlight, Jenny could just make out the rows of dead grapevines stretching toward a ridge of trees in the distance.

They were back at the Haunted Vineyard.

"Who's this asshole?" said Dinah, putting on a brave face.

In answer, he thrust a big stainless steel scalpel in her face. Dinah shrieked.

"I only know him as the Undertaker," said Jenny. He was wearing his same old shabby suit, glinting slightly in the dim light from too many dry-cleanings that had worn the cloth to a smooth, dull sheen. The balding man sneered down at her with beady, dead eyes.

"You should really learn to keep your mouth shut," he said, shoving the scalpel in Jenny's face now. "And your nose out of where it doesn't belong."

"Sorry, that's kind of my thing," she said in a shaky voice.

"Get up," said the Undertaker, hefting a small leather bag over his shoulder. "We're going for a walk."

Jenny and Dinah did as instructed, keenly aware of the razor-sharp blade at their backs. The Undertaker pointed them up the driveway, toward the burned and crumbling entrance to Pinefall mansion.

"Why did you bring us here?" asked Dinah in a small voice.

They stopped at the open doorway. Inside, the skeletal remains of the building loomed dark and dangerous, covered in dirt and grime from years exposed to the elements.

"I've got a theory," Jenny said.

"Really?" said the Undertaker with a nasty laugh. "Is it that I'm gonna kill you out here? Slowly, and painfully, where no one will hear you scream? How'd you put that one together, girl detective?"

He shoved Jenny forward. Dinah let out a whimper and hurried to keep up. Jenny had to concentrate on her footing as he forced them over loose floorboards and shattered masonry into what was once a big living room or ballroom.

"No, that's not the theory," she said.

Her eyes traveled around the dilapidated chamber. There were several gaping openings where the drywall had burned or rotted away.

"We don't get to see the basement?" Jenny asked the Undertaker. The hesitation on his face was all the proof Jenny needed to know her theory was right. "You're nothing but a bunch of frauds."

"You shut your mouth," the Undertaker said.

"That wasn't a denial," said Jenny, alarmed at her own insane moxie.

His eyes flashed, and he pushed the scalpel right up against her throat. She retreated from the blade into one of the crumbling walls. Dust rained down, and the structure creaked ominously.

Jenny let out a pained cry as the tip of the blade pricked her neck. A warm sensation trickled down onto her dirndl bodice and blouse.

"Stop it!" Dinah screamed.

The Undertaker withdrew the scalpel to show Jenny the drops of her own blood on it.

"Like I said," the Undertaker hissed. "Slowly and painfully."

Heartbeats of silence passed between the three of them. Jenny could feel the blood on her chest. She found Dinah's eyes and held them, willing her to hang in there.

The Undertaker's phone rang.

He frowned and stepped back, waving the scalpel at them to move closer together.

"Not a word!" he said, and with his free hand answered the call. "Hey, what's up?"

The three of them waited patiently for a response only the Undertaker could hear.

"Didn't those two bozos tell you? ...What? No. They're with me. At Pinefall. ...I had to. They were talking about the bottle."

Jenny moved closer to Dinah and whispered in her ear. "We have to split up. I'll be the bait."

The Undertaker looked back at them, a sickening lear on his face.

"Not yet... Horace, I told you, I'll handle this like I always do. Anyway, I gotta go. One of them looks like she's about to try something stupid."

He hung up and rummaged in his leather bag.

"Bear with me," the Undertaker said. "I've never done this while they're still alive."

"Oh gross!" Dinah shouted.

"What? Oh— Jesus, no not *that!*" the Undertaker cried. "What is wrong with you?!"

"Oh I'm sorry," Dinah said. "How rude of me!"

"I meant souvenirs!"

His eyes gleamed as he unzipped a case to reveal a syringe and a row of skinny vials, held in place by an elastic strap. Jenny's eyes were adjusting to the darkness, and she could see now that most of the vials were full of something dark, and labeled with a sharpie. Blood trophies.

"I'm a collector too, but not of books," he said with a chilling leer and licked his lips. "Now which one of you wants to go first?"

"Needles don't bother me," Jenny said. "Let's do it."

The Undertaker's eyes narrowed. "Try anything funny, and I'll gut your little girlfriend."

"Excuse me, I'm taller than you," Dinah said archly.

"Who do you got in there?" Jenny asked, nodding to his case of blood vials. "Let me guess: Rachael Martin?"

The Undertaker chuckled and prepped the syringe.

"You really *do* know too much," he said.

"And of course you've got a vial for Declan," Jenny continued. "Was he your first sale?"

The Undertaker spun her around, and Jenny felt him tapping the veins on her inner elbow. Then a slight sting as the needle broke the skin.

"We needed to test the merchandise," he said, his breath hot on her neck. "And Declan needed cash. We were all square until he started asking about *Ressort Rouge* again."

"His murder was real lucky for you, huh?" Jenny said.

"When God closes a door, he opens a window," said the Undertaker.

"What are you guys talking about?" asked Dinah.

"I'm solving the mystery," said Jenny. "I'll explain later."

The Undertaker snorted as he filled a new vial with Jenny's blood.

"Here's something you'll like," he said. Jenny turned to find him beaming like a proud collector as he deposited the vial of Jenny's blood into his case and withdrew another. "The crown jewel of my set."

Behind her back, where the Undertaker couldn't see, she was counting down to Dinah with the fingers on her right hand.

Five...

She glanced at the name on the vial.

RJ Valentine

"Bullshit," Jenny said. "You didn't kill him."

Four...

"Not for lack of trying," he said. "We sent him a dosed bottle of whiskey, but the idiot slipped and hit his head before he had a chance to drink it. You can do the honors instead."

Three...

"You forgot the number one rule of undertaking," said Jenny.

Two...

"What? Always be closing?"

One...

"Make sure they're dead first—NOW!"

Jenny sprang to the side.

The Undertaker lunged after her, fumbling the vials away and leaving himself wide open to a wicked high-kick to the face from Dinah's booted foot.

The scalpel dropped from his hand and clanged on the ground.

"RUN!" Dinah shouted.

Dinah went left. Jenny ran right, leaping through a hole in the wall and into the remains of the Pinefall kitchen. The shriek of rage behind told her the Undertaker was close in pursuit. She rushed headlong across the kitchen, arms still pinned behind her, and scrambled up the stairs to the second story.

The fifth step collapsed under her foot, and the Undertaker got ahold of her leg.

Jenny rolled over on the stairs and kicked out with all her strength. She got him right in the dome, and he stumbled back.

She rolled again and was back on her feet, racing up the stairs. The Undertaker tried to follow, but two more steps snapped under his heavier frame. Jenny laughed down at him as he slashed the scalpel in frustration, unable to reach her.

"There are more ways up!" he growled and ran back into the ballroom.

Jenny hurried down the second story hallway as fast as she dared. In some places, the building had burned away entirely, and she had to leap across gaps in the flooring to keep going. She just hoped she was making enough noise to draw the Undertaker's attention and help Dinah get away.

If there were still a roof on the building, she never would have been able to see where she was going. Fortunately, most of the ceiling had long ago crumbled and burned away, and the second story was open to the moonlight above.

Somewhere behind her, she heard a loud snapping of wood and metal as another section of the building collapsed. Jenny leaned against a brick pillar to steady herself as an angry bellow roared up from below.

She hoped Dinah had run and wasn't trying to fight back. There was a door at the end of the hall. If she could just reach it—

Three steps away, her foot snagged on a piece of rebar and she tumbled to the floor. The sudden shift in weight overcame the failing strength of the construction here, and she fell right through in an avalanche of dirt and moldy insulation.

A cry of pain escaped her lips as she landed back on the ground floor. She coughed and spit out the dirt in her mouth. Near as she could tell, she was still in one piece, but she was going to have some wicked splinters in her back from where her shoulder raked against a floorboard on the way down. If she made it out of this alive, that was.

Jenny grunted, trying to roll over and get back on her feet without the aid of her arms. The kanzashi sticks in her wig had come undone, and the long black locks were in her face. She shook the wig off and felt the cool air blowing over her own hair.

"Careful!" said the Undertaker's high, cold voice. "It's not safe in here!"

Jenny gulped and backed up against the wall. She'd fallen into some kind of bedroom, and the Undertaker was standing in the doorway. She was cornered.

"You're a real pain in the ass, you know that?" he said, wiping his face. His cheap suit was covered in dust and grime now, and blood was trickling from his sharp little nose.

Something poked Jenny in the back as she pressed herself against the wall. A jagged nail.

"That's what everyone tells me," Jenny said. She scraped her wrist bindings across the nail. With a *Snap!* The zip-ties broke, and her hands were free.

She held up her fists with a savage snarl.

"Pshh, please," said the Undertaker.

Jenny charged.

He kicked her in the stomach, and she collapsed to the floor in pain.

She could hardly move, gasping for air as his shrill laugh rang out above her. Regret washed over her. It couldn't end like this, it just couldn't. Her hands grasped out for something, anything to save her.

"Pathetic," said the Undertaker, leaning down to hiss in her ear. "Any last words?"

Her fingers brushed over something long and smooth. One of her hair sticks.

"Yeah," Jenny growled. "You talk too much, you fucking amateur!"

"Jenny!" Dinah shouted.

The Undertaker spun. Dinah was in the doorway, holding a concrete brick.

Jenny gripped the kanzashi stick and stabbed with all her might into the Undertaker's calf.

He howled in pain and reached for her, leaving himself open to Dinah. She swung the brick two-handed and caught him under the chin.

He let out a groan and crumpled.

"Are you okay?" asked Dinah, helping Jenny up.

"I'll live. We gotta go!"

She pulled Dinah away from the broken Undertaker. There was no telling when he might wake.

"How did you get your hands in front of you?" Jenny asked as they rushed back through the abandoned mansion.

"I'm a cheerleader," said Dinah with a smirk.

They found themselves back in the ballroom and Jenny skidded to a stop as she spotted something glinting from the floor.

"Hold on," Jenny said.

She snatched up the vial of RJ's blood, and they ran out into the misty night air.

THEY FOUND THE UNDERTAKER'S HEARSE WHERE HE'D PARKED IT ON the driveway about fifty feet from the mansion. The car was unlocked, which was good. They had no key for the ignition, though, which was not so good.

"Shit!" said Dinah. "We should have got his keys! Or at least his phone!"

They frantically searched the cab but found only a pack of smokes, a couple compact disks, and some breath mints. Jenny snapped a CD in half and used it to cut through Dinah's bindings.

"Thanks," said Dinah, rubbing her red wrists. "What was that all about Declan Dillion and Rachael Martin?"

"It's the racket he was running," said Jenny. "I think I figured it out."

"...And?"

"Annnnd would you hate me if I held off explaining it till I gathered just a little more evidence?"

Dinah exhaled in annoyance. "I'm not gonna tell!"

"I know that," Jenny said. "But if I don't tell you, you won't have to lie. Just tell the cops the Undertaker was a crazy psycho who tried to kill us."

"Tried!?"

The Undertaker had found them. His face was a mess of blood and dirt, but his eyes still shone in a maniacal fury. He was only a few meters away and limping closer. He'd found his scalpel too.

"I'm gonna make you watch!" he screamed.

"Come on!" said Dinah, flinging a Cranberries CD at the Undertaker and pulling Jenny into the vines.

Footfalls pounded behind them as they raced through the dead vineyard. Despite his limp, the Undertaker was doggedly on their tail, only a dozen meters behind.

They ran on, into the tree line and up the ridge. The scent of pine needles and sulfur burned in Jenny's lungs as they slipped and scrambled up the hill. Exhausted, they crested the plateau into steaming, alien terrain. They'd made it to the hot springs.

"Deja vu," Jenny said, hands on her knees, sucking in oxygen.

"He's still coming," said Dinah.

Back down the ridge, the Undertaker had gained on them. He was less than 20 feet away now, grunting like a stuck pig as he powered up the slope.

A shrieking whistle sounded behind them.

"Oh perfect," said Jenny.

"We can make it," said Dinah.

It was a mad dash across the geyser field, leaping over tiny crags and craters and jets of steaming air. Heavy mist surrounded them, but Jenny had a clearer picture of the hot springs in her head this time. She led them at an angle, toward what she was pretty sure was the front of the parking lot.

Sooner than expected, a wooden railing loomed out of the mist. This time, they both stayed on their feet when hurdling the fence. All that jogging had paid off.

Suddenly, sirens wailed, and lights flashed in their faces as several police cruisers pulled up. Sheriff Lockhart leapt out of his police SUV, pistol in hand.

"Jennifer!" her aunt screamed, hopping out of the passenger side.

Dinah and Jenny raised their hands and looked back. The Undertaker was still 30 feet from the edge of the hot springs. He saw the police and skidded to a stop.

Despite the deafening sirens and shouts, Jenny could still hear the man as he smiled and stepped astride one of the hissing steam vents.

"I'll see you in your nightmares, Trouble!" he shrieked.

The geysers erupted, and the Undertaker was lost in the massive blast of superheated water vapor.

A high, shrill scream rose up from the hot springs—

—and just as quickly cut off.

Maybe it was just a trick of the police lights that turned a section of the Minutemen geysers red. Maybe not.

Jenny turned to Dinah and smiled in relief. Before she lost her nerve, she leaned over and kissed her. Dinah's lips were just as soft and warm as she imagined, and tasted like cinnamon chapstick.

It was a perfect moment. It lasted all of three seconds before they arrested her.

Chapter Twenty-Six

Oh, Shelly

"**O**H COME ON!" JENNY PROTESTED AS THEY PULLED HER AWAY from Dinah.

"Blake, is this really necessary?" said Shelly, pushing the sheriff out of the way to envelop Jenny in a backbreaking hug.

"What happened with you and Chuck?" Lockhart asked.

"Who's Chuck?" asked Dinah.

"That guy you just steam-fried," said the sheriff. "The Undertaker."

"Oh. Fuck Chuck," said Jenny.

"Did he hurt you?" Shelly asked, wiping Jenny's face with a tissue.

"Um, *yeah*. I've got about 50 splinters in my shoulder, and I'm covered in dirt and blood," Jenny said. "Look, can we maybe do this tomorrow, after I've had like 50 showers and a hot bath? All that matters is that guy was trying to kill us, and he's dead now, so he can't."

It took another half-hour of questioning, but Lockhart finally let them go home with the promise that Jenny would give an official statement at the station tomorrow.

THAT NIGHT, JENNY USED UP ALL THE HOT WATER TWICE. A LONG shower to clean off the filth, and a long bath to daydream about Dinah. Other than the kidnapping and attempted murder, her evening had worked out rather well.

Afterward, Shelly used tweezers to pull out the splinters from Jenny's shoulder as she lay across her aunt's lap in a bra and sweatpants.

"I wish you'd let your hair grow out," said Shelly, running a hand over Jenny's head. "La La always had such great hair."

"Mom didn't need to wear wigs all the time," said Jenny.

"Neither do you," said Shelly.

Jenny sighed in contentment. She was feeling so good that she decided to tell Shelly about Dad's will and the contest. She'd have to find out sooner or later, right?

This turned out to be a miscalculation.

"THAT SON OF A BITCH!" Her aunt was pacing around the living room, fists balled in rage. "If he weren't already dead, I'd kill him myself!"

"Dude, relax," Jenny said from a safe distance. "This could set us up for life."

"Or get you killed!" She grabbed her glass of chardonnay, downed it, and hurled it into the fireplace in an explosion of cheap crystal. "He's a *monster!*" Shelly screamed. "An absolute monster!!"

"Don't say that!" Jenny could feel her own temper exploding between her ribs. "He did it for me."

"You are so much more than his stupid books and games, Jennifer."

"I DON'T WANT TO BE!" she shrieked at her aunt, knowing even as she said it how juvenile it sounded. "I mean— No. I don't— I don't want to *have* to be, for you to like me."

Shelly blinked away tears. "Jenny, I love you."

"Coulda fooled me," Jenny said weakly, her lip quivering.

A girl detective knew how to spot a lie, and Jenny's aunt was telling the truth, which only made it worse. She stomped to the staircase and hurried up to her room. Pausing on the landing, she had a cruel thought and unleashed it before she could stop herself.

"And by the way!" she shouted down from the staircase. "Blake knew about the will this whole time! Why do you think he's dating you?!"

Jenny slammed her bedroom door shut, regretting her words immediately. Maybe she was the real monster.

THE UNDERTAKER HAD LIED. JENNY'S SLEEP WAS DEEP AND dreamless. He never made an appearance.

She slept in late. Shelly didn't stop her. As noon approached, her aunt drove Jenny in silence to the police station to give her statement. Her JCO was there too. Shelly kept her distance from Sheriff Lockhart. From his stiff demeanor and sagging face behind his aviators, it was clear they'd spoken, and it hadn't gone well.

Sorry, Lockhart. But also, fuck you.

Jenny told them that the Undertaker admitted to killing Declan over money he owed. It wasn't true, but this was cleaner. She kept the solution to the wine bottle mystery to herself, for now. She still needed a few more things before she was ready.

She also explained the poisoning attempt on Val, and how Jenny had faked that whole scene to save her. On speakerphone, Val reluctantly admitted that Jenny had said something about poison that night.

"Now, who wants to do the honors?" Jenny said, holding out her ankle and the lojack monitor on it. "Tell you what: no more social worker visits, no more forced medication, and Val refunds that fine back to my lawyer, and we won't file a counter-suit."

The juvenile court officer bit his lip. She had him dead to rights. He nodded, red-faced, and took the lojack bracelet off.

"And I want my phone back!"

"I HAVE TO STOP BY THE SCHOOL," HER AUNT SAID AS THEY DROVE away from the station.

"That's fine, I want to see Drew and Dinah," Jenny said, engrossed in her phone.

"We should talk," Shelly said.

Jenny ignored her, scrolling through all the emails and messages she'd missed for the past month. She'd already fired off a few emergency texts, and now she was reading through what everyone had been sending her during her captivity, which wasn't easy since the screen was still broken and half of the display was a mess of glitchy random colors.

Drew had sent her a message every night at midnight, testing to see if she'd gotten her phone back. There was one from Penny, apologizing. That was nice. Jenny was saving Dinah's messages for last and hoping they included a photo or two.

"Did you hear me?" Shelly asked.

"School, yeah," Jenny said as they pulled into the teacher's lot.

"I said we're moving back to Glendale," Shelly said solemnly, watching Jenny closely for her reaction.

"What? No, we're not."

"I can't keep you here, Jennifer. It's far too dangerous. Your father was a madman for bringing you into this."

"Relax," said Jenny. "The Undertaker is dead, he can't hurt me now."

"You almost died!" said Shelly, eyes wide in concern. "Sure, you caught *a* killer, but he wasn't *the* killer, right? What kind of mother would I be if I let you live in this kind of danger?"

"You're not—" Jenny paused at the flicker of pain in Shelly's face. She took her aunt's hand. "You're not putting me in any more danger here than I would be in LA. Come on, you think if someone wants to get me, they can't drive 400 miles?"

"I've already made up my mind," said her aunt.

"So I'm being punished again, even though I've done nothing wrong?"

"Let's not call it nothing," said Shelly with a glare. "But this isn't punishment."

"Yes, it is! I like it here! I belong here!" It would be a cold day in hell before Jenny let herself get taken away from Blackbird Springs. "This is about Blake, isn't it?!" Jenny said. "You just want to run away from him because he lied to you."

"It is not just about that," Shelly said, turning scarlet.

"Look, I asked him not to tell you about the will because I knew you'd freak. He likes you."

"Oh, so now you're defending him? I thought you hated him?"

"I mean, I do," said Jenny. "But I... It was wrong, what I said last night."

"You just don't want to leave," said Shelly, shaking her head. "Blake is not your concern, and we're leaving for you, not for me. I'm submitting my resignation to the principal right now."

"I'll run away."

"Jennifer..."

"Gimme the weekend!" Jenny said, panic rising in her chest.

"What difference will that make?"

"Maybe all the difference," said Jenny, a sudden burst of adrenaline coursing through her veins as she saw a way out of this. "Just, please, don't resign until Monday. Give me one more crack at this. It's $272 million! Think about it!"

Shelly leaned back in the driver's seat, massaging her temples. But this time, instead of a lecture, she simply said "Fine. Spend the weekend with your friends, but on Monday we're leaving."

"Thank you," said Jenny, giving her aunt a kiss on the cheek and hopping out of the car.

There was a time limit now, and Jenny did her best work under pressure.

Chapter Twenty-Seven
The Bad Egg

SCHOOL WAS JUST LETTING OUT WHEN JENNY ARRIVED AT THE
front entrance. She had dressed lazily in a flannel shirt and jeans
today, but she didn't care who saw her like this. The first familiar face
to limp by was Alicia Aaron. She stopped a couple paces away from
Jenny, sizing her up as she tapped a pack of cigarettes against her
palm.

"Are you smoking today?" Alicia asked, gesturing with the pack.

"No," said Jenny.

The redhead shrugged and lit herself a cigarette. They stared at each
other for a moment while Alicia took a drag.

"I hear you stopped a killer," Alicia said.

"But not *the* killer," Jenny said.

Alicia gave a slight shrug. "Don't sell yourself short."

"Valerie Valentine said she was going to buy you off," Jenny said.
"Why didn't you take the deal?"

"I didn't like the terms," Alicia said. "And it's not like I haven't been
making progress."

"Have you now?"

Alicia allowed herself a small smile and held up her phone for Jenny to see.

It was a photo of Alicia standing in front of a cafe. The one where the Poison Pen used to be. As if the location wasn't enough of a hint, Alicia was giving a peace sign to the camera. Somehow, she had figured out where Jenny's photo clue was taken.

Jenny reached out, but Alicia yanked her phone back quickly, a smug grin on her face.

"You're wasting your time," Jenny said coldly. "That's not going to solve the mystery."

"I'll be the judge of that, Trouble," she said.

Alicia tottered away, snickering to herself. That little snake knew far too much for Jenny's comfort.

"Wow, I was gonna say hi, but you look like you want to stab someone," said a familiar voice behind her.

Jenny's anger evaporated, and she spun around with glee to find Dinah Black's wonderful face right in front of her own.

"Not anymore!" she said, giving Dinah a big hug. Her girlfriend turned bright red.

"Oh— sorry," Jenny said, feeling like a tool. "If you didn't want to— I mean, we haven't even gone on a date yet."

"What, Pinefall doesn't count?" Dinah said.

"I just meant... If you wanted to keep it on the DL for now..." Jenny was so, so bad at this.

"No, it's not that," Dinah said. "It's just that your brother is coming this way."

Jenny wasn't sure if it was entirely about Jack, but he was certainly walking toward them, holding Penny's books as she walked next to him.

"Oh, right," said Jenny.

"I mean, I don't want to make *us* about *him*, you know?" said Dinah.

"Sure," said Jenny.

"I can tell you don't believe me. I'm not embarrassed, Jenny."

She took Jenny's hand, lacing their fingers together just as Jack and Penny walked up. Her brother was staring at them with a confused look on his face. Penny avoided eye contact.

"You two sure are spending a lot of time together," Jenny said.

"Jack is like practically my next door neighbor now," said Penny, unable to hide the satisfaction in her voice.

"He never held my books," Dinah murmured to Jenny.

"Mom and I are in the Crow's Nest, right next to Pen's building," said Jack.

"How are you liking it?" asked Dinah.

"It's… I'm still getting used to it. But it's not so bad," he said, giving Penny a little smile.

"Jenny, I heard about what happened," said Penny. "I'm sorry. Not just for last night, but the Winchester. That was wrong of me. I thought I was helping you out, but I understand now that it wasn't my place."

"Thank you," said Jenny. "I saw your text already, but thank you for saying so. Apology accepted."

"Wait, so you got your phone back?" asked Dinah.

Jenny grinned and lifted up her leg to show off her lack of an ankle bracelet. "I'm a free woman again. And for the record, I'm not crazy," said Jenny. "I mean, I have my mood swings, but I always know who I am. There's no split Trouble personality. I *am* Trouble, and she is me."

"And *she* is mine," said Dinah, who then leaned over and kissed Jenny full on the lips. It was her turn to blush as Jack and Penny stood there watching, gobsmacked.

"She thought I was embarrassed," Dinah said with a laugh. "Sorry, did I not tell you I'm super possessive?"

"I think I'm embarrassed now," said Jenny, but she loved it.

Jack kept looking back and forth between them, his jaw hanging open. Penny looked pleased as punch.

"Look, this is happening," said Dinah. "Let's all be adults about it."

"Woooooo!!" cried a voice in falsetto. "Get it, girl!"

It was Mason Lockhart. He was bounding up to join them, and Jenny was surprised not only to see Drew with him, but both of them sporting wicked shiners too. They were laughing together like old friends.

"Is it true you guys murdered the funeral director?" asked Mason.

"No," Dinah said. "It was more of a suicide by hot springs."

"Nice!" said Drew and Mason together.

"What's this about?" Jenny asked, waving a finger between Drew and Mason. She was still buzzing from that kiss. She squeezed Dinah's hand tighter, and Dinah squeezed back.

"Ahh, you missed it," said Mason. "Some Harbor High fools thought they could crash the festival last night. Had us a little tussle."

"You got in a fight?" Penny frowned at Drew, disapproving.

"I didn't start it," said Drew, shrugging.

"But he finished it," Mason laughed and slapped Drew on the back. "My boy DrewTron laid some fools *out*! One of the bake sale MILFs was so impressed she slipped my dude her number."

"Did you call her?" asked Dinah.

Drew turned a bright shade of pink and said nothing.

"He totally did," said Jenny and was surprised to find that she and Mason were both laughing about it.

"Well at least you're not trying to kill my sister anymore," Jack said with a smirk.

"Mason and I came to an arrangement," Jenny said, giving Mason a wink. He furrowed his brow, shaking his head.

"You're lucky the insurance paid off," Mason said darkly. "Actually, I just got my new wheels. You guys want a ride?"

He walked over to his new ride, which was, of course, parked right up front in a disabled spot. It was a big open-top jeep.

"No more Challenger?" asked Penny.

"Dad said I had to get something more sensible," Mason grumbled.

"This is much better than that stupid penis metaphor car," Dinah said.

"It feels like the last day of school," Jenny said to no one in particular. There was no way she was giving this place up without a fight.

"It's October," said Penny.

"It is for her, though," said Mason. "Aren't you moving back to LA?"

"What?!" said Dinah.

"No, I'm not," Jenny assured her. "How did you hear about that?"

"Uh, let's see," said Mason. "My Econ teacher shows up at my house last night and gets in a big ole fight with my dad. Something about keeping secrets?"

Jenny winced. "Was it bad?"

"Well, they went in his room, and it got quiet for a while," said Mason, looking a little embarrassed himself. "Then they got loud... *You know.*"

"Oh my," said Penny.

"And then they started screaming at each other some more, and she stormed out," Mason said.

They all stood around in silence for a while, inwardly cringing at the thought.

"I didn't need to hear that about my aunt," said Jenny, though she had to admit she was a little impressed with Shelly for getting in some breakup sex.

"I didn't need to hear that about my teacher," said Drew.

"We should do a campout," Mason said, polishing the wheel well on his new lifted jeep. "Get out of town before all the little Trouble cosplayers show up for Halloween weekend."

"Totally," said Jack. "We can use my old treehouse."

Jenny's eyebrows shot up in alarm.

"Can't," said Dinah, turning to Jenny. "My mom is insisting on a weekend spa retreat after last night."

"Me neither," said Drew. "I've got a project due on Monday."

"Deadlines," said Penny.

Jenny's phone vibrated in her back pocket. She glanced at the screen and felt a rush of excitement when she saw who the email was from.

"What about you, psycho?" said Mason.

"Sorry, looks like I'm busy too," Jenny said, tucking her phone away.

"Everything okay?" asked Dinah.

"Yeah," Jenny said with a smile. "It's great."

"Fine, losers," said Mason, hopping into the driver's seat. "Text me when you get bored of being boring. You coming, Valentine?"

"Sure," said her brother. He whispered something in Penny's ear and joined Mason in his new ride. Mason backed out of his spot in a screech of rubber, leaving new skid marks on the asphalt as he raced off out of the lot.

"Douche," said Jenny.

"You gonna key that jeep too?" asked Dinah.

"I didn't!" Jenny said. "At least not the first time."

"Sure," said Penny.

"No, she didn't," said Drew, speaking up. "Actually… that was me."

"What?!" Jenny and Penny shouted in unison.

Drew shrugged, pretending to be contrite but obviously very proud of himself.

"He was being a dick to Jenny, and I was standing right there with my keys…" Drew said. "Your recklessness inspired me."

"Well done, sidekick," said Jenny. She turned to Dinah and gave her a quick hug. "I gotta go."

Dinah frowned, her hand lingering on Jenny's shoulder. "You better not be moving."

"I'm not. I'll text you."

She would have loved to stay but needed to get her shit from the treehouse before Jack and Mason got there.

And she had a very important person to meet.

Later that evening, Jenny walked into the Bad Egg, a dive bar a few blocks from Town Square.

The place smelled like stale beer and corn nuts. It was mostly empty. Just a few middle-aged guys playing darts, an old bartender with a silver-streaked ponytail, and a young brunette girl in the corner by the entrance. Jenny ignored her and took a seat at a table in the back, taking in the ambiance and the crunchy guitars of some old alt-rock band on the jukebox.

She ordered a cranberry juice and waited.

Fifteen minutes later, a slender woman with dark hair and an expensive purple Burberry trench coat entered the Bad Egg. It didn't escape Jenny's notice, or annoyance that this was the exact coat Trouble wore on all the book covers. And this chick had the tall, leggy body to pull it off, too. When she took off her big, white-rimmed sunglasses, she looked the spitting image of a young Valerie Valentine.

Her dark eyes roved the bar before honing in on Jenny. She strode over confidently and held out her hand.

"You must be Dee Dee," said Victoria Valentine. "I'm Tori."

Jenny was wearing her blonde wig in a ponytail this evening. It was the same style she'd worn a month ago when taking selfies as "Dee Dee Sharp," the made-up transferee to Blackbird Springs Academy who was obsessed with following in Tori Valentine's journalistic footsteps.

"Hello, Tori," said Jenny, adding a slight drawl to her voice. "Dee Dee Sharp. I'm a big fan."

Tori laughed in a husky timbre.

"Girls your age usually say that about my father, not me," said Tori. She spoke in a low, affected mid-Atlantic accent, like actors in old movies. Jenny found it to be a bit too much, while also totally coveting it.

"I was very sorry to hear about him," Jenny said. "My condolences."

"Thank you," said Tori, unable to hide a hint of annoyance. "What are you drinking?"

"Oh, just cranberry juice."

Tori turned without a word and stalked over to the bar. After some conversation with the bartender, she returned with two tall glasses of an orange and red concoction. A pink umbrella toothpick spearing a cherry and an orange slice floated in each. When Jenny tried hers, the aftertaste of vodka was unmistakable. She did her best not to make a face.

"What can I do for you, Dee Dee," said Tori, sipping her own drink.

"Well, I know how much you did for the school newspaper," she said. "And I just wanted to know if you could give me any advice at all on journalism, or school, or time management, or anything, really."

"Let's stick to one thing at a time," Tori said with another laugh.

"You've met Mr. White, I assume? Great teacher."

They began to talk, and Jenny was, in her opinion, pulling off an amazing performance as Dee Dee, the eager journalism student. They discussed all-nighters to make deadline, Mr. White's cheesy music taste, AP vs. Chicago Style Guides...

Jenny found Tori a delight to speak to, and just as sharp as advertised. After their second round of drinks, Jenny was half-convinced to devote herself to journalism and pursue a career in broadcast like her supposed idol Ashleigh Banfield. Anything to impress the incredibly cool and addictively charming Tori Valentine.

Jenny's southern drawl got thicker as they went deeper into their cups, and Tori let some NorCal slang slip into her vocabulary.

"It used to be hella crazy back in the day," she said, getting wistful. "We even had a key to the teacher's bathroom, and Lacey—my photo editor—was always sneaking off with her boyfriend Ben to make out whenever Mr. White fell asleep. I think she became a woman in the same stall Mr. Finch takes his morning constitutional in."

They both giggled furiously. Three drinks in, Jenny's watch vibrated with a special pattern, and she was forced to admit to herself that she was drunk. It felt amazing. She had never felt more confident and on top of her game.

"So tell me," Jenny said. "What made you get interested in journalism?"

"Oh, geez," said Tori, using her teeth to pull a cherry off the end of her pink umbrella. "Well, as you may or may not know, my father was a journalist way back when. He ended up preferring fiction, but I've always found the truth just as fascinating."

"Like true crime?" Jenny asked.

"Sure," Tori nodded, and this time Jenny caught a glint of malice in her smile. Her watch vibrated again in concern. "It used to just be a hobby, but now it's touched even my own family."

"What do you mean?"

"My poor father," Tori said sadly.

"You mean your real father?" Jenny asked, trying to play dumb.

"RJ Valentine is my real father," Tori said, the sweetness gone from her voice.

"Oh, sorry!" Jenny said, mortified. "I just thought—I mean—that was just an accident though, right?"

"Views differ on the matter," Tori said, full of disdain.

"What happened? Were you there?"

The conversation was finally turning to Jenny's purpose. She would get Tori's version of that fateful night at last.

"I talked to Dad earlier that night in his study," Tori said. "Then I went to the charity gala downtown and met Val. Everything was fine, and suddenly a few hours later Jack is calling me in a panic, says Dad's not moving…"

Jenny passed Tori a tissue and took another sip of her drink.

"But you think it wasn't an accident?" Jenny asked innocently.

"There's just no way Daddy would have fallen off that ladder," said Tori. "He climbed it 20 times a week, easy."

"And you were at the party the whole time?" Jenny asked, wiping her eyes. In her intoxicated state, Tori's story was really hitting her.

"More or less," Tori said, emptying her glass and tilting her head to study Jenny. "It's not as definitive an alibi as yours, but then, I got to eat my dinner with a fork."

Jenny's heart froze.

"What?" Jenny asked, a fake smile frozen on her flushed face.

"Don't get me wrong, I've been there," said Tori.

"Um…" Jenny had no idea how to react.

"But this is the end of the line for you, Jennifer."

Jenny gulped. The jig was up.

"Did you really think some cheap wig would fool me?" Tori asked. "Idiot."

"I've got a few tricks up my sleeve, Victoria," said Jenny, dropping the pretense and glancing at the tattoo on her arm. She'd hoped to sound menacing, but she'd slurred Tori's name. She was really wasted.

Tori sneered and gripped her wrist, examining her Ace of Clubs art.

"Sloppy," she declared. "I hope you didn't have to blow the tattoo artist for this. They're not supposed to ink little kids."

"I'm not that kind of girl," Jenny said, yanking her arm away and pulling it under the table to tap a panicked S.O.S. on her watch.

"Your southern accent sucks, by the way," Tori said, and Jenny noticed that she was much more collected and alert now, not affected by the booze at all.

"Oh, thanks, Haley Mills," said Jenny. "From you that really means a lot."

Tori yawned and got her compact out to touch up her flawless crimson lips. Jenny tried to focus on the table as the room began to spin.

"Why are you covering for Val?" Jenny asked through gritted teeth. "Where did she go that night?"

Tori's eye twitched. There it was: doubt.

"You don't know, do you?" Jenny said.

"Leave it alone," Tori said, but the conviction was gone from her voice.

"You know, I always did want a sister," said Jenny.

"I didn't," said Tori.

Jenny stood up unsteadily.

"Well it was nice meeting you anyway," she said, feeling nauseous. "I'd puke on you right now, but I don't think Dad would want us to fight."

She stumbled toward the sketchy-looking ladies room, about to vomit.

THE DOOR TO THE BATHROOM SHUT, AND JENNY'S RETCHING COULD be heard over the 90s grunge music blaring on the jukebox.

Tori retrieved her phone from her purse—the latest iPhone, of course—and tapped on the screen before holding it to her ear.

"Hey Blake," she said, cooing into the receiver. "That's right, I'm back, and I'm about to make your day... Just get over to the Bad Egg. There's a sloppy little *Troublemaker* over here just dying to get arrested for underage drinking."

Tori stood up and smoothed her purple coat.

"Exactly. A win-win."

Her stepsister hung up and tossed a $20 bill on the table. Before she left, Tori leaned over and dropped a small silver flask into Jenny's purse where she'd left it on the chair.

With a haughty toss of her long, dark hair, Tori Valentine strutted out, putting on those big white-rimmed sunglasses to block out the glare of the setting sun and never once glancing at the mousy brunette in the corner, who was hiding behind big bangs and bigger sunglasses of her own.

She counted to twenty before rising and walking to the ladies room.

Jenny was bracing herself with both hands over the sink. She turned at the sound of the door opening, her watering eyes full of relief.

Chapter Twenty-Eight
One Phone Call

A FEW MINUTES LATER SHE EXITED THE LADIES ROOM, WIPING HER mouth and adjusting her blonde wig. Jenny's purse was still on the chair, with the flask Tori planted in it. It was tempting to dispose of it, but getting caught in Tori's trap might be the perfect opportunity, so she left it in there as she exited the Bad Egg.

She'd hardly taken three steps before a siren whooped and a big Chevy Tahoe police SUV pulled up on the curb. Blake and a female officer exited, motioning for her to stop. She raised her hands in mock surrender.

"Come on, what now?" she said.

"Had some reports of a drunk and disorderly," said Blake.

"So?"

"So, they were about you," said the female officer, handing Blake a breathalyzer kit.

"Talk to the bartender," Blake said.

The officer nodded and entered the Bad Egg.

"I'm not old enough to drink," she said. "And like this town would care anyway."

"We take underage drinking very seriously here, Jennifer," said Blake. "Come on, blow."

He shoved a breathalyzer in her face. She rolled her eyes and blew on it, waiting for the result. It took all the discipline she had not to laugh when the device reported **0.0**.

"Maybe it's busted," said the officer, rejoining them.

"Okay then, I'll be going now," she said.

"Stop," said Blake, surprised but undeterred.

"Look, I wasn't actually drinking in there," she said. "It was just a ruse, and obviously it worked."

"Bartender says he could hear her puking her guts up in the bathroom," said the deputy.

Blake frowned and tapped the breathalyzer on his palm.

"Fine, let's do this the old-fashioned way," he said.

They put her through all the tests. The fingers on the nose, reciting the alphabet backward, walking in a straight line. She aced every one. Blake probably would have had to let her go if they hadn't found the flask in Jenny's purse.

"Hey, fourth amendment, man!" she protested.

"Probable cause," said Blake, getting his handcuffs out.

"Is this a good time to say I've never seen that before?" she asked.

"You have the right to remain silent…" the sheriff began.

"Oh this is bullshit! I passed all your tests! You probably planted that!"

"We'll do a full tox screen back at the station," Blake said to his deputy. "Even if you are some kind of drunken savant, you can't fake that test."

She sighed. It had only taken a day before Jenny was back in trouble with the law again.

Jenny had asked her aunt for one more weekend to talk her out of moving back to LA. It wasn't going well so far. Through a bureaucratic quirk that sounded entirely made up, the lady who processed the toxicology screens was out of town until Sunday. Since the cops could hold her for 48 hours, she'd be spending most of her weekend in a small jail cell in the back of the fancy downtown police station.

Perfect.

She didn't even ask for a phone call the first night. Blake told her that he'd called Shelly to let her know what was up and that her aunt had been so mad she'd declined to even come visit. It had to be past 10:00 PM by now, but he was still hanging around the station in his uniform.

"Was she mad at me, or at you?" she asked him.

"Very funny," he said with a scowl. "Thanks for the heads up on that, by the way."

"Oh don't get all 'poor me' now," she said. "You could have told her a long time ago if you hadn't been trying to use her."

"We're not having this conversation," he said and walked out of the holding area, flipping off the lights as he went.

"Prick!" she called after him in the dark.

Fortunately, no one else had been arrested, so she had the cell to herself. They'd taken her clothes and wig and given her an orange jumpsuit to change into. This outfit was probably inevitable, really.

Her first night in jail was full of niggling anxiety. It was impossible not to think about what would happen if the plan went wrong. If Blake faked the tox screen or cooked up some other evidence with Tori Valentine and she never got out of here.

In the morning, she was awoken by one of the deputies banging his baton on the cell bars. It felt like she'd hardly slept a wink. They let her use the restroom and fed her a breakfast of powdered eggs and imitation bacon, then it was back in her cell again.

She requested a book, and after a half hour, Deputy Mack handed her a dog-eared copy of *Here Comes Trouble* through the bars. It appeared to be Blake Lockhart's personal copy and was full of little notes in the margins, always in relation to the dopey Sheriff Lockhart character.

Bullshit
This would never happen
That's not the procedure
No one talks like this
I'm 6'2"

She allowed herself the small satisfaction of knowing how much Dad's books bothered Blake.

After lunch, they led her to a small room with a big mirror on one side and handcuffed her to the metal table within. A short while later, the door opened, and Blake entered, followed by Valerie Valentine.

"Great," she said. "This bitch."

Blake ignored her and held up a hand to stop Val.

"Your purse," he said flatly.

"Oh come on, you know me," Val said, annoyed.

"It's policy, Valerie," he said.

Val rolled her eyes and shoved her purse into Blake's well-sculpted stomach. He ignored the hostility and searched through her purse for a moment before setting it on the table and giving Val a cursory pat down.

"I'll be just outside," he said and left.

Val smoothed her cream-colored pantsuit and gingerly took a seat on the other side of the table, running a judgmental eye over her stepdaughter.

"Come to gloat?" she said.

"Hardly," said Val. "I wanted to thank you for stopping my cousin's killer."

"And saving your life?" she asked pointedly.

Val ignored the comment and went on. "I thought maybe I could return the favor by finding you facilities that are more... suitable to your needs."

Val pulled some brochures out. They looked like they were for fancy schools with names like the *Phoenix Behavioral Learning Center*, the *Bellevue St. Catherine's School for Proper Ladies*, the *Windsor Academy for Troubled Girls*...

"I like that one," she said, pointing at the last one.

"I thought you would," said Val. "The Foundation offers scholarships all the time. I'm sure we could work something out for you."

"Right, in a boarding school far away from Blackbird Springs," she said. "How convenient for you. This is a lot less than the $40 million you offered last time."

"Discipline and a good education are more than you deserve," Val said sharply. "And more than your pathetic aunt can offer. If you continue to cause problems for my family, you'll soon find yourself wishing these options were still on the table."

"You got a lot of nerve criticizing Shelly when it's *your* daughter who's a two-time rehab junkie."

Val slapped her across the face. Hard.

"How dare you bring Tori into this, you grasping little gutter trash!"

She could hear a commotion outside, and a moment later Blake was there, dragging Val out of the room.

"She hates you, Val! You know that, don't you?!" she called after her evil stepmother. "Your own blood loved my father more than you!"

The door to the interrogation room shut, and she was alone again with the boarding school brochures in front of her. A few minutes later, Aunt Shelly walked in with the sheriff. The tension between them was palpable. After gritting her teeth through a pat down and purse search, Shelly took a seat and stared at her with a sad smile on her face.

"You know, your mother had a temper just like yours," Shelly said.

"What was she angry about?" she asked. She knew so little about her mother.

"Everything," Shelly said with a far off, wistful smile. "Capitalism, Bush, the patriarchy, our parents, pop music..."

"Really?"

"I think it was always hard for Laura to reconcile her expectations with reality," said Shelly. "She just wanted so badly for the world to be a better place than it was."

Shelly reached over and brushed some hair out of her eyes.

"Sometimes I wonder what would have happened if she had made it back to RJ that day," said Shelly sadly. "He never told Laura that Val was pregnant too. And then suddenly, he's not returning her calls, and she hears that Val is in labor. Maybe it would have been your brother growing up without a mother."

Her jaw hung open. This was all new information.

"Do you think..." she paused, not sure how to put this without alarming Shelly. "Do you think maybe Val had something to do with the accident?"

"I don't know." Her aunt shrugged. "Maybe? No, I shouldn't say that. Look, all I know is, nothing good ever came from getting involved with that family."

She nodded, still thinking about Valerie Valentine and how to pay her back.

"Well, one good thing," Shelly corrected herself.

"What, the money?"

"Not the money," her aunt said, and squeezed her hand.

"Let's call it two good things," she said with a little grin. "What was she like? Mom, I mean. Besides angry."

"Laura was…" Her aunt swallowed hard. "She was the coolest girl I ever knew. She smoked cloves and listened to the Pixies and dated guys in bands. She could talk forever about politics or philosophy or Jane Austen and have us all hanging on her every word. You'd have liked her."

Shelly sighed and picked up one of the brochures.

"Maybe this wouldn't be such a bad idea," said her aunt.

"No way."

"You'd be pretty much guaranteed a good college if you graduate from one of these places," Shelly said. "And we could get Val to pony up for college too."

"I've got my own tuition plan," she said, pushing the brochures away. "Unless one of these places is literally effing Hogwarts, I'm not going."

"I'm still turning in my resignation on Monday."

"That's two days away. There's still tomorrow, once I get out."

Shelly shook her head and stood up. "I'm gonna go home and start packing. Do you need anything else while you're in here?"

"No. Wait—yes. Before you go, send Blake back in here," she said.

Shelly's whole body rippled in disgust.

"I should have listened to you," Shelly said. "He *is* a bastard."

"Don't worry. We'll get him back."

Blake returned a short while later to take her back to her cell.

"Hold up, I need something first," she said.

"You don't get to make demands here," said Blake.

"What about my one phone call?"

"You just talked to your aunt."

"That wasn't a phone call," she said. "Now come on, you owe me."

"Hamilton Webb isn't going to get you out of here any quicker if that's what you're thinking," said Blake.

"What I am thinking is none of your concern," she said. "Phone call. Now. ...Please?"

He groaned in annoyance and led her down the hall to his office.

"One call," he said, picking up the receiver and dialing a **9** on it.

She took the phone and leaned over the keypad, hoping she'd memorized the number correctly.

"I'd like some privacy, please," she told the sheriff.

He glared at her and walked a few paces away, keeping an eye on her as he talked to his deputy.

She dialed and crossed her fingers. After a few rings, someone answered.

"Hello?" said Drew.

"Hi, is this Mason Lockhart's new best friend?" Jenny said with a smirk.

"Very funny. Jenny? I thought you were like in jail," said Drew.

"I am."

"Then how are you— wait, am I your one phone call?"

"Yes, and you had better earn it," she said, knowing that Drew was easiest to deal with by simply ordering him around.

"I'm honored."

"Good, cause Trouble needs her sidekick. It's time for you to earn your ten percent."

"Uh sure. What do you need?"

"Lots," said Jenny. "In fact, you'd better grab a pen and paper. You're gonna want to write this down."

THE FOLLOWING MORNING, THE TEST RESULTS FOR HER TOXICOLOGY report came back: sober with flying colors.

"One of these days, you're gonna have to tell me how you pulled this off," said Blake.

"I told you, I wasn't drinking," she said.

"That's not what I heard," Blake said, grumbling.

"Look, Tori Valentine may think she's very clever, but she still fell for the oldest trick in the book."

"Which is?"

"The old switcharoo!" she said with a devilish grin. "Come on, Blake, are you a detective or what?"

He stared down at her, full of suspicion.

"I switched glasses when her back was turned," she said.

He clenched his fists, shaking his head at her.

"I know you're lying about something," he said.

"Well, I'm always lying about *something*."

Shelly arrived a short time later, and Mr. Webb was with her.

"Your 'lawyer' says our presence is requested at Valentine Manor," her aunt said, making finger quotes.

"I know, I requested it," she said. "But if it's all right with you, I'd really love to stop by the house real quick to shower and change. That is if you haven't packed up my clothes yet."

"This had better be good, Jennifer," said Shelly.

"Oh, it will be."

Chapter Twenty-Nine
An Impossible Bottle of Wine

A N HOUR LATER, JUST AS THE CLOCK STRUCK NOON, JENNY Valentine stepped back into her father's study. Almost everyone else was already here. Jack was seated in his father's chair at the desk, sipping something dark from a tumbler. Yvonne Griffin was on the couch by the fireplace, once again seated next to Alicia Aaron. Ms. Griffin was busy on her phone, but looked up and smiled at Jenny.

A large oil painting of RJ Valentine had been hung above the mantle. The artist had perfectly captured the mischievous grin tugging at the corners of Dad's mouth as he watched over them.

"Now what's this about, Hamilton?" said an older man with a snow-white beard sitting with his cane between his legs in one of the Louis XIV chairs: Mr. Carnegie.

"As I said on the phone, Horace, it concerns the disposition of RJ Valentine's will," said Mr. Webb.

Mr. Carnegie nodded, and though he noticed Jenny, he didn't seem pleased to see her this time.

"I still don't see what that has to do with us," said a young paramedic in uniform, leaning against the wall next to his partner. Jenny had passed by the ambulance in the big roundabout driveway outside.

"I'm told your services may be required," said Webb.

The paramedics shrugged and went back to checking football twitter on their phones. Shelly had followed Jenny into the study and was doing her best not to be impressed.

"Nice view, eh?" said Jenny, staring out the tall windows at the arresting vista.

"Don't get used to this," Shelly said.

"But what if you could?" asked Jenny, throwing an arm over her aunt's shoulder.

Shelly ignored her and wandered over to the fireplace because Blake Lockhart had just arrived. He was flanked by two of his deputies: Mack, and an older deputy named Calderon.

Lockhart took one glance at the room and scowled.

"You better not be wasting my time, Webb," he said.

"I'm told I will not be," said Mr. Webb.

Lockhart spotted Jenny, and the furrow in his brow grew deeper.

"Oh, screw this," he said, turning around.

"I promise it will be worth your while!" Jenny said.

"I highly doubt it," he said. "We just got a 211 on the radio, we don't have time for this nonsense."

"Wait!" shouted Jenny, following them out into the hall. "Come here."

She pulled the sheriff down to whisper something in his ear.

"ARE YOU FUCKING KIDDING ME?!" he screamed, eyes bulging.

"SHHH!!" Jenny hissed.

Shelly poked her head out of the study and gave the sheriff a scowl of deepest loathing. Jenny waved her away and angrily shushed the cop, hoping he didn't ruin her whole presentation.

"Relax, they have no idea," she whispered to him.

"WHY—why didn't you say so on Friday??" he whisper-shouted back.

"Because I didn't have proof yet, and I know how likely you are to take my word on anything," she said, fiercely locking eyes with him.

Lockhart held his head in his hands and groaned, rubbing his temples.

"Okay, when?" he asked after a little while.

"Soon, maybe a half-hour," Jenny said.

Lockhart nodded in disgust and turned to his deputies, talking softly to fill them in. They all rejoined the others in the study a minute later, and Jenny put on her best smile for Shelly to assure her that everything was fine. Deputies Mack and Calderon casually took up positions on both sides of the doorway.

"Can we get on with this," Mr. Carnegie asked. "This is a very difficult time for my family, and I need to get back to them."

"Still waiting for my assistant," Jenny said in chipper spirits. "Oh!" she turned back to Lockhart, remembering something. "When you get a call about that 211, tell them to bring the suspect straight here."

"What?" he asked.

"Bring the perp here," she repeated. "Trust me, it'll make sense when they call."

The sheriff heaved an extremely bitchy sigh and made it halfway to the mini bar before stopping himself and cursing under his breath. He walked behind the desk instead and took up a position in the corner.

"Hey Jack, come here for a sec," Jenny said, moving to the mini bar herself.

"What?" he said, strolling over.

Jenny waved at the many bottles and crystal decanters of expensive liquor.

"Which one of these would Dad have not been caught dead drinking?" Jenny asked.

He raised an eyebrow and surveyed the bar's stock.

"Uh, this, I guess," he said, pointing to an unopened bottle of Johnnie Walker Gold Label Reserve. "Dad never drank whiskey, only scotch."

"Hmm, okay. Don't drink any of this," said Jenny.

"You called me over here for that?" Jack said, annoyed.

"No, so I could steal your chair too!" said Jenny, springing back to the desk to grab dad's chair before he could.

Drew and Penny arrived shortly. They were walking slowly and carrying something long and narrow between them: the screen Jenny and Drew had used to make their Big Board.

"Oh, excellent!" said Jenny. "Set that up over there, against the bookshelves."

Drew frowned at the sight of the paramedics but did as he was instructed.

"Penny, what are you doing here?" asked her mother from across the room.

"Oh, just helping out," said Penny. "Hi, Jack!"

Penny waived to Jack, whose grim expression vanished at the sight of the yearbook editor. After a couple minutes, they had it all set up but Drew left it furled for now. They'd worked out a loose agenda on the phone, and he knew his cues.

Jenny stood, placing her hands on the mahogany desk surface. She glanced at the green banker's desk lamp, the calendar blotter, the crystal paperweight in the shape of a chess piece. Reaching out, she hefted the bishop, weighed it in her hand for a moment, and put it back, nodding. Everything was in place. Now to begin.

"Thank you all for coming," Jenny said, twirling to take in her audience. "As you all know, my name is Trouble. I've gathered you here today to solve not one mystery, but two."

"Shouldn't my mother be here for this?" asked Jack, who had found himself a seat in the other Louis XIV chair. He was leaning out from behind Penny, who had found herself a seat in his lap.

"She'll be along, Junior," said Jenny with a wink. "Don't worry, we've got a lot to cover. First, I wanted to talk a little about what happened with the Undertaker the other night. I know there are lots of rumors going around, and it's time you all heard the full story."

Jenny couldn't resist the urge to glance Mr. Carnegie's way. His face behind his fluffy white beard had flushed pink like a zesty rosé, best paired with grilled asparagus, warm brie, and criminal intent.

"If only there were some official avenue for you to tell that story. Like—oh, I don't know: the police statement you were supposed to give us on Friday," said the sheriff, still grumpy.

"Don't start with me, Lockhart," said Jenny. "You kept me in jail for two days on the word of a notorious lush."

"Eat me, Jenny," said a voice from the doorway. The two deputies' hands darted for their holsters—

—And relaxed just as fast when they saw it was only Tori Valentine striding in.

"I don't believe I invited you," said Jenny, who had nonetheless been hoping Tori would get wind somehow and show up. Excellent. This would all work much better if she could trigger a genuine reaction from her stepsister.

"This is my house," said Tori, taking a seat on the front of Dad's desk. "I don't need an invitation."

"Yeah, about that…" said Mr. Webb.

"Can we just get on with this?" said Lockhart.

"Niners just scored, if anyone cares," said one of the paramedics, looking up from his phone.

Drew pumped a fist.

"*Anyway*," said Jenny, "Where this story really begins is with a bottle of wine. An impossible bottle of wine."

She nodded to Drew, who took a big breath and reached up to unfurl the Big Board. Drew had argued against unveiling everything they had, but Jenny insisted that if they were going to solve the mystery, they had to put all their cards on the table. Jenny suspected he didn't entirely believe in her theory and wanted to hedge his bets.

The other contestants and guests stared at their handiwork: pictures of heirlooms and heirs, maps, documents, even a coaster from the Winchester. They'd used color-coordinated yarn to tie all the threads together. Nearly everyone present could find their own picture up there somewhere.

A gargled cry rang out on her right.

"Oh shit! Is he stroking out?" Penny shouted.

Mr. Carnegie had collapsed out of his chair into the thick carpet and was twitching like a stuck pig.

"Give him air!" someone cried.

"Yeah, I thought that might happen," Jenny said as the paramedics rushed over. "But you could have waited until I was done with my story, you old fraud!"

"Jennifer!" Aunt Shelly was appalled.

"That goldbricker tried to have me killed!" Jenny yelled, stabbing a finger at the man on the floor. "Who do you think his son-in-law was working for?"

"Shit, this guy's coded," said the other paramedic.

What followed was a couple minutes of half-hearted CPR, followed by an awkward silence.

"Call it," said the first medic.

"12:32 PM," said the other.

Tori craned her neck around from her perch on the desk to sneer at Jenny.

"You're doing great so far, sweetie," she said.

"Shut up," Jenny said. "Like you'd be doing better."

"I would be," said Tori.

"All right, get him out of here," said Lockhart in disgust.

The mood was decidedly less buoyant after they wheeled Mr. Carnegie's body away on a gurney, and Jenny worried that she was losing the room.

"Thus passes the paterfamilias of the Carnegie family," said Mr. Webb, raising his rocks glass.

Everyone else murmured a polite platitude or amen and took a drink. Jenny found a red sharpie in one of dad's desk drawers and marched over to a cluster of photos connected to Valerie Valentine's bottle of *Ressort Rouge*. She drew a big red **X** over Mr. Carnegie's photo and returned to her place at RJ's desk.

"An impossible bottle of wine," Jenny said again. "For the uninitiated, let me tell you a story about a Haunted Vineyard, and the bottle of red that made it fam—goddamnit!"

A crackle from the police radios had cut her off. She glared at the interruption. Lockhart ignored her and clicked the button on his shoulder

"Go ahead," the sheriff said.

"Hey boss," said a distorted female voice on the radio, "We just picked up a perp on that 211 at Easy Storage, and she's insisting on speaking with you."

"So? Book her," said Lockhart.

"But uh… It's Valerie Valentine," said the radio.

"What?" said Lockhart.

"What?" said Tori and Jack.

"The perp?" Lockhart was stunned.

"That's a roger, boss," said the radio.

Lockhart looked back at Jenny. She nodded.

"Bring her to Valentine Manor," he said into the radio. "We're in the study."

"You sure?" asked the radio.

"Yeah, over and out," Lockhart clicked off his radio and gave Jenny a significant look. "More of your handiwork?"

"Maybe," Jenny said. "Don't get ahead of me."

She paused, trying to remember how she had rehearsed this.

"An impossible bottle of wine..." she repeated to herself. "Fuck, this is taking too long, and now my timing is off... Okay, the basic points are these:

"One: *Ressort Rouge* wine can only be made at Pinefall because of some special dirt and stuff that Drew's mom could explain if you're really interested."

"The *terroir*," said Tori.

"Two," said Jenny. "Since Pinefall is a barren wasteland, no more *Ressort Rouge* can be made. Therefore, three: these bottles are so rare now they sell for at least fifty grand a pop."

Shelly whistled. Leave it to the Economics teacher to appreciate the supply and demand part of her presentation.

"Cut to a few months ago," Jenny said. "Horace Carnegie's housekeeper sends my dad a bottle of *Ressort Rouge* as a birthday gift from the Carnegies. See, she wrapped up the wrong bottle by mistake. There's no way that cheap bastard would send Dad a rare, expensive bottle like that. Carnegie flips out and fires the housekeeper, and RJ Valentine—sensing something funny going on—hires her on to work here. It that all correct, Mrs. Rivas?"

Mrs. Rivas poked her head out from behind the study door where she'd been eavesdropping in the hallway.

"Um, yes, I suppose," Mrs. Rivas said.

"Thank you, ma'am," said Jenny. "So. Dad's got this impossible bottle of wine. Where did it come from? He'd already bought the last one in existence a few years back for his 15th anniversary. Or so he thought. Enter Declan Dillion. Declan was the one who hunted down that bottle for Dad, and Declan Dillion had a gambling problem. So where did Declan get his bottle of *Ressort Rouge?* The Undertaker!"

"I'm already lost," said Jack.

"You should have saved Declan for later," Tori chided her.

"Hush!" Jenny yelled at them. "Rachael Martin, the last surviving member of the Martins—the family who used to run Pinefall—she wanted to be buried with the secret recipe of *Ressort Rouge.* And guess who handled her funeral?"

"The Undertaker," said Penny, getting it. "But the blind sommelier told us the recipe would be useless without the special grapes from Pinefall."

"Exactly!" said Jenny, getting excited. "This one really stumped me for a while. But if you'll recall, the blind sommelier also told us that they recovered a few cases from the Pinefall basement that were, quote, 'untouched by the fire.' If the basement was untouched by the fire, then the soil underneath it was too."

Jenny produced a blue and red LED lightbulb from her bag.

"That broken glass we found at the Haunted Vineyard: it's from one of these," said Jenny. "A grow light. The Undertaker has been running a secret grow operation in the Pinefall basement for months, with help from Mr. Carnegie and a couple other accomplices."

"Ohhh," said Ms. Griffin, putting it together herself now. "And the bottle they gave Declan was to test on your father. If they could fool

RJ and Valerie, they could fool anyone."

"And start selling the wine in secret for fifty thousand dollars a bottle," said Jenny. "They didn't have the room to grow many grapes, but at those prices, it was worth it. That's like half a million a case."

"It's six hundred thousand," corrected Tori.

"Wait, you're saying Declan Dillion was in on this too?" asked Lockhart.

"I'm not sure," Jenny admitted. "I don't think so though, at least not entirely. From the way the Undertaker talked, it sounded like the wine forgers used him to test a bottle and probably paid him off for it. I'm betting he hadn't thought about it again until the will reading. He started asking questions, and the Undertaker got nervous and killed him. It was only dumb luck that I was at the Cellars with him when it happened. They almost killed me too."

For Jenny's purposes, she had to put Declan's murder on the Undertaker. Only the Stranger knew otherwise.

"This all sounds fascinating, but you've offered no proof so far," said Deputy Calderon.

"I'm getting there," she said, walking over to the Big Board.

Before she could continue, they heard conversation coming from outside the study.

"Niners scored again," said a voice.

"Bout time we got us a real QB," said another.

Those two city workers rounded the corner and waved hello. Dave was sporting a tool belt. Andy was holding a clipboard.

"We hear you got a gas leak needs fixing?" said Andy. He glanced around the room, and his eyes widened when he saw the Big Board. "Aw shit!"

The two deputies and Lockhart already had their pistols out.

"Freeze!"

"Arrest those men!" Jenny yelled, relishing the moment. "For conspiracy to murder, money laundering, and wine fraud!"

"Wine fraud isn't a thing," said Lockhart through gritted teeth.

Andy and Dave's hands shot up in surrender immediately.

"We'll plead!" Dave said as Deputy Mack cuffed him. "It was all Carnegie's idea! We can give him to you on a platter!"

"Shut up, Dave!" yelled Andy. "We don't know nothing."

"Bad news, guys," said Jenny. "You got no one left to plead out on. Carnegie's dead."

Andy swore and sagged into Calderon's arms.

"Wait, before they go!" Jenny hurried over.

"I give you the Ghost of Pinefall," Jenny said and yanked off Dave's shoe. She held it up next to her plaster cast of the footprint they found at Pinefall. The sole of his shoe was a perfect match.

"What are those creases in the sole from, anyway?" asked Drew.

"Standing on telephone pole pegs all day," said Andy in resignation.

"Dinah and I must have surprised this guy at Pinefall, and he dropped the lightbulb," said Jenny. "And we couldn't see where the footprint came from because they'd hidden the cellar doors under a pile of old vines."

"Look, you got us," said Dave. "But can we get out of here? Gas leaks are serious business."

"Davey, there was no gas leak," said Andy.

"Oh. Ohhhhh," said Dave.

Jenny beamed. Even Aunt Shelly seemed impressed. Her aunt had always tried to discourage Jenny's namesake tendencies, and she was finally witnessing just how clever Trouble could be. Ms. Griffin was snapping photos with her phone, and Alicia Aaron had gotten up to get a closer look at the Big Board.

While the rest of them basked in her genius, Jenny walked over

293

to the mini bar and used a napkin to pick up that bottle of Johnnie Walker.

"If you need more physical evidence, there's this bottle that the Undertaker sent to Dad," Jenny said, carrying it over to Lockhart. "It's supposed to be poisoned. Also, there's a whole money laundering angle here that I won't go into, but would probably interest you, Mr. Webb. They were using fake *Trouble* memorabilia to launder the wine profits through The Poison Pen. It was all very ingenious, really. You can find ledgers and records that lay out the whole scheme in the basement under Pinefall. It's all waiting for you, untouched. Well, mostly untouched. You're welcome."

"That's good because the D.A. would throw me out of his office if I showed up with a footprint made out of play-doh," said Lockhart.

"So, is it your supposition that these wine forgers were responsible for RJ Valentine's death?" asked Mr. Webb, stroking his chin.

"Actually, no," said Jenny. "That's where the second mystery comes in, and our guest of honor is here just in time."

The others turned to witness Valerie Valentine being led into the room, followed by the female officer whose name Jenny had learned was Peña. Val looked flustered and hostile, like a cornered animal.

"What the hell is going on?" demanded Val, as haughty as ever.

"Hello, Valerie," said Jenny. "I was just solving your mystery."

Chapter Thirty
Double Trouble

JACK ATTEMPTED TO GIVE HIS MOTHER A BRIEF SUMMARY OF THE wine forgers until he botched it too many times and Tori cut in to take over.

"I still can't believe Horace Carnegie would stoop that low," said Val.

"I don't know, mother, the Carnegie vineyard has been struggling for years," said Tori. "They really took a bath on some real estate during the last housing bubble."

"Plus, the whole thing only works with Carnegie," said Lockhart, clearly annoyed that Jenny was right. "No one's buying rare wine from Chuck Slater and these two bozos. They'd need the Carnegie name and reputation. Not to mention his contacts in the wine biz."

Everyone nodded. Even Andy and Dave.

"All right, Mack and Calderon, get these guys out of here and check out Pinefall once they're processed," said the sheriff. "Darcy, you stay."

The male deputies escorted the city workers out, taking the bottle of tainted whiskey with them. Officer Peña stayed behind, remaining in position behind Val.

"Thus concludes the wine bottle mystery," said Jenny.

"I feel like it needs a name," said Drew. "*The Bloody Bottle*."

"Gotta have 'Trouble' in the title," Jenny corrected him.

"Trouble at the Haunted Vineyard," suggested Jack.

"Trouble isn't as Smart as She Thinks," said Tori.

"The Trouble with Tannins," said Drew.

Jenny snapped her fingers and pointed at her sidekick. "Nailed it."

"Hold on," said Alicia Aaron. "If the wine dudes didn't have anything to do with the real killer, then why'd you just spend all that time talking about them?"

"Because I thought it was an interesting story," said Jenny, glaring at the redhead. "And I almost got killed several times investigating it. Also, I was waiting for Val to get here. Also, shut up."

"I don't understand," said Aunt Shelly. "If those guys didn't kill your father, then why was the wine bottle one of the heirlooms?"

"Because Dad didn't know for sure which clue was the real deal," said Jenny. "Each of these heirlooms is a clue to *a* mystery, and he figured at least one of them was connected to whoever was threatening him, but he had no way of knowing which one. Otherwise, he would have solved it himself.

"Ironically, the Undertaker *did* try to poison Dad with that whiskey, but his tastes ran too cheap for RJ, and someone else got to Dad first."

"Who?" asked Val.

"You," said Jenny.

No one spoke. Everyone slowly turned to stare at Val.

"Oh not this nonsense again," said Val, rolling her eyes.

"Hey Val, where'd you just come from?" Jenny asked. "It sounded like you got caught trying to break into a storage shed like a common criminal."

"That has nothing to do with this!" Val hissed. "Just a stupid misunderstanding with that idiot at Easy Storage. And I don't appreciate being hauled around by your deputies like some low-rent hoodlum."

Lockhart offered the slightest of eyebrow raises, somehow communicating condescension, suspicion, and offense all in a single facial twitch.

"I'd say it's very relevant, but I'll get to it in due course," said Jenny. "First, let's walk through motive, means, opportunity."

"Fine, but I'm having a drink now," said Lockhart, heading to the mini bar. "Unless there's another surprise I'll need to be ready for?"

"Nah, you're good," said Jenny.

"Michelle?" Lockhart asked, gesturing to Aunt Shelly with a crystal scotch decanter.

Shelly communicated her distaste for the sheriff with a full body shiver and fixed herself a wine spritzer instead.

"Whatever," said Jenny. "The motive. Did Valerie Valentine have reason to want her husband dead? I'd say so. Forget about the money and the Stratford family's own diminishing coffers. You fucking hated him. Ever since he cheated on you with my mother. Go look at any photo of these two over the years. Talk about your frigid ice queens."

Val's hand darted out in a vicious slap, but Jenny had anticipated this and dodged it this time. Good, she needed Val angry.

"You have no idea what you're talking about!" Val said, invisible lightning crackling around her.

"Do you deny the relationship was strained?" asked Jenny.

"Marriages are hard work," said Val. "It's not all—you know what? I don't have to sit here and let myself be insulted by this little—"

"Hey!" yelled Shelly.

"Val, every player has the right to propose a solution to the mystery," said Webb, pushing his horn-rimmed glasses up on his nose and sipping his drink. "You'll be allowed the same should you ever wish to start playing instead of trying to pay off teenage girls to falsely accuse me."

Val's eyes widened in surprise.

"Yeah, I recorded that whole convo and played it back for the lawyer," said Jenny. "Really not helping your case, is it?"

Jenny walked back to her place behind RJ's desk.

"Is it agreed that the motive is sufficient?" she asked.

"When it's the spouse, you don't even need a motive," said Lockhart.

"Excellent. Now let's see…" Jenny bit her lip, trying to decide which piece of evidence to present next. The wine forgers were a fun test, but this would require her finest performance. She looked over at Tori, perched on the desk corner. "What do you think, little miss smartypants? Should I blow up her alibi first, or the locked-room part of it next?"

Tori had turned a shade paler and had no retort this time. Jenny shifted her attention to the portrait of her father over the fireplace. How would Dad have done it?

"Let's do the locked-room part first," Jenny said. She stepped over to the bookshelf by the window and knocked twice. "Come on out!"

There was a satisfying *clunk!* and the first five shelves swung outward to reveal a secret door. Dinah Black stepped out.

"Finally!" Dinah said, giving Jenny a saucy glare and handing her a crimson and black rose.

"Oh thank you!" Jenny said, blushing.

The tall cheerleader, who had stripped down to a couple layered tank tops, wiped her brow and tossed her purple Cheer windbreaker onto the desk.

"As you can see, this room isn't so locked after all," said Jenny. "Big mistake having that meeting in the conservatory where this passage let's out, Val. You can see in the soil where the other side opens."

Tori was staring at Jenny with the kind of bitter disappointment that could only mean Dad had never told his adopted daughter about the existence of this secret passageway.

"Did Mr. Carnegie really die?" asked Dinah, helping herself to an iced wine spritzer.

"Lol, yeah," said Drew.

Jenny walked a short way into the passage and lifted up a heavy cardboard box. She brought it back and set it on the desk.

"What's that?" asked Lockhart.

"It's a surprise!" Jenny said with sparkling eyes. "Of course Dad would have designed this place with secret passageways. And your brother was the chief architect of Valentine Manor, so don't pretend like you didn't know it was there, Val. Let's call that Means."

Val swallowed, perhaps a bit more cautious, but still defiant.

"I was at the gala all night," she said.

"Were you?" Jenny stalked over to the Big Board. "Mr. Webb, Lockhart, I'd like to draw your attention to these photos of the charity gala on the night of the attack, pulled from social media. Please note the time stamps."

"What am I looking for?" asked the sheriff, peering closer.

"Those are all of Val, right?" Jenny said.

"Sure," he said.

"Wrong. Look again. The one on the right isn't Val, it's Tori."

Jenny turned to face Tori Valentine, who appeared lost in thought now, lips pursed in confusion. Val's defiance had vanished along with all color from her face.

"I'm sure you have a good explanation for why you were pretending to be your mother that night," said Jenny.

Tori opened and closed her mouth, saying nothing.

"Honey…" Val began to speak, then stopped. "Maybe we should continue this with my attorney present."

"Well, you *do* have the right to remain silent, Valerie," Jenny said, feeling a surge of bitter hatred for the woman. She looked back to Mr. Webb and the sheriff. "You won't find a photo of Val at the gala after eight o'clock that night. Only Tori, wearing Val's outfit and masque."

"In case anyone forgot, Val called RJ Valentine from the gala at about 7:45 PM that night," said Drew, reading from a report taped to the board. "The housekeeper can confirm this. And Jack found RJ at about 9:10."

"Is that enough time to make it up to the mansion and back from the ballroom?" Jenny asked the room.

The study had gone deathly quiet.

Yvonne Griffin glanced up from her notepad.

Val's face was frozen; beautiful and unreadable.

Alicia Aaron looked to the sheriff, and he flinched as though something had passed between them.

Jack was gripping the arms of his chair, white-knuckled.

"I'd say so," said Lockhart.

"Oh wait—what's this?" Jenny said numbly, letting the excitement drain away from her performance. She reached out and moved a piece of paper aside on the board to reveal another photo from the gala. "I did find one more photo of Val at the gala. This one was taken at 9:04 PM. Have a look at her high heels."

Jenny grabbed a magnifying glass from Dad's pen holder on his desk and gave it to Mr. Webb.

"The left one," she said.

"Some kind of orange smudge?" said Webb

"Hey Dinah, can I have your shoe?" Jenny said.

"That's a little creepy," said Dinah.

"I'll give it back," Jenny said.

Dinah handed her shoe to Jenny. It was a white Keds cross-trainer. Jenny held it up for Mr. Webb and Lockhart to examine. Tori had joined them, looking intently at the evidence. There was a scuff of reddish-orange dirt on the heel of Dinah's shoe.

"It's the soil from the conservatory," said Jenny quietly. "Very distinct. The color comes from high iron content. It's good for flowers. Hard to avoid getting on your shoe if you're not careful, though."

Tori turned to Val, her eyes misting up.

"You told me it would be a fun game to see if people could tell the difference between us," Tori said.

"Be quiet, Victoria!" snapped Val.

Jack's jaw was hanging open in disbelief. This was going to hurt her brother, Jenny knew, but it was necessary.

"Just tell 'em where you were, Mom," Jack said.

"I... I received a threatening note that evening," Val said, her throat hoarse. "It said to come to the conservatory alone, and keep it a secret, so I did. I waited 15 minutes, and no one came, so I went back to the gala."

"You said you had a bathroom emergency and disappeared for a while..." Tori trailed off. She stood frozen for a moment before walking out of the study without another word.

Officer Peña looked to Lockhart in question. He shook his head, and she stayed put and let Tori go.

"Do you still have this note?" Lockhart asked.

"No, I burned it," Val said, her face a mask of bitter regret.

"Motive, means, and opportunity," said Jenny.

It was time for the coup de grâce. She glanced up at the portrait of RJ again. Dad would appreciate this.

"Now what about the murder weapon?" Jenny asked. "I've got a theory about this. With compliments to Drew for the suggestion, of course. And like any good theory, we can test it."

Drew glowed with pride as Jenny pulled a stapled document off the Big Board.

"According to the M.E. report, RJ was struck with something narrow, rounded and blunt," Jenny said. "Well, that sounds a lot like this guy."

She picked up the crystal paperweight of the bishop chess piece from RJ's desk.

The others leaned closer in wonder.

"RJ Valentine's paperweight is a well-known affectation of his. So popular that they gave away replicas of it at the gala the night of the attack. And this?" She tossed the chess piece up and down in her hand. "This is not the real one. It's too light. It's plastic. A replica from the gala."

No one spoke. She had them spellbound.

"I should also mention that when I sat at this desk two months ago, the real one was here," said Jenny. "So where is it now?" She laughed mirthlessly and nodded to Penny Griffin. "This is where I had to get a little underhanded to test my theory. Sorry Val, but that call you got from Easy Storage earlier today was actually Penny. She gives great phone."

Jenny could almost see the bottom drop out of Val's stomach.

"You set me up," Val said.

"You set yourself up," Jenny said. "Penny, what'd you say on the phone to Mrs. Valentine?"

Penny squirmed in her chair, feeling Jack's hot gaze of betrayal.

"I didn't know what this was for when I made the call," Penny said nervously. "I told her that I was the storage place and that Declan Dillion had a unit there. I said that Val was the emergency contact, and the rent needed paying or they'd auction off everything that was in it."

"That's why you got arrested at the storage place?" said Jack. He scowled at Lockhart. "Well, that's not fair. She thought she had a right to the place!"

"You're missing the point, Jack," Jenny said tenderly. "I thought if Val did have the murder weapon, the only way it would ever make another appearance was if she tried to frame someone else with it. I've been sorta trying to incept Val with the idea that Declan Dillion would be a good suspect in Dad's murder. The storage unit was a test, and I think your mother failed."

"Did she have anything on her, Darcy?" the sheriff asked.

"Some bolt cutters and her purse," said Peña. "It's in the truck."

"Go get her purse," Lockhart said.

The officer jogged out of the study.

"You planted it on me somehow," said Val quietly. "You're framing me."

"How? I've been in jail all weekend," said Jenny.

"You got out this morning," Val mumbled.

"Excuse me, but I've been with my daughter from the moment she was released," said Shelly. "I even went out back and watched her upstairs window while she was changing to make sure she didn't try to sneak out and run away."

"Hey!" said Jenny.

"You *did* threaten to," said Shelly.

"I was there too," said Mr. Webb. "I can verify that Miss Valentine came nowhere near you, Val."

"Before, then…" Val's voice had gone nearly inaudible.

Jack looked horrorstricken.

"Valerie, I checked your purse yesterday when you visited Jenny in the holding room," said Lockhart. "There was no crystal bishop in it then."

Peña jogged back into the room. She was wearing black latex gloves now and holding Val's leather Dolce & Gabbana Sicily Bag.

"You check it yet?" Lockhart asked.

Peña shook her head and set the purse on Dad's vast mahogany desk. She handed the sheriff a pair of gloves and took up position behind Val again.

Everyone had gathered around to watch.

Lockhart flipped over the purse and emptied out the contents. A loud object thumped onto the desk.

It was the crystal bishop paperweight.

Val began to cry.

Jack fainted. Penny caught him.

Peña had her handcuffs out, and Lockhart numbly read Val her Miranda rights.

For a moment, Jenny was overcome with emotion. She was sick to her stomach. She thought she might have another panic attack. She glanced at Dad's portrait. This was how it had to go.

The feeling passed. Barely.

"If that comes back with my Dad's DNA on it, would you say I solved the mystery?" Jenny asked Mr. Webb.

"I'd say so, yeah," said Mr. Webb.

"Well…" Jenny tore open the top of the cardboard box Dinah had brought with her through the secret passageway. "Anyone want to find out what a $50,000 bottle of wine tastes like?"

Lockhart glared daggers at her. Jenny pulled out a pristine new bottle of *Ressort Rouge*.

"Like I said, 'mostly untouched,'" she told the sheriff.

"That's evidence."

"You can have a bottle," said Jenny as Officer Peña led a whimpering Valerie Valentine away. "Everyone can. *Resort Rouge*, 2019 vintage. I hear it's a good year, for wine."

THE FORENSICS TEAM FOUND TRACES OF BLOOD ON THE REAL CRYSTAL bishop hiding in Val's purse. Someone had tried to wipe it down with bleach, but they missed a few spots in the little crannies of the bishop's hat. Or nose, whatever. DNA evidence came back on Wednesday. It was an absolute match for RJ Valentine.

Val was claiming now, through her lawyer, that she'd only gone to the storage unit to search for clues, and that she'd been set up somehow, which was why none of her fingerprints were found on the murder weapon.

There would be a trial, of course. But where Jenny was concerned, only Hamilton Webb's judgment mattered, and according to him, Jenny had done it.

She'd solved the mystery.

She'd won.

It would take a couple weeks to process all the financial stuff, and there were tons of documents to sign, but Jenny and Shelly were allowed to move into Valentine Manor right away.

Jenny's first request was that each of the other players receive two percent of RJ's assets as a token of good will, and a thank you from the Valentine estate for participating. Jenny hoped it would keep them happy, and unmotivated to ask further questions. Drew got his ten percent. They'd work on the bathtub with ass-jets part later.

Alicia Aaron immediately accepted her cut. Jenny still didn't trust her.

Jack wasn't speaking to Jenny now and had rejected the money outright. She even offered him his old room back, but he refused it. She hoped he would come around eventually. Meanwhile, Tori had disappeared again. If Jack knew where she was, he wasn't saying. He and Penny were nearly inseparable now, which meant she no longer spoke to Jenny or Drew much either.

Ms. Griffin and Sheriff Lockhart both asked for their shares to be put into trusts for Penny and Mason, respectively.

Val didn't get a share, obviously.

Shelly had threatened to do the noble thing and stay at the grandparents' house, rather than indulge in the frivolous opulence of Valentine Manor. That lasted until Jenny got her aunt to try the in-house chef's cooking. They moved in the Saturday after Valerie Valentine's arrest. Mr. Webb even arranged to hire movers for them, and they didn't have to lift a finger themselves. Jenny was able to simply walk right in, her brand new iPhone in one hand, an iced latte in the other, and claim her birthright.

She chose Jack's old bedroom for her own. Only until he wanted it back, Jenny told herself. The big naval painting had stayed when Jack moved out, and Jenny found herself staring up at it while chatting with Dinah on the phone all evening. Life had been so busy that there hadn't been time yet for a proper date. They had one on the books for next week, though. Jenny couldn't wait.

She drifted off to sleep under a wondrously soft comforter, thinking that her life was already a waking dream…

With a sudden start, Jenny's eyes snapped open. It was dark all around her, and she didn't recognize her surroundings. After several seconds of panicked breathing, she remembered that she was in Valentine Manor. Her brother's old room. She lived here now.

Her nightmare was already fading, but the horrible emotions lingered.

Guilt. Incredible guilt.

What had woken her up? She closed her eyes and tried to recall the noise she'd heard. A creaking sound on the windows, like from a change in the air pressure.

Someone else was in the mansion.

Jenny slid out of bed and groped for her clothes, not wanting to risk a light. She slipped on her track jacket hoodie and some jeans, tucked her new phone into her pocket, and padded silently out of her room on her bare feet.

There was a stairway a short walk down the hall. Jenny crept down to the first floor, stopping every few seconds to listen. All she heard was the rushing wind outside, and her own imagination playing tricks on her. In the silver moonlight, Jenny could see that the kitchen was empty.

She eased a carving knife out of the block on the counter and stole down the corridor with it, ready to stab the first thing that moved.

All the way to the foyer, nothing did.

The front door was closed tightly and locked. Jenny might have turned back then, if she hadn't caught a glint of light down the opposite hall, from the west wing of the mansion. She moved on, willing her fears aside. Had the Stranger come for her at last?

The door to RJ's study was ajar. Creamy yellow light shone from within.

Jenny eased the door open an inch or two wider and peered inside. The banker's lamp was on, illuminating the study in a soft, warm glow. Deep red curtains had been drawn over the tall windows. Dad's high-backed chair was facing away from his desk.

With reckless courage, Jenny slipped into the study; she crossed around to the side of the desk; the chair was turning; her knife was raised to strike—

The young woman in the chair covered her mouth to stifle a scream.

Jenny nearly dropped the knife, relief and annoyance flooding into her veins to chase the adrenaline away.

"Goddamnit, you scared the shit out of me!" Jenny whispered. "What are you doing here? I thought we agreed, not until tomorrow?"

"I'm sorry, Trouble, but I'm freezing my tits off in that treehouse! And plus, I— I just couldn't wait any longer."

She said it in the same voice as Jenny's, and with the same face. Because they were twins. Identical twins. With matching Ace of Clubs tattoos to boot.

Jenny set the knife down and embraced her sister.

"We did it," Jenny whispered in her ear.

"Do you think they suspect?" asked her sister.

"You? Not a chance," said Jenny. "But Val's gotta know we framed her somehow, and Tori's out there in the wind. We need to keep an eye on her."

"Alicia Aaron too," said her sister. She produced an open bottle of *Ressort Rouge 2019* from somewhere and took a swig. "That girl is way too nosy. She already found the spot from Mom and Dad's photo."

"She'll never figure out what it means. Still, it would help if you'd stop bumming cigarettes off her," said Jenny, lightly scolding her twin, who winced sheepishly.

"I quit, I swear."

"You better have," said Jenny. "Gimme some." She grabbed the bottle of wine and took a swig of her own. A crisp, tart sensation like pepper and warm cherry pie washed down her throat. "If someone figures it out—"

"The whole frame job falls apart, and we lose everything," said her sister, repeating one of Jenny's constant lectures. "Believe me, Trouble, I know. Hiding me isn't the problem."

"Then what is, D?" Jenny asked, frowning.

"That."

Her sister pointed behind Jenny. She looked over her shoulder and felt her heart freeze to the core. After all that mystery solving the week before, they'd left the Big Board in the study, moving it over by the fireplace so it was out of the way.

It was still there, lit dimly by the yellow light of the desk lamp.

Someone had made a bold new addition to the board. In big, blocky letters, in what she hoped was only red spray paint, they'd left her a message.

KiLLROY WAS HERE!!

Jenny clutched her sister's hand tightly.

"We knew he'd make his presence felt eventually," said her sister.

"The real killer," said Jenny, handing the bottle back.

"The Stranger," said her sister.

"*A tall, dark, and Strangesome menace. Beware,*" they quoted together without even meaning to. It was a twin thing.

"You think he's pissed?"

"That I stole his credit for killing Dad and framed someone else?" Jenny tilted her head at the defaced Big Board. "Yeah, I'm thinking so."

They stood in silence. Passing the bottle back and forth, and staring at the malevolent writing.

"Did we do the right thing?" asked Jenny after a moment. "I know

Val's a bitch, but I feel guilty as fuck. She was crying, and Jack won't even look at me."

"Don't feel too bad. For all we know, she was the one who had Mom killed."

"Yeah, maybe…"

"Shelly was going to take you away," said her sister, turning to face her with earnest conviction. "It sucks, but if Val is innocent, we can make it up to her later. You'd be even less safe back in Glendale and without any money or resources. We're gonna need those. We're in the real game now."

"A dangerous game," said Jenny.

A fiendish grin spread across her sister's lips.

"That's okay. Danger is my middle name."

To be continued…

ACKNOWLEDGEMENTS

None of this ever happens if we weren't invited to the Pretty Little Liars set by Norman Buckley in April, 2015. Marco and I were driving down to L.A. to visit Warner Bros. Studios when an alarming thought occurred. If you go to Hollywood, aren't you supposed to have a movie or TV pitch in your back pocket, just in case someone asks? We spent the next few hours brainstorming an idea for a TV show about a girl named Trouble who solved mysteries.

Norman has been a motivating presence throughout the writing process, offering industry insight and career advice. It was on his suggestion that we decided to turn the Trouble pilot script into a book. Fellow PLL alum Joseph Dougherty was incredibly gracious, providing detailed notes that helped us understand the story we were trying to tell. We are much indebted to Joe for the long skype sessions digging into the nitty gritty details of mystery.

Alex Ruhl and Allyson Nelson were two of the first people to read Trouble, and their enthusiasm and encouragement were so essential to keeping us going. Alex was the first person ever to hear about Danger, and she remains one of the very few who knows who killed RJ Valentine. And it's fair to say that Jenny owes some of her edge to Allyson's acerbic Chicago wit.

Major thanks are in order for my editors Amanda Saint, who forced me to ruthlessly jettison all but the most essential elements, and Karen Crain for the fantastic last-minute proof-read and polish job. And all credit is due to Michael Manuel for our amazing cover art. Amanda Chronister did a fantastic variant cover for us as well.

The book might not have been written without Krystal Pearson and Stacy Motsinger diligently reading every new rough draft chapter and keeping my worst male writer tendencies in check. I still think the "free handjobs" joke was funny, but fine. Michael Manuel and JJ Allendorf provided essential moral support, prodding and shaming me when I'd gone a week without writing. All this despite JJ's rabid anti-Drew partisanship.

I don't think I fully understood Jenny's relationship with her father until Kaitlin Reilly politely informed me that RJ was a monster. Shelly agrees, but Jenny would tell Kaitlin that she just doesn't understand.

I want to give a very special thank you to all the people I pushed drafts of Trouble on, desperate for feedback, only to email them a day later saying "read this version instead!" Rebecca and Jenny, Kristin, Peanut, Girl Michael, Leah and all the rest. And a big shoutout to all our wonderful podcast listeners who endured years of cryptic Trouble mentions before we finally put out the book.

My meager knowledge of tannins and terroir is courtesy of my sister Rachael, and my other sister Sara drove me around Sonoma County (the real life Blackbird Springs) and took me to my first wine tasting. I'm too embarrassed to let my parents read Trouble, but thank you to mom and dad nonetheless, and Marco's family as well.

Last, and greatest, Trouble is the daughter of two minds: myself and my writing partner Marco Sparks. Thank you for letting me take the wheel on this one, Marco. Can't wait to get to work on the sequel.

—James Taylor

ABOUT THE AUTHORS

JAMES TAYLOR is a writer and co-host of Bros Watch PLL Too, the #1 Pretty Little Liars podcast on the internet. His first memory of mystery stories was staying up all night when he was seven reading Howliday Inn. In another life, he was a professional gambler. These days, he's content to pass his time in cafes and multiplexes. He lives in Los Angeles.

MARCO SPARKS is a writer living in California. He's suspiciously tall. His fiction and non-fiction can be found in various dark corners of the internet. He is the co-host of several podcasts, particularly focused on teen murder shows. Also, he has the kind of cats where, when he suddenly ends up dead, no matter how much it looks like it was an accident, they were behind it.

CPSIA information can be obtained
at www.ICGtesting.com
Printed in the USA
LVHW110003250919
632199LV00001B/22/P

9 781733 066204